NAME
DROPPING

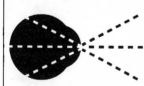 This Large Print Book carries the
Seal of Approval of N.A.V.H.

NAME DROPPING

Jane Heller

Thorndike Press • Thorndike, Maine

Published in 2000 by arrangement with St. Martin's Press, Inc.

Thorndike Press Large Print Basic Series.

The tree indicium is a trademark of Thorndike Press.

The text of this Large Print edition is unabridged.
Other aspects of the book may vary from the original edition.

Set in 16 pt. Plantin by Anne Bradeen.

Printed in the United States on permanent paper.

Library of Congress Cataloging-in-Publication Data

Heller, Jane.
    Name dropping / Jane Heller.
        p.   cm.
    ISBN 0-7862-2979-9 (lg. print : hc : alk. paper)
    1. Manhattan (New York, N.Y.) — Fiction. 2. Preschool
teachers — Fiction. 3. Mistaken identity — Fiction.
4. Women journalists — Fiction. 5. Apartment houses —
Fiction. 6. Blind dates — Fiction. 7. Large type books.
I. Title.
PS3558.E4757 N36 2000b
813´.54—dc21   00-064867

For Ellen Levine,
my friend and literary agent,
whose own funny story inspired this novel.

ACKNOWLEDGMENTS

The heroine of *Name Dropping* is a preschool teacher, and to find out what that profession is all about, I went straight to the experts. Thanks to my sister, Susan Alexander, and her assistants, Sergio Alati and Terri Resnick; my niece, Elizabeth Alexander; Nina Barcik; Ellen Birnbaum; Diane Hollowell; Pat Putnam; and Pam Ryan.

Thanks, as well, to those who fall under the heading of "miscellaneous advisors": Michael Barrett; Ruth Harris; Juli Morgan; Allison Seifer Poole; Louise Quayle; Karen Viener; Gordon Veling; and Renee Young.

A huge thanks to my editor, Jennifer Enderlin, the most positive person I've ever met.

Any my thanks and love to my husband, Michael Forester.

PART ONE

PART ONE

CHAPTER ONE

When the invitation arrived in the mail, I assumed it was a joke.

America's ambassador to Great Britain was requesting the honour of *my* presence at a black-tie reception at the United Nations?

Sure, and pip-pip to you too, I thought as I leaned against the tiny refrigerator in the tiny kitchen of my tiny apartment. What's next? Afternoon tea with the queen?

I examined the invitation, running my hand over it, holding it up to the light, checking for some indication of who might have sent it. All I could determine was that, yup, it was addressed to me — Nancy Stern, 137 East Seventy-first Street, New York, New York 10021 — and that it did seem authentic with its bold, black-scripted letters, heavy, wedding-invitation-type card stock, and official-looking seal. But how could it be authentic?

I was hardly a regular on the international circuit, hardly a pal of America's ambassador to Great Britain, hardly a pal of America's ambassador to *any*place. I was a teacher at Small Blessings, a nursery school on Manhattan's Upper East Side. I spent my days, not with foreign diplomats discussing trade agreements, human rights, or weapons of mass destruction, but with prekindergarteners singing "The Itsy Bitsy Spider." Moreover, the sort of diplomacy I practiced involved convincing four-year-olds that nose-picking, while not an inherently bad thing, is nevertheless a "poor choice" when socializing with others.

Me at a black-tie reception at the U.N., I scoffed as I tossed the invitation into the garbage. The last party *I* went to was when Lindsay Greenblatt turned five and her mother brought cupcakes to school for the class's snack.

Yeah, I'm a real party animal, I thought, mentally ticking off the more recent Saturday nights during which I'd stayed home with a good book rather than prowl the city's trendy clubs looking for love. Please. Shortly after I'd gotten divorced and found myself back in circulation, it became abundantly clear that Mr. Wonderful wasn't waiting for me on a strobe-lit dance floor. Call me old-fashioned but my idea of heaven isn't a guy in a sweat-drenched tank top, bumping and grinding and hip-

10

hopping to Puff Daddy Combs.

Not that I didn't go out now and then, do the things typical single-women-in-their-thirties do. I attended other people's weddings, spent the occasional weekend at somebody's summer rental, dated friends of friends, you know how it works. Unfortunately, my special man never materialized no matter how often I ventured out, and so, little by little, I stopped venturing out. Perhaps I had no romance in my life because I wasn't ready for a relationship. Perhaps I had no romance in my life because I was too picky, although it didn't seem *too* much to ask that the man not pierce his nipples. Or perhaps, like millions of other unattached women, I had no romance in my life because of the phenomenon I associate with warehouses: Overstocked! Too Much Inventory! Surplus! Yes, perhaps, it was simply that there was a surplus of single women and I didn't have the energy to fight the odds, unlike my best friend and associate teacher Janice Mason, a veritable Energizer bunny when it came to men.

Janice!

That's when it dawned on me: The invitation to the reception at the U.N. must be her handiwork!

A helium-balloon-voiced woman with

pixie-short blond hair, a trim, athletic figure, and a go-for-it, try-anything, follow-your-bliss attitude toward life, Janice loved fooling around on her computer, loved experimenting with different fonts and formats, loved printing out phony documents — sweepstakes come-ons, letters from the IRS, you name it — and sending them to people as a goof. A real prankster, that Janice. Such a kidder.

She also loved flirting with men over the Internet, hoping her overheated E-mails would lead to equally overheated responses, which would lead to in-person encounters, which would lead to marriage proposals. (They never did.)

We spent a great deal of after-school time together, she and I, and were compatible in many important ways, but where I couldn't care less about Web sites and chat rooms and dot com this and dot com that, Janice viewed her computer with the same sense of wonder as the kids in our class viewed their Pokémon paraphernalia. Yes, I decided. She mailed me the invitation. Ha-ha, Janice. Good one.

I confronted her at school the next morning while our sixteen young charges were crayoning pictures of turkeys in anticipation of the upcoming Thanksgiving holiday.

12

"I didn't send it, Nancy," she replied. "I couldn't have sent it. My computer's down."

"Tell me something," I said. "What's so great about computers if they're always *down?*"

"They're not always down," Janice said with conviction. "They run into problems every now and then, just like people do. What's important here is that they're our bridge to the rest of the human race, the linchpins of our intellectual infrastructure."

Intellectual infrastructure. This from a woman I'd once caught eating Play-Doh.

"Well, somebody sent the invitation," I said, getting back to the mysterious missive. "Do we know any jokesters besides you?"

"Forget jokesters. Maybe the invitation is on the level."

"Yeah, and maybe I'm Madeleine Albright."

"Okay, what about one of the other teachers, although none of them is a barrel of laughs."

Janice was referring to Victoria Bittner, the head teacher of the other group of four-year-olds. A painter who couldn't sell her paintings, Victoria took out her frustrations on the walls of her classroom, creating ridiculously over-the-top murals to tie in with each change of season. And then there was Nick Spada, the head teacher of one of the two groups of three-year-olds. Nick was a grad student at night, getting his masters in child psychology. He was much too busy, never mind deadly serious, to send jokey invitations to me or anyone else. And finally, there was Fran Golden, Nick's counterpart as the head teacher of the other group of three-year-olds. Fran was as sweet as they come but a tad on the syrupy side. If you're old enough to remember the teacher on *Romper Room*, you've got Fran to a tee. As for the assistant teachers who worked with Victoria, Nick, and Fran, they were just-out-of-college twentysomethings who spent their free time grousing about the low salaries they were earning in comparison to their friends who had chosen the corporate life.

"Of course, it's possible that the invitation did come from the embassy but that their computer printed out the wrong name," Janice added. "Why don't you RSVP and see?"

I was about to explain that I had already chucked the invitation when I noticed that a scuffle had broken out between two of the children, Fischer Levin and Todd Delafield, over which of them was entitled to use the black crayon.

"Fischer! Todd! Over here, please!" I called out to them as Fischer was in the act of punching Todd in the stomach. "Right now!" I was speaking in my authoritative, preschool teacher voice, the one that worked well with small boys but was less effective with grown men. (Ask my ex-husband.)

"I didn't do anything, Miss Stern. Todd was coloring on the *table* instead of on the paper like you said to. I was just trying to take the black crayon away from him so he wouldn't make a mess," claimed Fischer, who was articulate for his age but a big fat liar.

I know that sounds uncharitable, but Fischer Levin *was* fat and he *did* lie. All the time. He was a troublemaker, very disruptive, and whenever he was disciplined, he'd make up a whopper in an effort to cast blame on someone else. I asked his parents to come in and discuss his behavior, but they were Mr. and Mrs. We-Made-a-Bundle-in-the-Market and were too busy living it up to perform such a trivial errand. Instead, they dispatched Olga, Fischer's caregiver, who arrived for the conference in the same chauffeur-driven limo that transported Fischer to school every morning — a custom, silver Mercedes with POLO KING on its license plate. Olga was a plump, rosy-cheeked woman who had just joined the Levin household after immigrating from Latvia. She promised to convey my concerns to her employers, but cautioned me not to expect a response as she didn't have much clout with them. "Dun't forget, I am fourth or fifth nanny to Fischer in last six months," she said, her accent thick with her native land. "Not a lot I can do for child in situation like dat, you know?"

I turned to Todd, and asked him to tell Fischer how it felt to be punched in the stomach and what Fischer might say to get things back on track between them. This is what nursery school teachers do in the modern era: practice couples therapy. Never mind that the couples are four years old. Our job is to encourage the participants to express their feelings, to understand the consequences of their actions, to verbalize.

"All I know is Fischer socked me in my tummy," verbalized Todd, whose mother had given birth to twins the week before. Todd's mommy, like several of the mommies of the kids at Small Blessings, was an older, career mommy who had taken fertility drugs to get pregnant. Her twins were only the most recent multiple births making news at school; in September, Gabriel

Lester's mother had produced triplets.

"Fischer," I said, bending over to pat the boy's curly brown head. "Did you hit Todd?"

"No."

"Fischer, what have we been learning about lying?"

"I'm not —" He reconsidered. "That we're not supposed to."

"Very good. What have we been learning about hitting?"

"That we're not supposed to."

"Right. Now, what have we been learning about being mean to the other children?"

"THAT WE'RE NOT SUPPOSED TO!"

"I can hear you, Fischer. The next time you have a problem with someone in the class, I want you to use *words* to tell the person how you feel deep inside." I took Todd's little hand and drew him toward his bullier. "So how about using words with Todd and telling him you're sorry about what happened?"

Fischer's response was to stick his tongue out at Todd.

"Well, Miss Mason," I said to Janice, "I guess Fischer will have to sit in Time-out." For the uninitiated, making a child sit in Time-out is the contemporary equivalent of making a child sit in the corner. In other words, Time-out is teacher-speak for punishment, but we don't use the "P" word anymore. Too negative.

"Fischer, go sit in Time-out and think about how you could have handled the crayon situation differently," said Janice, pointing him in the direction of the group of empty chairs next to a poster of a Tyrannosaurus rex.

"Okay, but if you keep making me sit in Time-out, my dad will sue you," Fischer threatened as he marched away.

Janice looked at me and smirked. "Better get on the phone to a lawyer, huh?"

I laughed, shrugging. For all I knew, Fischer's father *would* sue. Small Blessings is an exclusive preschool that attracts the sort of parents who think being able to afford a hefty tuition entitles them to act like maniacs — litigious maniacs. For example, Tyler Snelling's parents sued the school because Janice and I permitted their son to prance around in a ballet tutu during costume play. (Their lawsuit accused us of "trying to turn him gay.") Emily Oberman's parents sued because Benjamin Weeks kissed Emily while they were swinging on the monkey bars. (They claimed we were promoting a climate of sexual harassment.)

And Samantha Klein's parents sued because their daughter got head lice. (Their lawsuit mentioned the utter humiliation associated with having to hire a professional nitpicker.)

I'm not saying that all the parents are nutcases, but the ones who are, really are, and their nuttiness rubs off on their "trophy offspring." I mean, these are people who are intense about seeing their kid at Harvard. They truly believe that once the little darling is accepted at Small Blessings, the rest is gravy. In their minds, getting into the right preschool guarantees admission to the right private school which guarantees admission to the right college, provided the kid doesn't do something stupid — like have ideas of his own. As a teacher, I always tried, as diplomatically as possible, to discourage them from projecting so far into the future; to stop putting pressure on their child and, instead, focus on his day-to-day accomplishments. Sometimes, I was successful; sometimes, not.

Fischer Levin sat in Time-out, and Todd Delafield went back to coloring his turkey. A few minutes later, Fischer trudged over to Todd and apologized for the crayon incident. A few minutes after that, he invited Todd to his apartment for an after-school playdate. Todd responded by holding his stomach and claiming he didn't feel well enough to spend the afternoon at Fischer's, even after I said I'd call both of their caregivers to get permission.

"Come on, Todd. You'll have fun," I coaxed, not wanting Fischer's act of contrition to go unrewarded. "Fischer did a brave thing by telling you he was sorry he hit you."

Todd shook his head, his lower lip beginning to quiver. "My tummy hurted before he hit me. It hurted me before I came to school."

I held Todd in my arms, rubbed his back soothingly. "I think I see the problem, honey. It's hard for you at home, with the two new babies around." I assumed his stomach ache was really an ache for his mother's attention, that he was merely feeling eclipsed by the twins. "Remember that you're the big boy in the family now, Todd, and your mommy's so proud of how well you're doing in school. Just wait until she sees the turkey you're coloring for Thanks—"

Before I could conclude my speech, Todd threw up in my lap.

"And people think this is a glamour job," I said to Janice as I hurried Todd and my puke-soaked self to the bathroom.

After I'd returned home from school that afternoon, hopped out of my stinky clothes, and showered and changed, I sorted through my mail. There, amidst the bills and magazines and catalogs promoting products for the house and garden, was yet another invitation addressed to Nancy Stern at 137 East Seventy-first Street.

This one — are you ready? — requested the pleasure of my company at a private screening of the new Harrison Ford movie, followed by champagne and a light supper. At the director's apartment in Sutton Place, no less.

What in the world is going on? I wondered, genuinely bewildered now. Why am I suddenly on the guest lists of people who don't even know I exist? Or do they?

I shook my head as I reread the invitation and then indulged in a brief fantasy, imagining myself actually attending the screening, mingling with the glittering Hollywood set, bewitching them with witty and clever anecdotes about my oh-so-fascinating life as a nursery school teacher.

Right.

I sighed as I put the invitation aside for

the moment and opened the rest of the mail.

And then I received another jolt: my American Express bill. According to the invoice, my tab for October was $10,560, which was pretty steep considering that the only item I'd put on my card that month was the fifty bucks I'd spent on plants hoping to perk up my dreary apartment.

I stood, open-mouthed, as I ran down the list of charges. The round-trip ticket to London. The hotel bill from the Savoy. The round-trip ticket to L.A. The hotel bill from the Bel Air. There were other goodies — dinners at New York's hippest restaurants, merchandise from Madison Avenue boutiques, visits to some hair salon I'd never heard of, let alone been to — but the trips to London and Los Angeles were what really jumped out at me. Could they be linked to the invitations from the ambassador to Great Britain and the Hollywood movie director? And if so, how?

I went back over all the charges, then checked the remittance slip yet again. As before, I verified that my name and address were correct. But this time, I noticed that the account number wasn't mine.

Ah-ha, I thought. What's going on here isn't a joke or an intrigue. It's a mistake. A clerical error.

I called American Express to report the mix-up and was informed that there was a simple explanation behind it. Another woman named Nancy Stern had recently moved into my building and her mail must have been placed inadvertently in my mailbox. The customer service representative apologized for the error and promised to advise the other Nancy Stern to include her apartment number in her address in order to avoid this type of confusion.

The other Nancy Stern, I mused after I hung up. A Nancy Stern who's chummy with ambassadors and movie stars, apparently. A Nancy Stern who travels, shops, dines fine. A Nancy Stern who, according to the American Express lady, lives in 24A, on the rarified penthouse floor of the building, not in 6J, on my thoroughly *average* floor. A Nancy Stern who, I'd be willing to bet, doesn't regularly get vomited upon by four-year-olds.

Yes, there was a simple explanation for the invitations and the $10,000 charge card bill that had appeared in my mailbox. The trouble is, simple explanations often obscure the complicated situations to follow. At least, that was the case with me.

CHAPTER TWO

"You'll never guess who I ran into last night," said Janice as we were setting up the classroom the next morning.

"Who?"

"Gary, the nutritionist I met in the Hamptons last summer. You remember."

I winced, remembering. Janice, who was also something of a nutritionist when she wasn't succumbing to Play-Doh, had not only slept with Gary on their very first date but told him she loved him, proposed marriage to him, and declared that she wanted to have his children. Needless to say, she'd never heard from him again.

"Where did this reunion take place?" I asked.

"At the Korean market at Seventy-sixth and Lex," she said. "Gary was cruising the salad bar."

"Did you have a conversation?"

"Yeah. I told him it was nice to see him and he told me it was nice to see me too. Of course, he didn't have a clue who I was."

"How could you tell?"

"He called me Linda and asked if I still liked working in real estate."

"Sorry."

She waved me off. "Obviously, Gary's a sociopath."

"Obviously." I paused. "What, exactly, *is* a sociopath?"

"Oh. A psychopath with really good social skills?"

I smiled. "Sounds reasonable. Listen, don't hate me for saying this, Janice, but the next time you go out with a man, maybe you shouldn't come on as strong as you did with Gary. I think your, um, *enthusiasm* scares guys off."

"Nancy," she said, running her fingers through her spiky blond hair. "I can't help how I am. If I feel something, I flow with it. Isn't that what we teach the kids to do? To express what they're feeling deep inside? To be open and honest human beings?"

"Yes, but in terms of adult male-female relationships —"

"Look, Nance. The truth is, I'm not like you. I don't hold back."

Hold back? Was that what I'd been doing? Was that why I was manless? Because I *held back?*

While Janice rambled on about Gary, I

considered her assessment of me, tried to take an unbiased look at myself. I certainly didn't hold back my feelings with the children, I decided, never with the children, not in the nine years I'd been a teacher at Small Blessings. I was crazy about all the kids, even the Fischer Levin types, and I put my love out there, unreservedly. But, I had to admit, I could see where someone might find me a little standoffish with men. Sweaty guys on dance floors aside, I suppose that ever since my divorce, I *was* wary of feeling too much, wary of letting my emotions overwhelm me, wary of getting hurt. I don't mean to suggest that I was romance-phobic, just guarded, undaring, the anti-Janice.

Oh, poor little Nancy, you're probably thinking. Another victim of an ugly breakup. Sob sob.

The thing is, I didn't see myself as a victim, nor was my breakup ugly or even especially dramatic. I didn't find John in bed with another woman (or man), didn't find him on a street corner selling drugs, didn't find him on a wanted poster. He didn't beat me, he wasn't a boozer, and he wasn't averse to doing the dishes. He just didn't love me.

Some people say that married couples don't love each other equally, not really; that

26

one spouse loves the other more; that one is the adorer and the other the adored. Well, for six years, I was the adorer of John Stern, and I was so busy adoring him, so busy saying "I love you," so busy asking "How was your day?" and "What do you want for dinner?" and "Does this feel good when I touch you here?" that I didn't notice he wasn't adoring me back. And then one day I did notice. I stepped outside myself and began to observe how we were together; how he was the receiver of my affection, never the initiator. And I said: Enough.

Why did he marry me if he didn't love me, you're wondering? Maybe because his parents were fond of me. Maybe because two of his closest friends had just gotten married and he wasn't about to be the odd man out. Maybe because I'm a decent person and I have a brain and I'm very pretty in a wholesome, girl-next-door sort of way. Maybe because he sensed early on that I would be the kind of woman who would dote on him, cater to him, let *him* be the high-maintenance spouse. What he didn't count on was that, eventually, I would figure out that I deserved better, deserved a man who wanted a wife, not a groupie.

"Nancy? You there?" I heard Janice asking

through the haze of my memories.

"Oh. Yes," I said, coming to.

"So what did you do last night?" she said as we both sat on tiny chairs cutting up pieces of yarn for the day's art project.

"Nuked a frozen dinner, watched a little TV, went to sleep," I said. "My usual highwire act. Wait. Something moderately interesting did happen last night." I told Janice about the movie screening and the American Express bill. "It turns out, another woman named Nancy Stern just moved into my building, and I've been getting her mail. Which explains the invitation to the party at the U.N. that I mentioned to you yesterday. It was meant for her."

"Wow," Janice remarked. "This other Nancy Stern must be well connected."

"Well constructed too," I said. "You should see the boobs."

"You met her?"

"I saw her. The doorman pointed her out as she was getting into a cab this morning, although *she* was the one doing the pointing, if you get my drift."

"They're implants, I suppose."

"I have no idea, Janice. I didn't reach out and touch them."

"What does she look like, besides the boobs?"

28

"Long legs, long blond hair."

"God, doesn't she understand that the *Baywatch* babe thing is totally been-there? Even the four-year-old girls in our class understand it. They come to school with Mulan on their lunch boxes now instead of Barbie."

"Except for Heather Wilcox. She has a Louis Vuitton lunch box."

Janice rolled her eyes. It never ceased to amaze us how extravagantly accessorized some of the children were. Alison Spitz's Prada backpack, for example, cost more than my rent.

"Anyway," I said, "the doorman told me the other Nancy Stern is a freelance writer who interviews famous people for magazines. I guess that's why she's invited to so many swanky parties. She's always doing a profile on some celebrity."

"She must know everybody," Janice sighed. "Picture her Rolodex."

"Right now I'm picturing *my* mail going into *her* mailbox. If I'm getting hers, she must be getting mine, right?"

"Yeah, but if you think that's gonna be a pain, wait until the phone calls start coming in."

"Phone calls?"

"Sure. If the other Nancy Stern is such a

hotshot, she probably has an unpublished number. Which means that anybody looking for her in the phone book is gonna call you instead."

"Swell. A similar thing happens to my father. He has a land title company that's listed in the Yellow Pages under 'Escrow Services.' Unfortunately, 'Escrow Services' comes right after 'Escort Services.' Talk about mix-ups."

"I bet," said Janice. "If I were you, I'd be prepared for some interesting wrong numbers."

I was contemplating the sort of wrong numbers I might be in for when the kids began arriving, and Janice and I turned our attention to greeting them and getting them settled in the classroom's various play areas. Forty-five minutes later, we all took our customary positions on the rug, gathered in a circle, clasped hands, and sang the "Good Morning Song," which goes like this:

"Good morning! Good morning!
It's another great day!
But which day is it?"

At this juncture, Joshua Eisen, the designated calendar person (we assign the children jobs each week), yelled out: "Thursday!" and we went back to the song.

> *"And now we'd like to know who is here!*
> *So let's count!*
> *Ready? Set? Go!"*

On cue, Alexis Shuler, the week's designated counter, glanced around the circle and counted how many children were present and how many were not. "Thixteen are here!" said Alexis, who had a lisp and was spending after-school time with Small Blessings's speech therapist. I asked her to take another look around the circle, as several of the children were out sick that day, and explained the concepts of addition and subtraction. She processed the information for a minute, or so I thought, and answered: "Fifty-hundred are here!"

After the matter of attendance was finally resolved, we moved to Melyssa Deaver, the week's designated weather person, who picked through the pictures of suns and raindrops and snowy streets that we kept in a basket and correctly chose the one of the snowy streets, which she then affixed to our calendar with Velcro. "Before coming to America, my nanny never even saw snow," giggled Melyssa, whose nanny was from Jamaica. "*My* nanny won't let me eat thnow," lisped Alexis, the counter. "She thays there's dog pee in it and I could die if I ate it."

Alexis's remark provoked a spirited discussion among the children about pee as well as doody, subjects they found hilarious, and about dying, a subject they found fascinating, ever since Small Blessings banned peanut butter from the lunch menu after a child with an allergy to nuts had gone into anaphylactic shock. (Each classroom was now equipped with an EpiPen Auto-Injector, as well as a list of each child's allergies and the name of his or her pediatrician.)

"Okay, everybody," I interrupted, after Fischer Levin had announced that he'd heard his mother say she was allergic to his father. "Before we sit down in the circle, we're going to do our warm-up exercises."

I was about to lead the class in our morning round of "Heads, Shoulders, Knees and Toes" when I heard Fischer bragging that his father, the wizard of Wall Street, was, "in real life," a pirate who hunted for buried treasure and brought it home to their apartment. James Woolsey, the boy standing next to Fischer, was unimpressed by this latest whopper, and his nonchalance inspired Fischer to sock him in the arm. James, a sweet boy whose twenty-one-year-old au pair had recently become his stepmother, started to howl.

"I didn't do anything, Miss Stern," Fischer maintained, on his feet the instant he saw my eyebrows arch. "I don't know what he's crying about."

After the usual lecture, I put Fischer in Time-out and got on with the activity.

Later, while Janice took the class down the hall to Creative Movement, I took the opportunity to speak to Penelope Dibble, Small Blessings's long-time director, about Fischer.

Her office, a suite of rooms on the first floor of the two-story building that housed the school, was decorated to resemble an English country house with lots of chintz, precious little antiques, and copper pots overflowing with plants. As for Penelope herself, if I had to describe her in one word, I'd say *pearls*. She always wore them — a single strand around her pale, scrawny neck. She wore them so often it wouldn't surprise me if she slept with them. In fact, it wouldn't surprise me if she slept with *them* but didn't sleep with men. Penelope was in her fifties and had never been married, and I had a suspicion that she had something going with her administrative assistant, a stocky, square-shouldered woman named Deborah who requested that everyone call her Deebo.

When I arrived at her office, Penelope was in conference with a prospective parent but saw me within a few minutes.

"Is there a problem, Nancy?" she asked as she motioned for me to sit in one of the two visitors's chairs opposite her Queen Anne desk. She was thin, small-boned, neat, tidy. Her straight, brown hair was cut crisply, bluntly, just below her ears. Her eyes were a watery hazel, her nose as long and narrow as a finger. And her lips were lipstickless and tight; when she spoke she did so without moving them, and I often thought she'd make a terrific ventriloquist.

"It's Fischer Levin again," I said.

She nodded. We'd discussed him before.

"The shame of it is, he's such a smart, imaginative boy," I said. "The most precocious, verbally advanced boy in the class, with the exception of Carl Pinder." Carl Pinder's parents were out-of-control yuppies who had taught their child to speak five languages before he was three. Unfortunately, Carl was yet to be fully potty trained; I had a hunch he might go postal someday. "But Fischer's so disruptive that I'm neglecting the other kids. I can't teach them if I'm always disciplining him, and teaching is what I do."

"Of course it's what you do. Small Blessings is a preschool not a *daycare center*," Penelope said contemptuously.

"I've tried to talk to the Levins, to encourage them to attend a parent/teacher conference, but I haven't had any luck," I said, remembering that the last time I'd called, they were out of the country, horseback riding in Patagonia. "I have a feeling that if *you* called them, Penelope, they might —"

"I?"

"Yes, since you're the director. Something tells me Mr. Levin is the type who only responds to people in charge."

"He does seem to have a lofty opinion of himself."

"If you would invite him and Mrs. Levin to come in and then let Janice and me talk to them about Fischer, it might work, Penelope. We'd explain — tactfully, of course — that if they would take a greater interest in their son's activities, give a boost to his self-esteem, he might perform better and we wouldn't have such trouble with him."

"You sound as if you're suggesting we tell

them that we're giving up on Fischer."

"Not at all. I think Fischer could thrive at school, *if* he got a little attention from his parents."

She shook her head vehemently. "The boy has been in your classroom for a mere two months, Nancy. It's far too early to admit defeat."

"Defeat? You're not listening, Penelope. I'm here because I want Fischer to succeed."

"I don't know."

"What's not to know?"

I regarded her, regarded the lips, the pearls, the strict, unyielding, headmistress-y demeanor. Having to interact with her was not the most rewarding part of my job.

"All right. I'll be candid with you," she said. "The Levins have been very generous to Small Blessings."

"How generous?" I said.

"They've offered to donate the new library."

"Donate it?"

"Pay for it. The Levin Reading Room, they'd like us to call it."

"Give me a break."

"I'm sorry, Nancy. I simply cannot drag those people in here and confront them with the fact that their son is a delinquent."

"He's not a delinquent."

"Fine, he's not a delinquent. The point is, I don't want you upsetting them or giving them the impression that we don't know what we're doing at Small Blessings."

"Because you're afraid they'll pull their kid and their money out of here and take them to some other preschool?"

"Let's just say that it would be a detriment to our school and to the children if the plans for the new library were suddenly scuttled. So there we are."

She stood, indicating our meeting was over. Then she came around to my side of the desk, placed her hand on my back, and, ever so gently, pushed me out the door.

"You're a wonderful teacher," she said, smiling now. "If anyone can turn that boy into a little angel, it's you, Nancy."

When I got home from school, I found several intriguing pieces of mail in my box. I brought them upstairs and opened them, only to discover that most of them were for *her*.

An invitation to a party celebrating the publication of a new novel. Yet another movie screening. A letter from her agent confirming a future assignment. And — I almost fainted when I took a look at this one

— a personal thank-you note from Kevin Costner for the "really neat" piece she'd done on him.

As if all that wasn't enough to make my own mail (the electric bill, the cable TV bill, the flyer from the neighborhood super-market promoting a special on Butterball turkeys) seem hopelessly mundane, the doorman buzzed me at about five-thirty. He announced that someone had sent me flowers and that the delivery was on its way up. Before I could point out that it might be the other Nancy Stern who was expecting flowers, my doorbell rang. I went to answer it and there stood a heavyset man clutching a vase full of long-stemmed red roses.

"Are you sure those are for me?" I asked him. It wasn't my birthday. I didn't have a boyfriend. I hadn't been named teacher of the year.

"You Nancy Stern?" he said impatiently.

"Yes," I said, "but —"

"This is 137 East Seventy-first, right?"

"It is, but there's another woman in the building who is probably the —"

"Please, lady. Spare me the speech. I'm double-parked."

He thrust the roses into my arms and waited. It took me a second before I realized that what he was waiting for was a tip — for a delivery that wasn't even mine! I set the vase down on the kitchen counter, retrieved a dollar from my purse, and handed it to him. Without thanking me, he took off.

As soon as he was out the door, I hurried over to the flowers and plucked the small white card from among their petals.

"Nancy, darling," it read. "A fragrant thank-you for last night. Dinner was delicious. You were even more so. Kiss kiss."

The card was signed, "Jacques."

So she sleeps with a French guy *and* interviews movie idols, I thought with naked envy.

I tried to keep my tongue in my mouth as I shlepped the roses into the elevator and pressed the Down button, spilling water on the floor in the process and nearly slipping and falling on my butt. When I reached the lobby, I handed the flowers to the doorman.

"They were for the other Nancy Stern," I told him. "The one in 24A."

"I'll buzz her," he said, looking sorry for me. "She came in a half hour ago."

"Oh?" It occurred to me that I should run right up to her place and introduce myself. She and I could have a good laugh over having the same name and living in the same apartment building. I could give her her mail and she could give me mine. We could establish a little friendship based on the combined coincidence-nuisance of it all. Yes. "Was she alone when she came in?" I asked.

He shook his head. "Had a gentleman with her."

Jacques, I thought. Kiss kiss.

I'd better call first, I decided, not wanting to barge in on the lovebirds. And then I remembered that I couldn't call first, since the other Nancy Stern had an unlisted phone number.

I'll stop by one of these days, I thought, taking a final, longing glance at the roses. Instead of going back upstairs, I hurried out of the building and, feeling starved in more ways than one, headed for the Chinese take-out place around the corner.

When I returned to my apartment twenty minutes later, loaded down with little white boxes, I discovered not only that the light on my answering machine was blinking but that I had three messages. As I didn't have an immense circle of friends and had only been gone a short time, I let the food sit on the kitchen counter while I pressed Play with great curiosity.

"Nancy, babe," said a male voice I didn't recognize. "You don't sound like yourself. Anyhow, it's your old pal, Bo. I know you sent me one of those change-of-address thingies but I couldn't find it, so I looked you up in the book. How are ya, sweet pea? Got a night free this week? Love to play in the sheets, feel that buff body. Give me a jingle."

My my, I snickered. The Nancy Stern in 24A is one busy gal.

"Hello, Nancy. It's Henry," came another male voice, this one older, more reserved. "I had my secretary track down your new number from Information. I hope that's all right, dear." He paused, cleared his throat. "No, I haven't forgotten what you said about refusing to see me until Helen agreed to the divorce, but I can't bear to be cut out of your life. I'm afraid I must see you, must be with you. I'll tell Helen I have a business meeting out of town and then you and I can spend a couple of days together. Just the two of us. Will you consider it, Nancy? Will you *please?*"

Jesus, I thought. She's even got one who begs. (I had never been begged by a man, unless you counted the homeless guy who worked the block between Small Blessings and my chiropractor.)

"Oh. Sorry," came the third and final message, a female voice that was youthful, girlish, with a lilting southern drawl. "I must have reached the wrong Nancy Stern."

The wrong Nancy Stern. Ouch!

For some reason, the words really stung. Sure, I was in a bit of a rut, personally and professionally, but it had never occurred to me to think of myself in such a negative light. It had never occurred to me that there might be a right Nancy Stern and a wrong one — or that someone would refer to me as the latter.

Oh, snap out of it, I scolded myself. This whole thing is funny. FUN-NY. Lighten up.

I grabbed a couple of pieces of paper, transcribed the messages from Bo and Henry, and added them to the pile containing the other Nancy Stern's mail.

And then the phone rang. I forced a smile, gave myself a pep talk, reminded myself that I was the *right* Nancy Stern and that, while I clearly wasn't as popular as *she* was, I, too, had people who cared about me.

"Hello?" I answered.

"Is this Nancy Stern? The Nancy Stern who has lived at 137 East Seventy-first for nearly six years?" said a male voice.

"Yes?" I said hopefully, now that I had confirmed that it wasn't the other Nancy Stern he wanted. My heart raced as I wondered if one of the countless men to whom my mother had given my number was actually calling.

"Good evening, Nancy," he said. "How are you this evening?"

"I'm fine," I said, thinking he was awfully polite — a refreshing change from the insensitive brutes Janice had introduced me to. "How are you?"

"I'm fine, thanks. I'm contacting you this evening, Nancy, to let you know that MCI is running a special this month. I realize that you've been using AT&T as your long distance carrier ever since you moved to this address, but if I could take a moment to —"

I hung up and made myself a martini. So much for the moo goo gai pan.

CHAPTER THREE

In an effort to draw positive attention to Fischer Levin and show him that *somebody* cared about him, I decided to give him a more prominent role in our Thanksgiving play. I designated him the pilgrim who sings the Thanksgiving song, "Oh, Turkey Tom," as opposed to the pilgrim who merely expresses gratitude to the Indians for an ear of corn. He greeted the news with his usual bravado, but I could tell he was thrilled. "I'm a great singer," he said. "I'll probably grow up to be in Hanson."

During rehearsal, Fischer was amazingly focused — for Fischer. Every time he sang the song's chorus — "Go gobble, gobble, gobble all day" — he waved his chubby hands in the air, then took a little bow. The other kids loved his act, and when I suggested that they give him a big round of applause, they did. For the rest of the day, he was a model student, except for a brief shoving match with Zachary Sinclair involving Legos. I was hopeful that he had turned a corner.

As for me, I did not have a good day. While the children were at gym, I was served with two subpoenas — the first from the attorney representing the mother of Hillary Heilbrun, one of the girls in our class, the second from the attorney representing Hillary's father. I had heard they were divorcing, but I had no idea they were suing each other for custody of their daughter — or that *I* would be forced to testify in the case as to which of them was the better parent. Like I needed to be put in that position.

When I got home there was more mail for the other Nancy Stern, plus a couple of phone messages for her. Like I needed to be put in *that* position.

Tomorrow, I thought, as I climbed into bed that night. Tomorrow I'll pay my namesake a visit and get things straightened out.

I woke up the next morning with a badly swollen right eye. I don't mean to gross you out, but it was red and oozing and crusty and, because I'd been a preschool teacher for nine years, I recognized the symptoms instantly.

I called Janice, catching her in the middle of her granola. "It's the dreaded conjunctivitis," I said. "I guess I'm the latest casualty." A quarter of the class had already come down with the condition, which is highly contagious and a fact of life if you spend any time around young children.

"I'm surprised I haven't gotten it yet," Janice observed between bites of her cereal.

"There's still time," I said. "Anyway, I just wanted to tell you I won't be at school today. I'll call Deebo now, so she can get a substitute, and I'll talk to you later, after I've been to the doctor."

"Okay, Nance. Feel better."

"Thanks. I will."

And I expected to. I went to the doctor, who prescribed drops in the infected eye four times a day and advised me to stay home from school until it stopped dripping. No biggie.

But then I returned to the apartment and who did I run smack into but the other Nancy Stern, whose right eye was not only *not* dripping but was clear, almond-shaped, and a breathtaking shade of blue, just like her other eye. She was leaving the building the moment I was entering it, and the doorman took the initiative in making the introduction.

"Lovely to meet you," she said. She extended her hand to me and then, noticing my eye, withdrew it.

"Same here. It sure is a coincidence about two Nancy Sterns living here."

"Is it? My impression is that the city is full of us. The name is quite commonplace, I fear."

I fear? What was up with that affected way of speaking? No wonder her callers were confused when they'd heard my voice on the answering machine.

"Are there really that many of us?" I chuckled, trying unsuccessfully not to feel mousy and drab and sickly standing next to this golden goddess who was swathed in pure white — winter white. Wool slacks, cashmere turtleneck, leather gloves, all the color of snow. I, by contrast, was more like slush in my sloppy gray sweats.

She wasn't beautiful, I decided, her nose and mouth and cheekbones not the stuff of runway models. It was the package that made her so striking — the legginess, the blond mane, the expertly applied makeup, the little *ding* her dangling earrings made when she moved her head, the sweet scent that floated up into the air from her body — an aura of gardenia or honeysuckle or some other flower that is not indigenous to the island of Manhattan. And, of course, there were the breasts — twin turbos, ripe melons, hooters, knockers, blue vein swellers. I apologize for sounding like an adolescent boy, but they cried out to be described in such terms because they were so large in proportion to her tall, thin frame and were, therefore, comical. Normally, I would have found them even more comical, but on this day I found them depressing too.

It's your eye, I told myself as she and I continued to make chitchat. You're self-conscious about it so you feel inferior.

Or maybe it's the fact that she looks incredibly put together and you look like a bag lady.

As I half listened to Nancy Stern catalog the other Nancy Sterns she'd run across during the course of her wildly exciting life, I tried to imagine how I did appear to her, how I *came across*.

As I indicated earlier, I am pretty in an informal, utterly nonthreatening way. I have glossy brown hair which I wear parted on the side and medium-length; white teeth with a slight overbite; big brown eyes; a straight nose with freckles across the bridge; and a dimple to the right of my mouth. I have a reasonably nice figure but I don't work at it. I have a reasonably nice complexion but I don't work at that either. What I also have is a certain you-can-trust-her way about me, a certain demeanor that suggests I wouldn't do anything crazy, a certain mien that, if thrust in a tough spot, I would be the sensible, responsible one. If I were casting me in *Charlie's Angels* I would give me the Kate Jackson part. If I were casting me in *Three's Company* I would give me the Joyce DeWitt part. If I were casting me as an anchorwoman on a network news program I would give me the Katie Couric part. In other words, I am The Brunette Who Keeps Her Head.

Or so I thought at the time, although at the time I didn't pay much attention to which celebrity was on which show. I didn't have to.

"I have some mail of yours," I told the other Nancy Stern. "A few phone messages too."

"I have a piece of mail for you as well," she said. "Your Kmart bill." She paused. "Frankly, I had no idea Kmart had charge accounts, but then I've never been to one of their stores. I'm a boutique shopper."

"So I noticed."

"Excuse me?"

"I read your American Express bill by mistake. I assumed it was mine. Sorry."

She nodded her forgiveness. "Mix-ups are inevitable in our situation."

"Right. When would you like to get together and swap mail?"

"Let me think." She tapped her chin with her index finger. "Why don't you come up to my apartment this evening for a cocktail? Say, seven o'clock? We could make the exchange then."

"Seven's fine." I was dying to get a look at her penthouse and hear all about Jacques and Bo and Henry, not to mention Kevin Costner.

"We'll have to hurry a bit though," she cautioned. "I have an engagement at eight, I fear."

"There's nothing to fear but fear itself," I chortled. "See you at seven."

I was supposed to be under quarantine, I know, but I couldn't resist Nancy's invitation, not possible. So I washed my hands a dozen times before leaving the apartment and wore sunglasses to conceal the offending eye and hoped that, since I wouldn't be staying long, I wouldn't be passing along unwanted germs.

Clutching her mail and messages in my hand, I rode up to the twenty-fourth floor and got off the elevator. Her apartment was one of four penthouses in the building, the one facing southwest, the one with the best view.

"Nancy. There you are," she said, ushering me inside the vast space that was more than quadruple the size of my apartment. "Come in."

I came in. I had expected to find cartons everywhere, since she had only recently moved in, but there were none.

She must have hired someone to unpack for her, I thought. She must hire people to do lots of things for her, judging by her surroundings.

Plush, that's what her apartment was, ultra plush, full of expensive furniture upholstered in expensive fabrics. I'm no interior decorator, but I know a money-is-no-object budget when I see one. I took a mental inventory so I could give Janice a full report.

"You're wondering about the photos," she said as she brought me a glass of white wine. The crystal goblet weighed more than she did.

"Yes," I said, although I had only just begun to zero in on the framed photographs adorning the canary-yellow walls.

"After I've done a profile of someone, up they go," she said, nodding at eight-by-ten glossies of, among others, Larry King, Robin Williams, the aforementioned Kevin Costner, Donald Trump, Tara Lipinsky,

John Grisham, Julia Roberts, Tina Turner, the Reverend Jesse Jackson. If the frames themselves hadn't been so ornate, I would have felt like I was in the sort of restaurant where they hang pictures of the celebrities who eat there and name sandwiches after them.

"You really do lead a glamorous life," I remarked, as I gazed at all the famous faces. "You must love your job."

"I do. It definitely beats spending day after day with a bunch of kids," she said. "By the way, what do you do, Nancy?"

"I spend day after day with a bunch of kids," I said. "I teach nursery school."

Her hand flew to her mouth, as if she couldn't believe she'd just committed such a social gaffe. But behind the supposed embarrassment, there was a little smirk. I spotted it. This other Nancy Stern had a mischievous streak, I decided. "I'm terribly sorry," she said, affecting remorse. "I had no idea what type of career you —"

"Forget it."

"No, please. I only said what I said because I'm not a child person, never have been. Whenever I hear women talk about their biological clock — this obsession with being a mother — I simply don't relate. I'm too selfish to be tied down to a home and a family, I suppose. My satisfaction comes from flying off at a moment's notice, traveling the world, expanding my horizons, meeting interesting people. The thought of teaching nursery school! Well, thank goodness there are those of you who consider four-year-olds intellectually stimulating."

"Speaking of interesting people," I said, so busy being envious of her that I ignored the fact that she had just insulted me. "I took these messages for you yesterday." I handed her the notes I'd scribbled down about Bo and Henry and the rest, along with the mail I'd collected. She colored slightly as she sorted through everything, then looked up at me.

"It would appear that, while you and I are virtual strangers, we have intimate knowledge of each other's activities," she said.

"Not to worry," I said. "I have no intention of telling anyone anything. Your personal business is your own."

"Oh, I do appreciate that, Nancy. I wouldn't dream of sharing your personal business with anyone either."

My personal business, I thought. Like what? That I'm a Kmart charge customer?

Just then, her telephone rang. She reached for the cordless phone resting on the end table and picked it up.

"Hello?" she said expectantly. Unlike me, whose calls were mostly for her, she had every confidence that the person on the line actually wanted to speak to her. "Oh. Hi there. Yes. Right," she was saying cryptically. I had hoped for a juicier conversation on which to eavesdrop. "No, not at the moment. In a few minutes though." She glanced over at me and smiled. I had the distinct impression that her caller had hoped to catch her alone. "I will," she went on, nodding. "No. Don't leave yet. I'll ring you back. Bye."

She hung up the phone and checked the time on her watch, a seriously bejeweled number. "My, how the evening is slipping away from me," she said. "I hate to be rude, but I must dash off to that engagement I mentioned."

Is she bored with me already? I wondered. Is she feeling edgy about the conjunctivitis? Or is she in a big rush to get rid of me so she can return that call?

"You said your engagement was at eight and it's only seven-fifteen," I pointed out, not wanting our meeting to end. I hadn't even begun to quiz her on the stars she'd met, the romances she'd had, the marriages she'd wrecked (perhaps Henry and Helen were not the only couple on the outs thanks to her).

"Yes, but the limo is coming for me at seven-thirty and I haven't finished dressing." She sure looked dressed to me. Black silk suit, black velvet pumps, a divine diamond necklace. "It's a dinner party all the way downtown, and the driver felt we might need a full half hour to plow through the traffic."

"I understand," I said, wishing I had the nerve to ask: Whose dinner party? Who else will be there? Can I come too?

As I was getting up from the sofa, her phone rang again. She picked it up. "I *said* I'll have to call you back," she snapped at the person, not even bothering with a hello. She was testy suddenly, jumpy. I wasn't sure if I was the irritant or the caller was. Either way, she seemed eager for me to shove off.

"This was just a quick how-do-you-do," she said as she handed me the Kmart bill and hustled me toward the door. "I'm sure we'll see each other again soon."

"At the very least in the elevator," I kidded. "Or the laundry room."

"Not the laundry room," she corrected me. "I have a washer and dryer here in the apartment."

"Of course you do," I said. And a laundress to operate them, I'll bet.

"It was a pleasure meeting you," she said.

"If I get any more mail that belongs to you, I'll give you a call. You do the same, all right?"

"Absolutely," I said. It wasn't until I was back in my apartment that I realized she hadn't honored me with her phone number.

I polished off the Chinese food that was left over from the night before and then called Janice.

"How's the eye?" she asked.

"Gorgeous. I'm the spitting image of E.T."

"Poor baby. You didn't miss much in school today if that's any consolation. I only had to put Fischer in Time-out once."

"That's progress."

"When do you think you'll be back?"

"I'll definitely be there Monday," I said, figuring that since it was Friday, I'd have the whole weekend to recuperate. "Now, before I forget, I've *got* to tell you about the other Nancy Stern."

"You finally met her?"

"I had a drink with her. At her penthouse. Talk about loaded."

"She was drunk?"

"No. Loaded, as in rich. God, you should see the apartment, the clothes, the jewelry."

"Where'd she get all this money?" asked

Janice. "I mean, so she interviews celebrities. She's not exactly Barbara Walters. I've never even heard of her."

"Neither have I. But I don't pay any attention to bylines. For all I know, she writes for *People* magazine."

"Or for one of those really cheesy publications that's inserted in Sunday newspapers."

"Right. She could be the type of 'journalist' who only does flattering celebrity profiles — puff pieces. Which would explain the gooey thank-you notes she gets from people like Kevin Costner."

"Thank-you notes from Kevin Costner," Janice sighed. "That wouldn't be hard to take."

"Neither would long-stemmed red roses from someone named Jacques."

"A French guy sent her roses?"

"Yes, but they were delivered to me, naturally."

She sighed again. "Getting back to her money, say she does write for a fan magazine. I still don't see how a journalist nobody's ever heard of earns that much."

"It's possible that she has family money. Or a generous ex-husband."

"Or she could be one of those people who writes everything off as a business expense, even the boob job."

"Could be."

"Okay, so tell me about the apartment. And don't leave anything out."

I proceeded to give Janice an exhaustive account of Nancy Stern's penthouse, as well as her wardrobe. After we had gorged ourselves on her material attributes, we moved on to the men who appeared to adore her.

"That woman leads a charmed life," said Janice. "The career. The money. The looks. The boyfriends. She's a lucky lady."

"I should be so lucky," I said, then laughed.

"What's so funny?" asked Janice.

"I just remembered the old expression: Be careful what you wish for," I said.

"That's a stupid expression," she said. "Wish for whatever the hell you want."

CHAPTER FOUR

Penelope Dibble, the director of Small Blessings, sat in on our class on Monday, presumably to monitor the Fischer Levin situation. While she watched from a tiny chair in the back of the room, I carried on with the daily plan, which included another rehearsal for the Thanksgiving play. Fischer performed the "Oh, Turkey Tom" song with great flair. I was proud of him. It wasn't until later in the morning, during snack, that he acted up.

He and Todd Delafield were sitting next to each other, eating raisins, when Fischer threw a handful of his at Todd, who reacted with such surprise that he proceeded to choke on the one he was in the process of swallowing. In a replay of the previous week's incident, Fischer punched Todd in the stomach. However, on this occasion, the punch paid dividends — it dislodged the raisin from Todd's windpipe and saved his life.

"You see that, Nancy?" Penelope said, fingering her pearls. "Fischer's a hero, a good boy. There's no reason whatsoever to bother his parents." And then she left the classroom.

Knowing full well that Fischer's motive for socking Todd in the stomach had not been noble, I summoned him for a little chat.

"Fischer, you made a poor choice when you threw raisins at Todd and hit him," I said. "Tell me what you were feeling."

"Mad," said Fischer, "because he wouldn't believe me."

"What wouldn't he believe you about?" I said.

"My daddy," said Fischer. "That he's a pirate."

"Your father is an investment banker, not a pirate, Fischer," I said firmly. "Didn't we decide you were going to stop lying?"

"I'm not lying," he insisted. "My dad has buried treasure in a special room where we live."

Here we go again, I thought. The buried treasure fantasy.

"What am I going to do with you?" I asked, shaking my head. Fischer *was* a bright, imaginative boy, just as I had told Penelope. It frustrated me to see his potential wasted, made me feel helpless and ineffective as a teacher.

"Are you putting me in Time-out, Miss Stern?" he asked.

"Is that what you want?" I said. "To have to sit outside the circle, away from your friends, while Miss Mason reads them a story?"

He said no, that wasn't what he wanted. What he wanted was for Todd Delafield to come over to his apartment after school and play with his turtles.

"Then go sit with the others," I said, letting him off the hook. "But first, I need a hug." I drew Fischer to me and squeezed him. He did not pull away. I realize that I appeared to be rewarding him for misbehaving, but I was trying to change the pattern we had established, do something different. "You don't get many hugs at home, do you?"

"No," he acknowledged, still in my arms.

"Then we'll make sure you get some at school, okay?"

He nodded and I released him. He was about to go and join the rest of the children when he stopped in his tracks.

"What is it, Fischer?" I asked.

He hesitated, then replied, "Miss Mason is a nice lady, but I'll probably marry you when I grow up."

As he hurried away, I felt a rush of pleasure. I had finally connected with Fischer on an emotional level, finally made contact with his feelings. All that and a marriage proposal too. Maybe things were looking up.

I was home for barely five minutes that afternoon when the doorman buzzed me.

"Dry cleaning delivery on the way up," he bellowed through the house phone.

"I don't have my dry cleaning delivered. It's too expensive," I bellowed back. To no avail. Seconds later, a young man carrying a garment wrapped in plastic was standing at my door. So much for the building's tight security.

"You've got the wrong Nancy Stern," I said churlishly as he handed me the bundle. Now I was even referring to *myself* as the wrong Nancy Stern.

"Whatever," he said, ignoring me.

"Aren't you forgetting your *tip?*" I called out to him as he beat it down the hall, to the elevator.

"It's included in the delivery charge," he yelled. "You already signed for it."

Of course I did, I thought as I slammed the door and lugged the cleaning inside.

I wasn't going to open the bag, really I wasn't, until I noticed the fur. The garment that had been dry cleaned was a coat, it turned out — a completely gorgeous, full-length shearling coat with a mink collar and matching cuffs. Clearly, the other Nancy Stern wasn't an animal rights activist, but she certainly had good taste in clothes.

I'm embarrassed to tell you that after I tore open the plastic and removed the coat from the hanger, I tried it on. (Please don't judge me harshly. You would have done the same thing, be honest.)

Since Nancy was a giantess as well as a beanpole and I am neither, the coat was too long for me, not to mention a bit snug. But as I stood there in front of the mirror, modeling it, striking various poses in it, having imaginary conversations in it, I felt like a contestant on one of those game shows — the contestant who wins the fur coat and then "comes on down" to claim her prize, drapes herself in it, caresses it, and thanks God she didn't get stuck with the luggage, the refrigerator, or the *Encyclopedia Britannica*.

Enough, I commanded myself. Take it off. It doesn't belong to you.

I ran the exquisitely soft mink cuffs along my cheek one last time and then took the coat off, placed it back on its hanger, and rewrapped it as best I could.

"The dry cleaning was for Nancy Stern in 24A," I told the doorman, after dragging the coat downstairs to the lobby. "You should have buzzed *her.*"

"Sorry," he said, lifting the coat from my arms. "I'll buzz her in a little while."

"Why not now?" I said.

"She's under the weather," he explained. "She said she was going to take a nap."

"Does she have a cold?" I asked. "Everybody seems to at this time of year, although I can't picture our glamorous celebrity journalist with a red nose."

"Then picture her with a red eye, because that's what she has," said the doorman. "Conjunctivitis."

"Oh," I said and slunk back upstairs.

That night, I went over to Janice's. She was hosting her monthly reading group at her apartment. Since the book up for discussion was *Cold Mountain* and I had already read it on my own, she suggested I participate, even though I wasn't an official member of the group.

I had been to a couple of other meetings of Janice's reading group and had not particularly enjoyed myself, which was why I wasn't a regular. My feeling was that Janice's reading group was a fraud; that, rather than critique books, what the women really wanted to critique was men.

However, since I didn't have any plans for the night that *Cold Mountain* was on their agenda, I went.

There were five other women present in addition to Janice and me and, like us, they were single women with baggage. After roughly twenty minutes of back and forth regarding the book's hero and his endless trudging through the Civil War–torn South, there was a split decision as to whether the endless trudging rendered the novel a literary masterpiece or a crashing bore.

"Speaking of crashing bores, I had the blind date from hell the other night," said one of the women.

And they were off. There was talk that all the good men in New York were married. There was talk that all the good men in New York were gay. There was talk that the term *good men* was an oxymoron.

Janice told everybody about running into Gary, the nutritionist, and his not remembering who she was. Her anecdote led to one of those unfortunate, extremely repetitive Mars/Venus discourses, which, in my opinion, are far more boring than *Cold Mountain* could ever be.

I know that "women's consciousness-raising groups," as my mother's generation used to call them, are meant to be uplifting; that having other women listen to tales of your failed romances and then shout: "You go, girl!" is supposed to be a show of support, of solidarity, of *validation.* But as I walked home that night, I felt disenfranchised, alienated, and the only thing that got validated was my instinct never to go to one of Janice's reading groups again.

When I entered the apartment, I found there were two messages on my answering machine. I replayed them. They were both from men, they were both for the other Nancy Stern, and they were both proof that there was at least one woman in the city who was having absolutely no trouble in the romance department.

I sighed as I wrote down the callers' names and their requests for an audience with Ms. Stern. And then I sat at the foot of my bed in the dark, staring out the window. It was a clear, crisp night in Manhattan. I could see the lights twinkling from the building next door, see the TV sets blinking, see the silhouetted bodies moving from room to room, see the people living their lives, and the whole thing depressed me more than Janice's reading group.

What's your problem? I asked myself.

What in the world is wrong with you?

Normally, I took comfort in the scene outside my window. Normally, I felt an odd kinship with my neighbors, as if we were all in it together, as if we had all made the decision to come to New York and put up with the craziness so we could be part of the action in some tangential way. Normally, I enjoyed the sense of specialness that being a New Yorker bestowed upon me.

But on this night, I felt distinctly unspecial — a grain of sand, a speck of dirt, just one from among the throngs of New Yorkers struggling to "make it."

I had grown up in small-town Pennsylvania, outside Pittsburgh, and had found it utterly claustrophic, suffocating. It wasn't that I yearned for stardom or wealth or The Big Time. What I yearned for was possibility, promise, hope, and I sensed I had to go elsewhere for that. The "elsewhere" turned out to be New York. I spent a week here with my college roommate during our senior year, and the minute I caught a glimpse of the city I said, This is it, Nancy. This is the place for you.

Corny, no doubt about it, but true.

Since I'd always loved kids, I got a degree in education, settled in the Big Apple, and found a teaching job at Small Blessings. A year later, I married John. Six years after that, I was single again. But even after the divorce, even after having to start over in my own little apartment, even after the heartache, the loneliness, and the therapy, I never considered going back to Pennsylvania. I still felt the possibility here, still felt the specialness.

But now there was the other Nancy Stern — a quasi alter ego living on the twenty-fourth floor of my building, a woman who bore my identical name and address but who, unlike me, appeared to enjoy a *genuine* specialness. Now I was the lesser of the two Nancy Sterns at 137 East Seventy-first Street. Now my specialness — my very uniqueness — was being called into question.

Maybe I should start using my middle initial, I thought, getting up from the bed to make some tea. From here on, I'll insist that I be referred to as Nancy Z. Stern.

Of course, I quickly ruled out the idea because the *Z* is for Zelda and who wants everyone knowing that?

God, would you listen to me? I thought. What a hypocrite! I've just gone on and on about the tragic loss of my identity when a side of me — the side that drooled over the other Nancy Stern's shearling coat — is dying to trade places with her, dying to see what it would be like to *be* her.

What *would* it be like to step into her shoes? I wondered as I plunged the tea bag into my mug of hot water. What would it be like to shed my Birkenstocks and slip into her Ferragamos, if only for a little while? It's human nature to live vicariously through others, isn't it? Particularly if the person you hope to live vicariously through lives right upstairs?

Don't get me wrong. I had no desire to trade places permanently with the other Nancy Stern. I wouldn't have dreamed of giving up my job at Small Blessings for an invitation to some movie screening. Still, maybe spending day after day with four-year-olds *was* growth stunting, as she had insinuated. Maybe I would have felt drab, colorless, ordinary, even if I hadn't been forced to confront the dramatic contrast between my life and hers.

I was pondering these weighty matters when the phone rang. I glanced at my watch: ten thirty-five. Couldn't her suitors call at a decent hour? I thought. Or were they so filled with ardor that they simply couldn't contain themselves until morning?

I padded to the phone. "Hello?" I said without enthusiasm.

"Hi. Is this Nancy?" said a man.

"Yup," I said, bracing myself for the I-must-have-the-wrong-Nancy-Stern routine.

"Oh. Good. Great," he said, sounding a little anxious. "I hope I haven't called too late. *Have* I called too late?"

"That depends," I said. "Who are you?"

"A reasonable question." He laughed apologetically. "Sorry for the fumbling around, but I'm not very adept at this blind date stuff."

Blind date stuff. My heart leapt.

"I'm Bill Harris," he said. "Joan Geisinger suggested I look you up when I got to town. I've just moved to New York from Washington."

Joan Geisinger. Joan Geisinger. Joan Geisinger. I racked my brain. Nope. No Joan Geisinger.

"She said she hasn't talked to you in a while," he went on. "She didn't even have your new number, so I got it from Information. She gave me the impression that you two have drifted apart since you worked together at — which magazine was it? *Cosmo? House & Garden? Ladies Home Journal?*"

Damn, so he *is* calling the other one, I thought, feeling a surge of disappointment. He had such a nice voice. A kind voice. The sort of voice that made you reluctant to hang up on it.

"Nancy? Are you there?" he asked. "I was trying to remember which magazine Joan —"

"*Cosmo*," I heard myself say in a moment of madness. "Joan and I started our careers there. In the secretarial pool."

What the hell do you think you're doing? I asked myself. Are you out of your mind?

"According to Joan, you're a freelance writer now," said Bill-Harris-with-the-kind-voice. "Celebrity profiles, isn't it?"

"That's right," I pressed on, my palms growing clammy. "As a matter of fact, I did a piece on Kevin Costner recently."

You're pathetic, Nancy, I derided myself. A hopeless liar, just like Fischer Levin. Stop this right now, before you make a total fool of yourself.

"Well, well. Kevin Costner." Bill Harris chuckled. "I guess you wouldn't consider going out with a mere mortal after being in his company."

"Yes! Yes, I would," I said quickly, realizing that my stupid name dropping might scare him off. "I've been interviewing celebrities for nearly a decade. After a while, they lose their luster, if you know what I mean." God, forgive me.

"I can understand that," he said, "although your work sounds pretty glamorous to me."

"Oh? What do you do, Bill?" I asked, continuing to play along, continuing to scare myself.

"I'm in the jewelry business," he said. "I was the manager of the Denham and Villier store in D.C. until the company transferred me here last month. I'll be managing the Fifth Avenue store for the foreseeable future."

Denham and Villier was a world-renowned chain of jewelry stores, on a par with Tiffany and Cartier, speaking of luster *and* glamour. Bill Harris had to have his own dealings with the rich and famous. "How interesting," I said. "I've never met anyone in the jewelry business."

"Terrific. Then I'll be your first," he said. "Are you free for dinner Saturday night?"

"Free for dinner Saturday night?" I repeated, stalling for time.

He groaned. "You see? I told you I wasn't very smooth with this blind date stuff. Leave it to me to cut right to the chase when I should have engaged you in witty repartee so you'd find it impossible *not* to go out with me. I'm a little overeager, I guess."

Gee, he seemed nice. So down to earth. So honest, unlike somebody else I knew.

"I really would like to take you out on Saturday night," he reiterated. "*Are* you free, Nancy?"

Okay, big girl. Now what? I thought. Are you going to keep this game going or tell him the truth?

"I hope your silence doesn't mean you're seeing someone," Bill remarked. "You're not, are you? Joan didn't think you were, but then she hadn't talked to you in a while."

"As it happens I'm not seeing anyone," I said. "Not exclusively, anyway." Well, I couldn't let him think I was a complete shut-in.

"Oh, but I'll bet you're busy because it's Thanksgiving weekend and you're spending it with your family. I forgot all about the holiday, what with getting settled in a new city and a new job."

"I will be spending the holiday with my family on Thursday and Friday, but I'll be back in the city by Saturday night," I had the nerve to reply.

"Then how about having dinner with me?" he said.

A deep breath. "I'd like that," I said, feeling exhilarated as well as excruciatingly guilty.

"Great. Now, since you're the Manhattanite and I'm the new kid in town, maybe you could choose the restaurant. Anywhere you say is fine."

This is insanity, I thought. He's asking the other Nancy Stern out, not *you*.

Still, he's never met her, I reminded myself, has no idea what she looks like. Even if this Joan Geisinger did give him a physical description of her, I could always say that my appearance — I mean, *her* appearance — had changed. Joan admitted that she hadn't been in touch with Nancy in ages. It was possible that the last time she'd laid eyes on her old pal was literally years ago — well before the boob job.

What do you have to lose? I asked myself in a feverish attempt to decide whether or not to pretend I was another person. Why not go out with him — as a lark? You can always worm out of the situation when the date's over, stop taking his calls, explain that you didn't feel there was chemistry between you, change your phone number. Why not have some fun, do something wild and crazy, just once?

"There's a cute little restaurant down the block from my building," I said hesitantly, then told him the name of the place.

"I'll make a reservation for seven," he said.

"Seven it is," I agreed.

"I'll come by and pick you up," he said.

"No," I said, panicking. "I'll meet you at the restaurant." Joan would have tipped him off to the other Nancy Stern's ritzy lifestyle, I suspected, and he would, therefore, expect a fancy apartment, wouldn't he? Besides, what if we ran into the celebrity journalist herself as we were leaving the building?

"Whatever you say," he replied. "I'm just glad I'll get to meet you. Joan told me so much about you I feel as if I already know you."

"Did she?" I said, my stomach churning.

"She sure did," he said. "For instance, she mentioned that you're tall, like I am."

Pause. "Oh, you know Joanie," I said off-handedly. "She thinks everyone's tall. She once told me she thought Robert Redford was tall and he's not. I know because I interviewed him during that film festival he organizes, Sundown."

"Sun*dance*, isn't it?"

"Right."

"Well, Robert Redford may not be tall, but I am," said Bill. "Six-four."

"Six-four," I said. "My, Joanie wasn't exaggerating in your case. What's more, I'm glad you shared the fact that you're tall. Now I'll be able to recognize you when I get to the restaurant."

"And how will I recognize you, Nancy?" he asked. "Other than that fabulous blond hair Joan told me about."

"Fabulous blond hair." I laughed as if the words were hysterically funny. "As I said, Joanie's quite an exaggerator. Not only that, she's color blind." Now I was a liar *and* a slanderer. "You'll be able to recognize me though. I'll be the woman in the black dress."

Gee, that narrows it down, I thought. Every woman in New York wears black. It's practically a uniform.

"I'm really looking forward to this," said Bill. "It can be pretty daunting moving to a new city, not knowing many people. Lonely too. Women aren't keen on having dinner with a strange man. I mean, a stranger who's a man." He laughed at his own awkwardness, which I found endearing. "What I'm trying to get across is, Thanks for going out on a limb here, Nancy."

Going out on a limb doesn't begin to describe it, Bill.

CHAPTER FIVE

The instant I hung up with Bill Harris, I called Janice. Her line was busy. I tried a few more times, then fell asleep.

Maybe it's just as well that I couldn't reach her, I thought as I drifted off. I want to see her face when I tell her what I've done.

But when I got to work on Tuesday morning, I didn't have the chance to tell her, because Tuesday was the last day of school before Small Blessings broke for the Thanksgiving vacation, which meant that things were more chaotic than usual. Not only did we have to costume and prepare the children for our class's much-rehearsed Thanksgiving play, we also had to greet and chat with the parents.

The play itself was performed in the gym, adjacent to the classroom. While the kids did their number on the little makeshift stage, the parents sat on folding chairs and Penelope paraded up and down the aisle. (I was surprised she didn't pass the hat.)

I was really proud of the kids, none of

whom flubbed their lines, burst into tears, or abused the scenery. I was especially pleased that Fischer's parents showed up. They were late — it was the chauffeur's day off, apparently, so they were forced to take a cab — but they arrived in time to catch their son sing "Oh, Turkey Tom," thank God.

Mr. Levin — Bob — videotaped the action and bragged to anyone within earshot that he had purchased the camera while he and Mrs. Levin — Gretchen — were in Hong Kong for the transfer of power. When he wasn't videotaping, knocking over other parents to get the best shot, he was talking loudly on his cell phone, reaming out some poor underling at the office. The only thing he didn't do of an irritating nature was to light up a cigar.

He was a nice-looking man, if unremarkable. Forties, good shape, large brown eyes framed by tortoiseshell glasses, curly brown hair just like his son's. And he was dressed for success, no question about that. His impeccably tailored, three-piece suit was befitting the partner of one of the country's largest brokerage houses, although I, personally, could have done without the polo players galloping across the tie.

As for Gretchen Levin, she was your basic arm candy — a vacantly beautiful woman at least ten years younger than her husband. She wore her extremely dark hair shoulder-length, parted down the middle, and loosely coiled in the Raphaelite fashion that Madonna favored during one of her incarnations. Like her husband, she, too, was dressed in an impeccably tailored suit, the difference being that she wasn't trotting off to work after the play; Gretchen Levin's career was spending her husband's bonuses.

"Oh look, Bob. Here's one of Fischer's teachers," she said as she saw me approaching. The show was over and Janice was back in the classroom, helping the children out of their costumes. "Bob," she said again, tugging on his sleeve. "Surely, you can conduct your business later." He blew her off and kept yammering on the cell phone, something about margin calls.

"Mrs. Levin," I said warmly, shaking hands with her. "I'm so glad you and Mr. Levin could make it today. Fischer was great, don't you think?"

"He was adorable," she agreed. "Wasn't he, Bob?"

Bob finally pocketed the phone and gave me one of those who-are-you looks.

"I'm Nancy Stern, Mr. Levin," I told him. "I'm the head teacher in Fischer's class. Thanks for coming."

"What's to thank?" he said. "My boy had a starring role in a play. I'm not gonna miss that, am I?"

You did miss it, I thought. You were too busy with your toys to enjoy your *boy*.

"Fischer's very fond of you, Miss Stern," said Gretchen. "He mentioned it to his nanny, who mentioned it to our cook, who mentioned it to me."

"I'm thrilled that his compliment made it up the chain of command," I chuckled. "I'm very fond of him too. Which is why I've tried to reach you several times, as a matter of fact. You see, in the few short months that Fischer has been in preschool at Small Blessings, my associate teacher and I have noticed that he tends to have problems relating to the other children."

Bob practically split a gut. "Problems? *My* kid? What kind of problems?"

"For one thing," I said, not having to guess where Fischer got his explosiveness, "he often resorts to hitting when he's feeling frustrated or upset."

Bob appeared relieved, proud of his son almost. "So you're saying he's not a sissy."

"No, Mr. Levin. I'm saying he's the class bully." I wasn't usually so blunt with parents, but this guy was asking for it.

He flicked his wrist at me, a thoroughly

dismissive gesture. "I was exactly the same way when I was his age and I turned out okay." Debatable. "Sounds to me like the problem isn't with Fischer; it's with you teachers. You're just not packaging him right."

"*Packaging* him?"

"Yeah, for the schools we're applying to for next year. Dalton. Trinity. Horace Mann. You know."

"Yes, I'm aware of the schools you're interested in, Mr. Levin, and how important it is to you that Fischer be accepted at them. But he's not a piece of merchandise to be packaged. He's a four-year-old boy."

I turned to his wife, hoping she would be more receptive. "There's another problem we've had to deal with, Mrs. Levin. Fischer is very bright, very imaginative, but there's a fine line between a fanciful thought and an out-and-out lie. I wonder if —"

"It's Mr. and Mrs. Levin!" Penelope interrupted, glaring at me as she rushed over to us. "How lovely to see you both."

"It's lovely to be here," said Gretchen, as if I hadn't just told her that her son was in trouble. "Bob, you remember Miss Dibble, the director of Small Blessings."

He snorted. "I should. After that fat check I handed over to her."

81

Penelope laughed too, and as she did she positioned herself directly in front of me, so as to literally block me from the Levins' sight, block me out of the conversation.

"How did you enjoy the play?" she asked them, her tone cheery. "Your son was quite the virtuoso."

"He sure practiced enough," said Bob. "I got a hunch I'll be hearing that damn turkey song the whole vacation."

"Are you folks going away for Thanksgiving?" Penelope chirped while I stood there steaming.

"Yeah, we're flying down to Aruba," he said. "I'll play my golf and Gretchen will play her tennis, and at night we'll do the casino so we can pay for it all."

"What about Fischer?" I inquired as I maneuvered myself from around Penelope's body. "What will *he* do in Aruba?"

"He'll play with the nanny," Gretchen explained. "We're taking her with us."

"Sounds like a dream vacation," Penelope exclaimed before I could get another word in. "Now, while you two are waiting for Fischer to come out and join you, why don't I show you the plans for the new library? Pardon me, the *Levin Reading Room*."

"We'd love to see them," said Gretchen. "Wouldn't we, Bob?"

He checked his watch, one of those huge Rolexes that did everything but microwave dinner. "Sure, sure. If we make it quick," he said. "I'm losing money every minute I'm out of the office."

And off they went.

No wonder Fischer's a mess, I thought sadly, as I watched his parents trail after Penelope. The father was an asshole and the mother was an airhead, although I sensed that Mrs. Levin might be more approachable than Mr. Levin if I could ever get her alone.

I considered writing her a note after the holiday, expressing my concern about her son. Penelope would be furious, but what was she going to do? Fire me?

On the other hand, maybe the note wasn't such a hot idea, given the scarcity of teaching jobs in the city.

Janice and I put the classroom in order before leaving for the long weekend. Afterwards, I suggested we go out for lunch.

"I've got to talk to you," I said with a sense of urgency. "Confess to you, actually. I've been holding it in all morning."

She eyed me. "What'd you do, steal something?"

"In a way," I said mysteriously.

We ate at Janice's favorite restaurant, a health-food place where virtually every dish was accompanied by some form of soy.

"So," she said as she munched on her veggie-with-soy on whole wheat pita. She was forgoing her usual side order of low-fat cottage cheese, having recently discovered, along with most of the population, that she was lactose intolerant. "What's the confession?"

I put aside my fruit-plate-with-soy and leaned over the table so I could talk to Janice without being overheard. "I got a phone call last night," I said, keeping my voice low. "It was from a man who said he was given my name by someone I worked with — Joan Geisinger."

"Who's she?"

"Beats me. That's the trouble."

"Oh, you mean because you don't remember her. Hey, we all have memory problems as we get older. Try Ginko biloba. They have a Web site."

"My memory's fine," I said. "I don't *know* Joan Geisinger because she's not someone *I* worked with. She's someone the other Nancy Stern worked with at one of those women's magazines."

Janice nodded sympathetically. "Another mix-up with the chick upstairs."

"Exactly."

"Sorry, but I still don't see what the intrigue's about."

"I'm getting to that. The man on the phone, Bill Harris, is a jeweler who moved here recently from Washington, D.C. He called to ask *her* out for dinner on Saturday night — and *I* accepted."

"You what?"

"I said I'd go out with him, that *she'd* go out with him."

Janice looked stunned at first, but then a smile crept across her face and she started to laugh. "You're saying you let him think you were the other Nancy Stern?" she confirmed between guffaws.

"I let him think I was like this" — I held up two fingers together — "with Kevin Costner."

That did it. We both burst out in hysterics, our bodies convulsing with laughter. Everyone in the restaurant turned to stare.

"I can't believe this," said Janice, barely able to catch her breath. "It's so unlike you to pull that kind of stunt. Maybe I'm rubbing off on you, Nance."

"Or maybe I'm lonelier than I thought," I said. I was about to signal the waitress and order us a couple of stiff drinks but then reminded myself that the stiffest drink they made was probably a cup of echinacea tea.

"What in the world provoked you to say yes to this guy?" asked Janice.

"He had a nice voice," I said, shrugging. "We didn't talk long, but he was very down-to-earth, very sincere. Besides, I'm tired of sitting home on Saturday night."

"I'm with you there," she commiserated.

"And there's another reason. I wanted a peek at the other Nancy Stern's life," I admitted. "I figured, why not pose as her, assume her identity, for one measly night? Bill will never be the wiser."

"Wow," said Janice, shaking her head. "This is going to be one *really* blind date." The remark inspired another fit of giggles which lasted for several minutes.

"You don't think any less of me?" I asked, after we had settled down.

"Think less of you? I'm proud of you," she said. "You're taking a risk for a change, putting some adventure into your life."

"But I'll be lying to the man."

"And men don't lie to women on a regular basis? Anyhow, this is different. All you'll be doing is playing an innocent game of pretend, the way the kids in our class do. You won't be committing the crime of the century, believe me."

"As soon as the date's over, I'll tell him the truth," I vowed.

"Right," said Janice. "If he has a sense of humor, he'll find the whole thing funny. If he doesn't have a sense of humor, he wasn't worth going out with in the first place."

"Good point," I said.

"What's more, by stealing someone else's blind date, you'll be taking an extremely creative approach to the shortage of eligible men in this city."

"Thank you. I don't feel quite as twisted now that we've talked."

She smiled. "Look, you'll have dinner with him on Saturday night, do your act, and that will be that. Which brings me to a crucial question: What are you going to wear on the date? I'll help you pick something out if you want."

"I'm all set, wardrobe wise, but I could use your help in another way."

"Name it."

"Could you search that computer of yours and find out whatever you can about the other Nancy Stern? Maybe *she* has a Web site. She has everything else."

"The magazines she writes for must have Web sites. I'll click onto them and see if she's there in connection with specific articles or profiles."

"That would be great."

"I'll also try and get some general celebrity trivia for you. So you can sound like you know what you're talking about."

"Even better."

"There's just one thing."

"And that is?"

"What if this guy turns out to be a total sociopath, like Gary, the nutritionist? That would be a downer."

"What if he turns out to be the man of my dreams, only he's repulsed by women who aren't completely honest with him? *That* would be a downer."

CHAPTER SIX

I left the city on Wednesday and drove to Pennsylvania to be with my family for Thanksgiving.

I have a loving family, with the exception of my father's widower-brother, Uncle Dave, who gets drunk and crabby and then passes out in front of the TV, and I don't mind spending time at the old homestead, now that I don't have to live there anymore. But my head wasn't into this visit; I was fixated on my upcoming dinner date with Bill Harris.

My mother noticed something was up the first evening, when I suggested we all watch *Entertainment Tonight* instead of real news.

"Not interested in current events?" she asked as she passed the meat loaf. We were eating in the kitchen/family room, she and my father and I, saving the dining room for the big meal the next day.

"Sure, I am," I said, "but for some reason I'm in the mood for one of those celebrity shows." For some reason — ha! I was hoping to do research in preparation for Saturday night, hoping to catch a few tidbits about Leonardo DiCaprio or one of those people, hoping to impress Bill Harris with my vast knowledge of Hollywood happenings — in case the conversation meandered in that direction.

Later that night, as I was reading in bed (the current issues of *People* and *Entertainment Weekly*), my mother knocked on the door and asked if she could come in.

"Of course," I said, sliding over so she could sit on the bed next to me. "Is anything wrong?"

"I miss you, that's all," she said wistfully. "You'll always be my special baby, even though you're grown up and living on your own."

Special baby. Here we go, I thought, sensing where she was headed: another spontaneous, unsolicited retelling of the story of the day I was born. I had heard it so often I could recite it word for word.

"They told me I couldn't have children," was how she always launched into the story, establishing for the listener *why* I was a special baby right off the bat. Next came the visit to her doctor, the confirmation that she was pregnant, and the joy she and my father experienced upon receiving this unexpected but longed-for news. Then came the morning sickness followed by the food cravings followed by the weight gain. Then came the thrill of having her water break in the wee hours of the morning, the flat tire on the way to the hospital, and the good samaritan who appeared out of nowhere to fix it. Then came the arrival at the hospital, the labor pains, and finally the moment the doctor said, "I can see the head now."

"You're our miracle, Nancy," was how she always ended the story, rendering me miraculous as well as special.

I once mentioned the story to the therapist I consulted briefly after my divorce. He said that children who are constantly hit with the specialness routine either grow up to be ne'er-do-wells who figure they can never fulfill their parents' expectations so why try, or they go through life accepting nothing less than achievement, excellence, and glory. In which category do you fall, Nancy? he asked me. I said I didn't know. He said I should think about it.

That night at my parents' house, I did think about it. I decided that I fell into the latter category. Why else would I covet the other Nancy Stern's life if I weren't the type to accept nothing less than achievement, excellence, and glory? Of course, it was *her* achievement, *her* excellence, and *her* glory I was after. Not a healthy sign, I concluded.

"I wish I could see you more often, Nance," my mother said as she got up from the bed.

"Then why don't you come into the city?" I said.

"Oh, honey," she said. "You know how hectic it is here."

What I knew was that the word *travel* was not in my mother's vocabulary. She was raised three houses down from the house where she had raised me, and her life revolved around my father, her charity work, and the little greeting card shop she owned and managed with the woman who had been her best friend since high school. She moved within a very limited radius, but unlike me she never seemed dissatisfied with small-town life. She would never have yearned to be someone else, for example, never have even been tempted to steal the other Nancy Stern's blind date.

"One of these days I'll come in and stay with you," she vowed.

"Whenever you want," I said, hoping she would but not holding my breath.

Thanksgiving day went pretty much according to past holiday gatherings. Uncle Dave polished off a fifth of Jack Daniel's, unleashed a barrage of attacks on the United States government, the Pittsburgh Pirates, and his own children (who were smart enough to have avoided spending Thanksgiving with him that year), and conked out on the sofa.

As I was getting ready to head back to New York on Friday afternoon, my father asked if I had a "beau."

"No. Why?" I said, surprised by the question. My father wasn't one of those hovering, overprotective fathers who felt challenged by the men in my life, nor did he tend to inquire about such matters the way my mother did.

He shrugged. "You've got a look about you," he replied, studying my face. "Like you've got a secret you're not ready to tell us about. I assumed it was a beau."

"No beau," I said. "But I do have a dinner date tomorrow night."

"Oh? Somebody you met through work?"

"Somebody I met on the phone. He was a wrong number."

My father shook his head. "That city you live in. Anything can happen there, huh?"

"Just about," I said.

"Well, this fella may have dialed the wrong number, but he's a lucky son of a gun that he reached Nancy Stern," he clucked.

"He has no idea what a great gal he's getting."

"None," I agreed.

When I returned to my apartment, there was a large envelope waiting for me. "Your friend Janice dropped it off this morning," said the doorman.

Must be her research assignment, I thought, figuring she'd been able to unearth some background on Nancy. I thanked the doorman and was on my way to the elevator when the celebrity journalist herself appeared.

"Oh," I said, somewhat startled to see her, given that I was holding an envelope that was intended to help me impersonate her that very evening. "How are you, Nancy?"

"Fine. Fine. How are you?" she asked. She was wearing the shearling coat, I noticed. The freshly dry cleaned shearling coat. It looked smashing on her.

"I'm great," I said, wishing I were. "Where are you off to?"

"Westchester," she said. "I finally got an interview with Susan Sarandon and Tim Robbins for *Parade*."

"How exciting," I said, being a fan of both actors.

"It is exciting, because I've been after

their publicists for years to let me come to the house to do an in-depth piece."

"Well, good luck," I said. "I hope it goes well."

"So do I. They've got children, and children can be such a distraction when you're trying to conduct a serious interview. Maybe I should take you along, Nancy. While I grill the parents, you could play little games with the kiddies or something."

I tried not to take her remark personally. Perhaps she wasn't condescending, just unenlightened about the appeal of youngsters.

I went upstairs, unpacked my things, and opened Janice's envelope. It contained several sheets of computer printouts regarding the other Nancy Stern. My best pal had come through, as usual.

According to the material, the other Nancy Stern did write for a variety of publications, did travel all over the world chasing down her subjects, did have a glamorous career. And, according to the material, she did, indeed, interview Kevin Costner. But it was another of her interviews that impressed me. *Floored* me. There in the envelope was a 1998 interview Nancy had done with Susan Sarandon and Tim Robbins! At their Westchester home! For *Parade*!

Why in the world did she just lie to me? I

wondered. Why did she claim to be heading up to Westchester to interview the couple for the first time when it was clear that she'd already done the interview? Where was she really off to when I'd run into her downstairs?

Apparently, the other Nancy Stern was mysterious as well as glamorous, but I didn't have time to solve her puzzle. I had a date.

Okay, I sighed, as I sank onto the bed and began to study the rest of Janice's material. Here I come, Bill Harris. Ready or not.

Keeping my word to Bill, I wore a black dress on Saturday night — a midcalf-length, black wool dress that was slimming and versatile and the garment I trotted out whenever I had dinner with a man for the first time. I wouldn't exactly call it my lucky dress, as these dinner dates rarely went anywhere, but I would call it my security dress in that nothing terrible ever happened to me when I had it on.

I arrived at the entrance to the restaurant ten minutes early. I am always early and, therefore, am always the one waiting. Even when I *try* to be late, I am early. I was sure that, in contrast, the other Nancy Stern was the sort of woman who waltzed in long after she was expected in order to heighten the drama of her appearance and make people appreciate her all the more.

I decided to take a leisurely stroll around the block, to kill time. It was a cold, nasty night, following an hour or so of sleet, and the sidewalks were slick, even icy in patches. Nevertheless, I drew my coat around me and forged on, aware that what I was doing was foolish but doing it anyway.

I was walking past the Korean produce market where Janice had run into Gary, the nutritionist-sociopath, when I slipped on a banana peel. You heard me.

I went down hard, the heel of my black leather boot skidding on the slimy underside of the banana skin, and I landed flat on my ass.

No, nobody helped me up — this was New York, after all — and so I sat there for a second or two, stunned by the fall, grateful that I hadn't broken any bones, anxious about explaining to Bill how I came to have a yellow stain on the seat of my coat.

I glanced at my watch. It was only six-fifty-five. I was *still* early.

I raced back to my apartment to switch coats and then raced back over to the restaurant, my hair damp with a mixture of sweat and drizzle. I looked like something that had just crawled out of a swamp.

It was five minutes after seven when I opened the door to the restaurant and made my entrance.

"I'm meeting Mr. Harris," I said breathlessly to the maître d'. "I believe he has a reservation for two at seven o'clock."

He scanned the book, found Bill's reservation, and smiled at me. "The gentleman has not arrived," he said, his accent French, his manner friendly. The place I had chosen was a neighborhood bistro that had been there for years — an old standby as opposed to a trendy newcomer. The food was reliable and not terribly expensive and the atmosphere lively — the perfect setting for a blind date, I thought.

As the maître d' led me to a table, I laughed to myself about the fact that even though I was late, I was early, yet again. I also wondered if Bill Harris had somehow found out that he'd been hoodwinked and decided not to show.

I ordered a glass of wine and played with the silverware, the tablecloth, and the ends of my still-damp hair, checking the door every now and then for a very tall man. At about seven-twenty, a very tall man appeared — a very handsome tall man wearing a trench coat.

God, is this Bill? I thought, sitting up straighter in the chair. Could this dashing figure with dark hair and dark eyes really be a kindly, self-deprecating jeweler?

He was much better-looking than I had imagined from the voice on the phone — I'd formed a mental picture of a *gangly* tall man as opposed to a *gorgeous* tall man — and his cool, knowing expression evoked those British actors who always play spies.

Nancy, Nancy, Nancy, I chastised myself. Did you forget he's the manager of Denham and Villier's New York store? No wonder he's dashing. All the people who work there are. Dashing, perfectly groomed, and impeccably dressed. Not a nipple piercer among them.

I tried to remain calm as the maître d' escorted him to the table. It occurred to me that most women would be angry with Bill for keeping them waiting for nearly half an hour, but since I was about to pass myself off to him as someone I wasn't, I didn't feel I was in a position to be sanctimonious.

"Nancy?" he said when he reached the table. It was truly a question and it unnerved me, as if he already suspected that I couldn't possibly be the person Joan Geisinger had encouraged him to call.

"Yes, I'm Nancy." I smiled. "Really."

"Good. I'm Bill," he said, shaking my hand, "and I'm very late, I know. You're probably wishing you'd never agreed to meet me."

"Hey, don't be so hard on yourself," I said, noticing that the cool, knowing expression had been replaced by an earnestness I responded to immediately. "Did you get lost or something?"

"I ended up on the wrong subway," he explained as he removed his trench coat, draped it over the back of his chair, and sat down. "My apartment is on the West Side and I figured that getting crosstown would be a breeze." He shook his head. "As I said on the phone, I'm not the smoothest guy on the planet when it comes to blind dates."

"Not to worry," I said reassuringly, even though I'd assumed that to be a manager of Denham and Villier you *had* to be the smoothest guy on the planet — or one of them. "I'm just glad you finally made it."

And I was. He was extremely sexy in his dark green wool turtleneck and black corduroy slacks. Very snappy. I found it hard to believe he even went on blind dates, given just *how* snappy.

He ordered a glass of wine when the waiter came around.

"This is a charming little place you picked

out," he commented, surveying the restaurant, which was bustling by then. "You must know all the best spots in town."

"Well, yes. I do," I said. "I conduct a lot of my interviews over lunches and dinners. The job does have its perks."

He grinned. "I still can't believe I'm sitting here with *the* Nancy Stern, the woman Joan's been championing."

"Neither can I," I said, meaning it. "Oh, if you're wondering what happened to the blond hair she mentioned — I was flippant about it on the phone the other day — I chopped most of it off about three years ago and let my natural color grow in. I decided that the *Baywatch* babe thing was pretty tired." I groaned to myself as I realized I was parroting Janice's remark.

"Your natural color's very pretty," said Bill, running his eyes over me. "As a matter of fact, I can't picture you as a blonde."

That's because I'm The Brunette Who Keeps Her Head. Yeah.

"What else did Joanie tell you about me?" I fished.

"Let's see. She said you always wanted to interview celebrities, even back when you two were at — which magazine was it again?"

"*Harper's Bazaar*," I replied, then remembered that I had told him *Cosmo* the last time the subject had come up.

"She said you had a knack for getting people to open up," he added. "What's your secret?"

"My secret?" I said. If he only knew.

"Your secret," he repeated. "The key to getting celebrities to talk to you."

"Oh. Right. Well, I hate to toot my own horn, Bill, but I suppose I'm a good listener," I said shamelessly. "That's probably the key to my success — in a nutshell."

"I'm sure there's more to it than that. For instance, I'm guessing the job requires a certain fearlessness, a refusal to be intimidated."

"Yes, fearlessness is important."

"And the ability to write under pressure."

"Absolutely."

"And you'd have to have an overall knowledge of the arts, as well as the political scene."

"No question."

He laughed. "Would you listen to me? I'm putting words in your mouth when you're the wordsmith. Why don't I let you tell me about this glamorous career of yours."

Bill took a sip of his wine. I took three or four sips of mine.

"Ah, where to begin." I sighed. "I do a

great deal of traveling and I put in killer hours when I'm on deadline, but it *is* a glamorous career in many ways. I get to meet my share of interesting people, charismatic people. Actually, you resemble one of them."

"I do?"

"Yes. You're sort of a young, American Jeremy Irons. I interviewed him in Tuscany a few years ago, on the set of *The English Patient*."

Bill looked confused. "Wasn't it Ralph Fiennes who starred in *The English Patient*?"

I drank more wine. "Did I say Jeremy Irons? Boy, do you believe that? Obviously, I meant that you remind me of Ralph Fiennes. A tall, American Ralph Fiennes."

"Well, thanks either way," Bill said shyly. "No one's ever told me I look like a movie star before, but I'm not going to try to talk you out of it. Was he a nice guy?"

"Ralph or Jeremy?"

"You've interviewed both of them?"

"Oh, yes. I did a lengthy profile of Jeremy when he was promoting *Notting Hill*."

Bill scratched his head. "I could have sworn Hugh Grant was in that one."

"Right you are." I chuckled. "I'm mixing up my Brits, as you can see, probably because I've interviewed so many of them.

Why just the other week, I was invited to a reception at the British embassy."

"And I've never even been to England," Bill lamented. "Too many things keeping me busy here."

"Like what?" I asked, eager to shift the focus onto him.

Before he could answer, we were momentarily interrupted by the waiter, who announced the evening's specials.

"Please, do tell me about yourself, Bill," I urged when he departed. "What made you go into the jewelry business, for starters?"

"Dumb luck, really. I got married right after college and my wife's father owned a couple of jewelry stores in Virginia. I went to work for him, discovered that I was good with clients and enjoyed being around all those diamonds, and continued to work for him for a short time, even after his daughter and I split up. Eventually, I moved to Washington to take a job at the Denham and Villier store there."

"Sounds like you had a friendly divorce from your ex-wife."

"Friendly enough. Jill and I have two kids, and we're determined to keep them on an even keel. So far, we've done pretty well, although now that I've relocated here I won't get to see them as often as I did."

"How old are they?" I asked.

"Twelve and fifteen. Both boys." He whipped out his wallet and handed me a couple of snapshots. "That one's Peter." He pointed to the older boy, a dark-haired teenager with his father's aristocratic features. "And that's Michael." The younger one was a redhead, with only a hint of Bill in his face.

"They're very handsome," I said. "Will they be coming up to New York to visit over Christmas?"

"I wish. Christmas is a zoo at the store, so I can't take off until New Year's. They'll be coming that week, and for presidents' week in February and occasional long weekends — if they can fit me in. They're active kids. They've always got something going on."

"And you miss them."

"And I miss them. More than I can describe."

I thought of the fathers of several of the kids in my class, fathers like Bob Levin who probably didn't even know what his son ate for breakfast. I had a hunch that Bill Harris wasn't like them, judging by the way his eyes looked both pained and proud when he'd displayed the photos of his boys. No, this was a man who cared. I suddenly remembered the other Nancy Stern's admission — that she wasn't a "child person" — and doubted very much that she and Bill would have clicked.

During dinner, he related a half-dozen funny anecdotes about his sons, prefacing each one with: "Are you sure this stuff isn't boring to you?" I assured him that I loved children and wasn't bored in the slightest. Which I wasn't. Bill was a good storyteller, I discovered, with a wry sense of humor and an eye for detail. He was especially interesting when he talked about his work, describing his transition from local jeweler to one of Denham and Villier's head honchos.

"Going from a mom-and-pop organization to a corporate retailer was an eye-opener," he said. "I thought I'd just glide into Denham's D.C. store, puffed up with my experience running a couple of suburban mall stores, and they'd make me king." He laughed. "Before they let me set foot in the place, I had to be trained at the GIA."

"Is that a branch of the CIA?" I asked, thinking he might have needed a background in covert operations so he could guard all that expensive jewelry.

He smiled. "It's the Gemological Institute of America. I did my training there, out in California, and then started at Denham at ground zero, gradually working my way up the ladder from a lowly polisher to a sales-person who more than met my quotas, which was how I got promoted to store manager. The slow and steady route."

"They put you through the paces, is that it?"

"They sure did, but it's understandable when you consider the value of the merchandise they sell. Denham isn't going to hand over the key to a showcase to someone they haven't come to trust over a period of years."

"Makes sense. I take it the move to the New York store was another promotion?"

"A nice one. The New York store is the jewel in the company's crown, to make a really bad pun. The D.C. store doesn't do nearly as much business, especially not any-more." He laughed again. "A lot of the cli-ents there were politicians buying baubles for their mistresses, but the minute the Lewinsky thing broke, they cut back on their extracurricular activities."

"God forbid they should buy baubles for their wives."

"Oh, they did that too, which is why dis-cretion is an important part of my job. It's a real no-no to stroll up to some guy's wife and say, 'How did you like that emerald necklace your husband bought you?'

Ninety-nine percent of the time she'll say, 'What necklace?' "

"Men."

"Men can be louses, I grant you, but the women who come in are pieces of work too. We get the type who tie up our salespeople for hours. They try everything on and can't decide what to buy or whether to buy, and then they pull out their cell phone and call their mother or sister or girlfriend to come over to *help* them decide. There are times when I have to step in to close the deal."

"So you must be a good salesman as well as a good manager."

His eyes twinkled. "You tell me, Nancy. Am I a good salesman?"

"You're doing all right," I said. He was doing more than all right. Whenever he looked at me, I turned to Jell-O. "Discretion aside, Denham and Villier must see a fair share of celebrities, Bill, especially at the New York store."

"We do. Sometimes, we put them in a private room with three or four pieces of jewelry and their favorite alcoholic beverage. Sometimes, we send a few trinkets to their home or office, accompanied by a sales specialist and a setter. Sometimes, as we did recently in the case of Barbra Streisand, we make an after-hours presentation, waiting until the store is closed so there can be complete privacy for the client."

Barbra Streisand? I tried not to look star-struck. After all, I was the one who was supposed to know everybody.

"But my contact with these people is pretty minimal. It's the sales staff that usually deals with them. I get stuck with the status seekers."

"And who are they?"

"They're the ones who shop at Denham so they can *say* they shopped at Denham. They won't deal with anyone but the manager so they can *say* they didn't deal with anyone but the manager. I'm talking about people who aren't comfortable with who they are, Nancy, people with such inferiority complexes that they have to *pretend* to be important. They're sad cases, let me tell you."

"You don't know how sad."

"What was that?"

"Nothing. I was just agreeing with you."

We were lingering over dessert and coffee when it hit me that the date was going so well that it was more than likely that Bill would want to see me again. But I ignored the matter of exactly what I was going to do about the situation, and instead responded to the question he was posing to me at that moment: Which celebrity did I enjoy interviewing the most?

I'm not a bad storyteller myself, having had all that experience in the classroom, so I made up a heartwarming tale about the afternoon I spent with former President Jimmy Carter — how he took me on a tour of the Carter Center in Atlanta, shared his thoughts about world peace over a couple of humble chicken salad sandwiches, and, when it was determined that I wouldn't be able to fly back to New York that day due to a freakish snowstorm, invited me to stay with him and Mrs. Carter in their home.

"It was amazing of him to do that," I concluded, marveling at the supposed memory of the president's supposed generosity.

"He must have enjoyed your company, the way I am right now," said Bill. "I doubt he opens his home to every journalist he talks to."

I shrugged in an ostentatious display of modesty. I was about to launch into another riff, this time about my interview with Princess Stephanie of Monaco, when I felt someone tap me on the shoulder.

"Nancy! Fancy meeting you here."

Damn. It was Victoria Bittner, one of the other head teachers at Small Blessings, the frustrated painter. What was *she* doing at the restaurant when she should have been home painting?

"Uh, hi, Victoria," I said awkwardly, as she stood there with her husband, a frustrated sculptor whose name I always forgot. "I didn't see you come in."

"Well, *I* saw *you*," she replied, eyeing Bill, eager to be introduced. "But I decided to wait and say hello on our way out."

"That was thoughtful. This is my friend Bill Harris," I said, putting her out of her misery. "He just moved here from Washington."

Victoria and her husband shook hands with Bill and said it was nice to meet him and that any friend of mine was a friend of theirs, blah blah blah. Then she turned to me. "So how did your Thanksgiving play go on Tuesday, Nancy?"

My Thanksgiving play.

Why hadn't it occurred to me that I might bump into someone I knew? Someone from school, of all places.

"It was a fine production," I said ambiguously, hoping to give Bill the impression that the play Victoria had asked about was a Broadway show starring a celebrity I'd be interviewing.

"So nobody acted out? Not even Fischer Levin?" she said.

"The acting was superb," I said. "Fischer was a revelation."

"Is this Fischer an up-and-comer?" said Bill. "A star of the future?"

Victoria smirked. "They're all stars of the future. Just ask their parents."

"I take it you and Nancy are in the same field," Bill said to her.

"Yeah," she said. "We both work with four-year-olds."

"Four-year-olds." Bill laughed. "I can see why you'd feel that way. From what I've read about your business, you must see your share of temper tantrums."

"Daily. That's why they pay us the big bucks," she said dryly.

I was growing edgy, impatient. It was time for Victoria and her husband to run along.

"Well, I guess we'll be running along," said Victoria, getting the message exactly. "Welcome to New York, Bill. See you at school on Monday, Nancy."

"Which school was she talking about?" Bill asked after they left.

"Dog training school," I said without missing a beat. "Victoria and I have Jack Russell terriers and we can't do a thing with them." I was getting good at this. Too good.

Bill signaled for the check. After he paid

it, he reached for my hand and gave it an affectionate squeeze. "I don't know about you, but I'm ready to do this again," he said. "Like, tomorrow."

I smiled, flushed with the compliment. He liked me. He did.

"All right, so how about the day *after* tomorrow?" he said. "I'm serious, Nancy. I had a great time."

"So did I," I said.

"Then it's a date? Monday night for dinner?"

Okay, Nance, I thought. Here's your chance. This is where you tell him the truth and put an end to your little game.

But if I tell him the truth, he won't want to see me again, I protested silently, convinced that Bill Harris wasn't just suave and sophisticated; he was the most honest and decent man I'd ever met, the type of kindhearted soul who wouldn't find it remotely amusing that I had spent the entire evening lying through my teeth.

I wanted desperately to see *him* again, that was a given. I hadn't felt so alive in a long time. Maybe it was the game playing that had heightened my senses and maybe it wasn't, but I wasn't prepared to give up the feeling.

"I'd love to have dinner with you on

Monday night," I heard myself say.

Bill sank back in his chair and positively beamed. "You know, you're not what I expected. From Joan's description."

"Well, I explained about my hair and how I —"

"I'm not talking about your hair, Nancy," he interrupted. "I'm talking about you, your personality, your *accessibility*. I had this idea that you would be snooty or self-absorbed or taken with yourself — and I see enough of that stuff at the store. But you're not. You're more than just a good listener. You're —" He stopped. "This is silly. I'm not going to start piling on the flattery on the first date. You'll have to wait until Monday, although the nicest surprise about you is that you like kids. Joan gave me the impression that you didn't."

"Joanie had me mixed up with someone else," I said.

"You think so?"

"Trust me."

CHAPTER SEVEN

Bill offered to walk me home, but I fed him a line about needing to stop at the twenty-four-hour market for a quart of milk. He asked if I wanted him to walk me there and *then* walk me home, but I said that I tended to take a long time when I shopped, was an inveterate browser, and usually ended up buying more than I came for.

Brother. I make the man sound like the most gullible turkey around, but the thing is, I was more adept at bullshitting than I ever imagined I'd be.

Janice called at eight o'clock on Sunday morning to find out how the date went.

"I'd rather tell you in person," I said, shivering because I was in a cold sweat. Janice had woken me out of a deep sleep, and I'd been dreaming that Jeremy Irons and Ralph Fiennes and Hugh Grant were chasing me across London Bridge, which, of course, was falling down.

"Was the date that good or that bad?" she asked.

"Both," I said. "Let's meet this afternoon and I'll explain."

"Great. How about the Barnes and Noble in Union Square?" she suggested. "I hang out there on Sunday afternoons now."

"So you can do research for your reading group?"

"No, so I can meet men. Barnes and Noble is the new pickup place."

"Ah."

"Then I'll see you there? Two o'clock?"

"If you're sure I won't cramp your style," I said.

"You won't. Just try not to cry," she said. "I think that's a turnoff."

At two o'clock, I met Janice in the magazine section of the store. When I came upon her, she was chatting up a disheveled man in combat fatigues, who was leafing through the latest issue of *Guns & Ammo*.

I grabbed her by the elbow and herded her over to the café. "That didn't look very promising," I said.

"I suppose not," she agreed, "although he had nice eyes."

We ordered a couple of coffees (well, I ordered a coffee; Janice ordered a V8), and I began to describe my evening with Bill Harris.

"He's much handsomer than I expected," I said, "but not at all conceited. The opposite, if anything."

"God. I absolutely love that when the really good-looking ones don't understand how good-looking they are. It's so — I don't know — *real*."

"That's the thing," I said excitedly. "Bill's real. A regular guy. A *nice* guy. He didn't spend the entire night obsessing about his washboard abs."

"Are they?"

"What?"

"Are they washboard abs?"

"Possibly, but I didn't lift up his sweater and measure his fat-to-body ratio."

"Oh, so you didn't have sex?"

"No. It didn't even come up. Not that there wasn't an attraction between us. But I sense that Bill is the type who likes to take things slowly, so he can get to know the woman first."

"Divorced?"

"Yes. With two kids. But even that part sounded normal, sensible. He and his ex-wife actually make a point of getting along, for the sake of the children."

"What a concept."

"The only uncomfortable part of the date had to do with the celebrities I supposedly interviewed. I screwed up their names a few times, but I straightened out as the night went along." I told Janice about the appearance at the restaurant of Victoria Bittner and her husband and how I managed to wriggle out of trouble there.

"Excellent. Now, what happened when the date was over and you told Bill you weren't the other Nancy Stern? Did he get the joke or go ballistic?"

"Actually, that's where things got a little rough."

"So he did go ballistic. You're not hurt, are you, Nance?" She checked me for bruises.

"I'm fine, Janice. Things got rough because I didn't tell him the truth when the date was over."

She sat back in her chair and stared at me. "No?"

"No."

"And the reason for this is?"

"Oh, Janice. I couldn't. The words just wouldn't come out of my mouth. I was enjoying myself too much, I guess. See, Bill and I established a genuine connection, right from the start. It was as if we were on the same wavelength."

"Except for one teeny weeny detail: He thought you were someone else."

"Yes, but aside from that, we were totally in sync. I realize I haven't dated as often as you have and that almost any man would look good to me these days, but I felt different when I was with him — more alive." I was so alive I was gesturing wildly with my hands and knocked my coffee cup over.

"Look, Nance," said Janice as I wiped up the spill, "I'm glad you had fun and it's reassuring to learn there are still nice guys out there — even if they had to import this one from Washington — but what are you going to do if he asks you out again?"

"He already did. We're having dinner together tomorrow night."

She immediately launched into the chorus of the old Motown song "Quicksand."

"I know, I know. I'm sinking deeper," I said sheepishly. "I hate lying."

"You're not lying," she maintained. "As I said the other day, you're having an adventure."

"An adventure," I repeated, nodding.

"Although, technically, you *are* lying," she added.

"Janice."

"But you're not doing it to trap Bill, like some pathetic *Rules* girl. You're doing it to satisfy your curiosity about the other Nancy

Stern, about what it would be like to live her life. That's accurate, isn't it?"

"It was. It is. It depends."

She laughed. "The important question is, how long do you think this curiosity of yours will last?"

I shrugged. "Bill insisted on picking me up at my apartment tomorrow night. Since I can't transform it into a penthouse, he'll figure out right away that I'm not rolling in money like the other Nancy Stern. In other words, my 'curiosity' could be over sooner rather than later."

"Not necessarily. Just tell Bill your apartment is a pied-à-terre — the cozy little spot where you hang your hat whenever you're in Manhattan. Tell him your primary residence is a big estate in the Hamptons or wherever. Oh, and call the house something — you know, one of those names like Green Meadows."

"That sounds like an assisted living facility."

"Okay, then *you* come up with a name," she said huffily.

I smiled. "Now that I think about it, there's no reason why Bill would expect Nancy to be rich. Remember, she's not Barbara Walters."

"Fine. So don't tell him about the big estate. But you are going to have to tell him who you are at some point. Who knows? Maybe he'll be happy that you teach pre-school. You said he loves kids."

"Yes, but he's definitely impressed with the other Nancy Stern's career, with all the celebrities she's rubbed shoulders with. I'm fairly certain that stories about Fischer Levin won't be as thrilling to him as stories about Gwyneth Paltrow."

"Probably not."

"Still, I will tell him the truth. Tomorrow night."

She patted my hand. "Of course you will, Nance. By the second date, men start to show their neuroses, anyway. I guarantee you: Bill won't look as good to you the next time around."

On Monday, Alexis Shuler, the girl with the lisp, turned five, and her mother brought a homemade birthday cake to school for the class's snack. When I say "homemade" I'm not kidding, either. Alexis's mother was one of those Martha Stewart mothers who makes everything from scratch and then decorates it as if it will be used as a prop for a photo shoot. For this particular creation, Mrs. Shuler assembled various ingredients atop the white cake and frosting to replicate the face of her daughter (red licorice for the mouth, a cashew nut for the nose, green grapes for the eyes, coconut shavings mixed with yellow food coloring for the hair), and she enveloped the entire masterpiece in a nest of spun sugar. By the time the children were through with it, the cake looked like mashed potatoes.

Later that morning, everybody sat in a circle on the rug and did a little show-and-tell about his or her Thanksgiving vacation. When it was Fischer's turn, he told us about his trip to Aruba.

"My dad found buried treasure there," he said. "He brought it home and put it in this giant box late at night. He thought I was sleeping but I saw."

I allowed him to finish his recitation instead of putting him in Time-out, but later I warned him about the pirate business.

"We're not going to lie about things, right, honey?" I said, feeling horribly two-faced, given my personal situation.

"I'm not —"

"Fischer?"

"Yes, Miss Stern," he said without further protest, then chugged over to the circle, where Todd Delafield made a space for him.

Next, it was Carl Pinder's turn at show-

and-tell. He was the kid who spoke five languages but wasn't fully potty trained. He told the class about his Thanksgiving at his grandparents' chateau in the Loire Valley, recounting the entire story in French. As the other children barely understood English, they became restless and fidgety a few minutes into Carl's story. I'm sorry to report that among the first to become restless and fidgety was Fischer, who socked Todd in the stomach and was put in Time-out after all.

When I got home, I glanced at my mail, had a cup of tea, and took a shower. I was about to change clothes for my date with Bill when the doorman buzzed, informing me that a delivery boy from the pharmacy was on his way up. As with other recent deliveries, I tried to fend this one off by barking at the doorman. But I was too late. Within minutes, my doorbell was ringing.

"Delivery for Nancy Stern," mumbled the young man, who was carrying not only a small bag containing the prescription but a very large boom box. He was a fan of rap music, apparently, and he had the bass turned up so high that I thought my head, never mind the building, would explode.

"This isn't for me," I shouted, meaning

the delivery not the music, although I could have done without both.

Naturally, he didn't hear me over the ear-splitting sound, but he did hang around until I came up with a tip. I stuffed the money in his hand and scowled.

"Hey, you're not gettin' jiggy wit it," he said.

"Whatever," I said and closed the door.

I carried the bag into the kitchen and opened it. It contained two prescriptions, it turned out, both for Nancy Stern at 137 East Seventy-first Street but neither for me, since I hadn't called in any. What's more, I didn't take Claritin, since I didn't have allergies, nor did I take Prozac, since I didn't have —

Prozac? *Prozac?*

Was the other Nancy Stern depressed? The Nancy Stern with the looks, the boyfriends, the career, the money? The Nancy Stern with the life I coveted? Had I been naive — okay, downright stupid — to think she was coasting along without any problems?

I thought back over the past few weeks and reminded myself that the tenant in 24A did act a tad strangely — from her anxiousness over the phone calls she'd received while I was in her apartment to her lie about

124

rushing off to interview Sarandon and Robbins.

Obviously, things weren't so ducky up there in the penthouse, and I had viewed the other Nancy Stern in a hopelessly simplistic light. Of course she was human. Of course she was vulnerable. Of course she was flawed — depressed, even. She had just seemed to me to be *less* flawed, *less* depressed than I was, which was why I intended to have dinner with a man who had intended to have dinner with her. I had assumed, without even knowing her, that she was the possessor of an embarrassment of riches and would, therefore, not miss yet another one.

Well, she can hardly miss Bill when she isn't even aware that he exists, I reminded myself. Not only that, just because she takes Prozac doesn't mean she's suicidal.

No, one less man in her life certainly won't put her over the edge, I decided. Besides, he'll be back on the market as soon as I tell him who I am — or, should I say, who I'm not.

CHAPTER EIGHT

For my second date with Bill I dressed casually, in jeans and a sweater, because we were going to a boisterous, pub-type hamburger joint up the street from my apartment.

"I know you're used to eating at all the best restaurants," he'd said when we were discussing where to go, "but ever since I moved here, I've been dying for a good burger, preferably with greasy fries and a side order of onion rings."

"And a room in Lenox Hill's cardiac care unit," I'd joked. "I've got just the place."

I'd thought it was sweet that underneath his finely chiseled features, wavy dark hair, and tall, lean frame lurked your basic meat-and-potatoes guy.

At seven o'clock on the dot, the doorman buzzed. "Bill's on the way up."

Right on time, I thought with a rush of pleasure. He must be looking forward to seeing me. Hubba hubba.

I made a quick check of the apartment, trying to see it through Bill's eyes. It was small but comfortable — an L-shaped studio, really, with a wall between the bedroom and the living room/dining area. It wasn't a penthouse but it was a "find" for a single gal with my meager salary, especially considering the high-ticket neighborhood it was in, and I'd felt lucky to have it — until the other Nancy Stern had moved into the building and rubbed my nose in her life.

I fluffed the sofa cushions, cleared away a couple of dust bunnies, and raced to the door after Bill rang the bell.

"Hi," he said as he stood in the threshold.

"Hi," I said as I stood there facing him.

Okay, so we sounded like a couple of imbeciles. What you're missing is the electricity that crackled between those "Hi's," the mutual I-didn't-expect-to-be-so-glad-to-see-you-again body language. It was incredible. There Bill was, in his blue jeans and ski sweater and brown leather jacket, gazing at me with his deeply set eyes, as if there were no one on earth he'd rather be gazing at. And there I was, one giant nerve ending, on the receiving end of his gaze and nearly bursting with the high octane–ness of it all. If you've ever been in this situation — where you had a blind date with a guy and you sensed it went very well but you weren't absolutely sure, and then you saw the guy a second time and the instant he walked in you knew, just *knew*, that your assessment of the first date was right on the money — you can appreciate the moment.

"It's good to see you in the flesh, Nancy."

"In the flesh?"

"Okay. The truth is, I was thinking about you so much yesterday I started to wonder if I'd conjured you up, if you were real."

I smiled. "I'm real, I promise." It's only my identity that's fake.

"Perfect. Since you're real, your apartment must be too. How about letting me come inside?"

"I think that could be arranged." I stepped aside so Bill could cross the threshold. As I did, I noticed he was carrying something in his left hand. "What's that you've got there?" I asked.

He held up a magazine. "It's the new issue of *TV Guide*. Your article's in it so I brought it over, not that you haven't seen it already."

"My article," I said, having no clue what he was talking about. The only time I ever read *TV Guide* was in the checkout line at the supermarket. "Actually, I haven't seen it. I never get to see my finished products."

"Well, here it is." He handed me the magazine.

I flipped nonchalantly through the pages

and stopped when I came upon a piece about Morgan Fairchild, written by none other than Nancy Stern. "My, they did a nice job with the layout," I remarked, settling into my Pretend Journalist mode. "And they seem to have used most of my material for a change." I glanced up at Bill and shrugged resignedly. "I do my interviews for these publications, but once I turn them in I have no idea what's going to be printed and what's going to be cut."

"I didn't know it worked that way," he said. "Hey, don't think this is goofy, but I brought the magazine over because I was hoping you'd sign it so I could send it to my kids. They get a kick out of stuff like that."

"Sign it? You mean, autograph it?"

"You do think it's goofy."

"No, it's just that I'm not the celebrity. It's Morgan Fairchild's autograph your sons would get a kick out of."

"No question they would, but since you wrote the article and your name is on it, I just thought —" He stopped, taking the magazine back. "You hate the idea. Forget I mentioned it."

"Don't be silly," I said, taking the magazine back from him. "I'll get a pen."

I went into the kitchen, grabbed the black Flair hanging from the magnetized holder on the refrigerator, and scribbled "Nancy Stern" across the close-up of Morgan Fairchild's face, hating myself for deceiving Bill and now his children too. When I returned to the living room, he was seated on the sofa, surveying the room.

"Oh, you're probably wondering about the apartment," I said, handing him the *TV Guide*.

"Wondering about it?"

"Yes. Why it's so small." Bill started to protest that he didn't think it was small, but I interrupted him. "It's my pied-à-terre. I've also got a house in the Hamptons. Down the road from Spielberg's place." Gag.

"No kidding?" said Bill. "Have you met him?"

"Oh, sure. At parties, movie screenings, you know."

Bill smiled. "What I know is that Nancy Stern goes where the movers and shakers are. The next thing you're going to tell me is that you've been to the White House."

"Well, yes. I have, actually." I said this shyly, demurely, so as to reassure Bill that he was right about me, that I wasn't snooty or self-absorbed or taken with myself. "But the surprise about the White House is how much it reminds you of your basic mansion in Greenwich or Beverly Hills. I mean, it's not that big, compared to the homes of some of the people I've interviewed."

"I guess that's why you think this place is small," said Bill, gesturing at our surroundings. "To me, it's a comfortable one-bedroom apartment."

"It is comfortable," I agreed. "And thank goodness it is, since I spend a lot of time here between trips."

Yeah, trips to and from Small Blessings, I thought. I was making myself ill. I needed some fresh air. Instead of offering Bill a drink and some hors d'oeuvres, I suggested we get going. "The restaurant doesn't take reservations, so we could be in for a long wait," I said.

"By the way, where's your dog?" he asked as he was helping me on with my coat.

"My dog?" I said.

"The Jack Russell terrier you send to dog training school."

One lie always leads to another, Nance. And before you know it, you really are in quicksand.

"Oh, you mean Taffy," I said, seizing on the name of the cocker spaniel we had when I was growing up. "He was such a discipline problem in school today that they decided to keep him there overnight, the little devil."

"Is he a biter or something?"

"Yes," I said. "A biter *and* a barker."

You should be ashamed of yourself, I thought. It's bad enough to lie about yourself. But to lie about poor old Taffy, well, that's about as low as it gets.

After I had pressed the Down button, Bill and I stood by the elevators and waited for one of them to stop on my floor. A minute or so went by and then one did stop. We had already stepped inside when I realized, to my utter horror, that the only other person in the elevator besides Bill and me was the other Nancy Stern — the very occurrence I'd been dreading.

"Why it's Nancy," she said gaily. Without a hint of depression.

"Yes," I said, forcing a smile as the doors closed us in. I don't recall ever feeling so claustrophic. "How are you?"

She was dressed to kill, that's how she was, her science fiction body arrayed in a very chic gray silk dress (chic because gray, according to the celebrity magazines I'd been reading, was the new black). Her long blond hair was pulled back into a tight chignon. And her earlobes were adorned with tiny sterling silver teddy bears, adding a touch of whimsy to the presentation. I glanced at Bill, to see if his tongue was hanging out. It wasn't, but he wasn't disinterested.

"I'm tip-top," she said, responding to my question in that affected way of hers. "Are you and your friend going out on the town?"

No, we're climbing Mt. Everest, I thought sourly, wondering how it could possibly take the elevator so long to transport us a mere six floors. "We're just going out for a hamburger," I said. I did not introduce Bill to her or vice versa. It was unnecessary, I felt. Unnecessary and dangerous.

"Any more mail for me?" she asked. "Or phone calls?"

You're looking at one, I wanted to scream. He's standing a foot away from you. What's more, if Bill had called you instead of me, the three of us would be riding down in the elevator under entirely different circumstances. "You had a delivery from the pharmacy a little while ago," I said. "I left it with the doorman." Plus someone did leave a cryptic message on my answering machine for you on Sunday afternoon — the same young woman with the southern accent who'd called before. She didn't leave her name this time either. Strange.

"Well, I have a piece of mail for you," said Nancy. "It's your rent bill, I fear." She giggled. "You'll have to excuse me but I'm giddy with anticipation about the person

I'm interviewing tonight."

Before I could muzzle her or change the subject or press the Alarm button on the elevator, Bill piped up. "You're an interviewer too?" he asked her.

"Yes," she said with interest. "Why? Are *you,* Mr. . . ."

"Harris," he said. "Bill Harris. And no, I'm not an interviewer but Nancy here has done interviews with —"

Mercifully, the elevator doors parted. I grabbed Bill by the hand and dragged him into the lobby, moving extremely quickly so as to leave Nancy in the dust.

"Have a lovely evening!" I called out to her when we were safely out of the building.

"Who was that woman?" he said as we walked up Third Avenue.

"A neighbor of mine," I said casually.

"I guessed that. But why was she talking to you about mail and phone calls?"

"Oh, because she used to live in my apartment before she moved upstairs to a bigger place. We're still getting each other's correspondence, deliveries, you name it."

He nodded. "And she's a journalist like you?"

"Not a journalist exactly. She writes a newsletter," I said, "for a national support group for people with psoriasis. I assume

134

the person she's so excited about interviewing is a dermatologist who invented a
new ointment.''

No, I wasn't proud of this explanation, although I was amazed by my ability to think
on my feet, as I've mentioned.

Bill took my hand and smiled. "I liked it
when you held onto me as we were getting
out of the elevator before.''

"Did you?" I said.

"Very much," he said. "So if it's all right
with you, I think we'll hold onto each other
on the way to the restaurant.''

"It's all right with me," I said in what was
clearly an understatement.

We ate burgers and fries and onion rings
and got ketchup all over our fingers, and,
while I was trying to wipe mine with a
napkin, Bill noticed the ring I was wearing.

"That's Tiffany's Étoile band ring with
diamonds set in platinum, isn't it?" he said.

"It is," I said. "I wear it because I think it's
a beautiful piece of jewelry, not because it
carries any sentimental value. Actually, it's
pretty dumb that I do wear it, considering
my lifestyle.''

"Your lifestyle? I would think a ring like
that would be a perfect accessory for all
those swell parties you go to.''

Oops. I had let my guard down for a moment. The "lifestyle" I'd been thinking of involved sticking my hands in Silly Putty.

"Not really," I said, recovering. "It's best for the interviewer not to outshine the interviewee, if you know what I mean. I learned that lesson when I did a piece on Mother Teresa a year or two before she died. There I was in this diamond ring, while a bona fide saint was speaking about poverty and hunger and the most extreme kind of need. Did I ever feel ridiculous." Sort of the way I feel now, I thought.

"You mentioned your ex-husband," said Bill. "I don't remember Joan saying you'd ever been married."

"No? Oh, well I was married all right," I said, deciding to go with the truth here. What was the harm? "John and I split up, essentially because he wasn't a very giving person. And by 'giving,' I'm not talking about jewelry, believe me."

"Then what are you talking about? Tell me, Nancy. I want to know about you, about who you *are*."

Who I am. Sheesh.

I looked at Bill before answering, studied his face, studied his demeanor, tried to gauge what his reaction would be if I told him who I was. The man reeked of sincerity, of straightforwardness — a genuine Honest Abe. Even after a couple of dates I could sense that he wasn't one for game playing, so how could I possibly 'fess up and reveal all? And yet I did want him to know a part of me, the part I felt it was safe to share. I wanted him to know something about the real Nancy Stern, no matter what happened in the future.

And so I told him about me, about growing up in Pennsylvania in a town that was devoid of possibility; about my mother who never went anywhere and my father who never minded; about my need to escape and my eventual arrival in New York; about my marriage to a man who didn't love me.

When I finished, Bill reached for my hand. "His loss," he said of John. "You realize that, don't you, Nancy?"

"I do, although there are still moments when I wonder if there was something I could have done to make him —"

Bill shook his head. "His loss. That's all there is to it."

"If you say so." Bill Harris was a definite ego boost.

Later, as we drank coffee and shared a slice of cheesecake, I asked Bill to tell me his story.

He said he grew up on the eastern shore of

Maryland; that his father was a cop who had made it clear he expected his three sons to be cops too; that two of them did go into law enforcement while Bill chose retailing; that he always felt he was the black sheep of the family even though *he* was the one who made money; that his marriage ended because his wife had been having an affair.

"That must have been a terrible shock," I said, my heart clutching with sympathy pains.

"Oh, it was," Bill said. "I asked myself over and over, 'How can you think you know someone and then find out you're way off the mark?' I have a lot of trouble with the concept. I can't reconcile myself to the fact that I thought I knew Jill, knew the kind of person she was, and it turned out I didn't know her in the slightest. I especially didn't know what an amazing actress she was, playing the part of the happy little wife while she was involved with another man. Was I ever misled."

I wanted to crawl under the table then, just crawl under the table and slink out the door. But I didn't because Bill continued to talk, and, since I was supposed to be such a good listener, I continued to listen.

"You must be wondering how I was able to keep on speaking to Jill after what she did," he said.

I nodded, wondering how I was able to keep on eating cheesecake after what I did.

"Simple: the kids," he answered. "They mean more to me than she ever did. I'm not going to screw up their lives by poisoning them against her. It's not their fault that she's a dishonest person."

That did it. I put my fork down. *This* dishonest person didn't deserve any more dessert.

"What is it?" Bill asked. "You look pale, Nancy."

"I'm fine," I said. "Just a little tired maybe."

"Then I'll get the check and take you home. Big day tomorrow?"

"Very," I said. Janice and I were introducing a new theme at school: How Animals Cope in Cold Weather. We were planning to focus on the bear, the rabbit, and the duck-billed platypus.

Bill and I left the restaurant at about nine-thirty and returned to my apartment soon after.

"Are you sure you're okay?" he asked as we stood in my foyer. "I sense a definite climate change."

"I'm sorry, Bill. It has nothing to do with you. I had a wonderful time tonight."

He stepped closer, lowered his head, and kissed me. "Me too," he murmured, then kissed me a second time.

I let myself enjoy his embraces, enjoy the feel of his mouth on mine, enjoy the sensation of being held and caressed and cuddled by a man I respected, a man who appealed to me on every level.

I could really fall for this guy, I thought as I kissed him back. He's warm and giving and nothing like John. If only . . .

"I want to see you again, Nancy," he said, stroking my hair. "My calendar's wide open until the kids come. Say when."

When I didn't say anything, Bill kissed me again. I heard myself sigh with pleasure as he wrapped me tighter in his arms.

"Friday night at seven?" he whispered.

"I can't," I managed, my brain struggling to focus on reality, my body cleaving to his. "I'll be out of town for three weeks on business."

"Three weeks?" He seemed terribly disappointed.

"Yes," I said, my rationale for the three weeks being that it would be close to Christmas by the time I supposedly returned. Bill would be putting in long hours at the store and then he'd be getting ready for his sons' arrival, and he'd be so busy with

140

all of that he'd forget about me, I figured. Out of sight, out of mind. End of story.

"If I have to wait three weeks, so be it," he said as he continued to hold me. "We'll see each other the minute you get back."

"But you'll be right in the middle of your craziest season at work."

"Seeing you will be the perfect respite."

"What about your sons? You'll have to prepare for their visit."

"Look, I'm not taking no for an answer," he said, foiling my plan. "Is it a date?" He asked this, then planted exquisite little kisses along the side of my neck.

"Yesss," I purred, foiling my own plan.

CHAPTER NINE

"You didn't tell him? Again?" Janice demanded at school the next morning.

"No," I said.

"You should have told him," she said.

"I can't believe you're being so judgmental all of a sudden," I said. "You were the one who encouraged me to have an adventure, to take a risk. You're Miss 'Just Do It,' aren't you?"

"Yes, and now it's time for *you* to just do it. Tell him."

"I'll handle the situation as soon as I come back from my quote-unquote business trip. I always figured I'd wait until our third date to tell him. The third time's the charm. Isn't that what they say?"

"No. Three strikes and you're out. That's what they say."

"Why are you being so hard on me, Janice?"

"I'm not being hard on you. I'm being protective of you. You're like Bambi when it comes to dating — an innocent little fawn. I really hate to think of this guy carving you up into pieces of venison."

"No venison," I assured her. "He's a burger-and-fries type."

"I'm serious, Nancy."

"So am I, Janice. Bill's not a monster. He's kind and caring and smart and handsome, and he has an excellent job at an established, prestigious company. Plus he's a loving father to his sons. He's exactly the kind of man I've been hoping for."

"Really? And what if he just hasn't shown his true colors yet? I told you, it takes a while for their neuroses to reveal themselves. You think he's gonna be pleased when he finds out he's been duped? Men go berserk when they think their manhood's been threatened."

"What does any of this have to do with Bill's manhood?"

"*Everything* has to do with a man's manhood. That's why they're so screwed up. Ask them to clear the table? You're threatening their manhood. Ask them to stop for gas *before* the tank is on E? You're threatening their manhood. Ask them to see any movie starring Meryl Streep? You're threatening their manhood. I'm telling you, Nancy. It's not a jungle out there. It's a padded cell."

"Bill is not nuts," I declared.

"All I'm saying is that the longer you keep him in the dark, the madder he'll be when he finds out the truth."

"He's not going to find out the truth."

"What are you talking about?"

"Well, I've come up with sort of an unorthodox strategy, not that this whole situation isn't unorthodox."

"What strategy?"

"I'll call him in three weeks and go out with him, just like I promised I would. When he brings me home, I'll break up with him."

"And the reason you'll give for breaking up with him is?"

"I'll say I can't get involved in a serious relationship because of my job, because I do so much traveling, because it wouldn't be practical to tie myself down."

"Nancy, if you're planning to say that, why go on the date?"

"I told you: I promised him I would. Also, I'm dying to see him again. Oh, Janice. Bambi has fallen in love."

She sighed. "Then why not just tell him you're not the other Nancy Stern instead of kissing him off? That way you'd at least have a fighting chance with him."

I shook my head. "You don't know Bill, know what he's been through with his ex-wife, know how much he values honesty. He'd hate me if he found out I'd been lying to him."

"But you *will* be lying to him if you tell him you don't want to see him anymore."

"Look, there are lies and there are lies. I'd rather lie about my feelings than lie about my identity, okay?"

She shrugged. "Either way, your nose is gonna grow."

I put my arms around her. "Then I'll ask the other Nancy Stern for the name of her plastic surgeon and have it fixed."

Fortunately, I didn't have a lot of time to dwell on the Bill problem, as the three weeks before Christmas were always hectic at Small Blessings. In our efforts to instill in the children a tolerance for all members of the human race, our holiday curriculum was multicultural, and we covered Christmas, Chanukah, Kwanzaa, even Ramadan through songs, stories, and art projects.

During one activity — the kids were making picture frames for their parents, gluing uncooked noodles to pieces of cardboard and spraying the whole business with gold paint — Fischer Levin threw a handful of pasta at Todd Delafield and a food fight ensued.

"Fischer! Todd! Over here! Now!" I said, arms crossed over my chest in my best drill sergeant pose.

They trudged over, listened to my harangue, and directed a few choice words at each other.

"Fine," I said. "Go sit in Time-out until you're ready to be with the rest of the class. Both of you."

They did as they were told, but it was Fischer who apologized first — right away, in fact — and I was pleasantly surprised by the development. Then he cupped his hands around my ear and whispered, "I'm giving you a special Christmas present, Miss Stern. Because I love you."

"Aw, I love you too," I said, hugging him. "But you don't have to give me anything, honey. All I want for Christmas is for you to behave."

He grinned. "Then I'll give you two presents — the one I'm talking about and the one you're talking about." He high-fived me and went back to his seat.

The next day, the class baked holiday cookies. Fischer was a model student.

The day after that, we taught the children how to make their own Christmas wrapping paper. Again, Fischer stayed out of trouble.

I was so optimistic about this trend that I

was actually looking forward to telephoning his mother. (Janice and I had divided up the parents list and were calling everyone on it about our Christmas party on the last day of school. We were asking them to drop off a gift for their child — we put a ten-dollar limit on the gift, but we knew the clueless parents would ignore it — so that when the janitor dressed up as Santa and appeared in the classroom, he'd have a little goodie for each child.)

I reached Gretchen Levin at seven o'clock in the evening, just as she and her husband were heading out the door.

"It's yet another charity gala," she said, apologetic about having to rush. "There's one every night, it seems."

Doesn't charity begin at home? I wanted to ask but did not, naturally. "I'm calling about our Christmas party." I gave her the spiel about the gift for Fischer.

"Of course," she said. "I'll have his nanny dash out and buy something and bring it to school ASAP. Let's see, maybe Fischer would enjoy one of those Mercedes for children. I think FAO Schwarz carries them."

I informed her about the ten-dollar limit.

"Oh," she said. "I suppose that is more democratic."

"The idea is to have Santa send the children off on their vacations with a big surprise," I said. "It's very exciting for them when he presents them with a gift with their name on it. We tell them he's rewarding them for being so good all year long. Speaking of which, we've noticed some improvement in Fischer's behavior."

"Fischer's behavior?"

"Yes, Mrs. Levin. Remember when you and your husband came to school for the Thanksgiving play and I told you we'd been having problems with your son?"

"I do, but I was under the impression that the problems had been resolved." I could hear her husband yelling at her in the background, telling her to hurry up and get off the phone. "Miss Dibble indicated that Fischer was doing beautifully at school now. She phones us on a regular basis, to keep us up to date on how well he's performing."

"Is that so?" I said, astonished not only that Penelope had been going behind my back and calling the Levins directly but that she was feeding them misinformation, just so they'd keep pouring money into Small Blessings.

"Yes, now I really do have to run," said Gretchen Levin, following a loud "Wouldja get off the goddamn phone!" from her husband. "I'll take care of that gift first thing tomorrow. Thanks for calling." Click.

Needless to say, I marched into Penelope's office the very next morning, storming past Deebo, insisting I had to see her boss. I'll spare you the gory details of the meeting, but, basically, Penelope admitted she'd been sucking up to the Levins yet maintained it was none of my affair. "You teach, I fund-raise," she said. I was really steamed and began to raise my voice in defense of all that was right and good and American about being an educator of young children. But when Deebo rushed into the office, looking as if she were about to wrestle me to the ground, I shut up. "You do your job and I'll do my job and everything will be just fine" was Penelope's parting shot. I didn't ask what would happen if I didn't toe the line. I didn't have to.

When I got home that afternoon, there were four messages on my answering machine. One was from Bo, the man who had wanted to play in the sheets with the other Nancy Stern. (Apparently, he had never heard back from her.) The second was from Henry, the married man who had begged Nancy to spend a weekend with him. (Apparently, he had never heard back from her, either.) The third was from the young girl with the southern accent. (Apparently, she was too reticent to leave her name or the reason for her call.) And the fourth was from Bill, *my* Bill. (Thank God I hadn't been home and picked up the phone.) He said he knew I was out of town but figured I'd probably check in for messages. He said he'd been thinking about me nonstop. He said he missed me, even though we'd only been out together twice. He said he couldn't wait to see me and would come racing over the minute I called.

I replayed his message five times, swooning after each listen. I couldn't get over how sweet he was, how completely open he was with his feelings, how utterly lacking he was in that vile macho posturing I'd observed in other men. Best of all, he appeared to be mad about me. Or was he mad about the woman he thought I was?

So as not to torture myself with fantasies about Bill, knowing the relationship was doomed and that I had designated myself as the doomer, I took the elevator down to the lobby with the two messages for the other Nancy Stern. "Would you buzz Miss Stern in 24A?" I asked the doorman, "and tell her I'd like to come up?" You can also tell her she would have made life easier for all of us if she'd listed her number in the phone book, I muttered to myself.

The doorman buzzed her. After a couple of tries, she finally answered and gave him the okay to send me upstairs.

Obviously, she's not off interviewing Mel Gibson, I thought as I ascended to the twenty-fourth floor, and it's a good thing she's not, considering the envy that's already built up inside me.

When I emerged from the elevator, there was Nancy, standing outside her apartment door waiting for me, her bionic body wrapped in nothing but a towel.

"Oh. Gee. I hope I didn't get you out of the shower," I said. She could have told the doorman she was indisposed.

"You didn't get me out of the shower. You got me out of bed," she said. "I was having sex. We were just finishing up." She reported this without a hint of embarrassment.

In response to *my* embarrassment, she flashed me a crooked, lopsided, drunken smile.

Yes, that's it, I realized as I caught a whiff of alcohol on her breath. She's smashed. And it's only four o'clock in the afternoon.

Was it Jacques who was inside the penthouse, partying with her? Or was it one from among the legions of other men in her life?

"I'd invite you in for some champagne, but my friend is in his birthday suit," she said, showing a side I hadn't seen before — a coarse, mocking side which, in combination with her snide, condescending side, made her someone whose life I no longer coveted as opposed to someone whose life I did.

"I understand completely," I said, although it had been eons since I'd had a naked man in my apartment.

"Good, because I think we're out of champagne." These words were accompanied by a genuine snicker.

"Champagne," I said, attempting to remain cordial. "Are you celebrating something, Nancy?"

"Yes, I am," she said, slurring her words. *I am* became *yam*. "I'm celebrating the end of another day in the life of Nancy Stern."

The woman is wacked, I thought. Say what you have to say and get out of here. "Listen, I didn't mean to interrupt anything, Nancy. I just came up to give you these messages." I handed her the piece of paper on which I'd written both Bo and Henry's entreaties. "And I keep meaning to tell you about the girl who's looking for you."

"What girl?"

"She doesn't leave her name. She calls my

152

phone number, hears my voice, figures out that I'm not you, apologizes, and hangs up. The only thing I know is that she has a southern accent and sounds young."

"Hmm. I can't imagine who she is or why she's bothering me."

"Actually, it's me she's bothering."

"Oh, come on, Nancy." She laughed. "You're enjoying all this newfound attention you're getting, aren't you?"

"What do you mean?" I said, my face flushing.

"I mean that you don't mind being the beneficiary of my calls, jotting down the messages, and trotting them up here like a doggie with a bone. That's right, isn't it?"

"As a matter of fact, I do mind," I said indignantly. A doggie with a bone. It occurred to me that the other Nancy Stern wasn't nice when she was drunk. It occurred to me that she wasn't nice, period.

"No, you don't mind," she contradicted me. "You're having lots of fun since I arrived on the scene. And from my perspective, you're quite the competent little message taker. So efficient. So on top of everything. How'd you like to be my executive secretary for a living instead of babysitting people's brats?" She threw back her head and roared. Okay, she was more than not nice. She was a bitch, talk about doggies.

"I'm happy with the job I have," I replied crisply, thinking how wrong my first impression of this woman was, how screwed up my priorities had been. I *was* happy with my job, except for having to put up with Penelope's nonsense. Why had I assumed that interviewing a bunch of self-absorbed movie stars would be so wonderful?

"Happy." She scoffed. "What's happy?"

Being with Bill, I answered silently, wishing he and I had met some other way, some way that didn't involve Nancy; wishing I had it all to do over again.

"What's the matter?" she baited me. "Is the nursery school teacher mad at me?"

"The nursery school teacher is bored with you," I said. "But before I let you get back to your friend in there, do you have any mail or messages for *me*, Nancy?"

She smirked. "Just one message: The grass isn't always greener, sweet pea."

She slammed the door in my face.

Sweet pea, I mused as I walked away from her apartment, shaking my head at what an awful person she turned out to be. Wasn't that Bo's nickname for her?

Oh, who cares? I thought, as I descended in the elevator. Not me, not anymore.

And I didn't care. Not exactly. I was curious, that was it.

Did Nancy make the grass-isn't-always-greener remark as some sort of warning to me? Because she sensed that I'd been drooling over her life? Because she found out that I'd stolen her blind date? Was *that* where all the attitude was coming from?

Or was it simply that she wanted me to know how rotten things were for her — rotten instead of glorious? Was her performance some sort of cry for help? Was she "acting out" like Fischer did, just to get attention? And if so, what was I supposed to do about it?

CHAPTER TEN

I received a slew of Christmas cards, the majority of them for the other Nancy Stern, but I didn't deliver them in person. Ever since the champagne-and-sex incident, I decided to keep my distance from my neighbor and, therefore, left her cards and all other communications intended for her with the doorman.

The person from whom I really wanted to keep my distance, though, was Bill, given that I was supposed to be away on business. New York is a big city, obviously, but it can metamorphose into an extremely small town if you're trying to avoid somebody. It's uncanny, really. There are millions of people in Manhattan, hustling and bustling and rushing hither and yon, and yet it never fails that you run smack into the single person you'd give anything to steer clear of.

Still, I had figured I *could* steer clear of Bill during my "business trip" because he lived on the West Side and I lived on the East Side and he worked in Midtown and I worked all the way Uptown. No problem, I thought. Piece of cake.

So imagine the swan dive my heart did as I was standing in the bathroom section of Gracious Home, an upscale hardware store on *my* side of town, looking for the kind of towel bar that adheres to the wall instead of screws into it, when there, in the kitchen section, stood Bill, who appeared to be looking at cutting boards.

Well, I nearly died, naturally. Not only wasn't I dressed for a reunion with him — it was a Saturday morning and I had just tumbled out of bed and I hadn't put on any lipstick let alone brushed my teeth — but I wasn't even supposed to be in New York. Besides, what in the world was he doing at the East Side Gracious Home when there was a perfectly nice branch store on the West Side, probably right near his apartment? Sure, the East Side store was the flagship store and it sold every product under the sun, but why not shop in his own backyard?

Finesse this one, I thought.

I placed the towel bar gingerly back on the shelf and tiptoed past the kitchen section, where a sales clerk was hyping Bill on the merits of Corian cutting boards as opposed to the butcher block ones. I had almost made it past them when I inadvertently kicked a stainless steel garlic press that some careless, neglectful customer had probably dropped and not bothered to pick up, and the damn thing went skittering across the floor. Bill and the sales clerk glanced up, to see where the racket was coming from, and I, grabbing the first item I could lay my hands on, hid my face behind an extra-large colander.

Great move, right, since colanders have holes and are, therefore, see-through.

Even so, Bill didn't recognize me, thank God. Continuing to hold the colander in front of my face, I resumed my tiptoeing past him.

And then I heard my name.

"Nancy! We keep bumping into each other, don't we?"

It was Victoria Bittner, the preschool teacher–frustrated painter, minus her husband this time. Obviously, the colander wasn't much of a cover.

I peeked over at Bill, to see if he was looking in our direction. He wasn't. Yet.

"So you're shopping for kitchen wares this morning?" said Victoria, who was becoming quite the nuisance. Wasn't it enough that she and I had adjoining classrooms at school and that she was forever running back and forth through our common door to borrow supplies, to return supplies, to gossip? Did she and I have to have adjoining lives too? Did she have to appear out of nowhere at the least opportune moments, turning up whenever I was posing as someone I wasn't? "Are you, Nancy?" she repeated. "Shopping for kitchen wares this morning, I mean?"

"Just this colander," I said in a cross between a whisper and a growl.

"What's wrong with your voice?" she asked.

"Sore throat," I croaked. "Gotta get home, take some aspirin."

She patted my shoulder. "And drink lots of liquids. Tea with honey is good."

I nodded my thanks and started to hurry past her, toward the door, intending to dump the colander in the light bulbs section on my way out. But I was intercepted by a sales clerk, who was either desperate to make a sale or convinced that I was about to walk off with the merchandise.

"Step right up," he said, herding me and the colander into the checkout line, before I could protest. I wasn't happy about having my escape thwarted, but I would have been less happy about causing a scene and even less happy about being arrested for shoplifting.

So I stood in that line, ducking my head like a criminal, only to have Bill and his stupid cutting board (he'd gone with the Corian one) step into the same line.

I was positively undone by this development.

Please don't recognize me, I prayed, grateful that the two men standing between Bill and me on the line were big men — tall as well as beefy — and provided excellent screening.

"Cash or credit?" asked the cashier when it was my turn to pay.

Terrific. I had brought just enough money for the towel bar, and now there I was buying a colander that wasn't your average wire-mesh job but one of those high-tech, hideously expensive kinds.

Wordlessly, so as not to call further attention to myself, I handed the woman my American Express card.

"We don't take American Express," she said, giving the card back to me.

I rummaged in my wallet for my Visa card and handed it to her.

Along with everyone in line behind me, I watched impatiently as she placed the card in the machine and waited for verification. After what seemed like an eternity, during which I was sweating profusely, she returned the card to me and said, "Not valid. Past the expiration date. Wanna try another one?"

At that point, I was so relieved that she hadn't shouted out my name and so frantic to get the hell out of there that instead of handing her another card, I handed her the colander and fled. It wasn't until I was safely inside my apartment that I allowed myself to breathe.

And then I cursed myself for not bringing home the towel bar — the reason I'd gone to Gracious Home in the first place.

That's what happens when you tell a lie, I thought miserably. You're forced to tell more lies, not to mention act like a crazy person.

After that episode, I was more determined than ever to end my relationship with Bill, as painful as I expected that to be. My phony three-week business trip was just about over. Before the next week was out, he and I would have our final date. I would break the bad news and go on with my life, as if he'd never walked into it.

I was not looking forward to this.

I called Bill at work the following Monday, and he sounded thrilled that I was back in town, insisting that we get together that very evening. We decided to meet at Rockefeller Center, so he could see the famous Christmas tree all lit up, and then get a bite to eat.

"I missed you," he told me after we'd said our hellos, punctuated by an immensely passionate kiss. We were standing beside the skating rink when this kiss took place. The night was chilly but clear, the rink and the tree and the shops were twinkling with Christmas lights, and the whole scene was very romantic. "I know it's strange to miss someone you've only spent a short time with, but it's the truth, Nancy."

The truth. Well, the truth was, I had missed Bill too. So much so that I almost didn't go through with my plan. During the entire day at school, it was impossible to concentrate on the kids, impossible not to feel conflicted about what I was about to do.

Why are you going out with him if you're dumping him? I kept asking myself. How can you do it? Why are you doing it?

You're probably asking yourself the same questions, wondering why I would put myself through the torture of being with Bill, only to tell him to his face that we were history.

The simple answer is I didn't see any other way of handling the situation. I wanted to go out with him one last time, but I needed to end the charade. I had to break up with him, but I preferred that he think me a cold-hearted witch than an imposter. We all have our quirks.

So there we were at a seafood restaurant near Rockefeller Center, not that I was hungry.

"And then there was the wild-goose chase Denham sent me on," Bill was saying.

I had drifted off for the umpteenth time that night, rehearsing my I-can't-see-you-anymore speech, but I pulled myself back to reality. If this is your last date with Bill, you might as well enjoy it, I decided. "This was when you were at the D.C. store?" I asked, trying to pick up the thread of his story.

"Right, when I was still in sales. We had a phone call from an extremely wealthy client of ours who lived in Texas. He was in the market for a particular size and setting of diamond that we didn't have on hand."

"Was this diamond for his mistress?" I said wryly.

"No, for his mother."

"How sweet."

"You haven't heard anything yet. We didn't have the piece he was looking for but we offered to get it for him and personally deliver it to his house."

"Wow, just like Domino's Pizza."

"Exactly. The setter and I flew to Houston, rented a car, and drove to this dusty, God-forsaken town where he lived. We drove and we drove and we drove, trying to find his place, based on the directions he'd given us. Finally, we ended up at the door of what looked like a crack house. We're talking about a rundown shack in the middle of nowhere."

"Were you scared?" I asked. "You had big-time jewelry with you, didn't you?"

"A seven-carat marquise diamond. You bet we were scared. We also had a handgun, but neither of us knew how to use it."

"Swell. So what happened?"

"We checked the directions again and re-alized that the dirt road we were on wasn't a dead end after all. We got back in the car and drove a little further and what do you know? We went over a hill and across an-other dirt road and there, like a mirage, was this guy's house, which, by the way, was the size of Madison Square Garden."

"You must have been relieved."

"We were, but we were kind of touched too. When we asked him about the shack, he explained that it had been his home when he was growing up. Instead of tearing it down after making his millions and building his mansion, he decided to keep it, to remind him of his humble beginnings."

"Aw, that's a nice story," I said. "For a minute there, I thought you were going to tell me he was a fraud."

"That's why it's a nice story. It's so rare to find a guy with that kind of money who's decent and honest and comfortable with who he is."

Yup, I've made the right decision, I thought as Bill was paying the check. It's better to break up with him than to have him find out I'm not decent and honest and comfortable with who I am.

Still, as I held his hand all the way back to my apartment, as I inhaled his scent, as I sensed yet again the intense mutual attraction between us, I was filled with regret — not that I wasn't the other Nancy Stern but that I wouldn't have met Bill without pretending I was. It was such a shame.

When we got to my building, Bill asked if he could come up for a while. I said yes, I wanted him to come up, because there was something I had to talk to him about.

He came up. We sat on the sofa. And then he reached for me as I suspected — hoped — he would. Not only reached for me, but murmured between caresses that he felt incredibly lucky that Joan Geisinger

165

had given him my name.

Lucky. If he only knew.

"Bill." I forced myself to pull away from him. "I guess the only way to say this is to just say it," I began, determined not to cry or tear up or even swallow hard. I would do plenty of blubbering later.

"What is it, Nancy?" he asked.

I cleared my throat. "I've really enjoyed the times we've spent together and I think you're a very special man, but I'm afraid I won't be able to see you anymore." God, I did it.

He smiled at me, as if I'd made a joke. "Anymore this *week*, you mean?"

"No, Bill. You and I are both aware that what's between us is becoming more serious than a couple of dates, and I feel I have to put a stop to it now. Before it goes any further."

His expression changed. He was no longer smiling. "Why, Nancy? I don't understand."

"Because of my job," I said. "Joanie indicated to you that I've always been an ambitious person. Well, she was right. I am ambitious. I can't let anyone or anything stand in the way of my success. I have my sights set on television, on becoming Barbara Walters someday." I tried not to choke. I sounded like a character from a Jackie Collins novel.

"I have no problem with that," Bill maintained. "I'm not one of those men whose manhood is threatened by a successful woman."

See, Janice? "I'm sure you're not, but this is about me, Bill. About the deadlines and the traveling and the pressures of my career. I can't get involved now. It wouldn't be fair to you."

"Shouldn't I be the judge of what's fair to me?"

He was being entirely too sensible, making things harder for me. "Look, Bill. I know how much you value honesty, so I'm being honest with you, okay? I don't want to be in a relationship at this point in my life. It's that simple."

He shook his head, refused to buy my act. "I don't think it's simple at all. In fact, I don't think you're telling me everything, Nancy."

"I am," I insisted. "I'm sorry."

"I'm not convinced," he persisted.

"Please, Bill."

He wouldn't take his eyes off me, as if he were studying me, waiting for me to say "April Fool's."

"This is really unexpected," he said instead. "I thought we were —"

"I'm sure you did," I cut him off. "But this is the best thing, Bill. Believe me."

"If it's the best thing, then why does it hurt so much?"

When I remember this conversation, replay it in my mind, it's that line of his, that question, that gets me. I'd worked with children for most of my adult life and couldn't bear to see any of them hurt — ever. And now, in Bill's case, *I* was actually doing the hurting, was actually *causing* the hurt. The guilt was unimaginable.

When I didn't respond, Bill rose from the sofa and walked very slowly toward the door.

"I'm sorry," I managed.

"You already said that," he replied.

"I mean it, Bill."

He shrugged. "You mean it. You don't mean it. It doesn't matter in the long run." He opened the door. "I hope you find what you're looking for, Nancy."

I already did, I thought as I watched him go.

CHAPTER ELEVEN

During the last week of school before the Christmas break, I found myself stuck in a somewhat unhealthy routine: I went to work, came back from work, ate dinner standing up at my kitchen counter, and thought about Bill.

I thought about Bill at his job, presiding over all those diamonds and rubies and emeralds. I thought about Bill at his apartment, getting the place ready for his sons. I thought about Bill in his bed, thanking his lucky stars that he'd gotten the heave-ho from Nancy Stern, the journalist-sociopath.

Every night I reached for the phone to call him, and every night I devoured a half-dozen Vienna Fingers instead. Why call him? I said to myself. What would be the point? Not only is he busy, but he probably hates you.

No, it's the other Nancy Stern he hates, I tried to convince myself. He doesn't know you exist.

Even if you finally told him the truth, he'd hate you, I always concluded by the time I drifted off to sleep. He hates people who lie. Give it up already.

And so it went, my interior dialogue. If it weren't for the kids in my class, I might have driven myself crazy, but they proved to be much-needed breaks from my preoccupation with Bill. Sure, they were hyper around Christmas, and they did talk an awful lot about gifts gifts gifts, but they arrived at school each day with an aura of expectancy — an infectious sense of awe and wonder at the approaching holiday. They sat on the rug, twitchy yet wide-eyed, captivated by the stories Janice and I read to them about reindeer and snowmen and sleighs full of toys. They were also full of stories themselves — stories about the time they got a puppy for Christmas or a new baby sister or a trip to Disneyworld. One of the reasons I love teaching four-year-olds is that they're like lab experiments, developing and mutating and transforming right before your eyes. There's so much going on in their brains at that age, such change, such a learning curve. When they start school in September, they're still little hatchlings, struggling to survive the separation from their mothers, but by Christmas, they're little people, able to form their own judgments about the world. I never tire of watching their growth, never cease to marvel at what precious gifts *they* are, speaking of gifts. That Christmas, most of all, they were the perfect distraction for me — the Christmas I spent pining for Bill.

On the final day of school before vacation, Hector Alvarez, the janitor at Small Blessings, was felled by a stomach virus and couldn't assume his usual role of Santa Claus. As a result, Deebo was pressed into service. She made a fine Santa, fortunately, and more than filled out the costume, especially in the shoulders.

"Ho-ho-ho! And look what I have for you!" she told each child, handing him or her the gift that had been brought to school by their parents.

"Ho-ho-ho! And look what I have for *you!*" said Fischer when it was his turn with Deebo/Santa. He was about to yank her beard off but, after catching my eye, thought better of it.

"You've been such a good boy lately, Fischer," I said when his caregiver arrived to pick him up at the end of the day. "I hope you have a great time on your vacation." The Levins were leaving that night for London. A "Dickens Christmas," Gretchen Levin had dubbed the trip.

"You're my favorite-est teacher, Miss Stern," he said. "I wrapped your present all by myself."

Small Blessings discouraged the parents from buying presents for the teachers, but they all did anyway — perfumes, scarves, gift certificates at Bloomingdale's, a "day of beauty" at Elizabeth Arden. I wondered briefly what Gretchen Levin had chosen for me, then remembered from an earlier conversation with Fischer that he claimed to have picked it out himself.

"Thank you, Fischer, honey," I said, hugging him again. "I can't wait to open it."

When the children were gone, back into the bosom of their families, I felt positively bereft, as if they were my own children and they'd just abandoned the nest. Janice took one look at my face and shook her head.

"You need some cheering up, kid," she said.

I nodded. "Any ideas?"

"We could start by dividing up our loot." She pointed at our pile of festively wrapped presents. "I brought a bunch of shopping bags. A couple of them for each of us."

"That was considerate of you, Janice. I forgot to bring my bags this year."

"I figured you would. You've had other things on your mind. Have you heard from him by the way?"

"Who? Bill?"

"No. Kevin Costner."

"No, I haven't heard from him and I'm not surprised. I blew him off, remember?"

"Yes, but some men don't give up so easily. Some men are persistent."

"Bill isn't 'some men.' He has self-respect."

"Whatever. I was only trying to make you feel better, Nance. Your body language screams *broken heart*."

"Does it?"

"Check yourself out in the mirror. You're so mopey your shoulders are down around your ankles."

"That's attractive."

"Hey, you can always call Bill and tell him the truth, you know. You have that option."

"Calling Bill and telling him I pretended to be someone else is not an option, Janice, so let's not even go there."

"Fine. Then let's go here." She sat down on the rug beside the pile of presents, and patted the space next to her.

I sat too, and we sifted through the Christmas gifts, depositing the ones with our names on them into our own bags.

When I got home, I stuffed my bags of unopened gifts into my hall closet and showered and changed for the Christmas tea party that Penelope was hosting for the staff. The soirée was an annual affair held at her place on Park Avenue — one of those high-ceilinged, bookcase-lined, prewar apartments that are so hard to come by in New York. (Penelope had come by hers by fawning over the head of the building's co-op board, who just happened to be the father of one of Small Blessings's pre-schoolers.) I would have preferred to skip the party this year but decided it was probably good for me to get out and mix with people, instead of staying home alone and sulking.

Penelope's apartment was reminiscent of her office at Small Blessings, which was reminiscent of Penelope herself. It was prissy, fussy, filled with teeny tiny objects from past centuries — crystal figurines, china cups and saucers, porcelain dolls — all of which were fragile-looking and scared me to death. Whenever I went near them, I was overcome by the irrational fear that I would freak out and smash the entire collection. Perhaps it was time for me to deal with my hostility toward Penelope, yes?

Everybody who worked at Small Blessings showed up at the party, except for Hector Alvarez, the janitor who couldn't play Santa Claus because he was home with a bug. In addition to the classroom teachers and the administrative staff, there was

Carrie Mosby, the creative movement teacher; Donna Davecky, the librarian; Shelley Sheinbloom, the speech and language therapist; and Dr. Isabel Leaf, the psychologist.

We chatted over tea and scones. Victoria Bittner, the frustrated painter, told me she was contemplating a divorce from her husband, the frustrated sculptor, because she found him in his studio with a nude woman who was not his model but his brother's wife. Nick Spada, the teacher by day/grad student by night, expounded on his theory that potty training is a political issue, akin to freedom of speech, and that children should have the right to remain in diapers as long as they like. And Fran Golden, the *Romper Room* throwback, revealed that she was now making Play-Doh from scratch for her class instead of using the store-bought kind. (Recipe: 3 cups flour; 1 1/2 cups salt; 3 tbsp. oil; 3 tbsp. cream of tartar; 3 cups water; food coloring. Mix all ingredients and simmer on stove until liquids take on solid yet squishy consistency.)

I wasn't avoiding Penelope per se, although, after our initial greeting, I didn't seek her out. The person I did seek out was Dr. Leaf, a talkative, outgoing woman whose ambition was to have her own call-in radio show just for young children. Never mind that young children don't listen to the radio for the most part, nor do their parents encourage them to place their own phone calls. What's more, young children don't do their own shopping, which would make advertisers unlikely to support such a show.

"I have this friend who's been fantasizing about leading a more glamorous life," I told Dr. Leaf. "In your professional opinion, does she have a psychological problem?"

"Of course not," she said. "Fantasizing is perfectly normal."

Normal. So far so good. "What if this friend wished she could trade places with a woman who she thought led a more glamorous life?" I said. "Would that constitute a psychological problem?"

"No," she said. "We all wish we could step into another person's shoes from time to time, just to get a taste of what it would be like."

"Okay, shifting gears now, say this friend fudged the truth about herself, in order to impress a would-be boyfriend," I said. "Would you consider that a psychological problem?"

"Well," she said, "I suppose it would depend on how much fudging we're talking about."

"Deep, dark, rich fudging," I said.

"I see." She reached inside her handbag for her business card and a pen. "Here," she said after writing something on the card and handing it to me. "I don't work with adults, but I'm referring you to a colleague of mine who does. Give her a call, Nancy. Before the fudge melts."

I nodded and walked over to Janice to report my conversation with Dr. Leaf.

"She's the one who's warped," Janice insisted. "You don't need a shrink. You need a drink. Let's blow this popsicle stand."

We made our way over to Penelope and thanked her for having us.

"Then you've accepted that you won't be calling Fischer Levin's parents with all that unpleasantness?" Penelope asked me.

"No, but I didn't think your party was the place to bring it up again," I said. "The good news is that Fischer seems to have calmed down a bit. Maybe the New Year will bring more positive changes in his behavior. If so, my calling his parents will become a nonissue."

Penelope fingered her pearls. "Your calling them is a nonissue now, Nancy. As we've already discussed."

She smiled that tight, bullshit smile of hers and moved on to her other guests.

Janice and I took that as our cue to split.

Janice agreed to throw nutritional caution to the wind, so we went to one of the zillion interchangeable Italian restaurants that have sprung up in Manhattan like portobello mushrooms, all of which have a name that ends in either -luna or -luma. We shared a bottle of wine (two bottles, actually), had dinner, and talked about our plans for the holidays, which weren't very impressive. Neither Janice nor I was leaving the city to spend Christmas with our family, and neither of us had a date for New Year's Eve.

"Do you think men hate the pressure of New Year's as much as women do?" she asked. "I mean, aren't we all sick and tired of feeling like we *have* to have a date for that stupid night?"

"Please. Not only do we *have* to have a date, we have to have the sort of date that's special, exceptional, memorable — on a par with the senior prom."

"I didn't have a date for that either," said Janice.

After deciding to spend New Year's Eve together at her apartment, surfing the Internet for cyberdates, we said good night and walked home.

It was close to ten-thirty by the time I

made the turn onto Seventy-first Street, only to find that the entrance to my building, not to mention the entire block, was swarming with cops and television news crews and curiosity seekers.

"What's going on?" I asked the doorman after elbowing my way through the crowd. "Was there a murder in the neighborhood or something?"

I was half joking when I'd said that. No, murder is nothing to joke about, but the crime rate in New York has gone down in recent years, and people have taken to thinking that they're no longer vulnerable — or, at least, that they're less so.

"In the building," said the doorman, his face flush with all the hubbub.

"What about the building?" I said.

"The murder," he said. "It was here in the building."

"A murder in *our* building? My God. How horrible," I said, stunned as well as alarmed, my mind focusing immediately on the creepy delivery men who were constantly wandering from floor to floor. In fact, after taking another minute to process the information, I realized I wasn't just stunned and alarmed; I was angry — downright furious that the lack of security in the building could have resulted in a death.

A death. Suddenly, the reality of *that* hit me and I experienced an overwhelming feeling of grief. The thought that someone I might have nodded to or exchanged pleasantries with or actually befriended could have been brutally, savagely killed was very upsetting.

"Which of the tenants was murdered?" I asked hesitantly.

"Miss Big Shot," said the doorman. "That's why the media's so interested."

"Miss who?"

The very instant the words were out of my mouth I knew, of course. I knew but I didn't want to know. I knew but I couldn't face knowing.

"The pretty one with the fancy job and the boyfriends," he said. "Your pal in 24A. The other Nancy Stern."

As I recall, I literally went limp after he uttered the name, not fainting exactly, but keeling over, in a sort of swoon. I probably would have sunk to the ground if the cop — one of the officers assigned to the case — hadn't caught me.

"You live here?" he asked as he stood me upright.

I nodded, still feeling dizzy, weak, nauseous.

"Name?"

My lips trembled but nothing came out.

"Your *name?*" he repeated, his pen poised to write in his notepad.

"The same as hers," I finally managed.

"The same as whose?" he said.

"The deceased's," I said, hoping he'd get it if I spoke in cop talk.

"Oh, so you're telling me *you're* Nancy Stern?" he said skeptically, as if he suspected me of being a sicko, a nut job, a crime scene junkie.

"That's what I'm telling you, Officer," I said as persuasively as I could under the circumstances. "I'm Nancy Stern."

And I'm not the wrong Nancy Stern, either, I thought with no small amount of relief. Not this time.

PART TWO

CHAPTER TWELVE

Sleep was out of the question, so I milled around the lobby for an hour or so, huddling with other tenants and exchanging remarks like "I can't believe this!" and "Isn't it awful?" and "Who could have done such a thing?"

Eventually, I went upstairs and called Janice, who said, "I can't believe this!" and "Isn't it awful?" and "Who could have done such a thing?"

"I don't know," I said in answer to the last one.

"You know more than you think," Janice asserted, "since you were getting her phone calls and letters. Maybe you have information the police could use, information that could crack the case."

"Me? Crack the case? I highly doubt it, Janice," I said. I felt *myself* cracking at that moment. I couldn't stop shaking. I was still in shock, I suppose.

"I'm serious, Nance. You should make a list of the people who called you thinking they were calling her, and give their names to the police. Including Bill, by the way."

"Bill? Why? He never met Nancy. Well, except for that time in the elevator. But even then he had no idea who she was."

"It doesn't matter," said Janice. "Some animal murdered the woman, some insane creature. I think you have an obligation to give the names to the cops — *all* of the names — and let them figure out who's a suspect and who isn't."

Bill a suspect? My Bill? The very notion was ridiculous, impossible, didn't make sense. He thought *I* was the other Nancy Stern. He thought *I* was the celebrity journalist. He thought *I* — I stopped, a new realization registering. "He's going to find out about me," I said numbly. "The jig is up, Janice."

"What are you talking about?" she said.

"Bill. *Bill.* The man I was trying so hard to impress. He'll read about the murder in the paper or watch something about it on TV, and he'll see that my face is different from her face and it'll dawn on him that I was an imposter!"

"You're right," Janice conceded. "The other Nancy Stern wasn't Barbara Walters, as we've said a thousand times, but her murder will probably get some publicity,

186

considering that she was white, lived on the Upper East Side, was better-than-average-looking, and hung out with famous people."

"Oh, they'll run her photograph and he'll see it," I repeated, my heart sinking. "He'll see her face, not to mention her hair and her boobs, and he'll think, Who was that flat-chested brunette I went out with?"

"It had to happen sooner or later, Nance."

"I guess so."

"Hey, chin up. If it turns out that he's the murderer, you did yourself a favor by dumping him."

"HOW COULD HE BE THE MUR-DERER IF HE DIDN'T EVEN KNOW HER, JANICE?"

"Okay. Okay. You don't have to bite my head off."

"Sorry. I'm not myself." I laughed rue-fully. "Actually, I *am* myself. And thank goodness I am or I'd be the dead one instead of her."

"Then there is a bright side to this after all."

"It would be brighter if the police caught the murderer," I said, "although they might have the person in custody, as we speak."

"They might."

"But if they don't, I'll call them in the

morning and offer whatever information I can."

"Good girl. Now, are you gonna be okay there by yourself? You sound a little jumpy."

"I'll be fine," I said, more hopefully than confidently.

"You sure? You can sleep at my place if you want to."

"That's sweet of you, Janice, but I'll stay here."

"Then I'd pull the plug on my phone if I were you."

"Why?"

"Because there may be media coverage of the murder where they *don't* run a photo of your dearly departed neighbor or mention her career. They may just do a quickie bulletin that says, 'Nancy Stern of 137 East Seventy-first Street has bought the farm,' and save the rest of the details for later. If it happens, everybody you know is gonna think *you're* the Nancy Stern they're talking about and call you to confirm that you're dead. Do you really want to put yourself through that tonight?"

God, what a mess.

"I'll make up the sleep sofa in my living room," Janice offered.

"I'll pack a few things and be right over," I said.

The next morning, Janice and I scoured the newspapers for coverage of the other Nancy Stern's murder. They all ran stories, but *the Daily News's* was the most lurid, complete with a photo spread of the deceased in happier times (my favorite was the one where she was standing arm in arm with Kevin Costner).

In fact, there was plenty in the article about Nancy's associations with celebrities, along with tidbits about her personal background (she'd never been married, it was her mother who identified the body, mourners were asked to make a donation to their favorite charity in lieu of flowers), but what interested me more was that she had been shot and killed in her apartment somewhere between 8:30 and 10:00 P.M., that the doormen on duty did not recall letting any visitors up to her apartment during the day or evening, and that the killer or killers were still at large.

"So nobody was seen going in or out of her apartment," I mused as Janice fired up the blender for a couple of orange smoothies with bee pollen. "How do you think the killer got to her?"

"She lived in the penthouse," said Janice. "Maybe he climbed in through the terrace."

"Maybe. Or maybe my doormen are asleep at the switch. The building doesn't exactly have the tightest security."

"That must be it then. Whoever was supposed to be guarding the door when the killer passed through was probably taking a crap."

I smiled. "I'll be sure to communicate that theory to the detective I'm going to see later."

"You called the police?"

I nodded. "While you were in the shower. I called my answering machine too. You were right, Janice: Everybody wants to know if I'm dead. I've never had so many messages, not even when people thought they were calling *her*."

"Want me to help with the call-backs?"

"That would be great. You call Penelope and I'll call everyone else."

"Penelope. Gee, thanks."

"You volunteered."

We ate breakfast, made the phone calls, and then I headed for my appointment with the police detective I'd spoken to. I was almost out the door when Janice asked me what I was doing that evening.

"It's Christmas Eve," she pointed out when I'd said I had no plans. "We could deck the halls or something."

"I really need a little time to myself," I said. "The last twenty-four hours have been pretty tumultuous."

"But Linda Franzione — you know, the one from my reading group whose ex-husband faked his own death so he wouldn't have to pay her alimony — is having a party and she told me I could bring a guest."

"I think I'll skip it, Janice. You go and have a good time, okay?"

"Okay, but I hate to picture you sitting home all by yourself."

I hugged her. "I'll be just fine. Besides, once the party gets going, you won't be picturing me doing anything. You'll be deep in conversation with some nice single man Linda invited."

"Linda doesn't know any nice single men. If she did, she wouldn't be sharing them, believe me."

"Merry Christmas, Janice."

"Merry Christmas, Nance."

I went to the police station and was interviewed by a rather paunchy, middle-aged detective named Burt Reynolds. Yes, that was his name, and because it was his name, he was extremely empathetic when I explained about the mix-ups involving the other Nancy Stern.

"Having the same name as someone better known than you is a pain in the ass," he commiserated.

"Were you ever tempted to pretend you were the other Burt Reynolds?" I inquired, eager to know if I had company in that regard.

"To get dates, you mean?"

"Yes. Exactly."

"That's how I met my wife," he said.

"Really?" I said.

"Yeah. One of the guys at the precinct gave me her number and I called her up for a blind date. I told her my name and she said, 'Are you *the* Burt Reynolds?' and I said, 'You betcha,' and she said, 'I'd love to go out with you.' We got together, she saw I wasn't the actor, but we hit it off and the rest is history."

I smiled. "Then in that case, having a famous person's name wasn't a pain in the ass."

"Sure it was. My wife and I have been separated for seven years, because she won't give me a divorce unless I pay through the nose. Not that I'm a cheapskate, but cops aren't millionaires."

I said I was sorry for his troubles, then told him everything I could think of that might be pertinent to the investigation:

Jacques, Bo, Henry; the flowers, the coat, the Prozac; the calls from the girl with the southern accent; the drunken orgy with the unknown reveler. It was only when he asked, "Anything else?" that I mentioned Bill.

"Oh," I said, as if the subject were an afterthought. "A man named Bill Harris called me one night looking for her." I explained about his job and his move from Washington to New York and the mutual friend he and Nancy shared in Joan Geisinger and the fact that he and I had dinner a few times.

"You actually went out with this guy?" said Detective Reynolds, putting down his pen so he could get a good look at me. "Even though he was calling the other one?"

"Well, yes," I said, feeling myself flush under his withering gaze. "After all, you went out with your wife, even though she thought you were the other one."

"That's different," he said. "She figured out I wasn't the other one the minute she laid eyes on me. You never admitted to the guy that you weren't the other one. You lied to him." He was crossing his arms over his chest and arching his eyebrows at me. I hoped he wouldn't put me in Time-out.

"I was planning to tell Bill the truth, but I

ended up breaking up with him instead. Not that it's germane to your investigation." I was defensive, I know, but *I* wasn't a murder suspect. I was simply trying to help. "If you have no further questions, Detective, I guess I'll be going."

"Yeah, okay. Thanks for coming in," he said, softening towards me — or so I thought. "Give me a shout if you've got anything else."

"I'm happy to cooperate," I said. "No idea yet who killed her, I suppose?"

"Nope. Could have been she had an enemy. Could have been she walked in on a burglary. We'll see what turns up."

"A burglary?" My eyes widened. If they could hit 24A, they could hit 6J, couldn't they?

"Her place was pretty torn apart, but nothing was stolen as far as we know."

"Nothing?"

"We're still checking things out." He rose from his chair to escort me to the door of his fetid office. "There is one thing I haven't asked you, Miss Stern."

"Yes?"

"How did you feel about the deceased?"

"How did I —"

"Feel about her, right. Other than the fact that you were put out by all the mix-ups."

"I didn't *feel* one way or another about her, Detective. We weren't friends. We weren't even acquaintances. We were just neighbors with the same name." Why go into some tortured explanation of my psychological conflicts over the other Nancy Stern? It was none of this cop's business that my self-esteem had recently taken a dip, that her life had seemed more desirable than my own, and that I'd fantasized — well, more than fantasized — about stepping into her shoes every once in a while.

"You say you didn't feel one way or another about her," he repeated. "And yet you were in sort of a tug-of-war with her over this Bill guy."

"Tug-of-war?" What on earth was he insinuating? "I merely went out with Bill Harris a few times, as I've already told you. Nancy didn't know a thing about it."

"And you wanted to keep it that way, didn't you, Miss Stern? Keep her in the dark, I mean."

"I didn't actually go out of my way to —"

"Sure you did. You let him think you were her so she'd never get together with him, so she wouldn't come between you two love-birds."

"No. No. That puts an entirely inaccurate slant on the situation."

"Then what *slant* would you put on the situation, Miss Stern?"

"Look, you're making my motive sound sinister and it was completely harmless. *I'm* completely harmless. I didn't do it, Detective. I'm a preschool teacher. A nurturer not a murderer." Talk about defensive! I was positively paranoid at this point. *He* seemed to be suggesting that I had reason to bump off the other Nancy Stern when all I was attempting to do was give him some leads. "Besides, I have an airtight alibi for last night."

"Good. Why don't you tell me about it?" he challenged.

"I will." I told him about the party at Penelope's, followed immediately by the dinner at — well, naturally I couldn't think of the name of the restaurant. "It's an Italian place that ends in either -luna or -luma." He looked skeptical. "You can ask my friend, Janice Mason. She was with me."

"I'll do that," he said.

"Swell. May I go now?" I said, not bothering to hide my hostility. The meeting hadn't gone the way I'd expected.

"Be my guest," said Detective Reynolds. "And have a merry Christmas."

"Yeah, right," I said.

I didn't go straight home. I was still pretty

freaked about the murder in the building or the burglary-gone-wrong in the building or whatever it was that had occurred in the building, and didn't relish the idea of setting foot in the place. Instead, I wandered the streets like a zombie, letting throngs of frantic, last-minute shoppers bang into me, sideswipe me, clobber me with their shopping bags. I was so tired I didn't have the energy to get out of their way (Janice's sleep sofa, like most sleep sofas, was about as comfortable as a bed of cacti), but I finally did duck the crowds by escaping into a movie theater. Unfortunately, the movie that was playing was one of those twisty, convoluted thrillers where the heroine isn't who she claims to be and gets her comeuppance in the end. Not much of an escape after all.

I stopped at a pay phone to call my parents and wish them a merry Christmas, and told them about the other Nancy Stern's murder in the event that news of the case made it to Pennsylvania. When they asked me about the crowd noise in the background, I said I was at a party — an outdoor party in the middle of winter. Sure.

"Are you with that new beau you mentioned?" chuckled my father. "The one who dialed the wrong number?"

"Yes, Dad," I said, deciding to surrender utterly to my game of pretend. "And we're having a wonderful time."

"Make sure he takes good care of you," my mother chimed in. "You're our special baby, remember?"

"How could I forget?" I said and signed off.

I stopped into a deli and had a sandwich and a root beer and lingered long enough so that the waiter got antsy about it.

"I'm going, I'm going," I sniffed, leaving him the modest tip he deserved. It wasn't as if Jewish delicatessens were mobbed on Christmas Eve.

It was dark by the time I got home — about seven. I flipped on the lights, sorted through the mail, and played back the messages on the answering machine. (There were none for the other Nancy Stern, thank God.) And then I got undressed, wrapped myself in my ratty bathrobe, and turned on the TV. There was nothing on except Christmas specials of the type that star Kathie Lee Gifford. I turned on the radio. There was nothing on except Christmas songs of the type that are sung by the Chipmunks.

I decided to meditate. Janice had tried to teach me how, but I'd never been able to sit there without thinking. Hoping I'd have more success on this particular night, I sat on the floor cross-legged, closed my eyes, and took a couple of deep breaths. I was just on the verge of not thinking when the doorman buzzed.

I nearly jumped off the floor, let me tell you, so unnerved was I by the sound of that buzzer.

"What?" I yelled into the house phone. "What *is* it?"

"Bill's on his way up," said the doorman, the one who'd been on duty the night before, the one who'd probably been taking a crap when the murderer passed through.

"Bill?" This time I did jump. "Wait! Hello?"

Too late. The doorman had already hung up.

Bill? I thought, pacing back and forth in my tiny foyer. What's he doing here? How does he know my name? And, more pressingly, why am I wearing this hairball of a bathrobe?

I dashed into the bedroom, stuffed the robe in the closet, and threw my clothes back on.

Should I act as if I'm on my way out? I wondered. To a celebrity-studded bash or, perhaps, to a quiet evening with my colleagues?

Of course not. He knows you're not the other one now, I reminded myself, unless he's been in a black hole.

Then what should I do? What should I say? How should I handle this?

Before I could come to any conclusions, the bell rang.

"Nancy?" came Bill's voice through the door. And it wasn't the kindly Bill's voice, either. "I know you're in there. Open up."

Yikes.

"Nancy!" he said again, more insistently this time.

"Just a second."

I gathered myself up, shoulders back, head erect, the picture of self-assurance except for the little muscle in my right cheek that was twitching in a thoroughly irritating manner, and went to let him in.

CHAPTER THIRTEEN

"Why, it's my friend Bill Harris," I said, throwing open the door quite theatrically, like some great lady of the stage. "Do come in."

He came in with a vengeance, storming past me and planting himself in the middle of my living room, his hands on his hips, his eyes boring in on me. He was a vision in his camel's hair coat and charcoal gray business suit, his dark wavy hair slightly windblown, a lock of it having fallen across his forehead. He must have come straight from the store, I guessed, straight from hoards of bonus-laden Wall Streeters procuring diamonds as stocking stuffers for loved ones. "I think it's time you told me what this is all about," he demanded.

"By 'this' you mean what, exactly?" I asked innocently. Well, I had to be sure which of my lies he was referring to. Maybe he hadn't read the newspaper or watched TV. Maybe he hadn't heard that the other Nancy Stern was dead. Maybe he was just stewing about the fact that I'd rejected him. I had to keep my options open.

"I'll make it simple," he said, continuing to glower at me. "Who the hell are you?"

"I'm Nancy Stern, of course." I made it sound as if he were the screwy one. "You asked the doorman to buzz me, don't you remember?"

"I asked the doorman to buzz the woman in 6J," he snapped. "I have no idea what your real name is. I only know that it's not Nancy Stern because *she* was murdered last night."

Ah. So he had heard. Scratch Plan A.

"But my real name *is* Nancy Stern," I insisted. "Nancy Zelda Stern, if the truth be told."

"The truth? Ha!"

"Bill, let me —"

"Stop it. Just stop it." He turned his back on me. He was muttering to himself, mulling over how he should proceed. "Okay," he said, wheeling around to face me again. He was giving me a dirty look. A filthy look. "Who are you? And no games."

"Listen, Bill. I'm sure you're upset with me and you have good reason to be, but I can explain, really I can. How about sitting down first, making yourself comfortable?"

"No."

202

"Then how about a snack or something?"

"No."

"I suppose a glass of eggnog would be out of the question?"

"I hate eggnog."

"So do a lot of people. I've always wondered why it's even served during the holidays, sort of the way I've always wondered about fruitcake. Show me a person who likes fruitcake and I'll —"

"Tell me who you are already!"

"Right." I plunged in. "The other Nancy Stern, the freelance celebrity journalist Joan Geisinger intended to fix you up with, moved into this building a month ago, and because we had the same name, there was a bit of confusion. We started getting each other's mail and phone calls. One of those phone calls was you, Bill. You called that fateful November night to ask her out on a blind date."

"But I got you by mistake?"

"Yes. And instead of being honest with you by telling you that you had the wrong number, I pretended to be the other Nancy Stern. To keep the conversation going."

"Why would you do a thing like that?"

Why indeed. "Well, you had a very friendly voice. A warm, soothing voice. I don't know if anyone has ever complimented you on your voice, by the way, but if you decide you've had it with the jewelry business I bet you could move into radio." I was rambling, sliding off the track, but I couldn't help myself.

"You did a lot more than keep the conversation going," he said accusingly. "You went out with me — not once but three times — all the while assuming the identity of another woman."

"I did, but you see I was —"

"You actually regaled me with stories about your oh-so-glamorous career."

"*Her* oh-so-glamorous career," I corrected him.

"Jimmy Carter. Mother Teresa. *Morgan Fairchild.*"

"Don't remind me."

"You're not a celebrity journalist, are you? Admit it, dammit!"

"I admit it. The only celebrity I've ever met is Miss Piggy."

Another filthy look. "You think this is one big joke, don't you?"

"No! I'm not joking. We took the class on a field trip to the local PBS station where Miss Piggy was taping a show. She's much thinner in person, incidentally, but they say the camera does add ten pounds."

"What class are you talking about? The

dog training course you and your friend send your Jack Russell terriers to? Or was that story total bullshit like the others?"

"Total bullshit. I don't have a dog, Bill. Neither does Victoria. She and I are both preschool teachers. We teach four-year-olds at a private school here in the city called Small Blessings."

He stared at me, shaking his head. "A preschool teacher. You had me completely fooled."

"I'm sorry."

"I mean, I really bought your act. You're very good."

"Thanks. Well, *thanks* isn't the appropriate word, because I'm not proud of what I did."

"Then why did you do it? Can you answer me that?"

"I was lonely, I guess. And I was up for an adventure. My friend Janice had been after me to be less withholding, to start taking risks. She's a Just-Do-It sort of person."

"How lucky for mankind."

"But mostly why I did what I did was because I had this notion that the other Nancy Stern had a more exciting life than I did, a more special life. I wanted a glimpse of that life, Bill, just a quick peek at it. And so I accepted the date with you and then I enjoyed myself so much I accepted another date with you and then I enjoyed myself even more and I accepted a third date with you. Everything kind of snowballed. Whenever I promised myself I'd tell you who I was, I'd chicken out; I knew how you felt about dishonesty, about people who misrepresent themselves, and I didn't want to lose you."

"Lose me? Honey, you were the one who blew me off."

"I had to. I was falling in love with you."

"Falling in love with me?" He stopped grimacing and laughed. Laughed!

"May I ask what's so funny?" I said indignantly, taking a break from the mea culpa business, briefly.

"*You* are. What makes you think I'd believe anything you say?"

"Because you were falling in love with me too. You were, Bill. I could feel it."

"You could *feel* it?" He laughed some more. "Well, *feel* this, Nancy Stern — or whatever your name is." In a flash, he was grabbing me by the shoulders and kissing me, kissing me hard on the mouth. At first, I was too stunned to react — obviously the last thing I expected him to do was display even a modicum of desire for me — but when the kissing went on for several seconds, progressing into actual "making out,"

I reacted by moaning and murmuring and crying out an honest-to-goodness "Oh, yes."

I was really hitting my stride in the sound effects department when he pulled away abruptly. "You liked that, didn't you?" he challenged.

"I liked it," I agreed breathlessly. I liked it so much that I was tempted to jump the guy.

"How do you think you'd *feel* if you thought I'd been killed — murdered — and you'd never be able to kiss me again? Would you feel shocked? Sad? Haunted by a sense of what if?"

"All of the above."

"Great. You have an idea of how *I* felt when I opened the morning paper and saw an obituary for Nancy Stern, celebrity journalist, who lived on Manhattan's Upper East Side. I felt shocked, sad, haunted by a sense of what if? I thought, I'll never be able to kiss that woman again because she's gone forever."

I reached out to touch his arm. He waved me off.

"And then — poof! — Nancy Stern wasn't dead after all," he went on. "At least, not the Nancy Stern I'd remembered kissing. It turned out that another newspaper ran a longer article about the murder, with a photograph of the victim, and I was so relieved that she wasn't you that I didn't know what to do with myself."

"Relieved? Really?" I said, my eyes brimming with tears. "That's so sweet, Bill."

"Oh, it was sweet all right — for about ten seconds. Then I got mad. I'm talking as mad as I've ever been. I realized that I'd been taken in, toyed with, treated as if I were an idiot — by *you*, the mystery woman in 6J. God, when I think back on all those whoppers you put over on me." He shook his head again. "You're either a terrific con artist or a complete sociopath."

"I'm not a sociopath," I declared, desperate not to be lumped together with Gary, the nutritionist. "And I'm not a con artist. I'm just a nursery school teacher who hadn't had a date in a while. People do strange things when they haven't had a date in a while."

"Apparently."

"It's true. You should be a fly on the wall at one of Janice's reading groups. You'd get an earful."

"I'll pass." He didn't speak for a minute. I assumed he was weighing his next move. I hoped it would be another grab for my lips. "The point is," he said after clearing his throat, "I didn't know what — or who — I was dealing with after reading about the murder, and so I came here to confront you, to get to the bottom of this."

"And boy, am I glad you did come here, Bill. It's wonderful to see you. You look —"

"I look like a man who's leaving."

He started for the door.

"Wait! There's a lot more I want to say to you." I hurried after him. When he didn't seem the least bit inclined to change direction, I blocked the door, splaying my arms and legs across it. "I'm sure that once you've simmered down and had a chance to see my side of the argument, you'll conclude that I meant you no harm, that I have the highest regard for you, and that I didn't set out to trick you — well, not in a bad way. In short, I'd like another crack at our relationship."

"Our relationship? We don't have a relationship. *'I can't get involved at this stage of my life,'*" he said in a high nasal tone meant to mimic me, mock me. " *'It would interfere with my career.'* Isn't that what you said the night you dumped me?"

"Yes, but that night doesn't count," I protested. "I was still pretending to be the other Nancy Stern."

"Right, and now I've had it with your pretending," he barked. "Find yourself another sucker."

He literally picked me up, plunked me down a few feet away from the door, and walked out of my apartment, without even so much as a merry Christmas.

Well, what did I expect? The scene had gone exactly the way I'd feared it would — heavy on the melodrama, light on the forgiveness.

Although he did kiss me. And it wasn't one of those dry, tight-lipped pecks on the cheek, either.

Yes, Bill was angry, and yes, he indicated that he had no interest in even contemplating another go-round with me, but that kiss — well — that kiss hinted that there might be a slight window of opportunity. After all, men don't kiss women they detest, do they?

I was about to pick up the phone to call Janice, my expert on generalities relating to men, then remembered that she had probably left for Linda Franzione's Christmas party.

You're on your own, kid, I thought, feeling oddly optimistic for the first time in months. You'll find a way to win Bill back, and you'll forge a new relationship based on respect and honesty and trust. And once you do, nothing will come between you.

CHAPTER FOURTEEN

On Christmas morning, I awoke to find that my positive outlook from the night before was still intact. As I scrambled a couple of eggs and toasted an English muffin, I flashed back to Bill's kiss and how he'd said he felt relieved when he realized I hadn't been murdered, and I began to whistle while I worked.

This holiday might not be a dud after all, I thought, and continued to whistle such seasonal favorites as "Jingle Bells," which less than twenty-four hours earlier I wouldn't have whistled for anything. Yes, this will be a jolly old holiday, I clucked to myself. Janice and I will take in a few movies, troll the department stores for after-Christmas sales, even drop in at the open house that Fran Golden, our drippy colleague at Small Blessings, is having. I'll get through it, I thought. In a matter of days, the New Year will dawn, Bill will be returning his kids to their faithless mother, and I'll have another shot at winning back his affection.

I knew I'd have to come up with a plan, of

course, an excuse to thrust myself in his path yet again. Simply walking into Denham and Villier and begging for his forgiveness wouldn't be empowering or effective, judging by the fact that I'd already gone the begging route and he had marched out of my apartment anyway. No, there had to be a better strategy, one that would put us on a level playing field. I had the rest of my school vacation to come up with it, I figured, and, by God, I *would* come up with it — or die trying.

Speaking of dying, I had just swallowed my first forkful of eggs when I opened the newspaper and there, staring me in the face, ruining my appetite, temporarily, was the other Nancy Stern. The photo accompanied a story involving the progress of the police's investigation.

I pushed my plate aside and read.

According to the article, Det. Burt Reynolds, while not ruling out the possibility of a burglary-gone-wrong, had conducted a preliminary interview with Nancy's daughter, who was not a suspect in the murder, per se, but was under "an umbrella of suspicion."

Nancy's daughter?

I put down the paper.

Nancy's *daughter?*

She'd told me she wasn't a child person. She'd told me that she would never tie herself down to some dreary domestic scene when she could be out gallivanting around the world, interviewing colorful characters of international renown. She'd told me she wouldn't dream of letting motherhood cramp her style. So how come she had a daughter?

I picked up the paper and read on.

Apparently, this daughter had stepped forward upon hearing the tragic news of her mother's death. Apparently, this daughter had been camped out in New York, hoping to make contact with her mother. Apparently, the reason this daughter had been camped out in New York, hoping to make contact with her mother, was that she had been given up for adoption the day she was born, was raised in Mississippi by abusive, alcoholic parents, and now wanted to confront the heartless woman who had handed her over to such monsters and, with any luck, extort money from her. Apparently, this daughter was maintaining her innocence in the murder but was not denying her long-held wish to make mommy pay.

I put down the paper again.

A daughter! I said out loud. A daughter from Mississippi!

She must have been the young woman with the southern accent, I realized, the one who kept calling my number but never left her name. Perhaps, she had been trying to stake out her mother, intending to shake her down. Perhaps, on the night of the murder, she snuck past one of the building's crack doormen, rode up to 24A, and announced her existence to the other Nancy Stern. Perhaps an argument ensued when the subject of money came up. Perhaps one thing led to another as they so often do. Perhaps the miss from Mississippi was packin' a pistol along with her hostility and ended up shootin' and killin' her very own ma! (Perhaps I was getting a little carried away.)

Boy, people are full of surprises, I thought as I resumed eating my breakfast. Who would have guessed that the other Nancy Stern had a daughter, for instance? And what other secrets had she been keeping?

On the day of Fran Golden's open house, there was more news about my murdered neighbor. I was dressing for the party and half watching TV when the local station reported an update in the investigation. The police were questioning Helen Quigley, the wife of Henry Quigley, who, it turned out, was not only the Henry I'd mentioned to the police — the adulterous lover desperate to spend an illicit weekend with Nancy — but the highly respected CEO of Span Publications, the international magazine group that had employed her from time to time. According to the report, Mrs. Quigley had learned of her husband's affair with Nancy — had caught the two of them in flagrante delicto! — and was now, along with Nancy's daughter, standing under that big golf umbrella of suspicion. The report's final note on the matter was that Henry Quigley was taking a leave of absence from Span Publications in order to put his personal life in order and assist in his wife's vigorous defense. (The family had retained Gerry Spence.)

"Have you heard the latest?" Janice asked as we huddled together in the corner of Fran Golden's living room while the others were locked in a fierce battle of Christmas charades.

"You mean, about Henry Quigley's wife?" I said.

She shook her head. "About Bo, the one who wanted to roll around in the sheets with Nancy."

My eyes widened. "What about him?"

"I heard it on the radio in the cab coming over here. He's a drug dealer. 'Coke supplier to the stars,' the reporter called him."

"Whoa. So Nancy *used*, as they say?"

"The police found traces of coke and booze in her body. Poor thing."

I pondered this new information and found myself feeling sorry for the other Nancy Stern. From afar, it had seemed that *I* was the one leading the lesser life when it was *she* who was. All that bizarre behavior, the furtive phone calls, the secrets. "Is this Bo a suspect?"

"I'm not sure," said Janice. "Joan Rivers interrupted the radio reporter to remind me to take my belongings."

"I hate those recorded messages they have in taxis now," I said.

Janice was about to respond when Fran Golden poked her head in. "What are you two doing over here by yourselves?" she asked in her syrupy sweet voice, the kind of voice that instantly made you feel as if you were one of the three-year-olds in her class — one of the slowest three-year-olds. Maybe it was the way she drew each word out that inspired a feeling of being talked down to, drew every single syllable out so you wanted to tear your *hair* out, wondering if she'd ever get to the point. Or maybe it was the high pitch of her voice that did it — that sort of sing-songy, baby-talky, icky-yucky simper I swore I'd never adopt. Of course, it could have been the combo of the voice and the smile — a "There, There" smile you'd bestow on a kid with a boo-boo.

"We're not doing anything," Janice told Fran. "Really."

You see? Fran made even Janice feel like a child. A guilty child.

"Good," said Fran, clutching each of our hands and shepherding us back to the rest of the group. "Now come and take your turns at Christmas charades."

As you might imagine, Fran's annual Christmas charades were charades where the title of each book or movie or song had a Christmas reference. Janice and I hung in there as long as we could stomach it — I, for example, acted out "Silent Night" by standing up in front of everybody and simply not speaking for several seconds — and then went home.

By New Year's Eve, the police had yet another suspect in Nancy's murder: Jacques, her sometime boyfriend, the one who'd sent her roses. Kiss kiss.

His full name was Jacques Devallier, he was a Eurotrash type who had family money but no particular interests (other than women), and he was the last person to see

Nancy alive — or so it was surmised. According to the latest newspaper article I read, he had the key to her apartment and showed up unexpectedly on the night of the murder, only to find her in the middle of writing him a "Dear Jacques" letter. He admitted to police that he was enraged that she was breaking off their relationship, but insisted that a Frenchman would shoot himself before he'd ever shoot a lady, as chivalry was alive and well in France unlike in America, where there was only lawlessness and impeachment hearings and salads served *before* main courses.

"Now I don't know which of them did it," I told Janice after I arrived for our New Year's Eve date.

"Neither do I," she said. "What I know is that the other Nancy Stern wasn't as popular as we thought. I told you to be careful what you wished for."

I stared at her. "You told me the exact opposite, Janice. You told me to wish for whatever the hell I wanted."

"Did I?"

"You certainly did."

"Oh. Then I gave you bad advice. What I should have told you is to be grateful for small blessings — and I'm not talking about our little cherubs at school. I'm talking about the other parts of your life — the fact that you may be disappointed after what happened between you and Bill Harris, but you have your health and a roof over your head and a family who loves you. Be grateful for those, Nance. Not everybody has them."

"Janice, no offense but have you started the party without me?" It wasn't like her to get gooey or sentimental unless she'd been drinking. Even one sip could get her going.

"No, I have not," she said. "I waited for you."

"I appreciate that."

"What you just heard was my New Year's Eve speech," she said. "Whenever I think about one year ending and another beginning, I become very philosophical, very *Chicken Soup for the Soul.*"

"Very deep, in other words."

"Don't be a smart-ass. What I was trying to say is that, for me, New Year's is a time when I remind myself that instead of bitching about the things I don't have, I should appreciate the things I do have, give thanks for the things I do have."

"Isn't that what *Thanks*giving is for?"

"Yes, but you don't get to make resolutions at Thanksgiving."

"True."

"So my resolution this year is, I will be

grateful for small blessings. And frankly, Nance, in view of your fiasco with the other Nancy Stern, I would make it my resolution too, if I were you."

"Point taken. There will be no more yearning to live other peoples' lives," I pledged.

"Right," said Janice. "No more envying people we assume have it better than we do."

"Amen."

"From now on, we'll feel good about who *we* are."

"And view problems as growth experiences."

"Absolutely."

"Okay. Let the party begin," I said. "We'll eat and drink and watch the ball drop in Times Square and then we'll go cruising cyberspace for a couple of hot dates."

Janice shook her head. "We'll eat and drink and watch the ball drop in Times Square but there won't be any cyberdates. My computer's down."

"Your computer's down *again?*"

"Yeah, but my ice bucket's full, talk about small blessings. Carl Pinder's parents gave me a bottle of Dom Perignon for Christmas. What'd they give you, Nance?"

My Christmas presents! I'd forgotten all

about the shopping bags full of gifts that I'd lugged home the last day of school and stuffed in my hall closet. What with the other Nancy Stern's murder and the police's investigation and, of course, Bill's appearance at my door, the gifts had completely slipped my mind.

"I don't know what they gave me," I said. "I haven't opened my presents yet."

"No?"

"No, but I'll open them tomorrow. It'll give me something to look forward to."

Janice and I ate and drank and watched the ball drop and toasted the New Year with the Pinders' champagne. It wasn't the most exciting evening of either of our lives, but we were grateful for it and said so noisily, as per our resolutions.

The next morning, I retrieved the bags of Christmas presents from my closet, brought them to the sofa, and proceeded to unwrap all my goodies.

Oh, boy, I thought as I opened the first gift. Let's see what Santa's brought me this year.

Lindsay Greenblatt's parents gave me a ticket to a Broadway show — one ticket. I guess they assumed I wasn't dating anyone; it was hard to be insulted by this, as they were correct in their assumption.

Todd Delafield's parents gave me a lucite pepper mill. My hunch here was that the Delafields had themselves been given the pepper mill as a gift, hadn't liked it, and thus decided to rewrap it and pawn it off on their son's teacher.

Melyssa Deaver's parents gave me a canned ham. The Deavers were in the canned ham business and gave all the teachers canned hams, even Nick Spada, who was a vegetarian.

Alexis Shuler's mother, the Martha Stewart mother, *made* me a gift, naturally. It was a pretty little needlepoint pillow with a floral background and an inscription that read, I Love My Teacher. I was very flattered, but I couldn't help wondering if Mrs. Shuler had handcrafted similar pillows for the other service people in her daughter's life and altered the inscriptions slightly (I Love My Computer Tutor, I Love My Speech Therapist, I Love the Lady Who Cuts My Hair, etc.).

James Woolsey's stepmother, the twenty-one-year-old who was formerly his au pair, gave me a beautiful sterling silver pen with initials on it — hers. (And they say today's young people are self-absorbed.)

Carl Pinder's parents gave me a bottle of Dom Perignon, just as they'd given Janice.

Joshua Eisen's parents gave me a lovely silk scarf — the same one they'd given me the year before when I'd had Joshua's sister in my class. Zachary Sinclair's parents gave me Calvin Klein's Obsession — the perfume, the body lotion, even the deodorant.

And so on and so forth.

When I reached the bottom of the shopping bag, I found Fischer Levin's gift. I say Fischer Levin's gift as opposed to Fischer Levin's *parents'* gift because he'd told me he'd picked it out and wrapped it himself, using the paper we'd made in the classroom out of newspaper and gold glitter.

He did a good job, too, I thought, grimacing as I nearly tore my rotator cuff trying to open the damn package. (Fischer had gone a little heavy on the Scotch tape. What's more, he had wrapped and rewrapped and triple-wrapped whatever was inside, making it an adventure to *get* to the gift.)

But I did get to it eventually, peeling off the layers of paper until I came upon my prize: a gaudy, glittery pin in the shape of a flower — a tacky piece of costume jewelry of the sort that's one step up from the stuff you get inside a Cracker Jack box or a gum ball machine.

I held the pin in my hand and examined it,

and the longer I did the more I considered the possibility that it wasn't quite as cheesy as I'd first thought. As a matter of fact, the petals of the flower could very well be cubic zirconia, I decided, not just slivers of glass glued together. The same was true for the enormous, round, yellow crystal that was set in the flower's center; it, too, could have been not colored glass, but one of those fake gemstones that sell for about twenty bucks.

I laughed. The Levins were rolling in money, and Gretchen Levin wouldn't be caught dead wearing such a hunk of junk. They probably sent Olga, the Latvian caregiver, out with Fischer to buy me a gift and never bothered to ask what he had chosen.

I pictured Olga hoisting her chubby charge onto a stool at the jewelry counter of some discount store and saying, "Okay, dumpling. Pick something nice for dat teacher," and then Fischer pointing to the biggest, shiniest object and yelling, "I want *that* for Miss Stern!"

Ah, Fischer, I thought. He was a handful but he was a good boy. Never mind that the pin was grotesquely large and screamingly cheap. It represented his expression of affection for me and I was touched by it in a way that the Pinders' hundred-dollar bottle of Dom Perignon couldn't begin to match.

I fastened the pin to the collar of my flannel nightgown and modeled it in the bathroom mirror. God, it was ugly. Really garish. Jewelry only a hooker would wear, or, at the very least, someone with truly trashy taste. Still, I would wear it with pride, on the first day back at school, I resolved.

It was after I'd just used the word *resolved* that I remembered the New Year's *resolution* Janice and I had made, about being grateful for small blessings.

It occurred to me at that moment that I had stumbled on a small blessing for which it wouldn't be a stretch to be grateful. You see, the piece of "jewelry" that Fischer Levin had bought me for Christmas was, I fervently hoped, my way back to Bill.

CHAPTER FIFTEEN

The first day back at school was a veritable Furby convention — Furby being the year's *it* toy, the year's Tickle Me Elmo, the year's must-have Christmas gift. A bizarre-looking interactive stuffed animal, Furby had been on every single kid's wish list, and even though there had been much ado in the press about its being impossible to find, the parents of the children at Small Blessings had managed to find it.

"Dah o-loh u-tye," said Fischer Levin's Furby as he shoved the hairy thing in my face. (Furby speaks a nonsense language called Furbish, and the nonsensical words Fischer's Furby had just spoken meant "Good morning.")

"Good morning to you too," I said to the toy, then turned to Fischer and pointed to the collar of my blouse, to which I had fastened his Christmas pin. "It's beautiful, honey, just beautiful." I hugged him. "Thank you for making me feel so special." Special indeed. All Fischer had gotten Janice was a rabbit's foot keychain.

"I knew you'd like it," he said excitedly, clapping his hands together. "It's shiny, right?"

"The shiniest," I agreed.

"Big, too."

"Oh, is it ever big."

"And I picked it out by myself."

"I'll treasure it always."

"Yeah, because it came from a box full of buried *treasure*." He puffed his chest out. "My dad was real proud of me when I told him about it on the airplane."

"I'm sure he's proud because you've been such a good boy lately." The reference to Mr. Levin inspired me to ask Fischer about his vacation in London. He said that his father was on the phone a lot and that his mother was out shopping a lot, but that he had fun with Olga, who let him race her up and down the halls of the hotel and stay up later than his usual bedtime.

Thank God for Olga, I thought, glad that somebody in the Levin household paid any attention to Fischer.

When school was over that day, I immediately grabbed my coat and gloves and said good-bye to Janice.

"Hey, where are you off to in such a hurry?" she asked.

"You see this pin?" I said, referring to Fischer's gift.

"How could I miss it?" She laughed. "That yellow boulder in the middle of it is blinding me. Who buys crap like that anyway? Except for little boys on little budgets."

"Who buys it? Women with no taste. Women with no money. Women who want people to think they're rich."

"Why would people think they're rich? Jewelry like that doesn't fool anybody, just like fake eyelashes don't fool anybody, just like fake nails don't fool anybody, just like fake boobs don't fool anybody —"

"Janice," I interrupted. She was obsessed with fake boobs, I decided. "Isn't it possible that *somebody* might mistake this pin for a real piece of jewelry?"

"Like who?" she scoffed.

"Like me," I said.

"You? I don't get it."

"Okay. You asked me why I'm leaving in such a hurry this afternoon. The reason is, I'm going to find out if this pin could be a real piece of jewelry."

"But that's crazy," said Janice. "You know damn well it isn't."

"Yes and no. Yes, I know it's not real. No, I'm not giving up on Bill Harris."

"Run that by me again?"

I took a breath, trying to calm myself. "I spent most of the holidays wracking my brain for an excuse to see Bill again, Janice, and when I opened Fischer's present I finally came up with one."

"I'm listening."

"I'm going to take this pin over to him at Denham and Villier and ask him to analyze it, appraise it, whatever it is jewelers do. So what if the thing's fake? The point is, it'll get me in the door. It'll give me a reason to be in Bill's company again. It'll allow me to reopen the lines of communication between us because I'll be in the store on business. I won't have to walk in there with my tail between my legs and beg him to forgive me for pretending I was the other Nancy Stern. I'll simply be a customer, asking him if he wouldn't mind sharing his expertise."

"His expertise." Janice nodded approvingly. "Not bad."

"Yeah?"

"Yeah. Men love that shit. They can't resist playing Mr. Know-It-All. It flatters them. It makes them feel important. It puts them in touch with their manhood."

I rolled my eyes. The manhood thing again. "What I plan to do is take this pin to him and say, 'I know how busy you are, Bill, and I also know you're not my biggest fan at the moment, but I was given this pin for Christmas and I was wondering if it's real or a piece of junk. Since you're the most knowledgeable person I've ever met on the subject of jewelry, I thought I'd come to you for help.' What do you think?"

"I like it," said Janice. "The 'I thought I'd come to you for *help*' is a nice touch. It places him in the role of the hero, and he probably has fantasies of playing the hero. They all do, except the dirtbags who have fantasies of playing the heel. Those are the ones I end up with."

"Poor baby."

"There is one little problem with your scenario though. Bill will take one look at the pin and figure out what you're up to."

"Why?"

"Nance, the pin isn't real and anybody with eyes can see that."

"Not necessarily. The first night Bill and I went out, he told me that jewelry is a blind item — and that's a direct quote. He said it's almost impossible for the average consumer to detect real gems from fakes because there are such variations in quality and clarity and setting. He said that's why people are always getting ripped off when they buy jewelry. He said it's key to find a jeweler or gemologist you can trust and then get him or her to evaluate the piece. Well, that's what I'll be doing, right? Getting him to evaluate this piece of you-know-what."

She smiled. "I've got to hand it to you. You've changed a lot since all this Bill stuff started. You used to be so passive about men, so who cares, so if-it-happens-it-happens. And now here you are, for the first time in all the years I've known you, really pursuing a guy."

"Maybe I finally found someone worth pursuing," I said.

I stopped at the apartment before heading over to Denham and Villier so I could change clothes, fix my hair, and apply a little makeup. I was rushing into the building, waving hello to the doorman, when there, standing in the lobby along with a half-dozen more cops, was Det. Burt Reynolds.

"Hey, Detective. How's it going?" I asked.

"It's going," he said.

I got the distinct impression that he didn't remember me, so I volunteered, "I'm the other Nancy Stern, the one who wasn't murdered." How could he not remember me? I thought. He had practically accused me of killing Nancy and actually went so far as to contact Janice to confirm my alibi.

"Oh, right. I remember now," he said

without much passion one way or the other.

"Anything new in the investigation?" I asked. "I assume that's why you're here."

"We've been here every day since the homicide," he said. "We're interviewing the tenants, the doormen, the super, everybody — plus the forensics people are still working the crime scene."

"But according to the media, you have a number of suspects already, some of whom I believe *I* was helpful in bringing to your attention." I wasn't looking for a pat on the back, exactly; a brusque "thanks" would have done the trick.

"I can't comment on that except to say that the investigation is ongoing. It won't be long before we have our man in custody and your building will be back to normal."

"You said *man*. Does that mean you've ruled out Nancy's —"

"Can't comment."

"What about the burglary thing? Have you ruled that out?"

"Can't comment."

"Did you have a nice Christmas or can't you comment on that either?" Boy, was he *withholding*, as Janice would say.

"I *can* comment, but I don't want to," he said and moved past me, out the door.

★ ★ ★

Denham and Villier's flagship store was on the corner of Fifth Avenue and Fifty-fifth Street, a stone's throw from Tiffany and Cartier and Van Cleef & Arpels. Its interior was decorated in an Old World, European style, with crystal chandeliers on the ceiling and silk tapestries on the wall and thick, ankle-deep carpeting on the floors of the landmark two-story building. Whenever I wandered around the store, which wasn't often given my salary, I always felt as if I were in Prague or Paris or some other grand capital abroad, but my sense of awe was usually reduced when I reminded myself that Mr. Denham and Mr. Villier were just a couple of good ol' boys from Shreveport, Louisiana.

"Excuse me," I said, flagging down a sales clerk. "Would you mind directing me to the store manager's office?"

He pointed me toward the elevator and told me to take it to the second floor, make a right turn, walk all the way past the sterling silver department, past the fine china department, past the repairs desk, and there it would be.

I thanked him and strode toward the elevator, as if I wasn't the slightest bit nervous.

Once on the second floor, I followed the

salesman's directions and found the manager's office with no trouble at all. I hoped the meeting with Bill would go half as smoothly.

There was no secretary outside his office, no gatekeeper, and the door to the office was wide open, so I simply stuck my head in.

But it wasn't Bill who was standing at the desk with his back to me, talking on the phone; it was a short blond man with a Germanic accent.

I ducked out and waited in the hall while I considered the situation. Perhaps this man was a client of Bill's who had asked to use the office to call his own office. Perhaps he was the store's assistant manager who shared the office with Bill for budgetary reasons. Perhaps he was one of Denham and Villier's European managers who was occupying the office while he was in town. Lots of possibilities.

When I heard the man finish his conversation, I stuck my head back in. "Hello," I said. He turned to face me. "I'm here to see Bill Harris. Is he around, by any chance?"

"Yes, yes. He's around but not —"

We were interrupted by Bill himself, looking fabulously debonair in his navy blue suit and red tie. I was struck once again by the enormous attraction I felt toward him, struck by the fact that a mere glimpse of him could produce such a physical reaction in me.

"Bill!" I said. "I hope I haven't come at a bad time."

He stopped in his tracks when he saw who his visitor was, his expression stunned but unrevealing; I couldn't tell whether I was a welcome surprise or a bummer.

"I'll just need a few minutes with you," I promised, walking straight into the office and sitting down, before he could cast me out.

The blond man seemed perturbed by my presence, but Bill took him aside, had a few words with him, and he left us alone.

"So?" said Bill, his dark eyes fixed on me now.

"He wasn't pleased," I said of the man. "Did I throw a monkey wrench into a big sale or something?"

"What are you doing here, Nancy?" he asked, ignoring my question. He was still standing by the door, one foot in, one foot out, unwilling to commit himself.

"I'd like to speak to you," I said.

He sighed. "Look, if this is about what happened between us, I said all I have to say at your apartment on Christmas Eve."

"It isn't about us," I asserted. "I came to

235

ask your advice about a piece of jewelry, to ask for your help in evaluating the worth of a piece of jewelry."

He appeared skeptical but not completely without interest, arching an eyebrow at me as he finally entered the office and perched himself on the edge of his desk. Maybe the word *help* had sucked him in, as Janice had predicted. "There are plenty of jewelers in New York," he said. "Why seek me out?"

"Because I respect your expertise, Bill. You seemed extremely knowledgeable whenever you talked about your work."

"That's pretty funny, isn't it?" He wasn't laughing. "You seemed extremely knowledgeable whenever you talked about your work. Unfortunately, 'your' work was somebody else's and you weren't knowledgeable, just clever."

Remember the kiss, I encouraged myself. Don't let his bitterness scare you off. He still cares. He does.

"I'd like us to try to get past what I did," I said. "I've apologized to you. The apology was genuine. But I'm not here to grovel, Bill; I'm here to discuss jewelry." No reaction. "Now, may I show you the piece in question? It shouldn't take long to determine whether or not it has value. Not for someone with your *vast experience*."

He didn't answer right away. He was probably soaking up the compliment, playing out his hero fantasies, getting in touch with his manhood.

"All right," he said, extending his hand begrudgingly. "Let's see the piece."

Victory. I unbuttoned my coat, unfastened the pin from my blouse collar, and gave it to him. "So. What do you think?"

I figured he'd take one look at the thing and toss it in the garbage. Instead, he seemed somewhat intrigued by it.

"Well. Well. Where did you get this, Nancy?" he asked in a way that suggested he was no longer angry at me or less angry at me than he was before. A definite thawing, at any rate.

"It was a Christmas present," I said, not bothering to add that the present was from a four-year-old. Why not let him wonder who the present was from? I thought. Why not let him wonder if it was from a man, a suitor, a competitor for my affections? Once I admitted it was from a child, he'd guess the pin was worthless, because what kind of a child buys his teacher an expensive bauble for Christmas? No, I was keeping the purchaser of the pin to myself, I decided, to create a little mystery, so Bill might be tempted to spend at least five more minutes with me.

"A Christmas present," he repeated, studying the piece, as if it were some incredible family heirloom. "That means you only got it a week or so ago."

"Yes." It occurred to me that he'd probably known right away that the pin was junk but was either tricking me, to pay me back for tricking him, or was humoring me, to make our visit last a while. "Is it worth anything?" I asked, getting up from the chair to stand next to him. I could smell his cologne — a subtle scent, not one of those dreadful designer-y fragrances that club you over the head with their muskiness.

"It's hard to say," Bill hedged. "Jewelry is such a blind item."

"Right. You told me that the first time we had dinner together."

"I would have to do some testing of the individual stones to be certain of their value or lack thereof."

"Okay." This was fun. We were friends again.

"First I'd examine the large yellow stone under a loup, to see if it's got a Gemprint."

"Gemprint?"

"It's like a laser fingerprint that makes diamonds easy to identify."

"Diamonds?" My jaw dropped.

Bill smiled — a first for the afternoon.

"I'm hardly saying you've got a diamond here, Nancy. I'm just laying out the sort of procedure we follow for appraising a piece like this. That's what you wanted, wasn't it? For me to give you a thorough evaluation of the brooch?"

"Oh, yes. Absolutely." I couldn't tell if he was pulling my leg or taking me seriously, but whichever the case, he had to be just as eager to patch things up between us as I was, or he'd have pretended to be busy and ordered me to scram.

"I'd also do a scratch test, of course."

"Of course."

"And a refractive index test, to measure how the light is reflected inside the stones."

"Naturally."

"And a specific gravity test, to measure the density of the stones."

"Density, yes."

"And then I'd need to test for the proverbial four Cs — carat, color, clarity, and cut."

"My goodness. I bet all that takes time."

"Just a couple of days, now that the holidays are over. You don't have a problem leaving the brooch with me, do you?"

"No. I'd be happy to leave it." Happy that we have this new connection, Billy.

"Good. I'll call you when the tests are done and you can come and pick it up. I still

239

have your number." He actually chuckled when he said that, about having my number, because, after all, it was the other Nancy Stern's number he'd thought he had. "Or, I could bring it by your place after work," he said more tentatively. "And then we could have dinner someplace in your neighborhood."

"Dinner?" I was beyond happy.

"Yes. Unless you've written me off as the spoilsport of the century."

I chuckled at that one. Oh, things were turning out sooo much better than I'd expected. What an amazing about-face he had done. "You're not a spoilsport, Bill."

"Not usually, but I've been ridiculously rigid about this, about what happened. I see that now."

"Oh, Bill. I don't think you've been rigid," I reassured him, marveling at how well this was going. "If someone ever lied to me about their identity, I'm positive that I wouldn't take it nearly as well as you did. In fact, I'd never speak to the person again."

"Don't say that. You don't know how you'd react."

"Well, all right. But I do know that I'd be delighted to have dinner with you."

"Great. That's great." He opened the top drawer of the desk, took out a Denham and

Villier envelope, and placed the pin carefully inside. "I'll call you when I've appraised the piece and we'll get together later this week."

"Your sons have gone back to Virginia then?"

"My sons?"

"Didn't they come for New Year's?"

He shook his head in disbelief. "How embarrassing is this? Your visit has gotten me so flustered I forgot about my own children." He shook his head again. He *was* flustered, embarrassed. My showing up here must have really shaken him up, I thought with no small pleasure. "Yes, Peter and Michael have gone back to their mother, but I had a terrific week running them around the city. They can't wait to come back."

I was about to say, "I'd love to meet them the next time they're here," but I kept my mouth shut. I had made major progress with Bill. I had no intention of pulling a Janice and scaring him off.

CHAPTER SIXTEEN

On Wednesday, two days after I'd dropped the pin off at Denham and Villier, Bill called to say he'd finished the appraisal.

"So? Did my Christmas present turn out to be the Hope diamond?" I teased.

"Sorry," he said with a chuckle. "It turned out to be a bad imitation of a bad imitation."

"In other words, all those stones — even the big yellow one — are fake?"

"Worthless," Bill confirmed. "I assumed they were the minute I saw them, but I went through the motions, because I didn't want to disappoint you. Not after what an ass I made of myself over your innocent game of —"

"Bill," I cut him off. "Don't. Let's just be glad that the pin reopened the lines of communication between us." And, therefore, served its purpose exactly.

"You're right, of course." He paused. "I am curious about something though. Did the person who gave you the brooch lead you to believe that the piece had value?"

"Not monetary value — that was my own

pie-in-the-sky idea — but sentimental value. Yes, he definitely indicated that it was a source of pride to him." *You're my favorite teacher, Miss Stern. I picked your present out and wrapped it all by myself.* The pin had value because Fischer had chosen it for me — Fischer, who had such trouble expressing his feelings; Fischer, who was starving for love; Fischer, who deserved to be loved. I would wear his pin regardless of its cheesiness. It would always be special to me.

"I have another question." There was a hesitancy in Bill's voice, as if he didn't want to pry but couldn't help himself. "You said *he;* that *he* indicated. I take it the person who gave you the gift is a man?"

My, my. Wasn't our Bill the inquisitive one. So he was wondering who'd been attentive to me over the holidays while he'd been mad at me. "Yes, Bill. The person who gave me the gift is a man." *A man who hasn't reached puberty yet, but the gender's correct.* "He's someone I've known since September."

"Ah. Is he someone you work with at school?"

"As a matter of fact he is. But he and I aren't romantically involved, if that's what's on your mind."

He laughed. "I'm pretty transparent, obviously."

243

So Bill *was* jealous! He wanted me all to himself!

I was pleased beyond belief, finally secure in the knowledge that he cared about me, felt stirrings of love for me. But I had promised myself that if he and I were ever to rebuild our relationship, it would be based on trust, not deception; on truth, not lies. On the other hand, nothing I'd said about the pin or the person who'd given it to me could be construed as a lie, not really. I was simply providing him with a minimum of details, in order to create a tiny aura of mystery around myself, in order not to *bore* him. That was fair during the courtship stage of a new romance, wasn't it? Besides, what possible difference could it make to Bill who gave me the pin? He had appraised it, found it worthless, and that was that.

"I propose that we change the subject and talk about when we're going to get together," I said jauntily, confidently, "so you can return the pin and I can thank you for bothering with it. Would you like to come here for dinner one night this week? I'm not a gourmet chef but you won't go away hungry." Gourmet chef. Right. I couldn't remember the last time I'd actually cooked a meal — a meal that didn't involve the microwaving of something frozen, something someone else, some corporation, had cooked.

"I'll be there," he said enthusiastically. "Is tomorrow night too soon?"

I smiled to myself. Yes, his willingness to forgive me seemed awfully sudden, especially given how angry he'd been, but I wasn't complaining. He was back. We were back.

Bill arrived at the apartment on Thursday night bearing gifts — a dozen long-stemmed red roses. As I opened the box and put the roses in a vase, I flashed back to the afternoon when I had mistakenly received the other Nancy Stern's dozen long-stemmed red roses. The memory was unsettling. Yes, it was swell that it was *I* whom a man had thought to woo with roses this time, but it was also just a little creepy that the man who was wooing me with them might well have wooed *her* with them if *I* hadn't insinuated myself into the situation.

"You didn't have to bring me flowers," I said, filling the vase with water. Bill was standing next to me at the sink, very next to me.

"Yes I did," he said softly. "I owe you an 'I'm sorry.' "

"I thought we decided to get past what happened between us," I said. "This is a new year, a new beginning. Let's forget about how we met and all the rest."

"I'll try." He lowered his head and kissed me. I set the vase aside and kissed him back. Our reconciliation was moving right along.

"I missed you over the holidays," he said.

"Even though you had your boys with you?" I fished.

"Even though. You and I had some real momentum going for a while there, Nancy. I'm hoping we can pick up where we left off."

"We already have." He kissed me again. God, love was grand. No wonder people did somersaults in the hope of experiencing it. Still, I had worked hard on dinner and wasn't about to see it ruined. "Bill," I said, gently pushing him away, "if I'm going to pull a meal together, we've got to save this for later."

"Okay," he conceded, "although we could keep doing *this* and save the *meal* for later."

I shook my head and ousted him from the kitchen. The space wasn't big enough for two, and besides I had to concentrate, really pay attention to what I was doing.

In preparation for the dinner, I had spent

the previous evening watching the Food Channel on cable, sitting there in awe as a parade of chefs famous for this four-star restaurant or that best-selling cookbook chopped, diced, and sauteed their way through recipe after recipe using ingredients, never mind kitchen tools, I'd never heard of. I mean, who, not counting Martha Stewart, has a fucking mandoline? After a thoroughly intimidating few hours of Emeril and Bobby Flay and Two Hot Tamales, it occurred to me that these professionals have raised the bar when it comes to inviting someone over for dinner. Thanks to them, ordinary people like me, who aren't totally sure what cilantro is, can't just roast a chicken and feel good about ourselves. No, we have to cut the chicken up with our very own poultry shears, then marinate the chicken in a "nonreactive" dish, spread the marinade on the chicken using a boar-bristled brush, blacken the chicken with grill marks that create a cute little criss-cross pattern, and finally serve the chicken on a plate painted with colorful squiggles. Well, fine, I thought. I'm a preschool teacher. I know about squiggles.

Bill and I kept our hands off each other while he sipped a cocktail and I did the chicken. (That's another thing about the chefs on these shows. They don't cook chicken or make chicken or even prepare chicken; they *do* chicken.) He ooh-ed and ah-ed as I brought the food out and said I must have spent a lot of time and effort on the meal, which, of course, was true and nice of him to notice. We sat in my living room at the small round table that doubled as a dining room table, ate the chicken, as well as the potatoes and green vegetables I had *julienned* with my brand-new *mandoline*, and talked about my job at Small Blessings. As this was previously uncharted conversational territory for us — the other three times we'd had dinner together I'd talked about my job as a celebrity journalist, remember — I had loads of stories to tell Bill, and, to my delight, he seemed even more engaged than when I'd prattled on about Kevin Costner. He loved hearing about the children, loved hearing about Janice and Victoria and the others, loved hearing about the conflicts I'd had with Penelope over the years.

After dinner, we adjourned to the sofa for coffee and dessert.

"This is so nice," he said contentedly.

"Oh, you like the apple pie." I'd gotten the recipe from my mother, not from the Food Channel.

"I love the apple pie, but I meant *this*. Being here with you. Restarting our relationship."

"It's wonderful."

"To think we wasted all that time during the weeks we were apart," he said. "To think *I* wasted all that time being angry when I could have been with you."

"Please don't beat yourself up about that, Bill."

"I know, I know. But I'd like to make it up to you, like to make up for lost time." He took me in his arms and kissed me, over and over and over. And then he unbuttoned my blouse and kissed my throat and neck and breasts. And then he . . . well. The point is, it soon became clear to both of us that the living room sofa was limiting, that we needed to spread out. I suggested we repair to the bedroom. "I don't want to rush you," Bill whispered.

"You're not rushing me," I said, panting.

"You're sure?"

"Very."

With a tremendous sense of urgency, I grabbed Bill's hand and led him to my bedroom.

"I've wanted this since the first time we went out," he murmured as we stripped out of our clothes and climbed between the sheets.

"Me too," I said breathlessly, "only I was pretending to be the other Nancy Stern so I didn't think my feelings were appropriate."

"Let's forget about the other Nancy Stern," said Bill as he began to make love to me.

"I already have."

Bill was a wonderful lover, thank goodness. It would have been tragic had he been so well endowed and then turned out to be clumsy or selfish or just plain dull as dishwater in bed. And, judging by the number of "Oh, Gods" he'd moaned, I must have been more than satisfactory in his opinion. Of course, there will be some of you who think it was ill-advised of me to sleep with him after only four dates, just as there will be others of you who wonder why I waited four dates to sleep with him. All I can say is, it felt right. My instincts told me to go for it. What's more, I was *due* for it.

As we lay there in my bed, which hadn't seen such activity since the men from Dial-A-Mattress installed my new box spring, I thought how lucky I was to have found Bill, how my life really had changed since I'd met him. Naturally, I wished I hadn't gotten together with him at the other Nancy Stern's expense, and naturally, if I'd had it all to do over again, I would have told Bill the truth after our first date — at least I hope I would have — but I was grateful for small blessings, just as Janice and I had resolved, grateful for what I had, not yearning for what I didn't; grateful that Bill Harris and I were in love.

Not that Bill declared his love that night at my apartment. Such a declaration would have been too trite, not worthy of him. Every Tom, Dick, and Harry is tempted to say "I love you" after terrific sex, but it's the men who mean it who don't feel the need to blurt it out. That's what I told myself anyway.

"What are you going to teach your kids about tomorrow?" he asked as he traced circles around my breasts with his fingertip, sending exquisite sensations throughout my body.

"Tomorrow?" I repeated, my excitement making me stupid. "Tomorrow we're finishing up a unit on money."

"Money?"

"That's right. We've been collecting coins all week and learning the difference between the penny, the nickel, the dime, and the quarter in terms of their color, size, and value." He was playing with my nipples now. I was losing consciousness, never mind concentration. "The idea is to familiarize them with numbers and the concept of counting as well as introduce them to actual currency."

"That's very practical," he said as he moved his hand down to my stomach and rubbed me there, rubbed me all around.

"Yes," I said, my breath quickening. "We're making little purses for the children, so they'll have something to put the coins in. We're taking cut-outs of old rags and tying them together with colored yarn."

"Old rags." He smiled lazily, his own excitement growing.

"Well, that was the hard part, getting the rags." I blushed when I said "hard part," given the situation. "Small Blessings mothers don't seem to have any."

"What do they do with clothes they don't wear anymore?"

"They call one of the high-end consignment shops in town and have the clothes picked up, sometimes with the price tags still on them." Bill's fingers had ventured further south at this point. He had reached paydirt, speaking of money.

"Go on," he urged.

"No, *you* go on," I said. "I'll finish the story later."

An hour later, as it turned out.

Since we both had to get up early for work in the morning, we decided it would be better if Bill didn't stay over that night. Reluctantly and after yet another round of serious kissing, he got dressed, I put on my robe, and we walked, arms around each other, to the door of my apartment. We were standing there planning the sequel to our torrid evening when my mind drifted and I caught myself trying to pick out my outfit for school the next day. That thought led to the silk scarf that Joshua Eisen had gotten me for Christmas, and *that* thought led to the pin Fischer Levin had gotten me for Christmas, and *that* thought led me to remind Bill that he'd forgotten to return the pin — the original reason for his coming over.

"Before you leave," I said, nuzzling my head against his chest, "could you give me back the pin?"

"The pin?"

"The *brooch*, as you would say."

"Oh, didn't I tell you?"

"Tell me what?" I said, still nuzzling.

"It didn't survive the testing," he said.

I looked up at him. "What happened?"

"Well, as I may or may not have explained to you, diamonds are the hardest substance — the only substance that can stand up to the testing. Since the stones in your brooch weren't diamonds or even moderately expensive knockoffs as you'd hoped, they melted. Disintegrated, actually. We tossed the whole piece."

"Tossed it?"

"It fell apart, Nancy. There wasn't anything to save."

"Gee, that's a shame. Even though it was junk, it was a gift and I wanted the person who gave it to me to see that I appreciated it."

"Aw, sweetie. You're upset." He kissed the top of my head. "I probably should have gone into the techniques we use when we appraise a piece and laid out the risks involved. My fault entirely."

I nodded. I did understand. And yet I felt awful that I wouldn't be able to wear the pin at school, awful that I wouldn't be able to show Fischer how much it meant to me. He was going to ask me why I wasn't wearing it, I was sure of that, and I'd have to come up with some lame excuse — like the dog ate it. Oh, well.

"One of these days, I'll buy you the real thing," Bill said, hugging me tightly.

"Why? Does Denham and Villier give its store managers a deep discount?" I kidded.

"Yes," he said. "So be a good girl and you might get lucky next Christmas."

Next Christmas. That was nearly a year

away. I wondered where Bill and I would be in our relationship by that time.

I suddenly pictured us living together, pictured us getting married, pictured his sons filled with adoration for their new step-mother, pictured us becoming the parents of our own dear children.

Yeah, I know. I was getting way ahead of myself. But that's what happens right after you meet a man and fall in love. You get way ahead of yourself. You dream. You dream that life will now be a bed of roses, a bowl of cherries, a picnic. You dream that love conquers all, that hope springs eternal, that the road will be paved with gold. You dream in clichés when you fall in love. And then you wake up and find that the road is paved with boulders, not gold, and the best you can do is drive carefully.

CHAPTER SEVENTEEN

Bill and I saw each other Friday night and Saturday night and, since it was his day off, virtually all of Sunday too. By Monday morning, I was as giddy as a honeymooner and every bit as exhausted.

"You look radiant," Janice commented when I arrived at school. "Radiant but racoonish."

"You're referring to the dark circles." I had applied a ton of concealer under my eyes, to no avail, apparently.

"Yeah, and I'm envious," she said. "You two must be in that we'd-rather-have-sex-than-sleep stage of a relationship."

I nodded shyly.

"You'd better enjoy it," said Janice. "It won't last."

"What won't?" I challenged, thinking she meant Bill and me.

"The marathon sex," she said. "After a while, you'll only have it once a day. Then once every couple of days. Then once a week, and so on. You've been married,

Nance. You know how these things go."

"Yes, but what Bill and I have doesn't even come close to what I had with John. Unlike my cold-fish ex-husband, Bill is affectionate. He initiates. And he's protective of me without being smothering. He's so concerned about my welfare that he insists I lock my door after he leaves the apartment, because the police haven't solved the other Nancy Stern's murder and there could be a psycho running around loose in the building. In fact, the other day we were supposed to meet in my lobby before going to a movie. When I showed up, he was in the middle of a conversation with that detective, Burt Reynolds, who's still hanging around interviewing tenants. I asked Bill what they were talking about and do you know what he said?"

"Not a clue."

"He said he told Detective Reynolds that his *special lady* lived in 6J and that he wanted to make sure she was safe. I mean, how nice was that of him to take it upon himself to speak to the cop?"

"Very nice," Janice agreed. "Very impressive."

"I realize I haven't known him that long, but if I made a list of the characteristics I was looking for in a man, Bill would have

257

every one of them."

"He almost sounds too good to be true."

"No. I just got lucky. I never thought I'd find someone like him, Janice, but I did find him. I still can't believe it."

She hugged me. "When do I get to meet this embodiment of perfection?"

"Whenever you want. Why don't we all have dinner some night this week?"

"Great. Let's do it Wednesday night. I've got a date and we could make it a four-some."

"A date? Who are you going out with?" I hadn't recalled Janice mentioning any new men in her life.

"His name is Cummings."

"What's his first name?"

"Cummings. He's from one of those families where they give each other last names for first names and first names for last names. Cummings Gilbert is his full name. It's confusing, I know. I've already slipped and called him Gilbert, but he was completely cool about it. I guess it's happened before."

"When did you meet him?"

"Yesterday at Barnes and Noble. Sunday afternoon's my day to cruise the stacks, remember?"

"I remember."

"Well, I got there at about two-thirty and immediately positioned myself in the business section, and that's where I met Cummings. I had decided on the subway ride over to the store that I'd had enough deadbeats for boyfriends and that it was time I went after a man of means for a change. I figured the best place to bag one was in the business section."

"Gee, you really thought this out, Janice. What does Cummings do for a living?"

"Nothing. He has a trust fund."

"So he's a rich deadbeat."

"Yes. My strategy was only partially successful."

I smiled. "I'll ask Bill about Wednesday night, but I'm sure it'll be fine with him. He's as curious about you as you are about him."

"Why? What have you told him about me?"

"That you encourage me to take risks."

"*Used to* encourage you to take risks. From everything you've said about your relationship with Bill Harris, your risk days are over, Nance."

Cummings, Janice's date, had a cowlick. That was the first thing that struck me about him. The second thing that struck me about him was that he was a good ten years younger than Janice — not long out of the University of Virginia as it turned out and still contemplating which career path to take, if any. And finally, I couldn't help noticing that he *was* a man of means, just as advertised, full of stories about the family place in Newport, the family place in Barcelona, the family place on Jupiter Island, egads. While Janice seemed genuinely awed by the apparent size of the Gilbert fortune, she was considerably less awed by Gilbert — sorry — Cummings himself, judging by the fact that she mouthed the word *asshole* to me the minute his back was turned.

Her attitude toward Bill, on the other hand, was decidedly more positive and the feeling was mutual. From the moment we were seated at the restaurant — the same neighborhood bistro where Bill and I had shared our first meal — the two of them really hit it off, chattering away like old pals. I was thrilled that my two favorite people liked each other.

We were in the middle of dinner when Cummings glanced across the table at Bill and said between bites of his veal medallions, "How long have you worked at Denham and Villier, sport?"

"Ten years total," said Bill between bites of his chicken paillard, "but only three months at the New York store. I was at the D.C. store before I relocated here."

"Is that right," said Cummings. "It's such a small world when you get down to it. When I was at UVA, I spent a lot of weekends in Washington, many of them shopping at Denham and Villier. I'd pop in to buy a trinket for Mother or for my sister, Perkins, or for the occasional fair maiden from Hollins or Sweet Briar." He washed the veal down with some wine. "Come to think of it, I was quite chummy with the sales people there and yet I don't recall ever seeing you at the store, sport."

"Probably because I had shorter hair then," said Bill, whose dark brown locks curled just under his ears. "I grew it for the new job. I thought I needed a more sophisticated look for Manhattan."

I reached out and finger combed his hair. He responded by leaning over and kissing my cheek. We were disgustingly demonstrative, I admit.

"You say you were the manager of the D.C. store?" Cummings asked him.

"Actually, I didn't say," Bill replied, sounding irritated now. And why not? Cummings was an irritating little twit. "But the answer is, yes, I was the manager there. *Sport.*"

"How odd. The manager I dealt with was Dennis Peet," Cummings persisted. "Quite a pleasant fellow, although a little light in the loafers, if you get my meaning."

"No, Cummings. Spell it out for us," Janice snapped. She was growing to hate him, money or no money. Thank God.

"Dennis was the assistant manager," Bill explained, more tolerantly than I would have. "He was promoted to manager when I left."

"Oh. Then good for him," said Cummings. "I'm all for equal opportunity. They have a right to earn a living just as normal people do, provided they don't call attention to themselves with that constant swishing."

Janice and Bill and I exchanged looks. Obviously, Cummings wasn't winning our hearts.

We managed to finish dinner without pummeling him, then the three of us went back to Janice's.

"Was he a piece of work or what?" She groaned as she handed Bill and me mugs of chamomile tea.

"I think I liked the last one you picked up at Barnes and Noble better," I said. "The one wearing combat fatigues. At least he had some edge."

Bill put his arm around Janice. "A woman like you shouldn't have to settle." He turned to me. "Your friend's a keeper, Nancy."

"He's not so bad himself," Janice said, thumbing at Bill. "If he ever finds out he's got a twin brother, let me know."

I sat there beaming. My best gal approved of my best guy and vice versa. What more could I ask for?

For the next few weeks, Bill and I spent nearly every night together. Sometimes, we had dinner at my place; sometimes, we had dinner at his place; sometimes, we went to restaurants for dinner with Janice, who continued to try out new men on us even though we kept vetoing them.

No matter what we did, we enjoyed ourselves, especially in the bedroom. I kept waiting for things to calm down between us, sexually, just as Janice predicted they would. But no. Bill Harris and I were drawn to each other, red hot for each other, and every night was an adventure in intimacy. Wherever Bill touched me became an official erogenous zone.

Things were going so well for us that I took the plunge and told my parents about our relationship. My mother, in particular, was ecstatic and wanted to know every detail about Bill. I volunteered the information I felt was relevant. She wasn't satisfied.

"What are his sons like?" she asked.

"I haven't met them yet," I said. "They're not coming to New York until February."

"What are his parents like?" she asked.

"I haven't met them either," I said. "They're from Maryland."

"How nice. Has he said the magic words?" she asked.

"Which magic words?"

"I love you, silly."

"I know you do, Mom. Which magic words?"

She sighed, frustrated. "Has he told you he loves you?"

"No, but I know he does. He's probably just waiting for the right time."

"And when do you suppose that will be?"

I sighed, frustrated. "When he feels like it, Mom. He went through a tough divorce. He may not be ready to say the 'L' word."

"Then don't you say it to him," she warned. "It's the man who has to say it first."

I laughed. "Is that a law?" My mother was sweet but she was rather provincial, as I've already explained.

"Fine. Make jokes. I only want you to be careful, Nancy. You're my —"

"Special baby. I know. I'll be careful."

I shook my head as I hung up with my mother, who, despite her obvious delight that her daughter, the divorcée, was finally in a relationship, had managed to put a damper on it with her questions about those dopey magic words. Before I'd opened my big mouth and told her about Bill and me, I'd been more than content with the course our romance was taking, more than happy to wait for him to confirm his feelings for me. And yet the minute my mother raised the subject, I suddenly started to doubt his level of commitment.

He does love me, doesn't he? I asked myself. Why else would he *act* as if he loved me? Nobody's that good at pretending.

I wandered into my living room where Bill was stretched out on the sofa reading a crime novel by Sue Grafton. I think it was the one that started with H. *H Is for Hernia* or something like that.

I snuggled up next to him. "Come here often, big boy?"

He put the book down and wrapped his arms around me. "Now and then," he said, playing along. "How about you, little lady?"

"Whenever I'm in town," I said.

"Can I buy you a drink?" he said.

"Sure."

He kissed me. "What do you say we get naked?"

"I say okay."

We were about to rip off each other's clothes when I abruptly called a halt to the proceedings.

"What's wrong?" said Bill, his face flushed with ardor interruptus.

I lay back on the sofa. "Is this just about sex?"

"Is what just about sex?" He lay back next to me after zipping up his pants.

"Us. Our relationship."

"Of course not. You know better than that, Nancy."

"Then what is it about?"

"It's about the connection that's been there between us from the moment we met."

"Connection," I said skeptically. "You make us sound like the phone company."

Bill looked at me as if I had two heads. "What's going on with you?"

"With *me*?"

"Yes. I was reading a book, minding my own business, when you undulated over here, got me all turned on, and then pulled the plug."

"Undulated! Ah, so we *are* about sex."

"How do you figure that?"

"Simple. You wanted sex, I denied you sex, and now you're angry at me."

"I'm angry at *you?"* He scowled. "Are you getting your period?"

I bolted up from the sofa. "God, that is so typical of men, so predictable. The minute women are the least bit critical of them, they blame it on our hormones." I had heard Janice say that once and decided it was worth quoting.

"Nancy, sit down, will you? I honestly don't know where this is coming from."

I sat down. It dawned on me that Bill and I were having our first fight and that it was all my mother's fault. "Where *this* is coming from is that I'm questioning the basis of our relationship, the real reason you're here." Much to my embarrassment, I started to cry at this point. Why couldn't I have left well enough alone? "I've been wondering (sniff sniff) if your feelings for me (blubber blubber) are as —"

"I love you."

"What?" I stopped crying.

"I love you. Does that help?"

"Not if you're just saying it, because you think you've been manipulated into saying it."

He kissed my cheek. "I love you. I

should have told you before, but I held back."

"But why, Bill? I love you too." There. My mother would be happy. He said it first and *then* I said it.

Bill got up and began to pace. He seemed unnerved by his admission. Maybe he *had* wanted to wait a while before telling me.

"Is it because of your divorce that you held back?" I asked tentatively. "Because of how your ex-wife betrayed you? Because you're afraid to be vulnerable to another woman?"

"That's it." He nodded. "That's the reason."

He wasn't especially convincing, but what other reason could there be? "Well, then I understand perfectly," I said, "having been hurt myself."

Bill rejoined me on the sofa and clasped my hands in his. "I do love you, Nancy Stern."

"And I love *you*, Bill Harris."

"But I'd like you to make me a promise."

"All right."

"That you won't forget that you love me. No matter what."

I squeezed his hand, poor baby. He really must have been stung when his ex dumped him for another guy. It was as if he wanted me to *guarantee* him that I'd never do the same thing.

"I won't forget that I love you," I said. "No matter what."

CHAPTER EIGHTEEN

The investigation into the other Nancy Stern's murder was continuing, according to the newspapers, but the police still hadn't made any arrests. The lab reports were either inconclusive or incomplete, and the Manhattan D.A. was unwilling to proceed without hard evidence. The only new development as far as I could tell was that Detective Reynolds and his team had completed their interviews with the tenants and finished scouring Nancy's penthouse for clues. As a result, there were no longer any cops hanging around the building, which was both a relief (who needed constant reminders of the murder?) and a source of anxiety (who wanted to be left at the mercy of our useless doormen?). Oh, and the other piece of news regarding Nancy was that she died without a will and that the daughter she hadn't seen since birth was claiming *she* should be the beneficiary. The nerve.

Bill was extremely busy at the store, as Valentine's Day was fast approaching and men were rushing in on their lunch hour to buy something — anything — for the women in their lives.

At school, we, too, were preparing for Valentine's Day. Each child was assigned the task of making a Valentine for another child in the class. The Valentines would then be placed in a shoebox covered with red paper, and on Valentine's Day Janice and I would take turns handing out the cards. We would also be baking cookies in the shape of hearts and coating them with red sprinkles, as well as reading a story about a magic cat who brings lonely men and women together in true love.

"I'd like to get my hands on that magic cat," Janice growled as we were setting up the classroom and discussing our lesson plan for the upcoming V-Day. She had hit a particularly bad patch in the romance department. The last two men who'd shown an interest in her at Barnes & Noble turned out to be married, but what was even more grotesque about them was that their wives were right there in the store at the time, blithely browsing in other sections!

"I have some news that will cheer you up," I said. "Bill is coming in today. He should be here any minute." I offered this information tentatively. Janice was extremely fond of

Bill, but acting lovey-dovey with your boy-friend when your best friend is feeling witchy-bitchy because she doesn't have one isn't always smart.

"He is?" She looked glad about it, thank goodness.

"Yes. He's been saying how much he wants to see the school and the kids, and since he doesn't have to be at work until ten this morning, today's the day."

"Great. We'll make him sing the 'Good Morning Song.' "

We were laughing, picturing Bill and his six-foot-four-inches splayed out on the rug next to the children, when into the class-room he walked.

"Is this the hotbed of learning that I've been hearing about?" he said, grinning.

I jumped up to hug him. Janice did too. We showed him around and explained how the day was structured. A few minutes later, the kids started trickling in. I greeted them and got them settled in the activity areas while Janice gave Bill thumbnail sketches of each child. He seemed to be en-joying himself, because he stayed through the play time and he stayed through the "Good Morning Song" and he stayed through the recitations by the week's desig-nated calendar person and the week's designated attendance person and the week's designated weather person. He even stayed through the little spat that broke out between Fischer Levin and Todd Delafield over which of them was standing next to me during "Heads, Shoulders, Knees and Toes."

"You can take turns," I told them. "Fischer, you stand next to me during 'Heads, Shoulders, Knees and Toes,' and Todd, you sit next to me during show-and-tell."

As I was mediating, I glanced over at Bill and Janice and guessed that she was giving him the lowdown about Fischer. He seemed genuinely interested in what she was telling him, but his smile faded as she talked and his expression grew serious, pensive, preoccupied — as if he were reliving special moments when his own sons were preschool age. Yes, that must be it, I thought, as he gave her a quick hug and motioned to me, pointing at his watch.

I told the children I'd be right back and hurried over to him. "Gotta go?"

He nodded. "Thanks for letting me observe. It was fun."

Thanks. Fun. The words were fine, but the tone was off; there was definitely something distant about it, about Bill. It occurred to me that maybe he missed his children so much that the visit to my class wasn't the best idea.

I whispered that I loved him, he whispered that he loved me, and we said we'd see each other later, at my place.

It wasn't until an hour or so after he left, during snack, that I asked Janice if she had noticed a change in his demeanor.

"Did I ever," she said. "I adore Bill, but he's a lot more controlling than I thought."

"Controlling? What do you mean?"

"Controlling. Possessive. You know."

"You'll have to be more specific, Janice. *How* is he controlling?"

"Well, we were standing in the corner of the room, watching you interact with the kids, when Fischer and Todd had their run-in. I said, nodding at Fischer, 'He's the one who gave Nancy that pin for Christmas.' Bill stared at me and said, 'That little boy gave Nancy the brooch?' I said, 'Yeah. Didn't she tell you?' Obviously, you didn't tell him, Nance. What's more, you didn't tell me that you didn't tell him. I don't understand *why* you didn't tell him, but the bottom line is, I don't think he believes that Fischer gave you the pin, for some bizarre reason."

"Oh, Janice." I sighed, ashamed of myself. "The bizarre reason is that I wasn't completely honest with Bill the day I brought the pin to his store to have it appraised. I was nervous and insecure, because I wasn't sure if he still cared about me, so when I explained that I'd gotten the pin as a Christmas gift, I sort of let him assume that a man had bought it for me."

"A man as opposed to a four-year-old boy."

"Yes."

"To make him jealous."

"Right. It was a stupid, stupid thing to do, especially after the way I'd lied to him about being the other Nancy Stern. He probably doesn't know what to believe about me now."

"I'll tell you what he believes about you: He believes you might be cheating on him."

"Come on."

"I swear. He was pumping me for information, asking a million questions like when Fischer gave you the pin and whether he'd ever given you jewelry in the past. It was almost as if he was testing me, trying to trip me up, trying to catch me in a lie so I'd have to break down and tell him the truth."

"But Fischer did give me the pin. That *is* the truth."

She shrugged. "All I can say is, if you wanted to know if Bill's the jealous type, the answer's yes. I felt like I was being interrogated."

"I'm sorry, Janice. I'll talk to him tonight and straighten everything out."

Unfortunately, I wasn't able to straighten everything out with Bill that night — at least, not right away — because there was another, more pressing matter with which I had to deal. When I entered my apartment just after three o'clock, I discovered that it had been burglarized.

At first, I wasn't exactly sure it had been burglarized. Yes, the door was open when I got home, but I often forgot to lock it, even after the awful business with the other Nancy Stern. And yes, the apartment had been messed up, but I wasn't a particularly good housekeeper and it wasn't out of the realm of possibility that I might have left clothes, magazines, or papers strewn about the place before rushing off to school.

But when I stepped inside and looked around, there wasn't any doubt that someone had been there — someone who ransacked my drawers and threw their contents everywhere and made off with the few decent pieces of jewelry I owned.

I was terribly shaken, naturally, and I called Bill immediately after dialing 911. He arrived at the apartment in a flash — management has its privileges, I thought

— and took complete charge of the situation, making sure I was safe, making sure the cops did this or that, making sure we got a guy over to change the locks on my door. What was especially comforting — a happy coincidence, it turned out — was that he actually knew one of the police officers, the balding one who had shown up to dust for fingerprints. The man was a friend of his brother's, he explained, reminding me that his father and two brothers were both cops. Whatever. I was just glad to have him to rely on, glad that he wasn't letting his suspicions that I might be cheating on him prevent him from coming to my aid.

Later that night, we learned that three other apartments in the building had been hit while their occupants were at work, their jewelry stolen as mine had been. In a strange way, this knowledge made me feel better. For one thing, misery loves company. For another, it proved that I, alone, hadn't been the target of some premeditated caper; the crooks had simply gone tearing through the halls, trying all the doors in search of those that were unlocked, and pounced.

"So you'll lock your door from now on?" Bill warned after we'd finally climbed into bed, exhausted from the day's drama.

"I promise," I said, cuddling up next to him.

He reached under the covers and began to touch me in all the right places. I returned the favor. Before we knew it, we were groping each other like teenagers, our exhaustion giving way to excitement.

"I never thought we'd have sex tonight," I said afterwards, marveling at our stamina. "Did you, honey?"

Bill didn't answer. His eyes were closed.

"Bill?"

"Hmmm?"

"Before you fall asleep, there's something I'd like to talk to you about." I remembered about straightening him out on the subject of Fischer and the pin.

"Can't it wait till tomorrow?" he said, opening one eye.

"No."

"Sure?"

"Positive."

He opened the other eye. "Okay. Shoot."

"It's about what happened when you came to school this morning."

"Oh. You're upset because I never got a chance to tell you how terrific you were with those kids."

"As a matter of fact you didn't tell me, but that's not —"

"You were terrific, Nancy," he interrupted. "So natural with them."

"Thanks, Bill. That means a lot. But I was referring to the questions you asked Janice about one of the boys in the class, Fischer Levin. Apparently, she told you that he was the person who gave me the pin for Christmas and you didn't believe her."

He didn't respond, didn't make eye contact either.

"The thing is, I don't blame you for not believing her, for not believing *me*. See, I didn't come out and tell you Fischer gave me the pin that day I came to your office because I —" I stopped. This was embarrassing.

"You what?" Bill prodded.

"I wanted you to think I had men lining up at my door."

He sat up in bed, was studying my face now. "Go on."

"Janice always says that men are like sheep; that they find you irresistible if other men find you irresistible. I wanted *you* to find me irresistible, Bill. That's the long and short of it."

"I already did find you irresistible," he said. "Without the games." He seemed disappointed in me, annoyed with me, but he didn't bolt out of the room, thank God.

"Look, I'm sorry about the deception. I feel horrible about it. Give me another

279

chance to show you that I *am* an honest person; that the way I've behaved recently is a total aberration."

"Well, I suppose it was only a white lie," he conceded.

"Not even a white lie," I maintained. "It was an off-white lie. An ecru lie."

He smiled as he lay back down next to me. "So there's no other man in the picture?"

"None."

"And the boy — Fischer Levin — really did give you the brooch?"

"He did, bless his little heart."

Bill looked relieved. "Janice indicated that he's been a troublemaker at school and that you've tried to communicate this to the parents with no success. Why don't you tell me about it."

"Now?" Only a few minutes earlier, he'd preferred sleep to talk.

"Sure. If you're not too tired." He kissed me. "I love you, Nancy. That means I have a vested interest in everything you do, including dealing with difficult four-year-olds. I may not have a degree in education, but I have two sons. Maybe I can help." He kissed me again. "Why don't you start by filling me in on the boy's parents."

"His parents?"

"Yes. My guess is that they're the types

who keep their child on a short leash, always insinuating themselves into his daily activities, then he rebels against their authority by making a nuisance of himself at school. Am I right?"

"Sorry, Dr. Freud. It's the opposite. Bob and Gretchen Levin don't spend enough time with Fischer, and the reason he makes a nuisance of himself at school is because he's starving for attention."

"Poor kid. What does the father do?"

"He's a big shot on Wall Street with an aggressive personality to match. Very new money."

"And Mrs. Levin?"

"Very happy to spend the new money. She's not as unpleasant as her husband — more ditsy than nasty — and I think she loves Fischer, deep down. He's just not a priority. She delegates everything to the caregiver."

"No wonder he's so attached to you, Nancy."

"I do try to be demonstrative with him, give him hugs, positive reinforcement when he earns it, that sort of thing."

"And the brooch was his way of thanking you."

"Right. That's why I wish it hadn't fallen apart during those tests you did on it.

Fischer asks me practically on a daily basis why I'm not wearing it."

"What do you tell him?"

"Oh, I say that it means so much to me that I'm saving it for a special occasion."

"Another ecru lie?"

"You bet. It would break Fischer's heart if he knew his present was in some Dumpster. In his mind, he's a pirate who stole the pin from a buried treasure chest to give to his teacher. He lives in a fantasy world."

"I suppose the director at your school isn't much help."

"Penelope?" I scoffed. Bill had already heard an earful about my battles with her. Still, he asked whether I'd tried this or that with her, suggested ways I might approach her the next time, shared a story about a former boss he'd tangled with.

As he spoke, I gazed at him with absolute adoration. Here was a man who was not only intelligent and handsome and trustworthy, not to mention gifted in the bedroom; he was willing to stay up on a weeknight, listening to his girlfriend's career problems.

I didn't know what I had done in my life to deserve Bill Harris, but I wasn't about to look a gift horse in the mouth.

CHAPTER NINETEEN

Valentine's Day brought highs and lows, but not in that order, since the lows came first.

At school, the handing out of cards went well until Fischer swiped the pretty, lacy one that Alexis Shuler had made for Todd Delafield, insisting that Todd shouldn't be allowed to have a Valentine because he was a baby.

After I took Fischer out in the hall to chat with him about why it wasn't nice to call other people names and how the giving of cards and gifts was even more rewarding than the getting of them, he asked me for the hundredth time why I wasn't wearing the pin.

"If giving is so great, how come you're not rewarding me?" he demanded, twisting what I'd said but not entirely.

I knelt down and tossled his hair. "I already explained to you about the pin, honey. It's such a beautiful piece of jewelry that I only wear it on special occasions."

"Isn't Valentine's Day a special occasion,

Miss Stern?" he asked.

He had me there. "It is a special occasion," I said, "and I am going to wear it, but not in school, because we're baking cookies today and it might get damaged."

"You mean it might melt in the oven?" he said.

"Maybe," I said, spotting the irony. The pin *had* melted and then disintegrated, according to Bill. "Instead, I'm going to wear it tonight when my boyfriend takes me out for dinner to a fancy restaurant."

Fischer's face lit up. "It's so big and shiny that everyone in the restaurant will see it," he said excitedly.

"That's right," I said.

"And everyone will think it's beautiful," he said.

"They sure will," I said.

"Did you tell your boyfriend where you got it?"

I smiled. "I told him I got it from one of the smartest, most generous boys in my class."

"Yeah, but did you tell him I was a pirate?"

"Fischer."

"Did you, Miss Stern? Did you tell him I found it in a chest full of buried treasure in the middle of the night?"

"Oh, Fischer." I had to talk to the Levins. It was one thing for Fischer to play make believe; it was another for him to keep harping on the pirate thing, to obsess about it, to let it blur his sense of reality and impair his ability to relate to others. "Are you ready to go back inside the classroom and behave yourself?"

He shook his head and pouted. "I want to stay here with you."

I reminded him about the cookie baking, and he changed his mind. Getting chubby Fischer to eat wasn't exactly a struggle.

After school, I had another go-around with Penelope. She and Deebo were in her office, sipping tea, when I asked if I might have an audience with her.

"Nancy. Yes, of course," she said, seeming in a pleasant mood. Perhaps she and Deebo had been exchanging Valentines.

Without being asked, Deebo vacated her chair and left me alone with Penelope. There was an awkward silence as she shuffled papers on her desk while I shifted in the chair.

Eventually, I broke the ice. "Penelope, I know we've been over this territory, but it's Fischer again."

She nodded, lips pursed, her mood deteriorating.

"Before Christmas I felt that he was making progress," I said, "but since he got back from the trip to England he's been as disruptive as ever."

Still no verbal response; only another nod.

"What I'm most concerned about, though, is that he's stuck in his fanciful thinking, stuck on his pirate fixation, to the point where I really feel his parents should be contacted."

That produced a verbal response. "We *have* been over this territory," she said irritably. "It is my opinion that his parents should not be contacted. It is also my opinion that young children often indulge in fanciful thinking and it needn't scar them for life." Her expression softened slightly. "You wouldn't be doing your job if you didn't report behavioral problems to me, Nancy, and I do appreciate the dedication you bring to your work. It's teachers like you who enhance Small Blessings's reputation."

I tried not to choke. What did she think flattering me was going to do? Shut me up?

"Then we finally agree on something," I replied. "Small Blessings's reputation *is* enhanced by its teachers, not by the size of its library or the size of the investment portfolios of the parents who put up the money for its library. What attracted me to this school, when I was first applying for jobs, was that everyone said it was a place where the parent-teacher relationship was nurtured, just as the children themselves were nurtured. But here you are, telling me not to contact the parents of a child who's lonely and isolated and needs help. Has the school changed its philosophy or have you, Penelope?"

"Fischer Levin is just fine," she said, gathering herself up in her chair, nostrils flaring, pearls realigning themselves as the veins in her neck bulged. It occurred to me that she was the one who needed help.

"I beg to differ," I said, then told Penelope about the pin, about how important it was to Fischer that I wear it and how he clung to his belief that he had pilfered it from a treasure chest instead of picking it out during a shopping errand with Olga.

"A pirate, a cowboy, a forest ranger." Penelope waved her bony hand at me. "Boys will be boys, Nancy."

How do people like her even get into positions of authority, let alone hold onto them, I thought. "So you refuse to let me call the Levins."

"It's not necessary for you to call them," she said. "As a matter of fact, I'll be speaking to Gretchen Levin soon regarding the school fund-raiser. She's on the decorating committee, you see."

No, I didn't see.

"If I feel it's appropriate," she added, "I'll mention your little dilemma to her then."

My little dilemma. I thanked Penelope for her time and left her office. I was halfway down the hall to my classroom when I knew with absolute certainty that I would call the Levins in spite of her forbiddance. I'd be risking my job if I called them, but I wouldn't be risking my life. It's important to keep things in perspective, I decided.

The high point of the day came the minute Bill walked in the door of my apartment to escort me to dinner. He was taking me to a hip new place in SoHo — the sort of "in" spot the other Nancy Stern used to frequent — and then we were spending the night at his apartment.

"Happy Valentine's Day," said Bill as he handed me a small lime-green box which I recognized right away as one of Denham and Villier's gift boxes, lime green being the store's signature color.

"Oh, Bill," I said, throwing my arms around him. "Thank you so much."

"Hey." He laughed. "How can you thank

me when you don't even know what I've gotten you?"

"It comes from Denham and Villier. How bad could it be?" I opened the box. Resting on the layer of cotton were a pair of crescent-shaped gold earrings, each dotted with a tiny emerald, my birthstone. They were tasteful, simple, authentic. Like Bill.

"I adore them," I squealed, putting them on immediately. "They're the best Valentine anyone's ever given me."

"I'm glad," said Bill, admiring his purchase, admiring them on me. "I wanted you to have them for two reasons."

"And what might they be?" I said, twirling around, dizzy with happiness.

"Number one, because you just had your jewelry stolen and I wanted to help you restock your inventory."

"Very noble of you. Number two?"

"Number two, because I love you, Nancy. I hope the earrings make that clear. I may work at Denham, but I don't go around throwing the merchandise at every woman I meet. I hope you know that."

I smiled at him, still not believing my good fortune. "I do," I said. "I really do." I flew back into his arms then, kissed him. "I didn't have this with John, didn't understand what it means to be in love with a man and be loved equally, in return. You've changed my whole view of love, Bill. You've changed me."

He held me close for a long time — until I remembered that I'd bought him a Valentine too.

I reached over to the foyer table and grabbed the box there. "Here," I said proudly, handing it to Bill. "Direct to you from Bloomingdale's."

He opened the box and grinned when he saw what was inside. It was a leather picture frame — a double frame designed for two photos. One for each of his sons, I told him.

He was thrilled with it, he said. Called it the perfect Valentine. Promised he'd take new pictures of Michael and Peter when they came to New York for their vacation the following week and install them right in the frame.

"I can't wait for you to meet them," he said as we left for the restaurant.

"Do you think they're ready for that?" I asked, even though meeting his boys was my ardent wish.

"Why not?" he said.

Why not? I thought.

Bill was working late the next night, so I took the opportunity to call the Levins, screwing up my courage as their phone rang. One ringie dingie. Two ringie dingies. Three ringie dingies. Either nobody was home or nobody was answering. I was mentally rehearsing the message I would leave on their machine when Bob Levin picked up.

"Yeah," he barked.

Don't you love when people greet their callers that way? Makes you feel all warm and fuzzy.

"Mr. Levin?" I said.

"You got him."

"Hi. This is Nancy Stern, Fischer's teacher at Small Blessings?" I hated that I put a question mark in my voice at the end of that sentence. *I* knew who I was, for God's sake.

"My wife's not here," was his response, even though I hadn't asked to speak to her. In the Levin household, matters pertaining to Fischer were handled by the womenfolk, apparently.

"When do you expect her back?"

"Don't have a clue. She's in Switzerland at some clinic."

"Oh. Is she ill?"

"Whadayoukidding? She's having a face-lift."

"I see." Gretchen Levin was younger than

I was. "Then I wonder if I might take a few minutes of *your* time, Mr. Levin. I know how busy you are, but there's a situation concerning Fischer that I'd like to discuss with you."

"Not that again," he boomed. "I told you, you teachers coddle the boy, don't appreciate what you've got there. A real tiger, that's what he is. A chip off the old block."

"Yes," I said with a little laugh, in order to give Bob Levin the impression that I thought being a chip off his old block was a plus. "But the problem I'm referring to isn't Fischer's aggressiveness. It's his fantasizing."

"Haw-haw. You're telling me he got his hands on a *Playboy* magazine or something?"

"No, it's nothing like that, Mr. Levin." You crude gasbag. "He fantasizes about being a pirate, and he communicates this both to the other children and to his teachers. Now, it's not at all uncommon for children to play pretend or have an imaginary friend. In fact, such behavior is a healthy part of growing up. It's only a problem when it interferes with the child's ability to function, his ability to enjoy real life. I'm afraid that's what's happening with Fischer, Mr. Levin."

"That's complete bull. Fischer's a great kid."

"But is he a happy kid? Happy kids don't talk incessantly about being a pirate. His entire self-esteem seems linked to this pirate fantasy."

I explained about the pin and Fischer's constant chatter about how he stole it from a buried treasure chest.

"Complete bull, like I said. Fischer got the pin from the Wal-Mart store in Branford, Connecticut. The nanny took him there to buy it on their way up to our weekend place. He told me about it on the plane to London just before Christmas. He was all keyed up about it."

"That was sweet of him."

"He's a sweet kid, I'm telling you. He even brought the receipt along to show it to me, because I taught him that the IRS comes after you if you don't keep receipts." He laughed at this, but I doubt he was joking. "Fischer doesn't pull any of that pirate fantasy shit with me. Which proves my point, Miss Stein."

"Stern."

"Yeah. My point is, you teachers baby the boy, so he acts like a baby and hands you all kinds of baby stories. But here at home? He's a normal kid."

I didn't have an easy comeback. I was feeling defeated, out of answers.

"Listen. About the pin," Bob Levin added before I had a chance to respond. "I didn't get a look at the thing, but it had to be a piece of junk, judging by what they paid for it. Sorry about that. The nanny's a nice-enough gal, but she's got taste up her ass."

Poor, poor Fischer, I thought as I hung up the phone. What must it be like to have that creep for a father.

The phone call didn't accomplish what I'd hoped, obviously, but it made me more committed than ever to watching out for Fischer, to doing whatever I could to see that his little life had meaning.

CHAPTER TWENTY

For the next seven days I was off from school for President's Week, but I couldn't stop thinking about Fischer, about the fact that he was spending his vacation without his parents. His mother was still in Switzerland, and his father flew down to Palm Beach for a little polo, which meant that he was left alone with Olga yet again. My heart ached for the boy.

Speaking of boys, Bill's sons arrived in New York for their much-anticipated visit. As he and I weren't engaged to be married or even living together in any formal way, we didn't think we should throw me at the kids but rather ease me into their lives, introducing me without fanfare, describing me simply as "a woman Dad enjoys spending time with."

"So you're Dad's squeeze?" said Peter, the older boy. He was not being disrespectful, just colloquial.

That's what you get for trying to fool kids, I laughed to myself. I should have remembered that they pick up on everything adults are feeling. He and his brother would have had to be blind not to see that Bill and I were crazy about each other.

Bill winked at Peter and admitted that yes, I was his girlfriend, and that we had grown very close since he moved to New York.

Peter, who at fifteen was a virtual clone of his father, with the same tall, lanky frame and dark good looks, studied me for a few seconds and said, "Cool." I didn't know whether he meant that *I* was cool or that his father's having a *girlfriend* was cool, but I took the word to be a positive assessment of the situation.

As for Michael, the twelve-year-old, he was a redhead with a sly, toothy grin — the spitting image not of Bill but of Britain's Prince Harry. He seemed delighted that I was in the picture, but then he seemed delighted by everything. He rated Manhattan "cool" and his father's apartment "cool" and the Hard Rock Cafe where we took them for dinner "way cool."

Over burgers, both boys demonstrated that they were not, in fact, monosyllabic teens and conversed easily about their school, their friends, and especially sports, which interested them more than girls, apparently. The only tricky moment came when one of them brought up their mother.

Bill tensed at the mention of her name, I noticed, but recovered quickly, asking how she was and then changing the subject. Yet again, I had reason to admire him. No matter how badly his ex-wife had hurt him, he wasn't about to poison his children against her.

Dinner was a rousing success. I liked Peter and Michael very much and they more than tolerated me. We got along so well that when Bill announced that he had to be at the store for part of the day on Saturday instead of taking the whole day off as he'd planned, Michael asked if I'd be willing to "hang out" with them. I was thrilled by the invitation.

I picked them up around noon, took them to lunch at Serendipity and then on to the motorcycle exhibit at the Guggenheim. As we were leaving the museum, it was beginning to snow, so I suggested we cab it over to my place and hunker down until Bill got off from work.

I was in the kitchen, making everybody some hot chocolate, when Peter ambled in and after a few back-and-forths commented that I was nothing like his mother.

The remark was a little unsettling, naturally, because I didn't know whether being nothing like his mother was a plus or a minus in his eyes. But I remained the very essence of the calm, domestic goddess, stirring the chocolate into the warm milk and pouring the mixture into coffee mugs.

"What's your mom like?" I said casually.

"She's mad a lot," said Peter.

"Mad. Oh. Do you have any idea what she's mad at?" I said, figuring it was standard-issue ex-wife stuff, having to do with alimony, child support, or dumper's remorse.

"My dad," he replied matter-of-factly, as if the answer were obvious. "She hates the kind of life he has, and she doesn't try to hide it. But you're different. You don't mind what he does."

The kind of life he has? What he does?

I stood there, attempting to figure out what Peter meant and couldn't. Why, for example, would the former Mrs. Harris be angry about what Bill did for a living? Managing a famous jewelry store wasn't exactly a career to be ashamed of. He made good money, he was an honest, ethical businessman, and he was a loving, responsible parent. What was there to find fault with?

"I'm sorry, Peter, but I don't understand what you're talking about," I said. "What is it about your father's lifestyle that upsets your mother?"

He cocked his head at me. "You don't

know? I mean, Dad hasn't told you?"

"Told me what?" I was getting nervous now.

"I, uh, just thought, well, since you're his girlfriend . . ." Peter was clamming up, becoming tongue-tied suddenly.

"Hasn't told me what?" I repeated, gently but determinedly.

"Nothing. Really."

Nothing, my ass.

My mind raced as Peter slunk out of the kitchen with hot chocolates for himself and his brother. Could there be a side to Bill that he hasn't shown me? I wondered. And if so, what sort of side is it?

The kind of life he has. . . . What he does.

Peter's words were puzzling and disturbing.

What if Bill's on drugs? I theorized, jumping to wild conclusions, my thoughts spinning instantly out of control. What if he's a hopeless gambler, a religious zealot, a fetishist of some type? Yes, what if he pays hookers to chain him to the headboard and spank him silly?

Stop it, Nancy, I commanded myself. Just cut it out. There's a simple, innocent explanation for what Peter said. There has to be.

I reminded myself that it's not unusual to experience doubts about one's beloved in the early stages of a relationship. The period is fraught with anxiety: Does he really love me? Does he really think I'm attractive? Is he who he appears to be? It's normal, normal, normal.

Still, I wanted desperately for things to work out between Bill and me, which meant that I did *not* want there to be anything seriously wrong with him. So whatever his ex-wife was angry at him about, I certainly hoped it was without merit.

To punctuate that hope, I gave my hot chocolate a shot of bourbon and went to join the boys.

An hour or so later, Bill showed up, surprising us with tickets to *The Lion King* for that very evening.

"A long-time client of Denham's is one of the show's producers," he said. "He did me a favor."

Great excitement filled my little apartment as we huddled together to decide what to wear to the show and where to eat before the show and whether we'd be able to get a taxi to the show, given the increasingly heavy snowfall. In other words, the conversation I intended to have with Bill, in which I would report Peter's comments and he would immediately allay my fears, would have to wait.

The Lion King was a spectacular production, but I'm not sure I caught every moment of it. I was distracted, preoccupied, not my customary engaged self. After the show, Bill dropped the boys off at his apartment and told them he'd be back as soon as he took me home. We were standing in my foyer when he reached for me. I was less than responsive.

"Tired?" said Bill.

"No," I said.

"Didn't like the show?" he said.

"Loved the show," I said.

"Don't like me?" he said.

Under other circumstances, I would have said, "Love you," but I didn't.

"Okay," said Bill. "Let's have it. Something's wrong, obviously."

"Yes." My arms were folded across my chest and I was tapping my foot on the floor. Nancy Stern, the stern school teacher.

"Are you going to tell me or make me guess?" he asked.

"It has to do with a few remarks that Peter made this afternoon."

"What remarks?"

"You're sure you're ready for this?"

He smiled tolerantly. "Just spit it out, Nancy."

301

"Fine. Peter indicated that your ex-wife is angry at you. Because of the 'kind of life you have.' Because of 'what you do.' That's exactly how he phrased it."

Bill looked surprised.

"So what did he mean, Bill?" I said, bracing myself. For the gambling addiction, the S&M stuff, anything.

"Why didn't you ask Peter what he meant?" said Bill.

"I did. He wouldn't tell me."

He smiled again. He didn't seem especially concerned, I noticed. "Could we sit down? It's been a long day." Without waiting for a reply, he sank onto the sofa in the living room. I followed him but remained standing. "Come here, Nancy. I won't bite." He pulled me down onto the sofa next to him. "I don't know why you're so spooked, but what Peter must have meant was my job with Denham."

"Really? And why would your ex-wife be angry about your job?" I said skeptically, hopefully.

"Because I left her father's jewelry stores to go to work for Denham, remember? She has this idea that I turned my back on the family so I could rub up against what she perceives to be the glitz and glamour of an international corporation. I swear to God, she thinks I'm some sort of social climber, which you know I'm not."

He was awfully convincing and I was awfully relieved, but I wasn't letting him off the hook quite yet.

"You told me that you and your ex-wife have a good relationship," I reminded him.

"We do, when there are issues involving the children," he said. "But I haven't forgiven her for committing adultery and I guess she hasn't forgiven me for finding a more challenging career. There's a lot of residual anger there. Peter probably gets an earful at home, even though she and I vowed to shield him and Michael from our battles."

He was more than convincing. He was telling the truth. And I was an idiot to have doubted him. I made a decision then and there to stop listening to Janice, who told me over and over that men were, by the very nature of their genetic makeup, liars and cheats.

"That must be difficult for Peter," I said as I drew myself closer to Bill, cozying up to him.

"It is," he said, wrapping his arm around me. "But what does any of this have to do with you, Nancy? What did you *think* Peter meant by his remarks?"

I laughed, as if my remoteness throughout

the evening had been a figment of his imagination. "I didn't think anything," I said and tried to prove it by involving Bill in a long, wet kiss.

I'll never mistrust him again, I pledged, wishing he could spend the night instead of going home to his place.

I saw Bill's kids three more times during their visit. Then it was back to school in Virginia for them and back to school at Small Blessings for me. I was glad to be back, glad to be with *my* kids again. It was nice to have a break but, despite my flirtation with the other Nancy Stern's seemingly more exciting profession, I really did love my own.

On a less positive note, Fischer was especially unmanageable on his first day back from vacation. He hit Todd Delafield during lunch, claiming Todd stole a piece of cheese from his Lunchables. And he was alternately clingy with me, demanding to sit next to me at every opportunity, or cross with me, demanding to know why I wasn't wearing the pin. His behavior provoked me to speak to Olga when she came to pick him up that afternoon.

"I'm worried about Fischer," I told her. "Did he have problems while he was off from school?"

"Nutting dat unusual," said Olga.

"Well, he's out of sorts today," I said. "He hit another boy and gave me a hard time."

She shrugged. "I say dis before to you: Da parents dun't pay attention to him. I do vat I can."

"Of course you do, Olga." I patted her arm, which was as solid as a tree trunk and about the same size. "It's just that I feel bad about that pin he gave me for Christmas. The one you took him to buy at Wal-Mart. He keeps asking me why I don't wear it to school, and the reason I don't wear it is because —"

"Excuse, Missus," Olga interrupted. "Vat pin?"

"The pin. The piece of jewelry you took Fischer to buy for me at Wal-Mart, near the Levins' house in Connecticut." It was possible that Olga didn't know the English word for pin, I realized. After all, I didn't know the Latvian word for it.

She looked at me blankly. "I dun't understand."

I was right, I decided. I grabbed a crayon and a sheet of paper and drew Olga a picture of the pin Fischer had given me. "You remember now?"

She shook her head. "Maybe another boy

in da class gave you dat. Not Fischer. I didn't buy with Fischer."

"Are you sure?"

"Sure."

"You didn't go with him to Wal-Mart before Christmas?"

"Val-Mart?"

"It's a store, Olga. A big discount store." God, where were interpreters when you needed them. "Mr. Levin said you took Fischer there to buy me the pin. Fischer showed him the receipt."

"Receipt?"

What was the use. "Never mind," I told her. I patted her arm again, then glanced over in the corner of the classroom where Fischer had overturned a glass jar full of plastic magnets. It was time for him to go home.

It was on *my* way home that afternoon that my purse was snatched right out from under me — or, rather, over me. It was a brown leather shoulder bag that I should have worn strapped across my chest, as many women wear theirs these days, but it was hanging loosely over my shoulder, just sitting there begging to be swiped. Still, begging or not, I was shaken by the mugging, really rattled.

What happened was, I was midway between Small Blessings and my apartment, walking carefully, with my head down, stepping over the occasional river of slush, when a man grabbed the purse, yanking it off me and, in the process, nearly breaking my arm. He was gone before it had registered what he'd done, disappeared into the crowd. I didn't even get to shout, "Stop thief!" or scream for help or run after him myself. He was such a nimble mugger that there was no way I could give the police a description of him, except that he was a man. Although I wasn't a hundred-percent sure about *that*. You can't be nowadays, according to Janice.

When I got to my apartment, I had to ask the super to let me in, as my keys were in the purse, along with everything else of importance — my money, my credit cards, my driver's license, my lipstick (it was a shade that had been discontinued and was, therefore, extremely valuable to me).

"This year ain't going so well for you," said the super. "First, your apartment's cleaned out, now this."

"You're right," I said, wondering if I had, indeed, hit a patch of bad luck.

"Could be worse though," he added. "Look what happened to the one in 24A."

I nodded. "Could be worse."

CHAPTER TWENTY-ONE

Miracle of miracles, my purse was lost but then it was found.

The day after the mugging, I received a phone call from a cop at my local precinct, saying that a sanitation worker had come across the handbag in a garbage can, plucked it out, and brought it over to the station.

"How did you know the purse was mine?" I asked, since I hadn't bothered to report the mugging.

"Your driver's license," he said. "It was in your wallet."

"My wallet?" I was confused. "The crook didn't take my wallet?"

"Nope. He didn't take the money out of it either. Or your credit cards."

"I don't understand," I said, genuinely mystified. "Isn't that why purse snatchers snatch purses? For the money?"

"Usually. But not this one, I guess."

"Then why in the world would he take the purse?"

"Well, could be he's one of those cross-dressers," said the cop, "and he was too embarrassed to walk into a store and buy a purse for himself."

"Now there's a theory." I rolled my eyes.

"Or maybe he's into black market sales. They steal the designer stuff right off your back and turn around and sell it on the street."

"But my purse wasn't designer merchandise," I said. "It was a Chanel knockoff."

"That's why it landed in the garbage," the cop said. "It was a small fish and the guy threw it back." He laughed. "Of course, there's another possibility."

"And what might that be?" I said dryly. This cop was annoying me.

"He was looking for something in your purse."

"Looking for something?" I said. "Like what? My lesson plan for my preschool class?"

"Who knows?" he said. "Whatever it was he was looking for, just be grateful he didn't find it."

I *was* grateful. Another small blessing.

An hour later, when I went to the police station to collect my purse, I ran into Det. Burt Reynolds and asked him if there were any breaks in the Nancy Stern case.

"No comment," he said.

"Oh, come on, Detective. Don't play hard to get. You can at least tell me if you've arrested anybody for the murder."

"No comment."

"Brother." What a waste of our tax dollars. "Okay, how about telling me if you've ruled out robbery as the primary motive? Several apartments in my building were hit recently — including mine — and I was wondering if there could be a connection."

"I'm not gonna comment and that's that."

"You know, you were much friendlier when I first met you."

"That's exactly what my wife says," he muttered and went on his way.

Bill was as confounded by the purse episode as I was, and since he wasn't an expert on crime or criminals, he didn't have any explanations for it either.

"I feel terrible about it," he said, with as much remorse as if *he* were the one who had mugged me.

"It wasn't your fault," I assured him. "You can't stand guard over me twenty-four hours a day."

"No, but maybe you should take cabs to and from school from now on," he said.

"That's ridiculous," I said. "I've lived in

the city for years and this was my first mugging. I view it as a rite of passage, sort of like losing my virginity."

"I'm serious, Nancy. There's no point in taking unnecessary risks."

I chuckled at that one. "If I hadn't taken an unnecessary risk, I would never have met you, baby."

The subject was dropped and life went on — uneventfully, thank God. Bill and I spent more and more time together, took it for granted that we were a couple, agreed that he would accompany me to Pennsylvania over Easter so he could meet my parents. Still, even during our most intimate conversations, he always stopped short of asking me to move in with him.

"Men." Janice sniffed when I mentioned his reluctance to formalize our living arrangement. She and I were out for dinner, just the two of us, as it was a Thursday night and Bill was working late at the store. "They're freaked out by commitment."

I smiled at my friend and her sweeping generalizations. "Bill isn't freaked out by commitment, Janice. He's just deliberate about what he does. He's not impulsive like you are. I really think that's all that's going on."

"You're so naive." She shook her head at

me. "Has it ever crossed your mind that as perfect as Bill seems to both of us, he might have problems?"

"Oh, you mean *neuroses?*" Janice's favorite word.

"It's possible. People aren't always what they appear to be. You found that out with the other Nancy Stern."

"Please. If Bill had psychological demons, they would have surfaced by now. Am I disappointed that he hasn't said he wants us to live together yet? Yes. Does the fact that he hasn't said it suggest that he's screwed up? No. The truth is, we haven't known each other that long — six months — and I've only just met his kids. He's got *them* to consider, don't forget. Maybe they're the ones who aren't ready for us to live together and he doesn't want to push them."

"That's not unreasonable, I suppose."

"I'm telling you, he isn't like the men you talk about all the time. When it comes to Bill Harris, what you see is what you get."

The next night, Bill and I had arranged that I would meet him for dinner at the Chinese restaurant around the corner from Denham and Villier. But I was early, as was my habit and custom, and didn't feel like getting a table, sitting by myself and playing with the silverware until he showed up. Instead, I decided to buzz by the store and wait for Bill there, so we could walk over to the restaurant together.

Having paid Bill a visit at work before — the time I'd gone to the store to ask him to appraise Fischer's pin — I knew right where his office was. When I got to it, though, Bill was nowhere to be found. It occurred to me that he might have left for the restaurant and that we had crossed paths.

"Excuse me," I said, stopping a pretty young redhead in a tweedy brown suit. "Would you happen to know if Bill Harris is still in the building?"

"Mr. Harris?" There was something sweet, almost worshipful, about the way she said Bill's name.

"Yes. Has he left yet?"

"Gosh. I don't think so," she said, trying to be helpful. "I'm Ms. Davis, the assistant to one of the salespeople here, and I'm almost positive he's in a meeting with my boss."

"Oh, good." I was relieved I hadn't missed him. "Is there someplace where I could wait for him?"

"Sure. I'll show you," she offered, then escorted me to a nearby reception area, where there were four empty chairs arranged around a square glass-topped table. "Make yourself comfortable."

"Thanks. I appreciate it." I'll have to speak to Bill about giving this Ms. Davis a promotion, I thought, making a mental note.

She gave me a little wave before leaving me alone. I waved back. And then I took a seat and waited for Bill to come out of his meeting. And waited. And waited.

I should have brought something to read, I thought, after I'd waited for ten minutes or so and gotten restless — as restless as I would have gotten in the restaurant but without any silverware to play with.

And then I noticed the glossy, full-color Denham and Villier catalogs that were fanned out on the table. I picked one up. Its cover announced "For Our Most Discerning Clients" in elegant script just beneath the company's name and logo. *For Our Wealthiest Clients* is what they mean, I smirked. Obviously, what I was holding in my hands was a custom catalog intended specifically for Denham's high-end customers.

Okay. Let's get a look at these trinkets, I thought, as I began to leaf through the catalog. Maybe I'll see something that suits me.

Ah, yes, I mused. How about this one?

I was referring to a little number described as an Art Deco bracelet, circa 1925, with 384 calibré-cut Burmese rubies (could there possibly be any other kind?) and 280 round and half-moon diamonds. The piece was priced at a mere $185,000 — a bargain.

I turned the page. Pictured here, according to the caption, was a 51-carat emerald necklace with 164 round, pear-shaped, and marquise diamonds. Its price: $415,000 — another steal.

Hey, this is fun, I thought, as I continued to flip through the catalog, my jaw dropping with each entry. There was exquisite jewelry offered — necklaces and bracelets, rings and earrings, even tiaras and hair ornaments, all sparkling with diamonds and rubies and emeralds and sapphires and stones so unusual I didn't even know what they were.

I was halfway through the catalog, so fascinated by the photographs that I'd forgotten all about Bill and the Chinese food, when I came upon a piece of jewelry that caused me to do a double take. The piece was a pin, "a platinum-and-diamond floral brooch," the caption read, "the center of which holds a 25-carat, extremely rare canary yellow diamond." The cost of this baby was a cool $550,000. Plus tax, of course.

At first, it was the intricate design of the pin that grabbed my attention; there had to have been literally hundreds of tiny, individual diamonds that made up the flower's shimmering petals. And then it was the size and shade of the center diamond that knocked me out; it was enormous — about a half-inch all around — and a rich, golden yellow, a color I'd never imagined a diamond could be. And then it was the price that boggled my mind. How many people can actually afford to buy this stuff? I wondered. And even if they can afford to buy it, why *would* they buy it? Why strut around in public wearing a pin costing over a half-million dollars unless you have a death wish? If someone thought my purse was valuable enough to steal, wouldn't every creep in the world be after a piece like that — and do whatever they had to do to *get* it?

I was studying the pin and contemplating these matters when it finally dawned on me what I was looking at.

You know how you can stare at something and yet you don't see it? Really *see* it? Well, that's what happened to me in that reception area at Denham and Villier. I was staring and staring and staring at the pin in the catalog, thinking this about it, thinking that about it. And all of a sudden it registered *what* I was staring at — an exact replica of the pin Fischer Levin had given me for Christmas.

Duh, I thought when I made the connection. I mean, *hello?*

But how was it possible? I held the photograph up to my face so I could examine it more closely. How in the world could the two pins be identical? One was worth a fortune; the other was a piece of crap.

A second or two passed and then I had an idea how: The same way my purse could be mistaken for a Chanel original. The pin Fischer had bought me at Wal-Mart was simply a knockoff. Somebody had copied the design of the Denham pin and mass-marketed it as cheesy costume jewelry. Yes, that had to be it.

But then why had Olga denied that she had taken Fischer to buy the pin when I'd spoken to her about it at school? Language barriers aside, she had seemed pretty convincing when she'd said she knew nothing about the pin, had seemed completely bewildered by the whole discussion.

But if she hadn't gone with Fischer to buy it, why had Mr. Levin told me otherwise, even relating that dopey anecdote about the receipt? Why would he make up a story like that?

317

He wouldn't, I decided. Olga had to be incorrect, forgetful, confused — or all of the above.

I placed the catalog on my lap and took a deep breath. Where's Bill? I thought, closing my eyes and resting my head against the back of the chair. And why is his meeting taking so long?

As I sat there, my mind remained fixed on the pin and the puzzle it presented. It was uncanny, really. Whoever Wal-Mart's manufacturer was had done an amazing job of copying the Denham piece — so amazing that if it hadn't been a four-year-old kid who'd given me the pin, I might very well have sworn it was the $550,000 jobbie. Jewelry was a blind item. Wasn't that Bill's motto? Because the ordinary person couldn't tell the difference between a real diamond and a fake?

The latter question prompted another question, a shift in my thinking, just for argument's sake. What if Fischer's pin were the real thing, the very same one that was pictured in the splashy Denham catalog?

Okay, the notion was far-fetched, but what if the boy did steal it from a buried treasure chest instead of buying it at Wal-Mart? What if this so-called treasure chest was Gretchen Levin's jewelry case and

Fischer filched the pin from his own mother? Kids at Small Blessings had been known to take things from their parents' drawers and bring them to school, without realizing that they'd done anything wrong. The previous Christmas, for example, a boy in Victoria Bittner's class had presented her with his mother's diaphragm — boxed and gift-wrapped.

But if Fischer did take a half-million-dollar pin from Gretchen Levin's jewelry case, why would Bob Levin have given me that spiel about how Fischer picked out the pin at Wal-Mart and showed him the receipt on the plane to London?

Maybe because he was lying to me.

I sat up straight in the chair and considered that possibility.

Maybe the pin didn't belong to Gretchen Levin, I thought, not that her husband couldn't afford to buy it for her. Maybe the pin was intended for another woman — his mistress — and he'd been hiding it in a drawer until he made his ostentatious presentation. Wouldn't that explain why he'd concocted the Wal-Mart story? So Fischer's mommy would never have to know that he was fooling around behind her back — and that he was keeping his little chippy in diamonds?

I was thoroughly turned off as I thought about Bob Levin, the jerk. How like him to buy a fabulously expensive bauble for some babe, who was probably even younger than his trophy wife. How absolutely revolting.

Hold your horses, Nancy Drew Stern, I cautioned myself. If Bob Levin's son stole a $550,000 pin out of his drawer and brought it to school as a Christmas gift for his teacher, wouldn't the guy have asked for it back, particularly since Fischer had confessed to doing the deed? Wouldn't Mr. Margin Call have called me, explained the situation and arranged for me to return the pin to him — discreetly? He was wealthy, but he wasn't *that* wealthy. A piece of jewelry that valuable wasn't some bad investment he could write off as a loss leader, was it?

Of course not. There had to be a factor I was missing, an element that was escaping me.

I continued to stew, weighing one theory against another. When I heard footsteps approaching, I glanced up, hoping it was Bill walking toward me, but it was the young sales assistant in the tweed.

"I came to tell you," she said with a perky smile. "The meeting has just let out. Mr. Harris should be with you in a couple of minutes."

"Oh, good," I said. "In the meantime, maybe you could give me some information."

"Me?"

"Yes, since you work here. I'm curious about a piece of jewelry featured in this catalog." I pointed to the page on which the pin was pictured.

"It's gorgeous, isn't it?" she said with genuine awe.

"It is, but I was wondering —"

We were interrupted by the insistent *click click click* of high-heeled shoes making their way down the hall toward us. They belonged to a humorless, harried-looking brunette in black slacks and a black cashmere sweater.

"What's the trouble?" the brunette said frostily, to Ms. Davis.

This ice queen must be her boss, I thought, pitying the young woman.

"There's no trouble, Ms. Knapp," said Ms. Davis. "I was just talking to a customer."

"A customer?" Ms. Knapp eyed me, as if I couldn't possibly have any business in a store like Denham and Villier. After all, I wasn't the wife of an Arab shiek or the mistress of a bonus-bloated Wall Streeter. I wasn't even a financially secure professional woman who could afford to buy herself a diamond tennis bracelet or two. That was the problem with Denham; if you didn't have the smell of a big spender, the personnel (excluding Ms. Davis) wasn't especially welcoming. I'll have to speak to Bill about that too, I thought, making another mental note.

"I was asking Ms. Davis for some information," I told Ms. Knapp.

"Information? What *sort* of information?" she said. So snooty. I was taking up her precious time, apparently. In the seconds she'd wasted on me, she could have sold some Donald Trump wannabe a five-thousand-dollar nose hair clipper.

"I'm very interested in a piece of jewelry from this catalog." I showed her the page in question.

"Ah, the catalog. How lovely." Instantly, the snootiness was replaced by a syrupy sweetness even Fran Golden, the syrupy sweet teacher at Small Blessings, couldn't match. It seemed that I had gone from a bothersome nobody to a *discerning client* in this woman's eyes. "I'm Ms. Knapp. It would be my privilege to help. What would you like to know about the piece?"

"Well, Ms. Knapp, if I were to purchase a brooch of this importance, I would want to be sure it couldn't be copied."

"Copied?"

"That's right. How easily could, say, a discount store create a knockoff of the pin and then sell it to the masses?"

"Oh, not to worry, Ms. . . ."

"Stern."

"Ms. Stern. The brooch you're interested in was designed for us exclusively by Marcus Grant, one of the world's foremost jewelry designers. It's a one-of-a-kind piece, protected by a vigorous copyright. If another retailer were to even contemplate reproducing it, we would know about it. And we would prevent it. You needn't be concerned that you'd appear at a formal function wearing the brooch and that a member of the hostess's staff would be wearing it too." She chuckled. "No, there aren't any counterfeits out there, I promise you."

So the pin Fischer had given me and the brooch in the catalog *were* one and the same? And Bob Levin's Wal-Mart story was a total fabrication? And the supposed hunk of junk I'd asked Bill to appraise *wasn't* worthless after all, even though he'd assured me it was?

I was short of breath, suddenly. Sweating too.

"Is everything all right, Ms. Stern?" asked Ms. Knapp.

"Yes. Fine," I said, struggling to pull myself together.

"I'm delighted I could clear up that copyright matter for you," she said. "Unfortunately —"

"Getting back to the brooch itself," I said, cutting her off, ignoring the awful tightening in my chest, pushing myself to continue, propelling myself toward the last conclusion in the world I wanted to come to. "You mentioned that it's a one-of-a-kind piece."

"One of a kind and museum quality," she said proudly, "because of the yellow diamond. It's not a new piece, you know. It's had a handful of owners, including a member of one of America's first families of the theater."

I did not ask her to elaborate. I was not in the mood for celebrity trivia. I was looking for information. Hard facts. Right away. "But it found its way back to Denham and Villier?"

"Yes. Through an estate sale. The thing is, Ms. Stern, it sounds as if you have your heart set on the brooch, but —"

"Yes, I do have my heart set on it." I cut her off again, feeling an overwhelming sense of urgency now, a sense of dread.

"I understand," she said. "It's beautiful, one of the most beautiful pieces we've offered, but what I'm trying to tell you is that it's not available at this time. We would have taken it out of the catalog but it had already gone to the printer."

"Not available? Why not?" I said, my anxiety level rising with her every word and gesture. If only I could stop the tape, pull the plug, shut her up, I thought miserably. But I couldn't. I had to hear more. I needed to hear more. My future depended on it.

"Because it's been sold," she said. "Now. Why don't we leaf through the catalog and see if there aren't other pieces that might suit your needs?"

I shook my head. "I'm only interested in that piece."

"Perhaps if you would allow me to show you —"

"No."

"Well." Ms. Knapp's big phony smile faded. "If I can't help you, then I'll just run along."

"You do that."

I sank into the chair as I watched her *click click click* back down the hall.

Sold? I thought, trying to tie things together. The piece had been sold? When? To whom?

"Ms. Stern?"

It was Ms. Davis, the assistant, and she was speaking in a whisper.

"Yes?"

She leaned in close to me, so she wouldn't be overheard. "I shouldn't be telling you this, but the piece you wanted wasn't sold, the way my boss said it was."

I sat up straighter. "It wasn't?"

"No. It was *stolen*."

My heart thudded. "Stolen?"

"Yes. A couple of months ago or thereabouts. That's why we don't have it in the vault."

I was too stunned to respond.

"Nobody's allowed to talk about it," she went on in a hushed tone, "but since you were so curious about it . . ."

Stolen? Not in their vault? How could this be happening?

But it was happening, I reminded myself. Had already happened. And no amount of wishful thinking on my part was going to change it.

I had handed the pin over to Bill myself, right there in the store, a couple of months ago — the "couple of months ago" that coincided with Ms. Davis's time line. As we'd sat together in his office, he had given me the impression that he'd never seen the pin before, didn't acknowledge that it was a famous piece, didn't let on that it had been owned by one of America's first families of the theater. He'd said he would test it, to determine if it had value. And then he'd called me two days later, claiming it was made of such cheap materials it had disintegrated during the testing. That was why he'd been unable to return it to me, he'd said, because there was nothing left of it to return. And now here was Ms. Davis, in her tweed suit and eagerness to please, with an entirely different version of the truth — a version that was about to shatter my trust in the man I adored, a version that was about to destroy my happiness.

Why did Bill tell me the pin was worthless if it wasn't? I asked myself, my eyes brimming with tears. Why did he pretend not to recognize a piece straight out of his own catalog? Why did he hang onto it instead of giving it back to me? And, most crucially, why, oh why, did he hang onto it instead of *putting it back in the vault* as he should have?

The answers were devastating, all of them.

Because if Denham and Villier's prized, one-of-a-kind, $550,000 brooch was not in the store where it belonged, then Bill Harris, the love of my life, was not only a liar; he was a thief.

CHAPTER TWENTY-TWO

I ran down the hall toward the elevator, Ms. Davis running after me. "What about your appointment with Mr. Harris?" she called out, obviously perplexed by my abrupt departure. "Was it something I said?"

It was something you said, all right, but it was something *he* did, I thought bitterly as I kept going, kept heading for my escape.

I cried as I rode down to the first floor and I cried as I rushed toward the store's exit and I cried as I stepped out into the cold night. My heart was breaking.

As I stood there on Fifth Avenue, tears pouring down my face, I felt sick, really sick to my stomach. (No, this isn't yet another story where someone bends over and starts retching right in the middle of the street. Personally, I hate it when people throw up in public in response to hearing bad news. But a quiet queasiness is acceptable, in my opinion.) I didn't know how to ease my pain, didn't know where to go, where to turn. I felt as if I had to unburden myself, had to have a shoulder to lean on, had to have a sympathetic ear to help me cope with Bill's treachery, his *criminality*.

Janice, I decided, ruling out parents, shrinks, and clergy in favor of my best friend in all the world.

I spotted a taxi and raised my arm to catch the driver's attention. He pulled up to the curb, tires squealing. I got into the cab and gave him Janice's address. He took off by flooring the accelerator and, in the process, nearly herniating a disk in my neck. But I didn't care. I was so wracked with emotional pain, what was a little whiplash?

It occurred to me as I was getting out of the cab in front of Janice's building that I had no idea whether she'd be home. It was a Friday night, and, although she hadn't mentioned specific plans for the evening, that didn't guarantee that she didn't have any.

Please be there, I prayed as I approached her doorman. Please be there for me in my time of need.

"Is Miss Mason in?" I asked him between sobs. I couldn't stop crying. I had hoped the chilly air might snap me out of my hysteria, but no dice. I was too far gone.

"Yes," he said to my great relief. "And you are . . . ?"

"Nancy Stern," I said. He was new; her

other doormen would have recognized me, even with the red face and swollen eyes.

He picked up the house phone. I heard Janice's voice say "Yeah?" which brought on another bout of sobs.

"Nancy's coming up," the doorman told her.

"Nancy?" said Janice. I could tell she was surprised. And why not? I was supposed to be having dinner at some stupid Chinese restaurant with Bill, the cat burglar. I shuddered at the very thought of it, of him.

I took the elevator up to Janice's apartment. When I reached the third floor, I stepped into the hall and turned right. She was standing at her door, looking concerned.

Just the sight of her was enough to send me into absolute paroxysms of crying. She held out her arms to me. I flew down the hall into them.

"Nancy," she said, hugging me. "Oh, Nance. What's the matter, hon?"

I couldn't answer right away. I was too busy leaking snot onto her nice blue sweater.

"Would you please tell me?" she demanded. "You're scaring the hell out of me."

"I'm sorry," I blubbered, wiping my eyes

and nose with the back of my hand. "Something's happened."

"I kind of figured that," she said. "*What* happened?"

"Remember how you're always going on about men's neuroses?" I sniveled. "How they take a while to come out?"

"Yeah."

"Well, Bill's finally came out."

"You're kidding."

"No, I'm not. They came out, only they're worse than neuroses."

"Worse than neuroses?"

I nodded. "They're *criminal impulses*."

Janice stared at me for several seconds, to make sure I wasn't drunk or otherwise impaired. When she determined that I wasn't, she pulled me into her apartment and closed the door behind us.

I expected that she would be alone, that I'd be able to pour out my heart to her in private, but no. As she helped me into her living room, I was stunned to find five other women sitting there. I felt as if it were my birthday and Janice had organized a party without telling me and everybody was going to leap out of their seats and yell, "Surprise!" But they hadn't come to a party; they had come to Janice's for their monthly reading group and I had just burst in on it.

"Oh. I didn't mean to interrupt," I said, embarrassed and angry. Embarrassed that I had intruded on their meeting; angry that they were intruding on my misery.

"That's okay," said one of the women, Linda Franzione, the one whose ex-husband had faked his own death. "We're doing *Memoirs of a Geisha*. You've read it, haven't you? It's been on the best-seller list forever."

"Well, yes," I said, wanting to be polite as well as wanting them to beat it. "I *have* read it, but —"

"It's a disgrace when you think of how men use women," said Linda, just as Janice was plunking me down in a chair. "That's what *I* got out of the book — how these Japanese men have an almost pathological need to dominate. Not that American men are any different, naturally. Look at Clinton. Look at all of them. As far as they're concerned, women are put on this earth to service them."

As I've indicated, the book up for discussion was always incidental at Janice's reading groups. What the members of the group were really interested in wasn't exploring literary themes; it was trashing men. The difference on this particular night was that *I* suddenly wanted in. Why limit my audience to Janice when I can have a roomful of supporters? I realized.

"Nancy has something she'd like to get off her chest," Janice told the other women, sensing my need to vent. "And it's not about the book; it's about her boyfriend."

The five women laid down their copies of *Memoirs of a Geisha*. "We're all ears," one of them said, while the others nodded.

I reached into my purse for a tissue, gave my nose a good blow, and began.

I told them how Bill had been irate when he'd learned that I wasn't the Nancy Stern I'd pretended to be, even after I'd explained to him why I'd pretended to be someone else.

"So judgmental," everybody responded in unison.

I told them how he'd claimed to be devastated by his wife's infidelity and given me this big speech about truth and honesty and trust and how important they were in a relationship.

"Her infidelity was probably *his* fault," everybody responded in unison.

I told them how I'd believed in him, how I'd believed he could do no wrong, how I'd hoped to become his wife and the stepmother to his two sons.

"So he's in the market for a *slave*, like the

rest of them," everybody responded in unison.

Between *my* telling and *their* responding in unison, I felt like I was Odysseus and they were the Greek chorus. Or, to put it in a musical context, I felt like I was Diana Ross and they were the Supremes. Whatever.

I wound up the story by telling them about the pin and how Bill had deceived me about its worth, deceived me about why he couldn't return it to me, and then deceived his own employer by actually stealing it instead of putting it back in the store's vault.

"The guy's a crook?" everybody responded in unison.

"Apparently." I was sobbing in earnest now. Janice got up from her chair to comfort me. "And I thought he didn't have a phony bone in his body. I was a complete fool," I said, then asked if anybody had a tissue. I was all out. Several of the women handed me some. The kind with the lotion built right in.

"You weren't the only one he fooled," said Janice. "I thought he was pretty special too. He had real charm, a lot of class. Not the type you'd figure for a jewel thief."

"Oh no?" Linda Franzione piped up. "What about Cary Grant in that movie with

Grace Kelly? He stole jewelry on the Riviera and he was as charming and classy as it gets."

"I hate him," I said.

"Cary Grant?" said Linda Franzione.

"No. Bill," I said. "I hate him."

"I hate him too," said Linda.

"Me, too," said everybody else, not in unison but practically.

"I think it's a given that we hate him," said Janice. "What's not clear is what we're going to do about him."

"Do?" I said. "I don't want anything to *do* with him ever again."

"What I mean is, he's a criminal, Nancy," she said, "and criminals have to be dealt with. The minute he talks to that saleswoman who spilled the beans about the pin and saw you run out of the store, he's gonna know you know. He's gonna come after you. Maybe to silence you."

Everyone gasped, including me.

"You're saying Bill might harm me?" I asked, my anger and hurt turning to panic.

"I'm saying I wouldn't bet against it," Janice replied.

The seven of us sat there, speculating, for another hour or so. *Memoirs of a Geisha* was not mentioned. At nine o'clock, there was a knock at Janice's door. We all jumped.

"See who it is," I whispered to her.

"Who is it?" she called out to the person.

"It's Bill, Janice. Is Nancy there with you?"

Everyone gasped again, *especially* me.

"How did you get up here without the doorman noticing?" Janice shouted. "Nobody buzzed me."

"The doorman was outside having a cigarette," he said. "Now, just tell me, is Nancy in there? I have to talk to her."

"Well, she doesn't want to talk to you," Janice answered, before I had a chance to.

"Please, Janice," he said. "This is important. There's been a terrible misunderstanding."

"Oh, there's been a terrible misunderstanding all right," said Janice. "Nancy thought you were a paragon of virtue and it turns out you're a common criminal."

"No, Janice. I'm not a criminal," said Bill. "If you'd let me in I could explain everything."

She looked over at me. I shook my head.

"No way," she told him.

"I'm not leaving," he said and demonstrated this by continuing to knock on the door.

"He's giving me a headache," one of the women complained. "Tell him to cut out the knocking."

"Cut out the knocking," Janice yelled to him.

"I will — if you'll let me speak to Nancy. Please, Janice," he pleaded.

She looked over at me again. I shook my head again.

"She's not in a speaking mood," Janice told him. "She wants you to get away from the door, get out of this building, get out of her life."

"I'm sure she does, but that's because she doesn't know the truth," said Bill. "I've got to talk to her, Janice. Make her understand."

"Understand what?" Janice challenged.

"That she's in danger," said Bill.

"Sure, she's in danger. Because of *you*," Janice snapped.

"Listen to me, Janice," Bill persisted. "I'm not the one who's out to get her. I only want to protect her. So if you care about your friend, if you care about her well-being, you'll let me in."

Janice looked over at me a third time, but I couldn't make the decision; I was too close to the situation. So I solicited the opinions of the other women in the room. After a few minutes, we reached a consensus: We would let Bill in and he could explain himself to *all* of us. He wouldn't dare kill off the entire membership of a *book* group, would he? No, we figured. That would be too heinous a crime even for him. Besides, there was safety in numbers, wasn't there?

Bravely, Janice went to the door and opened it. "In there," she said, pointing inside the apartment, letting him go first so she wouldn't have to turn her back to him.

Bill hurried into the living room. His eyebrows arched in surprise when he saw that I had company — a veritable phalanx of females.

"You bastard," Linda Franzione hissed, before he knew what hit him.

"You dirtbag," another woman chimed in.

"You rotting sack of shit," volunteered a third.

"I thank you all for your comments," said Bill, recovering, "but do you think I could speak to Nancy alone?"

"No!" everybody responded in unison, the Supremes back for an encore.

God, he still looks good to me, I thought, wishing he didn't. He still appeals to me, still makes my pulse quicken the minute he walks into a room, still *gets* to me. I started to cry again when this dawned on me, just buried my head in my hands and bawled.

"Nancy, don't," Bill murmured, moving toward me.

I picked my head up and glared at him. "If

you take another step, buster, I'm dialing 911!"

He seemed not to take my threat seriously and kept coming toward me.

"I mean it!" I warned him. "If you don't stop right where you are, I'm calling the police!"

"I *am* the police," he said, having made it over to my chair, his six-foot-four-inch frame towering over me.

"Sure you're the police," Janice scoffed. "Tell us another one, asshole."

"Actually, I *was* the police," he corrected himself. "I'm a private investigator now."

"A private *dick*, you mean," Linda Franzione snorted.

"Exactly," said Bill.

"Prove it," said Linda.

Bill fished inside the jacket of his dark gray suit and pulled out his wallet. When he'd retrieved his private investigator's license, he held it up for everyone in the room to see — a grown-up show-and-tell.

"I really would like to talk to Nancy alone," he said, breaking the hush that had descended on the room. He turned to me. "I have a lot of explaining to do."

I was a wreck at this point, dazed and confused as they say. How could Bill be a private investigator when he was a manager at

Denham and Villier? And what had he meant when he'd said I was in danger?

"Nancy?" he asked again.

"I'll let you explain under one condition," I said.

"Name it," said Bill.

"That Janice is there."

He shook his head. "Some of what I have to tell you is confidential."

"Janice can keep a secret," I said. "Maybe not as well as you, Bill, but well enough." I put some extra sting in the word *secret* in case he didn't get how pissed off at him I was.

"Fine," he said. "Janice stays. The rest of you ladies go. Now."

There was a lot of grumbling and name calling and finger pointing, but the five members of Janice's book group finally got up and left, taking their *Memoirs of a Geisha*s with them.

"Okay," I said when the three of us were alone. "Start talking, Bill."

He pulled up a chair next to mine, sat in it, and reached for my hand. I batted him away. "I said *talk*."

He nodded. "First, I want to say how sorry I am that I couldn't tell you the truth about my job."

"Your job as a jeweler or your job as a private investigator?" I asked accusingly. I still didn't believe a word this creep was saying.

"My job as a private investigator. I've been undercover, Nancy. I couldn't exactly go around handing out business cards."

"So you *weren't* lying when you told me your father and brother were cops, but you *were* lying when you told me you weren't?"

"Right. I was a Washington Metro cop for thirteen years, the last six as a detective."

"A detective," said Janice, who was standing over Bill, watching his every move. "How macho."

"During those six years," Bill went on, ignoring her sarcasm, "I investigated gem thefts, among other things. That's how I learned about jewelry, became a specialist in it, got the department to send me to the GIA in California so I could learn more about it. Eventually, though, I got burned out from being on the force, and I quit, retired, picked up my pension and walked. A week later, I got a call from the Denham and Villier store in D.C."

"Oh, goodie," I said. "This must be the part where your lying really kicks in."

Bill tried to touch me again. I edged my chair away from him.

"Denham had been having its share of thefts," he said, plowing ahead, "and the

MO was always the same. A guy claiming to be the representative for some rich joker would come into the store and ask the manager to put together a presentation of four or five pieces and bring them to his boss's home or office or wherever he was most comfortable doing business."

"You did say that Denham made house calls," I remembered.

"They have to," said Bill. "When you've got a client that's willing to spend a million dollars on a necklace, you'd *better* cater to him. The problem is, you send the pieces to the client's house with a salesman and a setter and a polisher — a security guard, too — and every now and then the so-called client turns out to be a member of a gang of very clever gem thieves. The pieces are stolen, the personnel from the store are bound and gagged, and the company is out of valuable merchandise. What's more, their insurance rates go sky high. So they hire people like me to catch the bad guys."

"Why don't they just bring in the police?" I asked.

"Because the minute you bring in the police, you also bring in the media — and the attendant negative publicity. Retailers like Denham are all about discretion. They have a policy of keeping thefts quiet."

I suddenly thought back to Bill's son Peter's words that day in my kitchen. *My mom is mad about the kind of life Dad has, about what he does.* If it were true that Bill put himself in danger on a regular basis, the remark made sense. Because if I were married to a man whose job it was to catch crooks, I wouldn't be so crazy about it either.

"So Denham hired me as their private security investigator," said Bill, picking up the story. "My first job there was to pose as the manager in the D.C. store, to track the specific gang that was hitting them and then haul the whole bunch of them in. I guess I did a good job, because the New York store called me about eight months ago to help them out. And here I am."

"Here you are," I said. "Sounds like the basis for a nifty TV series. But you haven't explained why you told me the pin I got for Christmas from the boy in my class was worthless. According to your Ms. Knapp, it's anything but."

He sighed. "I don't think I'll ever forget the day you brought that brooch in. I almost had a heart attack."

"A very subtle heart attack," I said with attitude. "You barely blinked when you saw it."

"What was I supposed to do? Jump up

and down and say: 'Well, well. If it isn't Denham's one-of-a-kind, half-million-dollar piece'? That brooch had been stolen a month or so before, Nancy — the way I just told you the other Denham pieces had been stolen. I'd been tearing my hair out trying to get a lead on the case, but I wasn't about to tell you that."

"Why not?" I said.

"For starters, I couldn't admit I was working undercover. And number two, I had no idea where you'd gotten the brooch. All I knew about you, my sweet, was that you'd pretended to be your neighbor, the celebrity journalist. I didn't have a clue what your real story was, if you recall."

"What I recall is that you made me feel like a horrible liar over the other Nancy Stern thing. And now I find out that *you're* the horrible liar. How about *that!*"

"Come on," said Bill. "I had to conceal the truth from you. Especially after Janice told me you'd gotten the brooch from Bob Levin's kid. I had my lead, finally, and I wasn't about to blow it."

I felt my throat close up, my mouth go dry. "Your lead?" I croaked out the words. "Are you saying that you suspect *Fischer Levin's father* of being part of this gang you keep talking about?"

"That's exactly what I'm saying. Thanks to both of you" — he nodded at Janice and me — "Mr. Levin is now under surveillance. It's just a matter of time before I nail everybody in his organization."

Janice and I exchanged glances. We hadn't been Bob Levin's biggest fans, but we'd never suspected him of being a jewel thief.

"Why would a successful Wall Street guy steal jewelry?" she asked.

Bill shrugged. "Maybe he does it for sport. Maybe he does it to keep up appearances, because he and his wife are living beyond their means. Who knows? But he's in on these thefts. The brooch proves it."

I thought of Fischer then, of how crushed he would be if his father were convicted and sent to prison. There were no winners here.

"If you're convinced that Bob Levin is a jewel thief," I said, "why don't you turn him over to the cops and have them arrest him?"

"Because they'd only get *him*," said Bill. "I want all of them, everyone who works with him. That's why I'm keeping up the surveillance on him and keeping my eye on you, Nancy. I was hoping to trap the whole nest. That was the plan, anyway."

I stared at him, wondering if I'd heard him

correctly. "The plan?"

"That's right."

My face burned. I was hot with fury. "Let me get this straight," I said, my eyes narrowing with rage. "I was just part of some plan, some strategy of yours for catching a bunch of thugs?" My mind flashed back over the previous six months, to the loving, intimate moments Bill and I had shared. Suddenly, I was viewing them in a decidedly different light. Had I, in fact, been his prop, his tool, someone who had access to Bob Levin and was, therefore, useful to him? Had he only stayed close to me in order to stay close to Levin? Was our relationship a lie like everything else?

"I love you, Nancy," said Bill. "Whatever else you believe about me, believe that."

"Go fuck yourself," I said.

"I'll second that," said Janice.

Bill remained undaunted. "I love you," he repeated. "If I didn't, I wouldn't have busted in here and faced the wrath of seven women."

"Go fuck yourself," I said again, in case he didn't get it.

"I can't do that," he said. "I've got to protect you."

"Nancy's a big girl," said Janice. "Why would she need protecting?"

"Because her apartment was broken into and her purse was stolen," said Bill, his expression dead serious now. "And they were not acts of random violence, in my opinion. Neither was her neighbor's murder."

I grabbed for Janice's hand. "What are you saying?" I asked, my voice trembling, not with rage but with fear.

"I'm saying that you, not the Nancy Stern in 24A, were the one they were after," Bill said slowly, drawing out every word, so there was no possible way either Janice or I could misunderstand him. "Fischer told his father he gave his teacher the brooch. His father phoned one of his goons and ordered him to get the brooch back. He had the guy ransack the apartment of Nancy Stern at 137 East Seventy-first Street, and he didn't care whether or not she was present during the ransacking. The goon hit *her* place, not *yours*, Nancy. He made a mistake."

A mistake. This revelation took a while to sink in. I required water, then a couple of scotches, then a nap on Janice's bed before I could even process it.

It was not simply that it was a shock; it was that it was the height of irony. After I had received phone calls and letters and flowers that were meant for the other Nancy Stern, the murder, it turned out, was meant for me.

347

PART THREE

CHAPTER TWENTY-THREE

It was well after one o'clock in the morning by the time Bill and I finally left Janice's. I was drained, spent, absolutely wiped out, but I was no longer conflicted over whether or not Bill was telling me the truth — about himself, about Bob Levin, all of it.

To help erase my doubts, he had given me the home phone number of the *real* manager of Denham and Villier's New York store — the German-accented man I had seen in Bill's office the first time I'd stopped by. He confirmed both that Bill had been hired as the store's private security investigator and that the stolen brooch was currently in a special vault — a vault to which neither Ms. Knapp nor Ms. Davis had access.

After that call came the call to Bill's ex-wife, who was kind enough to corroborate his police background but couldn't resist taking a swipe at him. "If I were you, honey, I'd wear a bullet-proof vest to sleep," she said snidely. "When you're with Bill Harris, you never know who's gonna crawl out of a hole and bite 'cha." I thanked her for taking the time to speak to me so late in the evening and chalked her comments up to sour grapes.

"What happens now?" I asked wearily as Bill and I rode back to his apartment in a taxi. "Do I ever get to go home or will Bob Levin's henchmen be there waiting for me?"

"I have no idea. They've already checked your apartment and your purse and still haven't found the brooch," he said. "The problem is, they know you can trace it back to Levin, whether they find it or not. And that puts you in the hot seat."

"Swell."

"So you'll stay at my place for a while, okay?"

"Sure," I said. I was numb at this point.

"And you'll quit school, take a leave of absence or something."

"What?" I was no longer numb.

"You'll tell the director at Small Blessings that you've got a medical emergency, a family emergency, whatever you want."

"Not a chance, Bill."

"Think about it."

"No, *you* think about it. My job is just as important to me as yours is to you." I was feeling feisty, suddenly; wide awake; pumped with adrenaline. I appreciated the seriousness of the situation, but I wasn't sitting out the rest of the school year, no sir. Fischer Levin needed me more than ever, and I needed my job more than I realized. What's more, Levin's goons weren't going to come after me in the classroom and put the guy's own son in danger, were they?

"I'm trying to protect you, Nancy."

"Fine. Then why aren't you bringing in the police? You've got a suspect now, not only in the Denham thefts but in the other Nancy Stern's murder. Why aren't you going straight to Detective Reynolds and letting him handle the case from here on? I'd be protected then, wouldn't I?"

"I've already talked to Reynolds," said Bill. "The guy's got total tunnel vision, plus he's not the most communicative person I've ever met. He's stuck on his own theories about who killed your neighbor and he essentially told me to butt out. So that's what I'm doing."

"You're saying Detective Reynolds doesn't even know about Bob Levin, aren't you?"

"That's what I'm saying. I'm keeping Levin's name to myself until I've identified the rest of his buddies."

"And how do you propose to do that, big shot?"

Bill smiled. "By being very smart."

Well, all right. He *was* smart, smart enough to have fooled me about who he really was. But I was smart too. After all, hadn't I fooled him about who I really was?

"What's on your mind?" he asked, sensing something was.

I straightened my posture. "I want to help you get Levin and his 'nest,' as you referred to them earlier."

"Nancy," said Bill with a rather patronizing sigh. "You're a nursery school teacher. You're not trained to —"

"Listen to me," I interrupted. "My life is at stake. That gives me more than a passing interest in catching Levin and company, wouldn't you agree?"

"I would," he conceded.

"Besides which, I'm Fischer Levin's teacher. That gives me more than a passing interest in seeing him emerge from all this unscathed, or at least relatively unscathed."

"So?"

"So I've decided that you and I are going to work as a team."

Bill tried to squelch another smile. "Have you?"

"Yes."

"You wouldn't be afraid to work with me? I mean, we're not talking about fun and games here. Catching bad guys is not for the fainthearted."

"I'm not fainthearted," I said. "In other words, I'm not your ex-wife, Bill."

Before he could respond, the taxi arrived at his building. He paid the fare and escorted me up to his apartment.

We made love all weekend. Well, not every second of the weekend. Personally, I find it hard to believe people who claim to have nonstop sex; it's simply not possible, given our other needs, so let me clarify and say that we made love several times over the course of the weekend. To be honest, I think the revelation that Bill was in law enforcement as opposed to retailing was a turn-on for me. Maybe I was one of those women with a cop-cowboy fantasy but never realized it. What I did realize was that the minute Bill showed me his gun — his piece — I was ready for action. Even more so than usual.

"You don't look like a cop," I said while we were resting up after a particularly acrobatic encounter.

"No? What does a cop look like?" said Bill in a bemused tone.

"A marine," I said. "And don't ask me what a marine looks like. I have a specific image in my mind and it's very effective in terms of arousal."

Bill laughed. "Well, for your information, you don't look like a preschool teacher."

"No? What does a preschool teacher look like?"

"A nurse. And don't ask me what a nurse looks like. I have a specific image in my mind and it's very effective in terms of arousal."

I wrapped my legs around Bill's. "I think we should fix up your marine with my nurse."

"You name the place."

"I'll point to the place."

And so it went. Throughout the entire weekend, as I've indicated.

By Sunday night, we had not only increased our carnal knowledge of each other, we had agreed that I would help Bill catch the bad guys.

"Okay," he said, as we huddled together in bed. "Our first objective is to find out when there's a meeting."

"A meeting between Levin and his accomplices?"

"Exactly. As I've said, we want to nail everybody in the group, which probably includes a cutter and a setter and a polisher, plus a fence and a couple of mopes."

"Mopes?"

"They're the guys that get their hands dirty breaking into apartments, snatching purses, handling the grunt jobs."

"We want all of them," I said, nodding.

"Right. So we have to find out when they're planning a little gathering and then pounce."

"Sounds good. Why don't we bug Levin's phone? He's bound to contact his pals or vice versa."

"Because it's illegal, number one. And because whatever we got wouldn't stand up in court, number two."

I thought for a minute. "You've tried sitting in a car outside his apartment and then following him around?"

Bill smiled tolerantly. "I can't always get a parking spot outside his apartment, but, yes, he's been under surveillance. So far, I've followed him to his power breakfasts, his squash games, his manicures, that sort of thing. Not the stuff arrests are made of."

"What about inside his apartment? Have you actually gone in there?"

"Nancy, I explained that to you. I can't put a wire in his lampshade or anywhere else in his place. It's illegal, not to mention a waste of energy."

"I'm not talking about putting a wire in his lampshade. I'm talking about snooping around in his apartment. Have you done that?"

"Of course not. I'm not a cop. I don't have a search warrant."

"Well, I'm Fischer Levin's teacher and I don't need a search warrant."

"What are you suggesting?"

"I'm suggesting that I make up an excuse for stopping by the Levin place. I'll say that Fischer forgot to bring his art project home and I'm just dropping it off. I'll think of something."

"And then what? Bob Levin won't be thrilled to see you. It could be dangerous, Nancy."

"Not if I pick a time when he's not home — like in the late afternoon when he's still at the office."

"Okay. Let's say you do go there. Levin's not going to leave incriminating information taped to the refrigerator."

"No, but maybe Fischer will show me where he found the pin he gave me for Christmas," I said. "Maybe I'll get a look at his father's 'buried treasure chest,' as he calls it. That would give you additional evidence against him, wouldn't it? If I found more stolen jewelry in the house?"

"Sure, but after what happened with the brooch, he's not about to leave any more of it hanging around. My guess is that he's transferred the gems to a different location by now."

"It's still worth a visit, isn't it?"

"You'd go in the afternoon?"

"Definitely."

"And you'd phone the apartment first, to confirm that Levin wasn't around?"

"Yup."

"And since I'd be waiting in a car down the street, you'd come right out if there were any trouble?"

"I would. Now, may I ask you something?"

"Go ahead."

"Do you think you could kiss me?"

"I think I could, yes."

On Monday afternoon, about an hour after school had let out and Fischer had gone home with Olga, I called the Levin household.

Olga answered the phone. I explained that Fischer had forgotten his Rugrats lunch box and that, since I would be going right by their apartment, I would be glad to drop it off. (I had made sure Fischer had forgotten the lunch box; I had hidden it in Janice's gym bag.)

"Thanks," said Olga. "You leave lunch

box with doorman, okay?"

"Oh. I was hoping I could come up and chat with Fischer for a few minutes," I said. "I do think it's important that he sees that I've returned the lunch box, that I *cared* enough to return it."

Olga agreed.

"Although I'd hate to disturb Mr. or Mrs. Levin if they're at home," I added.

"Da parents are not home," said Olga. "Just Fischer and me, and da cook, da driver, da maid, and da laundry lady."

"Good. I'll be there in a half hour or so."

I called Bill to fill him in. We arranged that he would be parked just down the block from the Levins' during my visit — if he could get a parking space — and that if I didn't come out of their apartment after twenty minutes, he would come in and get me. I felt a frisson of excitement as I prepared for my first assignment as Bill's partner in crime — his partner in *solving* a crime, I mean.

The Levins lived in a Trump building — Trump Plaza, Trump Tower, one of them. Suffice it to say, the structure was tall and gleaming and didn't have a sign out front declaring "For those with serious assets only!" but it might as well have.

Their apartment was on the twenty-seventh floor. It was two apartments, actually. The Levins had bought the unit next door and broken through, and the result was an enormous living space with enough room for family members and staff, not to mention half the population of a tiny country. The other thing I noticed about it was that it was spotless, spectacularly neat, museumlike in its lack of dirt and clutter, as well as white — white walls, white ceilings, white wall-to-wall carpet. Very minimalist or very monotonous, depending on your taste in decorating. Either way, I couldn't imagine how a young child would feel comfortable in such a sterile environment, but then there was much more going on in that apartment than fastidiousness.

Fischer bounded to the door in his bare feet after Olga let me in, seeming very happy to see me. I leaned over to give him a hug and handed him his lunch box and asked if I could visit with him for a few minutes. He was delighted, led me down a long hall to his room and showed me his toys and his books and his fish tanks.

"I know something else you could show me," I said quickly. Bill had only allotted me twenty minutes to do my thing and get out. I had to hurry.

"What, Miss Stern?" asked Fischer.

361

"Your daddy's buried treasure chest. I'd love to see where you found my beautiful Christmas pin."

Fischer looked confused. "You always tell me I'm lying about the treasure chest. You and Miss Mason put me in Time-out if I say my dad's a pirate."

The kid had a point. "Miss Mason and I may have made a mistake," I acknowledged. "Grown-ups make mistakes too, honey. Now, do you want to show me this treasure chest before I go?"

He shrugged. "I can't. It's not here anymore. My dad moved it."

"Moved it? Where?"

He shrugged again. "Even my mommy doesn't know where it is."

"She doesn't?"

"Nope. She doesn't know my dad ever had it. Only I know."

So Gretchen Levin was in the dark about her husband's criminal activities. According to Fischer, anyway.

"How come you're the one he told?" I asked.

" 'Cause I'm the one who saw it. Dad said it would be our special secret. But then he moved it. So I can't show it to you, Miss Stern. I can't show it to you or my friends."

Fischer didn't have any friends. "That's okay, honey. Maybe you can help me in another way."

"How?"

I took a deep breath before posing my next question. I didn't want to get Fischer in trouble with his father, didn't want to make a bad situation worse, but I had no choice. Bill needed to know when Bob Levin was meeting with his fellow crooks, and I'd pledged to help him find out. Which meant sneaking a look at Levin's calendar. No, it wasn't likely that he would write down: "Meeting with other felons regarding jewelry heists." But I had to start somewhere. "You could show me your dad's office here in the apartment," I said. "He must have a room where there's a desk and chairs and a telephone and maybe some business papers, doesn't he, Fischer?"

"Yeah, he has a big office," Fischer said excitedly, then frowned. "But I'm not allowed in it."

"No?"

He shook his head. "I could get punished if I go in. No TV for a week."

"I wouldn't want that to happen," I said, trying not to be discouraged.

"Why do you want to see my dad's office, Miss Stern?"

"Why? Oh." Think. "Remember I told you about my boyfriend? The man who took me out for dinner on Valentine's Day?"

"Kind of."

"Well, he has a big office in his apartment too. His birthday is in a few days and I bet he would like a present for his big office but I don't know what to buy for him. If I went into your dad's big office, I might get a couple of ideas. Understand?"

"I guess. But I'm still not allowed in there."

"And I appreciate that, Fischer, honey. Rules are rules, just like we have at school. But how about if you tell me where in your apartment your dad's office is and I go in there by myself?"

He wasn't sure about this.

"It'll be fine," I said. "I won't make a mess, I promise. I'll be really careful, so no one but you will know I've been there. It'll be *our* special secret, the same way you and your dad have a special secret about the buried treasure chest." I hated myself for tricking him, but in the long run I was doing him a favor. Sending his craven father to prison would save the boy's life, I reasoned.

"Okay," said Fischer.

He told me where the office was. I thanked him and said he should wait for me in his room, that I'd be right back.

I hurried down the white-carpeted hall, past the exercise room, past the billiard room, past the media room, until I came to a room with a large leather-top desk and three or four upholstered chairs and gold-framed photographs on the wall of Bob Levin playing polo. This must be the place, I thought, and tiptoed in.

I went straight for the desk. No calendar. I opened the desk drawers. No calendar. I riffled through a stack of papers. Nothing worth talking about. I gave up on the desk and walked across the room, to a table covered with magazines. I flipped through them and shook my head in bewilderment. I mean, the guy actually kept back issues of *Cigar Aficionado*! I was about to take a peek inside his credenza when a voice stopped me cold.

"Fischer!"

It was a woman's voice — a shrill, high-pitched woman's voice that most certainly did not belong to Olga.

"Fischer! Come here this instant!"

There it was again. It wasn't pleased.

I raced back to Fischer's room, and as I did I noticed that there were brown footprints all along the white carpet — footprints that were accompanied by an unmistakable rankness.

"Quick! Mommy's home!" Fischer whispered when I ducked into his room. "If she finds out you were in my dad's office, she won't let *you* watch TV for a week."

"She won't find out," I said, patting his head. "Besides, I don't watch that much TV, so I won't miss it."

"Fischer! I asked you to come!" screeched Gretchen Levin.

He took off down the hall toward the entrance foyer, toward the voice. I followed him.

"Fischer! Look what you've done!" she said before realizing she had a guest. "Just look!" She was nodding at the brown footprints, her cheeks flushed with fury.

"I didn't do anything," her son protested. "I'm not wearing any shoes. And my feet aren't as big as those."

That's when Mrs. Levin glanced up at me — and then down at my size 8 feet. Without having to be asked — her withering stare spoke volumes — I checked the bottom of my shoes. Yes, indeed. *I* was the one responsible for the soiled carpet. It seemed that I had stepped in doggie doo on my trip over to the Levins' apartment and had tracked the stuff throughout their pristine palace — including Bob Levin's off-limits office.

Some undercover agent.

"Miss Stern?" said Gretchen Levin. She was surprised to see me. She was equally surprised to see her filthy carpet. I wondered if she'd call Penelope and have me fired. I wondered if she'd tell her husband and have me killed. I wondered if I could disappear.

"I stopped by to return Fischer's lunch box," I said, backing up at this juncture, edging toward the door. "I'm so, so sorry about the carpet. I'm sure the footprints will come out." I reached for the doorknob and turned it. "Those industrial-strength cleansers they sell nowadays can take out any stains, even blood. Well, not that you people have to worry about blood. I don't even know why I said blood. It just popped out of my mouth, the way words do when you're not thinking clearly. I should be more mindful of my words, since I'm a teacher. Which reminds me: I've got a staff meeting to attend to and I really have to be going. Have a nice afternoon." And I was out the door.

I was perspiring heavily by the time I got to Bill's car.

"What's the matter?" he asked as I slid onto the seat.

"I stunk," I said.

Bill squeezed my hand. "It was only your first assignment. You'll improve."

"No. I *stunk*," I said. "I left shit all over the place."

"Oh. You mean you recovered more stolen jewelry and then left it out in the open, where Levin could see it?"

"No."

"Then what, Nancy?"

I took off one of my shoes, turned it over, and showed the sole to Bill. "The Levins have white wall-to-wall carpet. I went snooping around in Bob Levin's office figuring he'd never find out."

He nodded, getting the point as well as the smell. "You weren't his favorite person anyway," he said.

"I suppose not," I agreed.

CHAPTER TWENTY-FOUR

I was determined to do a better job of helping Bill catch Bob Levin and his gang, but mostly I was just eager to see the bad guys get punished as soon as possible. I was uneasy knowing they were out there, in my city, contemplating their next move. I was also haunted by the now-irrevocable link between the other Nancy Stern and me. Even though she turned out not to be the shining example I'd thought she was, I felt guilty that she was murdered because of me. Well, not *because* of me, really; *instead* of me. The notion that she wouldn't have been killed if her apartment hadn't been mistaken for mine weighed on me, and as the days passed I couldn't shake it. I mean, if you had to guess which of us was more likely to die young, given *her* lifestyle, which involved drug use and multiple sex partners and a liaison with at least one married man, and *my* lifestyle, which involved reminding four-year-olds to say "please," there would be no contest. And yet, as risky as my lifestyle wasn't, *I* would have been the one to die young if Levin's goons hadn't been so sloppy.

"Hey, you," said Bill, waving his hand in front of my eyes. We were stretched out on his bed. He'd been reading. I'd been thinking. "You've got that faraway look."

"It's not a faraway look. It's a pensive look."

He put down his book, another Sue Grafton. *I Is for Indigestion* this time. "What's on your mind?"

I told him. "I want to get the case solved for obvious reasons," I summed up. "But I especially want to get it solved for Nancy. As a way of saying I'm sorry."

Bill smiled. "I want to get the case solved too, you know that."

"Then what can we do to hurry things along?"

"Actually, I do have an idea. But it's risky. Especially for you. That's why I haven't mentioned it before."

"Whatever it is, I can handle it," I said enthusiastically.

"Well, our objective remains the same: We want to manipulate a meeting between Levin and the other members of his group in order to catch them in the act, photograph them together, get hard evidence against them. Right now, they know Levin's

370

being watched, so they're staying away from him and each other. What we've got to do is provoke them into *having* to meet, to *scare* them into meeting."

"Great, but you still haven't told me your plan."

"My plan is to use you as bait."

"Ah." I attempted to look nonchalant.

"I said it was risky."

I nodded. There were risks and there was risks. "Could you be more specific about how we would use me as bait?"

"Sure. You've been talking about the spring fund-raiser coming up, the one you're going to at your school."

"Right. It's a black-tie dinner dance in the gym at Small Blessings. Gretchen Levin is on the decorating committee."

"And her husband will be there too."

"I would assume so. All the parents are invited."

"Good. I want Levin to see what you're wearing."

I laughed. "I doubt he'll be impressed by my black velvet dress. It's seen better days."

"He'll be impressed by the brooch that'll be pinned to the dress."

I stared at him. "You want me to wear Denham and Villier's five-hundred-thousand-dollar brooch to the Small Blessings spring benefit?"

"I can't think of a more appropriate place to wear it."

"But what if Levin grabs me, drags me out to the street, and kills me, so he can have the brooch back?"

"I'll be your date for the party, and I'll stick close to you. The idea is for you to walk into that room and parade around in the brooch as if you don't have a care in the world. It'll be like waving a red flag in front of a bull. Levin will go berserk when he sees it, because you'll not only be surprising him with it, you'll be flaunting it in his face. He'll be crazed enough about it that he'll *have* to convene a meeting with his guys, so they can decide what to do next."

"I get it," I said, nodding. "We'll be flushing them out."

"Trying to, yes."

"Oh, Bill. You're a genius. And you're not bad-looking, either."

"No?"

"No."

"What are you gonna do about it?"

"This." I picked his book up off the bed and placed it on the floor, then rolled over onto him, pressing my body against his and giving him a couple of bumps and grinds. He was all smiles as I unbuttoned his shirt, unzipped his pants. "You know, I wasn't always like this," I said, stripping off the man's clothes. "I used to be sort of apathetic about sex."

"I don't believe you," said Bill, who then watched with anticipatory glee as I stripped off my own clothes.

"It's true. You've put me in touch with my inner slut."

"Show me."

I did.

I was a nervous wreck the night of the fund-raiser, even before I put on the brooch. While Bill looked like a fashion model in his Ralph Lauren tuxedo, I looked like a fashion mistake. I had sprouted a run in my only pair of pantyhose, my blow dryer died, leaving my hair damp as well as unruly, and my dress didn't fit me as well as it used to, my having lost a few pounds since I'd moved into Bill's apartment and could no longer pig out on Vienna Fingers in the privacy of my own home.

But when he pinned the brooch just to the left of the buttons going down the center of the dress, my blood pressure really shot up. For one thing, I felt ridiculous that I had originally mistaken the piece of jewelry for a piece of crap. Now that I was seeing it again for the first time in months, I couldn't imagine how I'd thought it was a fake, and it was only Bill's reminding me for the tenth time what a blind item jewelry is — "Anyone in your position would have made the same mistake" was how he put it — that allowed me not to seem like a complete fool.

For another thing, I felt as if I were an imposter wearing such an expensive brooch, like a commoner prancing around with a crown on her head. I wasn't used to having a half-million-dollars' worth of diamonds affixed to my bosom, didn't have the posture for it. The other Nancy Stern could have carried it off with ease, but not *this* Nancy Stern.

And then, of course, there was the uncertainty of what Bob Levin might do when he saw the brooch, of what he might do to me. I had read enough crime novels to know that plans such as the one Bill had come up with often backfired, leaving the bait — in this case, me — dead.

Still, armed with numerous assurances from Bill that everything would be all right, combined with my own determination to do a better job as his investigative partner than I had previously, off I went to the party.

We arrived at school to find that the gym had been transformed into an African jungle, thanks to Gretchen Levin and her enthusiastic committee members. As the theme of the party was Safari Night at Small Blessings and the grand prize to be won in a silent auction was a two-week trip to the wilds of Africa, the room was decorated with mosquito netting as well as lions and tigers and bears — oh, my — all constructed out of papier-mâché especially for the event. There was also a band playing African music, which wasn't African music at all but rather Peter Duchin music that was heavier than normal on the bongo drums. And there were black waiters in loincloths and black waitresses in nose rings. If you ask me, the whole affair was as tasteless, never mind politically incorrect, as it gets — the very antithesis of the sort of curriculum we taught at school.

"This is typical Penelope," I whispered to Bill as I surveyed the sea of people milling about, decked out in the latest designer formalwear. "She'd sell her soul to raise a buck."

And speaking of Penelope, she and Deebo were talking to Janice and her date, a creator of crossworld puzzles whom she had met at — where else? — Barnes & Noble in — where else? — the bookstore's crossword puzzle section.

"Should we go over and say hello?" I

asked Bill, since he was running our little undercover operation.

"Okay, but keep your shawl tied across the dress. I don't want anyone to see the brooch until Levin does — it's the element of surprise we're looking for, don't forget — and I don't think the guy's here yet."

We made our way through the crowd to Janice and the others, exchanged greetings, then were quickly sidetracked by some of the parents of the kids in my class. At some point, Bill asked if he could get me a drink at the bar. "Yes," I said. "And make it a double." I had always wanted to use that expression and now I had.

"Make what a double?" said Bill. "You didn't tell me what you wanted."

"Oh. I'll have some white wine," I said.

Bill smiled and went off to the bar. He was away from my side for exactly two seconds when Mr. and Mrs. Levin entered the room and headed in my direction.

So much for sticking close, I thought, willing myself not to move a muscle. I was going to stand my ground, deal with Levin with or without Bill.

"Hello, Miss Stern," said Gretchen Levin when she reached me a minute or two before her husband did. Her tone was cool, distant. She was still upset about the doody on the carpet, I figured.

"Hello to you too, Mrs. Levin," I said, determined to project a thoroughly pleasant and carefree demeanor. "You look lovely," I added. And she did — if your idea of lovely is a potato stick.

"Thank you."

"And what a terrific job you and your committee did on the decorations."

"Thank you again," she said. "It was hard work, I must admit. I've never decorated a gymnasium before, and the project presented its share of challenges."

I smiled, thinking this chick was in for some real challenges, once hubby was behind bars. Speaking of whom . . .

"And here's Mr. Levin," I said as Bob Levin swaggered over to us. "How are you this evening?"

"Fine. Just fine," he said, as if he didn't know that I knew that he knew what I knew. "You by yourself tonight, Miss Stern?"

"No," I said. "I brought a guest, but he's over by the bar at the moment." We all glanced at the crush of people waiting in line for cocktails. Bill was somewhere among them. I tied the shawl tighter around my shoulders, as I was not supposed to expose the brooch while Gretchen Levin was looking on.

And so I made chitchat with the two of them for a few minutes, tried to engage them in conversation until Bill came back. But they grew bored with me eventually and drifted off to talk with the other, more socially important revelers. When Bill finally brought our drinks, I told him what happened. "So much for springing the brooch on him," I said.

"Not to worry. It's going to be a long night," said Bill. "There'll be other opportunities."

"Yeah, but who wants to keep this dopey shawl on?" I complained. "It's hot in here."

"You'll survive."

"That's a given, isn't it?"

He took my arm. We mingled, we nibbled, we waited for another shot at Bob Levin. But then Penelope stepped to the microphone, and all eyes were on her.

"First, let me thank every one of you for coming tonight," she said. "This benefit is our only major fund-raising event of the year and I couldn't be more pleased with the turnout." Applause. "As you know, the proceeds from this grand evening are vital to Small Blessings, providing funds for scholarships, program enrichment, new equipment, and teacher endowments. Due to your support, Small Blessings will remain the premier nursery school in New York." More applause, then Penelope invited us to take our seats at our assigned tables so dinner could be served.

Bill and I sat at the teachers' table. He was on my right, Janice on my left. We were munching on salad greens when she asked, "What's with the shawl? You're getting the fringe full of dressing."

I raised my arm. Sure enough, the black fringe of the shawl was soaked with balsamic vinaigrette.

"I'm chilly," I said, as I wiped the fabric with my napkin. "I'm keeping it on until I warm up."

"Chilly? It's a thousand degrees in here," she said. "They wanted it to feel steamy, like Africa, so they've turned the thermostat way up."

"Whatever," I said. Yes, Janice knew about Levin and the brooch, but I hadn't tipped her off about the plan for the party. Bill had advised against it.

Dinner went along. Then there was dancing. When I noticed that Bob and Gretchen Levin had taken to the dance floor, I turned to Bill and whispered, "We're running out of time. After the dancing comes the auction, and after the auction everybody goes home. Bob Levin has to see the brooch and he has to see it now."

"What are you thinking?" said Bill.

"That we should dance — and then we should switch partners."

Bill nodded, understanding. I grabbed his hand and led him onto the dance floor. I felt giddy suddenly, secure in the knowledge that Bob Levin was not about to hurt me in front of a gym full of people. Besides, I loved to dance and hadn't done nearly enough of it in recent months.

"What kind of half-assed music is this?" Bill grumbled, "and how are you supposed to dance to it?"

The band was playing a little ditty with what I assumed was an African beat.

"Let's try the samba," I said.

"I never learned how to do the samba," he said.

"Neither did I," I said. "Just follow the others."

We observed the couples around us, dipping and bumping and gyrating, and then launched into a pretty good imitation of whatever they were doing. *Da da dah. Da da da dah.* "This is fun," I said, moving to the beat, kicking my foot out to the side every once in a while. *Da da dah. Da da da dah.*

"You ready?" said Bill as he maneuvered

us right next to the Levins.

"As ready as I'll ever be," I said.

He released me. I sambaed over to our targets.

"May I have this dance, Mr. Levin?" I trilled. "I make it a practice of dancing with all the fathers of the children in my class. You don't mind, do you, Mrs. Levin?"

She looked dubious at first, and Bob Levin looked just plain pissed off, but then Bill swooped down on the conversation, introduced himself, and whisked Gretchen Levin off. *Da da dah. Da da da dah.*

"Now, isn't this nice," I said after we had swapped partners and Bobby baby and I were tripping the light fantastic.

"Look, I don't know what you're up to," he said, gripping me tightly around the waist, "but maybe we should go outside and talk."

"Talk?" I said as we danced. "What on earth would we have to talk about?"

"Don't play innocent with me, kiddo. I know you have that damn brooch. Either you have it or your boyfriend has it."

"You were right the first time," I said. "I have it."

He smirked. "Are you gonna tell me where you have it or do I have to send my friends to find it?"

"I'm gonna *show* you where I have it. Right now, in fact."

Emboldened by how well things were going, I untied the shawl and let it slide off my shoulders, exposing the goods. Before Bob Levin knew what had hit him, the brooch was in his face.

His eyes bugged out.

"Surprised?" I grinned. "I thought you'd be. So. I was wondering how you'd react if I showed the brooch to your wife. She'd be interested in seeing it, don't you agree? Interested in hearing how I got it too. Actually, I'll bet everybody at the party would be interested in that story."

"You don't have the balls," he said, his words tough but his expression one of a man genuinely caught off-guard.

"I wouldn't be so sure," I goaded him, flashing the diamonds at him, enjoying myself immensely. "Because I'm thinking about walking up to that microphone and telling every single person in this room what I know. Would you like that, Mr. Levin?"

He didn't respond this time. I really had ambushed him. *Da da dah. Da da da dah.*

"What's the matter?" I chuckled. "Cat burglar got your tongue?"

He was breathing heavily all of a sudden and his color wasn't good. But he kept moving to the music. *Da da dah. Da da da dah.*

"Okay, so I'll make a deal with you," he said, huffing and puffing as we danced. "You give me back the brooch, I'll have my people lay off you."

"I have a better idea. You have your people turn themselves in to the police and I'll skip the trip to the microphone."

He shook his head. His breathing was raspy, congested. "You don't get it."

"Get what, Mr. Levin?" I said sweetly, punctuating the question by kicking my foot off to the side, with the flair of a ballroom dancing champion, if I do say so.

"I've got to have that brooch back. I'm not the guy in charge."

"What's that supposed to mean?"

"Jesus. What do you think it means?" He coughed once, then twice, then loosened his tuxedo tie. He was sweating, having a hot flash. *Da da dah. Da da da dah.*

"You feeling poorly, Mr. Levin? Is the shock of seeing me out in public with the brooch you stole making you sick?" I taunted. "Or are you just a little winded from all the dancing?"

"I'm not the guy in charge," he repeated.

"If I don't get the brooch back, he'll —"

"He'll what?"

"He'll —"

"Who'll?"

"I don't feel —"

"Finish what you were about to tell me, Mr. Levin," I demanded. "Are you saying that you're not the one who's running your organization? That the man who is will do something to you if you don't —"

Before I could complete the thought, he made a choking sound, a gasping-for-air sound, and then his hands slackened from around my waist and he went down, face first, onto the gym floor.

"Oh my God!" I heard myself yelling. "Stop the music! This man needs a doctor!"

Bob Levin's collapse and my yelling caused a great commotion, as you might imagine, and put a definite damper on the festivities. Several of the fathers at the party *were* doctors and rushed to Levin's side to perform CPR on him. (They took turns, although there were two who hung back, claiming concerns about medical malpractice.) Gretchen Levin was so consumed with worry, waving her arms around like a hysteric, that she got herself caught up in the mosquito netting and one of her committee members had to disentangle her.

And then, of course, there was Penelope, who was apoplectic that her biggest donor was out of commission.

"This is *your* fault, Nancy," she said, wagging a finger at me. "If you hadn't wiggled and jiggled him across the floor like some cheap dance hall girl, he wouldn't have taken ill. You'd better hope he doesn't die."

Oh, I hope he doesn't die all right, I thought. If he goes, there'll be no way to catch his accomplices, never mind this boss he was mumbling about.

"I've done it again, haven't I?" I said morosely as Bill and I watched the EMS people cart Levin off to the hospital. "I've screwed up the plan."

"You were magnificent," he said, putting his arm around me. "You got him to give up that tidbit about the real head of the organization. Now we know there's another layer, another level."

"But if he doesn't pull through, we'll never find out about any of it."

"He'll pull through."

"What makes you so sure?"

"Because we're not done with him yet."

Da da dah. Da da da dah.

CHAPTER TWENTY-FIVE

Levin did pull through, just as Bill had predicted, but his doctor kept him in the hospital for a couple of weeks, after which he recuperated at home for a few more weeks.

"So young to have a heart attack," Victoria Bittner remarked as we were leaving school together one afternoon. "He's only in his forties, isn't he?"

I nodded. "And in decent shape, being both a polo player and a squash player."

"You'd think. Maybe he had one of those congenital abnormalities you hear about," she offered. "One minute, those people are fine; the next minute, they're an obituary."

"Could be," I said.

"Although it's possible that it was his Type A personality that brought on the heart attack," she reconsidered. "That and the fact that he's in a very stressful line of work."

"Very stressful," I agreed. I wondered whether being a crook was more stressful than being a stock broker or whether being a stock broker was more stressful than being a crook. And then I wondered whether I was comparing apples with apples.

Fischer was extremely disruptive in the classroom following his father's sudden illness. I assumed that he was acting out because there was chaos at home, that nobody was bothering to tell him what was going on, and that he was left to fend for himself, as usual. As I felt partially responsible for this — it was my flashing the brooch in Levin's face that triggered the heart attack, after all — I didn't put him in Time-out whenever he made trouble. Instead, I nurtured him, tried to draw him out, tried to get him to express his feelings.

"Are you scared about your daddy being in the hospital?" I asked him shortly after Levin's collapse.

"Kind of," he said. "But he's in a big room — the biggest room in the whole hospital."

"Oh, so you've been to visit him, honey?"

"Yeah. My mommy took me."

"That's great. How's he doing?"

"He goes beep beep beep. From the machines."

"The machines will make him better," I said. "And then he'll come home and everything will be back to normal." I practically gagged on my words. Bill and I were doing what we could to send Levin away for good, which caused a real crisis of conscience for me as Fischer's teacher. In the long run, I knew I was doing what was best for him, his father being a killer and a thief, but in the short run, I felt like a rat.

In any case, Bill and I figured that since Levin was under the weather, he wouldn't be holding any meetings with his bad-ass buddies and that our plan to nab the entire bunch of them would be in a sort of holding pattern for a while.

Wrong. Bill and I came home one night to find that his place had been ransacked.

"Welcome to the club," I said, surveying the mess. "I guess Levin isn't *that* under the weather. He managed to get in touch with his mopes, as you call them."

"Which means our plan was partially effective," said Bill. "Levin saw you with the brooch at the fund-raiser and he also saw you with me. He must have told his people that the brooch might be here."

"I'll say one thing for his 'people.' They're pretty incompetent, the way they try and fail and try and fail. Not that I'm not glad they fail. Plus, if they'd shown up when we were home, we could have gone the route of the other Nancy Stern."

"But they didn't show up when we were

home, because murder isn't their game. They didn't set out to kill your neighbor, I'm sure of it."

"Well, the main thing is, they're not giving up on getting the brooch back. Levin seemed desperate to get it back, as if this boss of his, this kingpin, was putting the squeeze on him to get it back."

"If I could just find out who the guy is," Bill mused. "Then I could knock them all out of operation."

"You will, but in the meantime I really think you should involve the police, before one of us does end up like Nancy."

Instead of answering, he started picking up the articles of clothing that had been strewn around the apartment.

"Bill." He wasn't paying any attention to me. "Bill?"

He looked up.

"Why are you doing all this housekeeping when you should be on the phone to the police?" I asked.

"I explained that to you before," he said, returning to his straightening up. "Reynolds told me to butt out of his investigation. Cops don't like us private guys interfering."

"But you have new evidence. He'll listen to you now, won't he?"

"Doubt it."

I regarded him, watched him tune me out, and as I did his ex-wife's crack echoed in my mind. *If I were you, honey, I'd wear a bullet-proof vest to sleep.* Had she been warning me about Bill, not merely sniping at him? Was he more interested in playing the hero than in reacting sensibly to a dangerous situation?

"I think I understand what's going on here," I said. "You'll be off the case if you turn all your information over to the police, isn't that true?"

"What's your point?" he said.

"My point is that if you tell the police everything you've got on Levin, they'll take over and you'll be out of it. You can't stand the idea of that."

"Look, Nancy. I thought I made this clear in past conversations. I was hired by Denham and Villier to do a job. That job was to bust the *organization* that's been costing the company millions in stolen gems. Fingering Bob Levin alone won't cut it."

"No, but there's another side to this. If Bob Levin's got a boss who's pressuring him to get the brooch back, he'll become bolder, take more chances, and the assaults on us, on our property, will only escalate. He's not going to stop at a couple of break-ins and a

390

purse snatching. Are you willing to risk my safety in order to do your *job?*"

He sighed. He seemed exasperated with me. "You know, you're really giving me mixed signals here. On one hand, you act all turned on by my job, by my cop background, by my gun. You even tell me you want to be my partner in solving the crimes. 'I'm not your ex-wife,' I believe you said, as if to mean that you, unlike her, have no problem with the way I earn my money. On the other hand, you want me to stop right in the middle of *my* case and turn it over to the police who, at this point in time, have absolutely no interest in it. Sorry, but I can't figure out where you stand."

I came toward him, put my arms around his waist. "I stand with you," I said. "I love you. But Levin's going to up the ante here. I feel it."

"Then let me do my job," said Bill, kissing the top of my head. "Trust me to handle this my way."

"All right," I said. "I will." For now.

With the brooch back in its vault, Levin still at home recuperating, and both Small Blessings and Denham and Villier closed for Easter vacation, Bill and I decided to drive out to Pennsylvania to spend the weekend with my parents, get a change of scenery.

As I didn't want to worry them, I continued to let them think Bill was the manager of Denham's New York store and told them nothing about the cops-and-robbers shenanigans we'd been up to.

"So this is the man who stole my daughter's heart!" my mother exclaimed when we arrived at about noon on Saturday. "She's my special baby, Bill."

"He's heard," I said as Bill shook hands with both of my parents and expressed how delighted he was to meet them at long last. He was in full charmer mode, every bit the debonair executive of an internationally famous jewelry store. It occurred to me as I watched him that we were meant for each other — two people who were uncommonly good at pretending.

My mother had made lunch, which we ate in the kitchen with the television on in the background, as usual. On this occasion, the set was tuned to CNN Headline News, which delivered the news on the half hour. By the end of our two-hour lunch, I had practically memorized the day's top stories.

"So, Bill. Tell us all about yourself," my mother urged as she deposited ice-cream scoopers full of egg salad, tuna salad, and shrimp salad onto his plate, then suggested that the rest of us serve ourselves. Bill was God, apparently, being the first legitimate suitor to come along since my divorce.

"Oh, there's not much to tell," he said self-effacingly, then proceeded to trot out the same bullshit story he'd handed me on our blind date.

"I've always been interested in the jewelry business," said my father, who had never been interested in the jewelry business, at least not that he'd ever let on. He asked Bill all sorts of questions like: "What's your markup?" And: "Who's Denham and Villier's biggest competitor?" And: "Is there much theft and, if so, how do you handle it?"

The last question provoked me to kick Bill under the table, but he remained unflappable, answering my father with a matter-of-factness that really impressed me.

After my mother and I cleared the table and did the dishes, the four of us adjourned into the living room so my parents could continue the grilling of Bill. Well, they weren't grilling him exactly; they were just trying in a very enthusiastic way to elicit information from him, to get to know the man with whom their daughter was shacking up.

By the middle of the afternoon, I was tired of sitting around the house, so I asked Bill if he wanted a tour of the town, the idea being that he and I could steal some time alone.

"What a wonderful idea," said my mother, clapping her hands. "We'll all go. Uncle Dave is coming over in a little while — I invited him for dinner so he could meet Bill too — but he's got a key and can let himself in if we're not back."

Uncle Dave, my father's widower-brother who drank too much and acted crabby. Oh, well.

"We'll start out by taking Bill to see my shop," my mother said proprietarily.

"He's not interested in greeting cards," my father disagreed. "I've got to run over to Home Depot to pick up a few things. I say we start out by taking him there. He can help me find what I need."

They were fighting over my boyfriend. I found this sweet.

"Actually, sir, I'm not much of a do-it-yourselfer," said Bill.

"Nonsense," said my father, who was not much of a do-it-yourselfer either. I had never known him to run over to Home Depot to pick up anything. I chuckled to myself as I realized that he was showing off for Bill, being a manly man for Bill, hoping to bond with Bill over nails and screws and paint spackle. He was, it seemed to me, courting Bill because he liked him and regarded him as a good candidate for the position of son-in-law. I may have been my parents' special baby, but Bill was the key to their having special grandchildren.

After our itinerary was set, we all got into the car and headed off.

My father drove. My mother narrated. Here's the elementary school Nancy went to. Here's her junior high. Here's her high school, where she got straight A's except for the C in Latin and the D in home economics.

"I don't think Bill's interested in every single aspect of my childhood," I told my mother. "Maybe you could just hit the high points."

She hit the high points. Eventually, we came to her greeting card shop. She had taken the day off, but the store was open, so she dragged Bill inside and introduced him around. After that, we buzzed by my father's office. It was not open, but my father insisted that Bill see it, so he unlocked the doors and let us in. Throughout, Bill was patient and polite and respectful of my parents. The perfect husband for Nancy, they were probably thinking. I wondered how perfect a husband they'd think he was if they knew *who* he was.

Our last stop was Home Depot. My father and Bill went off to the nails and screws and paint spackle sections of the giant warehouse, while my mother and I wandered off to the nursery to check out the plants. After what seemed like an eternity, she glanced at her watch, declared that it was nearly five o'clock, and said we should "find the boys" so she could get home and start dinner.

We went to find the boys. We couldn't find the boys. We looked in nails. We looked in screws. We looked in paint spackle. No go.

We tried lumber. We tried electrical. We tried plumbing. There was no sign of them.

"Let's split up," I suggested to my mother, knowing how easily you could lose someone in a store the size of Home Depot. You could walk down one aisle while the other person was walking down the aisle right next to it and keep missing each other for hours. "I'll take this side of the building. You take that side."

It was a terrible plan. After a half hour of what felt like a game of hide-and-seek, I had not only lost my father and Bill, I had lost my mother too.

I was standing by myself in the aisle where they sell drawer and cabinet knobs, thinking I should probably ask one of the employees to make an announcement over the loud-speaker, when a man darted over to me, appearing out of nowhere.

"You're Nancy Stern, right?" he said breathlessly.

"Yes," I said with a certain wariness. The man was extremely grubby-looking — his face unshaven, his hair lank and greasy, his clothes torn and stained — and he smelled as if he hadn't bathed in days.

"I just wanted to make sure," he said with an odd little laugh, sort of a *hee-hee-hee*.

It was as he was reaching for me, lunging at me, that I recognized him. He was the same man who had snatched my purse in New York! The goon Bob Levin had sent to find the brooch! He must have followed me to Pennsylvania, waited until I was alone, and was now going to kidnap me or something equally unacceptable!

I screamed, naturally, which brought dozens of Home Depot employees dressed in bright orange aprons running to my aid. (I don't advocate screaming as a method for getting a salesperson to wait on you, but it's food for thought.)

"Get this man away from me!" I said, which prompted a rather burly employee to grab the man by the arms and wrestle him to the ground.

It also prompted my father, my mother, and Bill to follow the commotion and find me and each other in the knobs aisle.

"Nancy! What on earth is going on?" my mother asked.

I looked at Bill and directed my reply to him. "This man was about to attack me," I said, pointing at the culprit. "I think he wanted to *steal my jewelry*." Not that I was wearing any, but I knew Bill would catch on. "He's a hardened criminal, at any rate."

"A criminal?" My mother turned pale.

I put my arms around her, gave her a little hug. "I'm okay," I reassured her. "Nothing happened. It's over now. They'll take him away and put him in jail."

"Put him in jail?" She wriggled out of my arms and kneeled down on the floor, next to the bad guy. I couldn't believe what I was seeing. She turned toward the Home Depot employee who still had the man in a hammerlock. "Release him this minute!" she instructed the employee.

"Mom. Please stay out of this," I said. "Without going into details, this man is part of a group of cunning and dangerous individuals."

My mother ignored me. Some special baby. "Release him," she told the employee again. "I'll vouch for him."

Bill and I stood there openmouthed as my mother helped the man to his feet. "Are you all right?" she asked him.

He nodded, all right but shaken.

My mother faced me. "I don't know what kind of craziness you're talking about, young lady," she said in her scolding voice, as if I were ten, "but this 'criminal' is Christopher Iverson, who has lived in our town his entire life. He was in your class in high school, was president of the audio-visual club, used to give you a ride every now and then. He was only coming over to say hello after so many years. Isn't that so, Christopher?"

Christopher said it was so, that he hadn't meant to upset me. Then he apologized for his scruffy appearance, explaining that he'd been working on the new bathroom he was putting in at his place, realized he'd bought the wrong toilet seat, and didn't bother to shower before rushing back to the store to exchange it for the right one. He asked if I remembered him now. I said of course I did and how were his folks. He said they were dead. I said I was sorry. And I *was* sorry. Sorry that they were dead; sorry that I had mistaken him for one of Levin's goons. I was so sorry that I invited him and his wife and children to join Bill and me and my parents and my uncle Dave for dinner. It was the least I could do, wasn't it?

Unfortunately, I had to call Christopher a little later, rescind the invitation, and ask him if he would take a rain check.

It wasn't that we didn't want Christopher and his family to have dinner with us. It was that we were not going to be having dinner, at least not at a reasonable hour. You see, when we pulled into my parents' driveway, we came upon Uncle Dave's car — with Uncle Dave in it, lying across his own backseat, his head at an odd angle, his feet out the window. "He must have gotten drunk and passed out," I suggested as we peered into the vehicle.

"Nancy," my mother scolded. Well, it wasn't as if it hadn't happened before.

"He's unconscious, all right," said Bill, after opening the car door and examining Uncle Dave more closely, "but he doesn't smell of alcohol."

"Look," my mother said, pointing to the back of her brother-in-law's head. "He's got a big bruise."

"He sure does," said Bill. "A nice purple egg."

"He must have fallen at home, poor bastard," said my father. "He's alone so much these days."

"If he fell at home and knocked himself unconscious, then how did he drive himself over here?" my mother asked.

"Yeah, and what's he doing in the backseat of his car?" I wanted to know.

"The important thing is to get him to a hospital," said Bill. "I'm guessing it's a concussion and he'll come out of it just fine, but let's not waste any more time. Nancy, why don't you and I stay with him while your parents go inside and call 911."

My parents hurried up the driveway, but when they entered the house, they discovered a second reason to call 911: Somebody had made a mess of the place, overturning furniture, emptying drawers, the works. It didn't take a genius to figure out what had happened: Levin's people *had* followed Bill and me to Pennsylvania, in search of the brooch, and Uncle Dave had arrived on the scene at precisely the wrong moment.

It was a long night, what with dealing with the police and keeping vigil at the hospital, but we all got through it. Uncle Dave came to shortly after being admitted, and the doctor deemed his concussion "mild." My parents were extremely relieved that he was okay, which took the sting out of the fact that some of my mother's jewelry had been stolen — and that Uncle Dave couldn't remember anything about the men who'd stolen it. As for Bill and me, we kept silent about what we suspected — at his insistence — which made me feel horribly conflicted.

"This whole thing is mystifying, because there's hardly any crime in our little town," said my mother.

"If you ask me, it was the gypsies," said my father, who believed that gypsies were responsible for most of the world's problems.

"I suppose we're lucky," said my mother. "At least none of us was killed."

"Very lucky," my father agreed, then turned to me. "Isn't that right, Nancy?"

"Very lucky," I repeated, thinking it was one thing for me to risk bodily harm while Bill diddled around with his investigation, but it was quite another for me to expect the people I loved to do the same.

CHAPTER TWENTY-SIX

The ride back to New York wasn't pretty. I was furious that my family had been victimized by Levin's goons — a situation that could easily have been prevented if Bill had just gone to the police weeks before — and I vented my anger in no uncertain terms.

Bill's response was that Uncle Dave hadn't been seriously hurt and my parents hadn't been hurt at all and their insurance company would reimburse them for the stolen jewelry, so what was I getting all excited about.

"I'm excited because you and I just stood there, knowing what we knew but not saying a word," I replied, trying unsuccessfully not to shout at the top of my lungs. "I *told* you Levin was going to up the ante. Didn't I say that just the other day? Didn't I predict that he'd get more and more desperate, because of this boss breathing down his neck?"

"Try to calm down, Nancy. I'm right next to you."

"I'm not calming down. Members of my

family could have been killed, Bill. The same way the other Nancy Stern was."

"Nancy, I've made this point over and over," he said wearily. "Levin and company aren't interested in killing anyone. They're interested in getting the brooch back. If they'd wanted to kill your uncle or your parents, they would have, believe me. You keep harping on your neighbor's murder, but that was a mistake these guys made. It was an aberration for them, a screwup. We're talking about jewel thieves here, not people who go on killing rampages."

"Well, how the hell do you think I feel about putting my own parents in a position where *they* could become a 'screwup,' as you call it?"

"I'm sure you feel awful about it. So do I. But there's a plan in place to solve the case and we're sticking to it."

"Maybe you're sticking to it, but I'm not so sure about me."

"No?"

"No. How can I stick to a plan that places the people I care about in jeopardy?"

"I've already —"

"Listen to me, Bill. The bottom line is that your idea of how to handle things is at odds with my desire to protect my loved ones. You think that the only way to solve the case is *your* way, which is to do everything yourself — without the police — and I think you're being incredibly stubborn."

His expression tightened. "The police have their job to do, and I have mine, as I've told you and told you."

"Your job is not to compromise people's safety."

"For the hundreth time, I'm not! I've had a little more experience at this than you have, Nancy. These cases aren't dangerous for the most part, but they do take time — months, years even. You have to be patient if you want to nail everybody in an organization like Levin's, especially if the organization has levels of authority, like his seems to."

"Well, my patience is running out."

"What's that supposed to mean?"

"You figure it out."

We didn't speak for the next hour, except when we stopped for gas and Bill muttered that he was going to the men's room. If there's anything more uncomfortable than taking a long car trip with someone you're not getting along with, please tell me.

It wasn't until we got back to Bill's apartment late Sunday night that he picked up the conversation.

"I'd like it if you weren't quite so angry," he said.

"I'd like it if you weren't quite so rigid," I countered. "It's time to call the police, Bill, before there's another *event*."

"I can't do that, Nancy. Not yet. Just give me another few weeks to crack the case. That's all I'm asking. This kind of job has to be nursed along, not rushed. I've explained that."

Nursed along, I thought. Someone's going to *need* a nurse if he doesn't act soon. A nurse, then an undertaker.

"So will you hang on a little longer?" he prompted as he opened his arms to me, cocked his head at me. "I love you. I need your support. I want us to be a team on this."

God, whenever he looked at me with those dark, soulful eyes, I couldn't refuse him anything.

I love you too, I said to myself as I gazed at him. I love you more than I thought I could love anyone. Even though you're pig-headed. Even though you have to be the hero. Even though you're a much bigger risk taker than Janice. Even though you're probably deranged, a mass of *neuroses*.

I stepped into his outstretched arms, into his embrace. "I just hope you know what you're doing," I said as he held me close.

The weather during the rest of April was

downright balmy, with unseasonably warm temperatures and light, soft breezes. Romance weather, that's what it was — the kind that makes you vulnerable to love.

I was already in love, as I've just described, but Janice was not, and the weather seemed to inspire her to step up her efforts to find a man. As an example, instead of limiting her forays into Barnes & Noble to Sunday afternoons, she added Friday nights to her regular routine.

"They have singles then too," she told Bill and me while we were having dinner at her apartment one Wednesday evening.

We'd had a wonderful time that night, as a matter of fact — a carefree time, just the three of us. No one talked about Levin or the brooch or Bill's job. No one brought up any unpleasantness. We laughed at bad jokes and drank too much wine and acted silly. The Three Stooges, Janice dubbed us.

The following Friday night, off she went to Barnes & Noble, ever hopeful. As luck would have it, after stationing herself in the New Fiction section, she met a dentist — a single who was not only presentable but earned a good living. What's more, this dentist — Stan was his name — was a health nut, just like Janice, and a computer enthusiast, just like Janice, and a person who liked to jump right into relationships, just like Janice. They hit it off so beautifully, according to her, that they dispensed with formalities and went straight back to his place and had sex. Safe sex, she assured me.

If only her return home later that night had been as safe.

After making a cup of herbal tea, she undressed, got into bed and read for a while, trying to wind down after her passion-packed evening. When she could no longer keep her eyes open, she turned off the light and went to sleep. About two-thirty she was awakened by the feel of something cold against her right temple. It was the barrel of a gun — and the man in the black ski mask made it clear that he knew how to use it.

"Scream and you're dead," was how he greeted her, speaking of all-time-worst wake-up calls.

Since he had his hand over her mouth, she couldn't do much in the way of screaming. Besides, she was too terrified to scream. She just did what she was told, which was to get out of bed, walk into the bathroom, and stay there while he searched her apartment for guess what.

She curled up in her bathtub, scared shitless, and forced herself not to cry as she heard the guy open every drawer and cabinet in her place, not knowing whether or not he'd shoot her when he didn't find what he was looking for. That was the biggie, she told me later — the uncertainty of what might happen to her, the possibility that she might die without ever determining if Stan was a one-night stand or Mr. Right.

No, Levin's mope didn't shoot her or even bop her on the head, like he bopped Uncle Dave. But he did slap her around a little, demanding to know if I had given her the brooch for safekeeping the night Bill and I had been over for dinner. Eventually, after saying "What brooch?" often enough that he either believed her or gave up, the guy tied her wrists to the tub's hot and cold water faucets, stuffed a sock in her mouth, and left, stealing her nice pearl necklace while he was at it.

It was Stan who found her. They had made plans to have breakfast together that morning. He showed up at her apartment, found the door unlocked, and walked in.

"When he first saw me, bound to that bathtub, he thought I'd had a double-header with some guy who was into bondage." She laughed. Laughed! She was amazing, my friend Janice. She told Stan she'd been robbed and he called the police and they questioned her about the events of the evening, and she never breathed a word about Bob Levin or the brooch. She knew that Bill's strategy was to keep the cops out of it, so she went with the program.

I, on the other hand, had had it with the program. Janice's near-death experience was the absolute last straw.

I confronted Bill once we were back at his apartment, after we'd seen Janice and heard her story. "She could have been killed — because of *your* singleminded pursuit of a bunch of crooks," I said hotly.

"But she wasn't killed," he said, raising his voice to defend himself.

"Fine. She wasn't killed. She was bound and gagged and threatened at gunpoint. Piece of cake, right?"

"Of course not. I'd give anything if she hadn't been attacked."

"You'd give anything." I laughed scornfully. "Anything except turn the case over to the police."

"We've been all through that, Nancy."

"Sorry. Well, since there's nothing more to hash out, I'm moving back to my place."

He looked stung. "What are you talking about?"

"I'm talking about leaving, Bill. I've had enough. You say it won't do any good to call the police. I say it won't do any good for me to keep asking you to. So go ahead. Hunt down Levin's organization. Do your job. Take all the time you need. But I'm out of it."

He reached for me, touched my arm. "You're not out of it. You're the key to it. If you leave, how will I protect you?"

"Why would I need protecting? You told me Levin's people aren't interested in killing anyone, that they're only interested in getting the brooch back. Well, I don't have the brooch. You do. So I'll be hunky dory."

"I don't want you to go."

"Then call the police."

"I can't do that."

God, this was hard, impossible. I didn't want to leave Bill, but how could I stay when he wouldn't bend?

He tried to kiss my mouth, but I turned away. As his lips brushed my cheek instead, I felt the same old stirring, the same old yearning for him that I always felt. But I couldn't surrender to it. Not this time.

"Do you remember when you promised you'd love me no matter what?" he asked in a voice that was so pained it nearly broke my own heart. "It was before you found out about my real job."

I nodded.

"What happened to that promise?"

"Nothing," I managed, the tears coming now. "Nothing happened to it. I do love you no matter what."

"Then why —"

"Because we can't agree on something very important."

"And because you don't trust me."

When I didn't deny this, he walked away, across the room, so as not to have to be near me. "It's ironic, you know," he said. "When we began our relationship, I was the one who didn't trust you." He coughed, cleared his throat. "You were pretending to be someone else, someone I wouldn't have loved as opposed to someone I do."

I thought of the other Nancy Stern then, thought of how I had coveted every aspect of her life, thought of how she would still *have* a life if it weren't for me. She would have had a life, but she wouldn't have Bill.

And now neither of us had Bill.

I waited before rushing off to pack, to think clearly about what I was about to do. I desperately wanted to come up with a compromise, a solution that would address both of our concerns. But I couldn't, because we weren't fighting over who should do the dishes or whether we should move into a bigger apartment or what kind of car we should buy. Those were domestic issues, the sort of problems people tackle on a daily basis, the sort of problems that don't sink relationships. Bill and I, on the other hand, were far apart on a life-and-death issue, and no matter how I spun it around in my head, I felt he was in the wrong.

"I'm sorry, but I have to do what I feel is right," I said and went into the bedroom and threw my clothes into a suitcase. When I brought myself and my belongings back to the living room, Bill was still standing in the corner, exactly where I'd left him.

"I'm going to worry about you," he said hoarsely.

"No need to. I'll be okay. Busy. We're winding down the school year. Only a month and a half left, if you can believe it. Janice and I have to get the kids ready for the end-of-school celebration. We're having a Middle Ages day with costumes and food and music."

"I'm sure it'll be a big success."

"Thanks."

I turned to go, my hand on the doorknob.

"Nancy?" came Bill's voice from across the room.

"Yes?"

"Is this temporary? This splitting up or whatever it is we're doing? I mean, when the case is over, I'm hoping we can pick up and move on."

"The trouble is, Bill, we don't know when the case will be over. You said it could take months, years even, to round everybody up. That's a long time to put a relationship on hold, isn't it?"

"It might be."

"Then why don't we just see how it goes?"

"See how it goes," he repeated halfheartedly, as if all the wind had been knocked out of him.

I stood there staring at him, taking a good look at him, in the event that Levin's goons might hurt him and I'd never see him again. The notion was excruciating.

And so I made one last overture. "If you change your mind about the police . . ." I trailed off.

"I can't," he said. "Not yet, anyway."

I nodded, heavy with sadness that we were at such an impasse. And then I opened the door to his apartment and walked out.

I had always wondered how it was possible for two people to love each other and still not be able to make things work. Now I knew.

Once resettled in my own apartment, I assumed my life would revert back to the old days when Janice and I would spend the occasional Saturday night together. But just because I was alone now didn't mean she was.

Following the attack, Stan had been incredibly solicitous of her, insisting that she stay with him until she felt safe enough to go home. As a result, she almost never went home. Stan was her last shot, her big chance, her best hope, she said, and she wasn't about to blow it by admitting that she had no qualms whatsoever about going back to her apartment.

Actually, I could see why she wanted to grab him. He was a nice dentist and he treated her like a queen, especially compared to the barbarians she'd been with. What's more, they really did share interests, have a lot in common, embody similar personality traits. They finished each other's sentences and laughed at the same jokes and talking to one was like talking to the other. I was very happy for my friend. She had waited a long time for Stan, just as I had waited a long time for Bill, the difference being that she was at the beginning cycle with Stan, the wash cycle, whereas I was at the ending cycle with Bill, the rinse cycle. Yes, that's it, I thought. Being in a relationship is like doing laundry; when it's over you hope that everything comes out clean.

Of course, I wouldn't be honest if I didn't admit to feeling just a twinge of disappointment that Janice had chosen my time of need to get cozy with Stan. I missed Bill terribly and wished she were around to let me cry on her shoulder. In the past, she'd always been able to lift my spirits, help me put things in perspective. But now the only time I had her attention was at school and even then she was distracted, the way people are when they're in the wash cycle.

So I pressed on by myself, sucked up my loss and loneliness. Every night, I would think about calling Bill and then decide there was no point. And every time the phone rang, I would think it was Bill on the line and then realize there was no point in that either.

One night the phone rang and, as usual, I wondered if it might be Bill. But when I picked it up, there was a woman on the other end.

"Is this Nancy Stern?" she asked.

"Yes," I said.

"Hi. My name is Joan Geisinger."

Joan Geisinger? *The* Joan Geisinger? The matchmaker who'd tried to set Bill up with the other Nancy Stern? What on earth did she want with me?

"Hello, Joan," I said, not knowing what else to.

"I'm an old friend of Bill Harris's, as he must have told you," she said.

"Yes, he told me," I said, feeling a catch in my throat. Even the mention of Bill's name hurt.

"Bill gave me your phone number. I hope you don't mind."

"Not at all." He'd given her my number, but he couldn't pick up the phone and call me himself? Things were worse than I thought. "I'm very sorry about the Nancy Stern that lived upstairs, Joan. She was an old friend of yours too."

"Oh, yes. Poor Nancy. Naturally, I was shocked when I heard she'd been killed. She and I hadn't been in touch in ages — actually I did write her a letter not that long ago, which she didn't answer — but when we were first coming up in the magazine business we spent a fair amount of time together. She was such a dynamo, so full of life. It's hard to believe she's gone. She seemed to lead such a charmed existence. Charmed but troubled."

"Troubled? How?"

"I never could quite put my finger on it, but there was an unhappiness there, even with all the beauty and brains. I'm a romantic, I guess, and so I thought that if she and Bill were to hit it off, her unhappiness or emptiness or whatever it was would evaporate. That's why I attempted to fix them up."

"And then he ended up with me instead," I said. "Sorry to have spoiled your plan."

"Nonsense. I'm delighted you and Bill found each other. But now he tells me you two have had a bust-up. He's awfully down about it."

"I'm not ecstatic about it myself."

"Which brings me to the reason I'm calling you, Nancy. You must be wondering."

"I am curious."

"Well, he's been such a friend to me that I just wanted to help in some way, to take a stab at getting you to patch things up between you. I'm sticking my nose in where it doesn't belong, but I thought that if I explained about Bill, about how he and I met and became friends, it might shed some light on him, on why he does what he does for a living, for example."

I didn't see how her story could affect the situation, but I wasn't about to hang up on her. "Please, Joan. I'd be grateful for your input."

"Okay. Let me begin by asking if Bill has

ever told you how he and I know each other."

"No. Actually, he hasn't."

"I'm not surprised. It probably depresses him to talk about it. Anyhow, I met him through my husband. Bill and Jack worked together, Nancy, when Bill was on the force down here in Washington."

"Your husband is a policeman?"

"Used to be."

"Oh, is he one of those private investigators now, like Bill?"

"No. He's dead. He was killed several years ago. In the line of duty."

Good one, Nancy. Way to go. "I'm sorry, Joan. I had no idea, as I said."

"Of course you didn't. Bill and my husband were detectives together, as close as brothers, closer than Bill is to his own brothers. They worked a lot of gem thefts, and both of them became experts on the subject, specialists. They took pride in what they did, but they also *enjoyed* what they did because they had each other. Then all of our lives changed. Jack was killed while he and Bill were investigating a group that was dealing in stolen gems."

"My God. I'm so sorry," I said again. I was sorry for Joan, but sorry for Bill too. "What went wrong?"

"They were brought into the case by the private security investigator who was working undercover for a jeweler — the jeweler from whom the pieces were originally stolen. What went wrong was that the P.I. brought them in too early, Nancy. He didn't have the case nailed down first. He didn't know what he was up against. He just sent the police in to do *his* job, essentially, and they were unprepared, didn't have enough men with them, went in like lambs to the slaughter. Bill made it out alive, obviously. Jack didn't. Bill was so devastated by Jack's death that he quit the force."

"He left the police force because of your husband's death?"

"Yes. He vowed that he would never let what happened to Jack happen to another cop. So he became a P.I. He hired himself out to jewelry companies. He stayed within his area of expertise. He caught his share of bad guys. And he *always* waited until he had enough evidence — enough information — before bringing in the police. Just the way he's doing now with this case that you and he are at odds about, the case that killed Nancy, the other Nancy."

"So he told you about the Levin case."

"He did. And there's no question that it's a complicated one, between his responsibility to Denham and Villier and your responsibility to your friends and family as well as to that child in your class."

"It's been difficult," I acknowledged.

"Yes, but what I'm telling you, Nancy, why I'm calling you, is that it's not recklessness or insensitivity that you see in Bill's behavior. It's a compulsiveness, a zealousness to ensure that all the i's are dotted and the t's are crossed so that he doesn't make the kind of mistake that killed Jack."

"That's very admirable but —"

"He knows what he's doing," Joan went on. "It must be hard for you to understand, because investigative work isn't your field, but he's a first-rate investigator with first-rate instincts. At the beginning of my marriage, I didn't agree with the rationale behind some of the decisions Jack would make. I was a writer for women's magazines. I knew about health and beauty, not cops and robbers. It took a while for me to 'get it.' "

"Joan, I appreciate that Bill is protective of cops, but what about innocent citizens like my parents and my friend, never mind me?"

"Oh, he's protective of you. Of all of you. Don't ever doubt that. He's trying to wind up the case as quickly as possible, for everybody's sake."

"Maybe so, but I've reached the point where I can't stand by and wait for someone I love to get killed."

"What if that someone's Bill?"

"That's not fair, Joan. You're asking me to choose between him and my family, him and my friends. I can't do that."

"I'm not asking you to make those kind of choices, Nancy. I'm simply asking you to keep in mind that men like Bill Harris don't come along every day."

CHAPTER TWENTY-SEVEN

The next morning at school, I told Janice about Joan Geisinger's phone call.

"She did give me new insight into Bill's behavior," I conceded, "but she didn't convince me that I should rush right back to him."

"You shouldn't," Janice agreed. "It's too dangerous."

Janice had rebounded well from the attack and, while she didn't harbor any ill will toward Bill because of his handling of the case, she was glad that I had cut my ties to him for the moment. The situation had become too risky, even for her taste.

"That's my feeling," I said. "No matter how well intentioned he is, I have to stay away from him until he brings the police into the case."

"In the meantime, you can't just wait around. You'd be wasting your good years."

"My good years?"

"Your marketable years. You're in your thirties, Nance. By the time Bill solves the case, you could be in your forties."

"So?"

"So, once women are in their forties, the only men they attract are in their fifties and up. And men in their fifties and up aren't looking for a soul mate; they're looking for someone to take them to the doctor. Their bodies don't hold up the way ours do, medically speaking."

"A fascinating viewpoint, Janice." She really had rebounded. She was her old pontificating self.

"And then there's the problem with having children. Men in their fifties and up either don't want to have children anymore, because they've already had them with the first wife, or they can't have them anymore, because their sperm counts have dwindled to nothing. Of course, some men in their fifties and up do want to have children, but they don't live long enough to see the kid graduate from high school and, therefore, aren't any help when it comes to the college tuition."

"Where are you going with all this, Janice?"

"Where I'm going is that you should let me fix you up now, before you're stuck with men in their fifties and up."

"Fix me up? Please."

"Why not? Stan has nice friends."

"I'm in love with Bill, that's why."

"But you're not *with* Bill, remember?"

"I'm not ready to date other men."

"Just one date."

"No."

"Come on. You can't sit home by yourself every night."

"I've done it before. I can do it again."

"Stan has one friend in particular I think you'd like. His name is Dan, which is easy to remember because it rhymes with Stan. Dan. Stan. Isn't that cute?"

"I'm not interested, Janice. Really."

"Dan's an opthalmologist," she said, continuing either to ignore or misinterpret my responses. "He's very bright, very knowledgeable."

"Great," I said. "When I feel a case of macular degeneration coming on, I'll call him."

"I'll have him call you," said Janice. "You can get acquainted over the phone and then the four of us will go out this weekend, okay?"

I looked at her and sighed. "Should I even bother to answer you?"

"I wouldn't."

Before long, the children began arriving. After our morning routine, we got right to work on our Middle Ages end-of-school project by reading a story about the period and discussing what it was like to live during that time. Next, we decorated the classroom's play area. We had about a month to make it look like the great hall of a medieval castle, and step one was having each child draw his own coat of arms and hang it on the wall. Later that morning, we held our first rehearsal for the song the children would sing at the celebration — the song that would be followed by the handing out of their diplomas, always an emotion-packed moment for the parents.

"Okay, everybody," I said, as Janice and I joined the children on the rug, rounding out the circle. "Miss Mason and I are going to sing you the special Middle Ages song and then explain what all the words mean, so it will be easier for you to learn it over the weeks ahead. On the day of the performance, you'll all be stars."

"What about our costumes?" asked Lindsay Greenblatt.

"We'll talk about that tomorrow," I said.

"Will my mommy come and see me?" asked Todd Delafield.

"Of course she will," I said. "All of your parents will come for the last-day-of-school celebration. That's why you have to learn the words to the song, so they'll say, 'Oh, my. Look how smart my child is. He or she is definitely ready for kindergarten.' "

"I don't want to go to kindergarten," wailed Fischer Levin. "I want to stay with you, Miss Stern."

"I'm going to miss you too, honey," I said. "Miss Mason and I are going to miss every single one of you, but kindergarten will be a wonderful adventure and you'll make lots of new friends there and learn lots of new things." Anxiety about moving up to kindergarten always reared its head a month or so before graduation, when the children realized that everything that was familiar to them about their school experience was about to disappear. It was scary for them to contemplate leaving Small Blessings for parts unknown, but it was going to be even scarier for poor Fischer, whose future would be truly uncertain once his father was arrested. "Now, are we all set for our special Middle Ages song?" I said, getting back to the lesson plan.

"Yeah, but Todd farted," said Fischer. "Tell him not to."

Janice asked Todd if he had to use the bathroom. He said he didn't because it was Fischer who had farted and tried to cover it up by blaming him.

427

After mediating this latest spat, Janice and I did a dry-run of the song, which we wrote to the tune of "I've Been Working on the Railroad." It went like this:

Way back in the Middle Ages,
Being a kid was great.
Serfs and peasants had to work hard
And they'd better not be late.

Kings and queens lived in castles.
They had knights to hunt and fight.
Girls were not allowed to do that
And it really wasn't right.

But!

(chorus)

That was long ago.
We'll tell you what we know.
Armors, shield, and coats of arms.
That was long ago.
We'll tell you what we know.
Feasts and colors bright.

No bathrooms. No stores.
No heat. No electric eyes . . .
No TVs. No VCRs.
And there weren't any cars.

But!

(chorus)

That was long ago.
We'll tell you what we know.
Armors, shields, and coats of arms.
That was long ago.
We'll tell you what we know.
Feasts and colors bright.
Hooray!

The children clapped when Janice and I finished singing. As I scanned their faces, faces I had come to know almost as well as my own, I felt a pang of sadness just as I always did as I neared the end of the school year. I had been with these kids since September, had been their teacher, their protector, their surrogate mother for several hours each day. Now they would go off to kindergarten and I would welcome a new crop of students and life would go on. It was the natural order of things, but even the natural order of things can make you a little melancholy, especially if you've just broken up with the man you love and your best friend wants to fix you up with an opthalmologist.

★ ★ ★

Dan did call me. He was very nice on the phone, very chatty. Yes, chatty is the perfect adjective to describe how he communicated. He spoke quickly, manically, barely took a second to catch his breath between sentences. He was zipping along about cataracts and how having them renders one's vision cloudy, as if a film has been placed directly over the eye, when my mind wandered and I remembered my first phone conversation with Bill. Unlike Dan, who had taken my question: "Tell me about your work" literally and gone into great detail about glaucoma and detached retinas and ocular nerve damage, Bill had been self-deprecating about being a jeweler, shy about it. He had wondered why someone who was on a first-name basis with Kevin Costner would go out with someone like him. Of course, he wasn't a jeweler at all, as it turned out, and I wasn't on a first-name basis with Kevin Costner, but our conversation had struck me as having a certain appealingly teenage quality to it.

Don't, I told myself. Don't start thinking longingly about Bill. He's in a dangerous profession, a crazy profession. That's why you're not with him. Dan, on the other hand, dilates people's pupils for a living.

The only crooks he deals with are the folks from the HMOs. Go out with him.

He suggested that we join Janice and Stan for dinner on Saturday night. I said I'd be delighted, but what I really was was beaten down by Janice. I couldn't face another lecture about men in their fifties and up. Dan, by the way, was thirty-nine. He had never been married, he told me, and was eager to settle down, start a family. "I want the wife, the kids, the house, the dog, the whole enchilada," he said in his rapid-fire way of talking.

And *I* want a man who doesn't use the expression "the whole enchilada," I thought as I hung up the phone.

Three out of four of us adored Thai food (I was the lone hold-out; putting scallions in tuna salad was about as exotic as I got). But the majority ruled and we went to a Thai place on Third Avenue that was all the rage, according to Janice, Stan, and Dan. Like Stan and Dan, the name of the restaurant rhymed. Jai-Ya Thai, it was called.

"The food here's incredible," said Dan as he was pulling out my chair for me. He was short and wiry, as was his reddish-brown hair, and he had a pointy nose and pointy teeth (the incisors, anyway). He wasn't unattractive by any means; he just wasn't Bill.

As for Stan, he was short and wiry too, and just as tightly coiled as Dan. In fact, I had never been in the presence of two men who were so wound up, so constantly in motion, so energetic. I actually whispered to Janice that I thought they must be on cocaine. "No," she assured me. "They're just high on life."

They were high on Thai food, that much was clear. The menu at Jai-Ya Thai rates the food for spiciness by placing one, two, or three stars next to each dish. Stan and Dan insisted on ordering three-star items, while Janice and I opted to play it safe with one-star entrees. The waiter tried to talk the men out of their choices, explaining that even the Asians who frequented the restaurant stuck with one stars. "We're not wusses," Dan told him, slapping the man on the back. "Give us the fire, man."

The waiter brought the fire for Stan and Dan. Then he brought the tamer stuff for Janice and me. Two minutes into the meal, I noticed that both Stan and Dan were weeping. The food was that incendiary, apparently.

"Are you all right?" I asked Dan.

He shook his head and gulped down an entire glass of water.

"Maybe you shouldn't have gone for the three-alarmer," I said.

He shook his head again. "This is what it's all about," he said, coughing and gagging and then drinking more water. "If I'm going to eat, I want to *feel* the heat." He shoveled another forkful into his mouth and started weeping all over again.

To each his own, I thought, as Stan and Dan turned the meal into a spectator sport. Janice and I watched as the two of them went head to head over their mee krob and dancing shrimp, eating and crying and eating and crying.

"Done," said Dan when he had cleaned his plate. He had beaten Stan to the finish line by a nose, his pointy nose. "How'd you like yours, Nancy?"

"It made my lips vibrate," I said.

"Excellent," he said approvingly. "Next time you'll move up to two stars."

There won't be a next time, I thought as we left the restaurant. I'd rather be home counting the fibers in my bedroom carpet.

I didn't say that to Dan, naturally. When he brought me back to my place, I invited him in for some tea and he described more maladies that bring people to the eye doctor.

"As a matter of fact, I think you've got a

broken blood vessel in your left eye," he said, sliding closer to me on the sofa. "Mind if I take a look?"

Before I could respond, he was in my face, peering at my eye.

"See anything?" I asked.

"Nope," he said without budging. "You're all clear."

"That's a relief." But it wasn't a relief because Dan didn't return to his original position on the sofa. Instead, he kissed me.

"Dan," I said after pulling away. "You're a terrific guy, really sweet, but I'm not available for a relationship right now. I'm involved with someone else. Janice should have told you."

He seemed surprised. Janice must have told him just the opposite.

"I'm sorry," I said as he got up from the sofa. "But I did enjoy meeting you. I hope you don't think our date was a total waste of time."

"Not total," he said as he walked toward the door. "You're getting up there in age."

"Excuse me?"

"You're in your late thirties, right?"

"Yes." I braced myself for a Janice-type lecture on my good years, my marketable years.

"Then it won't be long before you'll be

needing an opthalmologist," said Dan, who handed me his business card. "If I can't score with you one way, I'll score with you another, huh?"

He winked at me. I winked back. I did not bother to tell him that I already had an eye doctor, the one who'd treated me in November for the conjunctivitis.

"Give my office a shout," said Dan as he stepped into the hall. "In the meantime, maybe I'll run into you at the Thai place."

"Maybe." I smiled. And maybe not.

CHAPTER TWENTY-EIGHT

Going out to dinner with Dan on Saturday night made me miss Bill even more. (It made me swear off Thai food too; I nearly overdosed on Pepcid AC Chewables.) I longed to hear his voice, hear him tell me he still loved me. I was also, I had to admit, extremely curious how his investigation was coming along — whether he'd made progress in identifying the big shot who was jerking Levin and the others around. Most of all, I needed to know that he was all right. And so when I got home from school on Monday afternoon, I decided to break my vow of silence. I picked up the phone and called him at Denham and Villier.

"Hello," I said nervously when the switchboard operator answered. "Bill Harris, please."

"He's not in," she said. "I'll give you his voicemail."

Just like that. *I'll give you his voicemail.* Without even asking me if I wanted his voicemail. This is progress?

I hung up and redialed the number.

"Denham and Villier," said the switchboard operator.

"Hello. I'm calling for Bill Harris but I'd rather not leave a message," I told her. "Could you possibly tell me whether he's out for a few minutes or gone for the rest of the day?"

"I'll connect you with reception," she said and launched me into Muzak land.

A few seconds later a woman cut into an instrumental version of "Raindrops Keep Falling on My Head."

"Hello," she said. "Executive offices."

"Yes, hello," I said. "I'm calling for Bill Harris."

"Mr. Harris is out of the office," she said. "I'll give you his voice —"

"Wait!" I interrupted, before she could transfer me. "Will Mr. Harris be back today?"

"No, he won't," she said.

"Will he be back tomorrow?" I asked.

"No, he won't," she said.

"Will he be back on Wednesday?" I asked.

"No, he won't," she said.

"Look," I said, exasperated. "You could make this a lot easier for both of us if you'd just tell me when Mr. Harris *will* be back."

"I don't know, ma'am," she said. "He's

taking some time off."

"Time off?"

"That's right, ma'am. Would you like his voicemail?"

"No."

I hung up and considered this new development. Did Bill take time off to work on the case? I wondered. Was he down in Virginia seeing his kids? Or was he stretched out on a beach in Bali contemplating his navel?

As Bill's sons were coming to New York in a few weeks for the Memorial Day holiday, and as his work ethic was such that he would never fly off to the South Pacific and shirk his responsibilities, I narrowed the three possibilities down to one: He had gone undercover to wind up the case.

I was terribly conflicted, which wasn't uncommon for me since I'd met Bill. On one hand, I was thrilled that the end might be in sight, that he and I would be together sooner rather than later, that the whole mess would be over and done with. On the other, I was worried sick that something might happen to him. Men like Bill Harris didn't come along every day, as Joan Geisinger had rightfully pointed out. I could deal with the thought of our not working out our differences, if I had to, but I couldn't bear the thought of his being hurt — or worse.

I called his apartment. His answering machine picked up.

"Hi, Bill. It's Nancy," I said after the beep. "I hope you're okay. I love you. That's it, I guess."

And that *was* it. Days went by, then weeks, and Bill still didn't call me back. All I could do was wait. Wait and see how everything would turn out. I felt hopelessly passive.

At Small Blessings, Janice and I were busy getting the children ready for the Middle Ages celebration. We mailed a letter home to the parents asking them to send their child to school with an old pillowcase that we would make into a tunic. Of course, Small Blessings parents couldn't send their kid to school with just *any* old pillowcase; it had to be an old Ralph Lauren pillowcase, an old Pratesi pillowcase, an old pillowcase that was in far better shape than one of my *new* pillowcases. We had each child cut holes in his pillowcase for his head and arms, slip it on, and tie a rope around his waist to keep the tunic in place. Instant costumes.

We also had the children make swords out of pieces of cardboard and spray them with gold paint. We used the same materials for their crowns. Instant accessories to our instant costumes.

We had a Middle Ages feast instead of our regular lunch period. We cooked chicken legs and roasted potatoes and apple tarts, right next door to the classroom in the school's kitchen, and to wash everything down we served grape juice ("pretend wine") in plastic goblets I'd bought at a party store. The children were allowed to eat with their hands, because there was no silverware in the Middle Ages, we explained, and they got to dance to music which sounded medieval but was actually Mozart.

And every day leading up to the last day, we rehearsed the Middle Ages song that the children would be singing for the parents. They were learning the lyrics. They were learning the melody. They were learning their last lesson at Small Blessings. They were counting down to good-bye.

Oh, and there was one other order of business before graduation day. Each of our sixteen charges had to tell either Janice or me what they wanted to be when they grew up, and we would then write out their message in fancy script and insert the piece of paper inside their diploma.

Lindsay Greenblatt said that when she grew up, she wanted to be a vet and take care of people's dogs and cats but not their snakes.

Todd Delafield said that when he grew up, he wanted to be a man who drove race cars and have his mommy bring him chocolate milk when he got tired.

Alexis Shuler said that when she grew up, she wanted to marry Todd Delafield.

And so on.

What did Fischer Levin want to be when he grew up? A pirate who hunted for buried treasure, just like his dad. I had trouble writing that one down, but I didn't have much choice.

Eventually, Friday, May 22nd, the last day of school at Small Blessings, arrived, and it was chaos as expected. Ours wasn't the only class having a last-day celebration, so there were crowds of parents and guests and caregivers milling about the halls.

And then there was Victoria Bittner dashing frantically between our rooms, asking to borrow some paint, then some brushes, then some turpentine. She had created yet another mural in her classroom and was not only behind schedule but out of supplies.

That's her problem, I thought. I've got enough of my own today. It wasn't simply the last-minute preparations that had me rattled; it was the suspense of whether or not Bob Levin would show up to watch his kid graduate — and, if so, what he would say or do to me. I hadn't seen him since the notorious samba incident at the spring fundraiser, and so much had happened since then: Uncle Dave's concussion, my parents' robbery, Janice's night visitor, my breakup with Bill. Would he keep upping the ante as I kept predicting? Would he be desperate enough to do it on his son's last day of school?

My anxiety level rose as Janice and I got the children dressed in their tunics and crowns and swords and positioned them in the play area, amid their coats of arms. When everybody was in place, I punched Play on the tape player, and sounds of our medieval/Mozart music heralded the start of our ceremony.

"You may all enter the great hall!" I said, summoning the waiting parents inside the classroom.

They filed in. Mr. and Mrs. Shuler. Mr. and Mrs. Delafield. Mr. and Mrs. Woolsey. But no Mr. and Mrs. Levin. Where were they? And what did their absence signify?

I didn't have time to figure it out. I was busy greeting everybody and inviting them to sit in the little chairs we'd set up on the other side of the room or, for those with video cameras, to stand near the chairs.

I was about to begin the program when I finally spotted Bob Levin. My heart did a flip in my chest. Where was Gretchen Levin? I wondered as he made his way into the classroom, eyeing me with malicious intent. Where was Olga? And who were the five badly dressed men flanking him — men I didn't recognize as any of the other children's daddies?

I nodded in their direction and whispered to Janice, "Do you know those guys huddled together over there next to Bob Levin?"

"No," she whispered back, "but there's something fishy about them. I overheard Mrs. Shuler ask one of them which child he was here to see, and he said they were all here to see Fischer because they were his uncles!"

"Fischer's uncles. Yeah, right." I knew it, knew the bastard would pull something.

"You think they're Levin's guys?"

"What else?"

"But why would they come here?"

"To scare me. To intimidate me into returning the brooch. How better to get me to do what they want than by giving me the impression that they're willing to put the children at risk? That's what they're doing, I bet. They're saying: 'You don't hand over the brooch, we'll hurt the kids.' "

"But what about Fischer? Levin isn't evil

enough to let anything happen to his own kid, is he?"

"No. They're bluffing, I'm sure of it. Bill says they're not interested in hurting anybody, just getting the brooch back." Pretty ironic that I was suddenly taking his position, huh? Was it wishful thinking or did I finally trust him? I didn't know.

"Jesus, Nance. What should we do? Call security?"

"I have a better idea. Bill's hope was to manipulate a meeting of these guys, get them in a situation where they're seen together, incriminated together, photographed together. Well, here they are in our very own classroom. How perfect is that?"

"Perfect? Are you crazy?"

"No, I just want this case to be over. So here's what I want you to do."

"Me?"

"Yes. You're Miss Just-Do-It, remember?"

She rolled her eyes.

"I want you to tiptoe over to James Woolsey's father and ask him — very quietly — if you can borrow his video camera. And then, when I start the program, I want you to focus the camera lens on Fischer's *uncles* and catch them talking — to each other and to Levin. Got it?"

"Yeah, but what if Mr. Woolsey won't part with his video camera?"

"Tell him I'll flunk his kid."

She nodded and did as I asked. Mr. Woolsey gave up the camera, and I gave her a discreet thumbs-up.

I stepped to the center of the room.

"Good morning, ladies and gentlemen," I said, "and welcome to our special Middle Ages graduation ceremony. The children will be performing a song they've worked hard to learn, and after that we'll be handing out their diplomas. But first, I'd like to say what a wonderful class we've had this year and how much we'll miss each child." I went on about how well the kids did in all aspects of our preschool curriculum and what a breeze kindergarten was going to be for them. Blah blah blah. I had made the speech a thousand times, but this time I was more than a little distracted. "And now, without further ado, here are our stars!"

I walked back to the rug, knelt down in front of the kids, and asked them if they were ready.

"Yes, Miss Stern," they said, including Alexis Shuler, who had been cured of her lisp and could now pronounce my name correctly.

We began to sing. I tried to keep my mind

on kings and queens and serfs and peasants.

We were in the middle of the chorus when we were interrupted by Penelope, of all people. Or, rather, by Penelope's voice. It came blaring over the intercom that was used only for emergencies.

"Attention! Attention!" she bellowed. "I'm sorry to report that there's been a gas leak in the basement and we'll have to cut all our graduating ceremonies short in order to evacuate the building. Children will go first, accompanied by teachers. Once again, children first. As soon as every child is outside and accounted for, parents and other visitors may join them on the street. Please do not panic. Everyone will be fine provided they remain calm. Once again, children first. Children first."

What in the world is this? I thought. A gas leak? On the last day of school? We'd never had a gas leak in all the years I'd worked at Small Blessings.

My gaze went straight to Levin and the "uncles," to gauge their reaction, to determine if they were somehow responsible for the interruption in the program. They looked as stunned as the rest of us.

There was complete bedlam as Janice rushed over to help me herd the children out of the room. Some of the kids were scared and wanted to stay with their parents. Some of them were relieved that they wouldn't have to remember the rest of the words to the Middle Ages song. Either way, there was gridlock as we attempted to assemble all of our crowned and sworded and tunic-ed graduates, lead them down the hall, and keep them moving once they merged with the children and teachers from the other three classrooms.

"I didn't even know we had gas in this building," I heard Nick Spada remark to Fran Golden. "The place has oil heat and electric kitchen appliances. So what's there to leak?"

Nick had a point, but I couldn't address it at that moment. I had to concentrate on the children.

When we got the class out to the street, I was startled to see a dozen cops spilling out of the police cars that had come screeching up to the curb in front of the building.

"They sure are taking this gas leak seriously," Janice mused as the cops raced inside.

"I'll say. I guess the parents will be evacuated next. Fischer's uncles, too."

I was about to add that it was too bad the cops weren't there to arrest them instead of overseeing a gas leak, when Janice and I saw

Bill — Bill — running into the building, right on the cops' heels.

"My God!" I said excitedly, as the light in my brain finally went on. "This gas leak thing is a setup, a trap. Bill must have identified the uncles, found out they were all going to school with Levin today, and decided the time was right to call in the police."

"And the cops must have given Penelope that script to read over the intercom," she said.

"I've got to go back inside," I said. "If Bill *has* turned the case over to the police, he shouldn't even be here. Essentially, he's out of it now — or supposed to be."

"Yeah, but what can you do, Nance, except put both of you in the cops' way?"

"I can help him, Janice," I said, thinking of Joan Geisinger's poor husband. "I don't know how, but I'm about to find out. Can you handle things here without me?"

She nodded. "I've got the other teachers around, plus the parents are starting to come out of the building. There'll be plenty of us to watch the kids."

"Thanks. I owe you one."

"You owe me two," she said. "You never thanked me for fixing you up with Dan."

I blew her a kiss and ran back inside Small Blessings.

CHAPTER TWENTY-NINE

As I reentered the building, I noticed that there was an eerie calm about the place. I didn't see a single cop, either. It was as if all the tumult had died down, as if the commotion had drifted out onto the street, leaving the school with an echoey, deserted feeling.

Still, as I made my way back to my classroom, I knew full well that there were about to be fireworks and I began to tense up, gear up for what lay ahead.

Please let Bill be okay, I repeated over and over. Please let him have the sense to step aside and watch the action from the sidelines.

Doubting that he would even consider such a plan, I sped up my pace, scurrying down the hall until I finally neared my classroom.

I stopped when I heard loud, combative voices coming from the open door. I took a deep breath and peered inside.

There was a batallion of cops with their backs to me. I couldn't see their faces but I could see their pieces. That's right. The police had Bob Levin and the five uncles at gunpoint. Gunpoint! In *my* classroom! In *my* nursery school! Even though the only guns allowed at Small Blessings were glue guns, staple guns, and the very occasional squirt gun!

But that wasn't the whole story. One of the uncles had a gun too, and he was pressing it against the side of Penelope's head! The man was actually threatening to shoot my boss if the cops didn't let everybody go! Of course, what gave the scene an even more bizarre twist was that instead of pleading with him not to carry her off, Penelope was pleading with Bob Levin to make one more donation to Small Blessings before the cops carried *him* off! She wasn't worried about losing her life; she was worried about losing her library!

"Drop the gun, buddy," one of the cops told Levin's goon. "You're not going anywhere and you know it."

"My friends and I are gettin' outta here," he countered, tightening his grip around Penelope, "or else this bitch's brains are gonna go *splat* all over the ceiling."

As the cops and Levin's people fired threats at each other, I looked for Bill. I knew he was around somewhere, but where?

I ducked back out into the hall and went in search of him, sticking my head in the kitchen, sticking my head in the utility room, sticking my head in the neighboring classrooms. I was sticking my head in Victoria Bittner's classroom when I heard a chair tumble over onto the floor.

"Hello?" I said tentatively, figuring one of Victoria's kids might be hiding, afraid and alone as a result of all the confusion. "It's okay to come out now. It's only Miss Stern from next door. I'd be glad to —"

Before I could finish, Bill emerged from his crouched position behind the piano. "Nancy, what are you doing here? You should have been evacuated with the others."

I ignored the question and ran to him, threw my arms around him, hugged him tightly. It had felt like ages since I'd seen him. He looked haggard, exhausted, impossibly handsome. "You did it," I said jubilantly. "You engineered the meeting of Levin's guys, didn't you? You got all of them together, cracked the case, and called the police. Oh, Bill. It's over."

He gave me a quick kiss, then shushed me. "It's not over," he whispered. "First, Levin's boss is still at large. I got all of them together *except* him. Second, there's a goddamn standoff in progress, right in your class-room. One of them's got Penelope."

"Yes, but the police will take care of her," I said. "They'll track down the head guy too, now that they're up to speed on the case. They can do their job now, Bill. Yours is finished."

"That's not how I operate and you know it. I'm not leaving until everybody who should be in handcuffs is. Once that happens, the cops *can* go after the head guy by offering one of these guys a plea bargain. The main thing is to get them in custody."

I wanted to talk him out of staying. I wanted to persuade him that he and I should run for our lives. I wanted to tell him that he didn't have to be the hero, that he already was the hero. But why bother? I couldn't change who he was and didn't really want to, not anymore.

"If you're staying, I'm staying too," I said.

"Go home, Nancy. I'll call you as soon as we're done."

I shook my head. "You need me."

"No, I need to get into your classroom. I've got to end that standoff in there, got to distract Levin's guys so the police can regain control of the situation."

"Fine. I'll distract them. I'll yell Boo! and Levin will have another heart attack, although he looks as if he's recovered. He's probably on medication or something."

"Nancy." He sighed. "Time is running out. I've got to get into your classroom, whether it's through a window, an air conditioning duct, whatever."

"Forget windows and air conditioning ducts. You can get in through here." I pointed to the interior door that opened into my classroom. It was camouflaged by one of Victoria's masterpieces — a painted mural of the beach scene she had created especially for the last day of school — so it was easy to mistake it for one of the walls that was covered with her artistry. "The door leads right where we want to go," I said. "The two rooms are adjoining, Bill."

"Adjoining?"

I nodded and started poking around Victoria's classroom, in the cubbies, in the play area, in the book shelves.

"What are you doing?" said Bill.

"Looking for weapons," I said.

"Weapons?" He permitted himself a wry smile. "Ah, so your plan is to sneak in through this door and pelt the bad boys with *Thomas the Tank Engine* storybooks?"

"Do you have a better idea?"

"Not yet."

"Then why don't you zip it and give me

another minute?" I continued to search for something to use against the crooks, something that would unnerve them, make them vulnerable, make them putty in the police's hands.

"Putty! That's it!" I said, forgetting to keep my voice down.

"Shhh."

"Sorry."

"Are you talking about Silly Putty?" asked Bill.

"Close. I'm talking about Space Mud," I said. "It's a little softer than Silly Putty. Wetter too."

"Look, Nancy. I'm sure you mean well, but —"

"Come here." I pulled Bill over to the sand table, which is a furniture staple in most preschool classrooms. It's basically a rectangular frame on legs with a plastic tub that fits inside. Sometimes, we fill the tub with sand. Sometimes, we fill it with finger paint. Sometimes, we even fill it with chocolate pudding. The point is to have the children stick their hands in it, stick their toys in it, play touchy-feely in it. "A sensory experience" is how the teachers' manuals describe it. On this last day of school, Victoria had filled the tub inside her sand table with Space Mud. "It's slime, Bill," I explained when he continued to seem bewildered. "You must have seen it when you visited my class in January."

"I've probably blocked it out," he said.

"Oh, stop. It's supposed to look gross, but it's just a combination of Elmer's glue and water and Borax. Judging by this batch, Victoria added some green food coloring to hers." I removed the cover from the sand table, took hold of Bill's hand and dunked it in the squishy, goopy, blobby Space Mud.

"Yech," he said, withdrawing it instantly. "What do you propose to do with this stuff?"

"How about moving the table right next to the connecting door, opening the door as surreptitiously as possible, and then grabbing handfuls of the Space Mud — balls of it — and hurling it at Levin's guys? If it lands in their eyes, it'll either bounce off them or stick to them — blinding them for a second or two with any luck. If it lands on their face, it'll adhere to their skin and then drip down onto their clothes — not a comfortable sensation. And if it lands on the floor in front of them, it'll make them slip and fall — also good for our team. It'll distract them in any event. You did say you wanted to distract them, didn't you, Bill?"

He stared at me, his expression skeptical, but he stuck his hand back into the tub and swished it around in the slimy substance.

"See? It's kind of fun," I said when he wasn't so quick to pull his hand out this time. "And best of all, it's not a gun. I know you must have one on you, Bill, but I'd rather you didn't use it unless it's absolutely necessary. We *are* in a nursery school."

"I left the gun at home. I have kids of my own, remember?"

I was about to tell him what a wonderful, sensitive, caring man he was when we both heard Penelope scream. Things were not going well inside my classroom.

"Okay. The Space Goo is worth a try," Bill conceded.

"Space *Mud*," I corrected him.

"Right. It's not exactly the armament of choice for resolving a hostage situation, but we've got to do something."

"When in Rome," I reminded him.

We lifted the sand table and carried it over to the door between the two rooms, then opened the door and peeked through. Sure enough, the goon was still holding the gun to Penelope's head.

"How's your arm?" Bill whispered to me.

"I won't be pitching for the Yankees this season, but it's not bad," I said.

"How about your aim?"

"We'll see."

We plunged our hands into the tub of Space Mud, pulled out blobs of the green glop, reared back, and fired.

"Whoa, baby!" I said, after chucking my first slime ball and watching it make contact with Bob Levin, the primo slime ball. It landed smack on his head — on top of his curly brown hair — and stuck to it. Stunned, he reached up and tried to yank the glutinous stuff off, only to yank off his toupee!

"Well, what do you know?" I laughed, nudging Bill. "The Polo King wears a rug."

He barely acknowledged me. He was more concerned with his own targets. He had missed the guy with the gun on his first try and ended up hitting Penelope — in the mouth. Talk about stunned! She had been ranting about how the scandal would kill enrollments at Small Blessings when the goop shut her right up. It clung to her lips, then oozed down her chin, into her neck, onto her precious *pearls.*

We kept going back for more Space Mud and flinging it — and causing a major uproar in the process. All the participants were ducking now, trying to defend themselves, but we didn't give up the fight until Bill shot his wad, so to speak. He threw a fastball at

Penelope's gun-wielding assailant — at the guy's family jewels, to be perfectly candid. His intention wasn't to maim him (Space Mud does get hard the longer it's exposed to the air, but not *that* hard); he just wanted to make him drop the gun. Mission accomplished.

Once Penelope was freed, the cops descended on the bad guys, although they had their ups and downs getting to them — literally. Some of our errant throws were now gooey, sticky puddles on the floor, and navigating across the room was a little treacherous. I felt sorry for Mr. Alvarez, Small Blessings's janitor, whose final day of the school year would include the cleanup of my otherwise tidy classroom.

Det. Burt Reynolds, who arrived at the scene as Levin and his partners were being handcuffed and led away, offered Bill a begrudging thanks for his help in the Nancy Stern murder investigation.

One look at their body language and I could sense immediately that Bill had been right about how territorial cops and private investigators are; neither side really wants the other's input, and both sides really want the credit for solving cases.

Or was it something else I was sensing? The minute Bill spotted the detective, he seemed angry at Reynolds — angry as opposed to competitive — and I didn't know why, other than that the cop wasn't exactly Mr. Congeniality.

"Hey, buddy. Nancy here deserves a thank-you too," Bill told the detective in an uncharacteristically challenging tone. "Your guys wouldn't have been successful today if it hadn't been for her ingenuity."

Detective Reynolds seemed amused by Bill's remark. "So she's pretending to be a cop these days." He chuckled. "A few months ago, she was pretending to be a celebrity journalist. What's she gonna pretend to be next week? A professional wrestler?"

Obviously, the detective hadn't forgotten our first conversation, when I had confessed to making believe I was the other Nancy Stern. It wasn't very nice of him to try to embarrass me with it now, I thought. He was a pain in the ass, as a matter of fact. No wonder Bill hadn't wanted to deal with him.

"For your information, Detective Reynolds," I said, straightening my posture, "I pretended to be another woman because I felt that my life was inferior to hers. I'm sure I don't have to explain what it's like to feel inferior. Not to you, Detective. You must have plenty of days when you'd rather be anyone but yourself."

I smiled sweetly, linked my arm through Bill's, and left the building with my man by my side.

CHAPTER THIRTY

Since our graduation ceremony had been so
rudely interrupted, Janice and I were forced
to mail the children's diplomas to them. We
did not mail Fischer's, however. I wanted to
stop by his apartment and deliver his in
person, to show him I still cared about him
no matter what his father had done. I was also
eager to see how he was managing now that
Levin and his cohorts were behind bars; how
he and his mother were coping with the
scandal swirling around them. Co-op boards
aren't particularly forgiving when a resident
of the building turns out to be a felon, and I
could easily imagine the board that oversaw
the Levins' opulent digs tossing Gretchen
and Fischer out on the street.

When I arrived at their apartment the
Friday before Memorial Day, I found that
the family was, indeed, packing up.

"We're moving to the Connecticut
house," Mrs. Levin informed me after
thanking me profusely for bringing
Fischer's diploma. She not only didn't hold

a grudge against me for my part in her husband's downfall, she seemed downright grateful.

"For the summer?" I asked as we stood in the foyer.

"For the foreseeable future," she said. "The house is in *my* name. Bob's lawyers can't touch it. And the public schools are excellent up there."

"Public schools? I thought Fischer was going to Horace Mann. Wasn't that why you and Mr. Levin donated so much money to Small Blessings? So Penelope would write Fischer a glowing recommendation? Wasn't it extremely important to you that your son got into the best private schools?"

Gretchen Levin smiled wistfully and invited me to sit down in the living room. I checked the bottoms of my shoes before following her onto that white carpet.

"A lot of things used to be important to me," she said with a deep sigh. "But discovering that the man you married is a thief and a murderer, not to mention a sniveling coward, can alter your priorities significantly."

The bit about the sniveling coward referred to Bob Levin's willingness, within seconds of his arrest, to surrender the name and whereabouts of the organization's kingpin. I'd nearly fainted when Bill came home that night and told me who it was.

"Detective Reynolds?" I gasped after he'd broken the news.

"The very same," he said. "I suspected him from the get-go but didn't have a stitch of proof."

"But what made you suspect him?" I asked. "He's a cop, for God's sake."

"You spend enough time around cops, you can smell the bad ones a mile away. According to Levin, who gave Reynolds up hoping to save his own skin, the detective needed money and figured gem thefts would be a quick way to make some."

I flashed back to the first time I'd met Burt Reynolds, in his office at the police station just after Nancy's murder. He'd told me he needed money, come to think of it; griped about having a wife he was dying to divorce; claimed she wanted big bucks in alimony but he wasn't a rich man. Yes, that's what he'd said. I remembered distinctly.

"Now it all makes sense to me," I'd mused to Bill. "The way Reynolds blew off your theories about the case. Obviously, there was more than professional rivalry going on between you. He was afraid you'd find out what he was up to."

I was replaying that conversation in my

mind when Gretchen Levin asked if I wanted something to drink, drawing me back to the present.

"No, thanks," I said, feeling bitter on her behalf about what a rat her husband turned out to be. "All this must be very traumatic for you and Fischer."

"We'll be fine. Truly."

"I hope so. I worry about that little guy, you know. He's very dear to me."

"You're dear to him too, Miss Stern. But I do think he'll be fine, once he adjusts to our new situation. The fact that he and I are going to family counseling should help."

"Counseling? When I had suggested therapy for Fischer during the school year, Penelope gave me the impression that you weren't a fan of it."

"I wasn't, but that was before." She paused. "As I said, your priorities change when you've been through what I have. Since Bob's arrest and my decision to divorce him, I've had to reevaluate every aspect of my life, including the way I've raised Fischer. And what I've concluded is that I've been a selfish woman. I intend to do things differently from now on."

"I'm glad to hear that, really I am, but how will you be able to support yourself and Fischer, even if you do scale back your lifestyle? Are you planning to work?"

She laughed. "I said I've been a selfish woman, not a stupid one. I didn't fritter away *all* of Bob's money on clothes and lunches and cosmetic surgery. I kept some for a rainy day, believe me."

I believed her. Apparently, Gretchen Levin wasn't the complete airhead I'd thought she was. I was about to ask her if Olga would be staying on after she and Fischer moved to Connecticut, but then the caregiver herself opened the front door, her young charge waddling along beside her.

Fischer broke out into a huge grin when he saw me and chugged into my arms.

"How's my graduate?" I said, wrapping him in a hug. "You doing okay, honey?"

He nodded but kept his head buried in my arms.

"I brought your diploma," I said, rocking him. "Your mommy can buy a nice frame for it and hang it up in your room." I didn't add that I had removed the what-I-want-to-be-when-I-grow-up testimonial in which he had aspired to being just like his dad.

"I won't be living in my same room," he said, finally coming up for air.

"Then you can hang it in your room in Connecticut," I suggested. "I bet it's pretty up there, Fischer, with all those trees and lakes and biking trails. Will you let me come for a visit sometime?"

I had hoped that by inviting myself to his house, I would be giving him a sense of continuity, a sense that I, unlike his father, was not abandoning him. But instead of reassuring him, my question made him cry. As he had never cried during the entire school year, I was terribly shaken by his tears.

"What is it, honey?" I said, rubbing his arm, choking back my own tears. No matter how successfully Gretchen Levin rehabilitated herself, Fischer had a tough road ahead of him. It wasn't going to be fun being the only kid in class with a jailbird for a father.

"I just wish . . ."

"Wish what?"

"That it was the last day of school all over again, only this time, Miss Dibble wouldn't make us leave because of the gas leak."

The gas leak. Right. I wiped away his tears, but what I wanted to wipe away was the memory of his father in handcuffs, the fact that a day that should have been his proudest was his cruelest. "Nothing can take that day away from you, Fischer. Nothing and nobody. You finished preschool. You learned everything you were supposed to learn. You're all ready for kindergarten just like the other children."

"But we never finished the song. Miss Dibble made us stop in the middle."

"So you don't *feel* like you really graduated, is that it?"

"Kind of."

"Well, that's a snap to fix." I took his hands in mine. "How about if you and I sing the whole song for your mommy and Olga?"

"The whole song the whole way through. No stopping."

"You got it."

We sang the whole song the whole way through. When we were done, Gretchen and Olga clapped and Fischer beamed.

Hold this picture in your mind, I told myself. Remember it the next time you think your job is drudgery, the next time you're bored in the classroom, the next time you long for a career that's *glamorous*. Remember that you made it possible for a little boy with an uncertain future to feel as if he accomplished something.

Nothing small about that blessing.

Bill's kids came for Memorial Day weekend — a quickie visit as they had to get home to Virginia to finish their school term in mid-June. Since there wasn't time for a major excursion outside the city, they stayed at Bill's apartment and took day trips — to a Yankees game in the Bronx, to Sherwood Island State Park in Connecticut, to the South Street Seaport in lower Manhattan.

I'd asked them if they wanted to pal around, just the three of them, but they insisted I join them for every activity. "You're practically part of the family," said Peter, the older boy. "You're like Dad's *wife*," his younger brother Michael chimed in.

Michael's comment provoked nervous giggles. It's always a little awkward when people speak of you as if you're married even though you and your partner haven't discussed getting married.

Which brings me to the night that Bill and I did discuss getting married. Peter and Michael had gone to bed, and I was about to head back to my apartment for the night. I didn't feel comfortable staying at Bill's when his sons were there, didn't think it was appropriate for their father and me to sleep together during their visits. Bill didn't understand why.

"Because we're not married," I explained as we stood in the lobby of his building. "Call me old-fashioned, but I'd rather your sons view me as a role model, not as some woman who's having sex with their old man."

468

"The two aren't mutually exclusive," said Bill. "You can be a role model *and* have sex with their old man. Besides, they must have figured out that you have sex with their old man. They're not babies."

"Yes, but I don't have sex with their old man when they're right in the next room and can hear everything."

"But you would if we were married?"

"I guess so. Quietly."

"Look, why don't we get married then."

"Just so we can have sex when your kids are in the next room?"

"Nancy. I'm asking you to marry me. I'm sorry this isn't a more romantic setting, but if you say yes, we'll find a romantic setting for the wedding. The important point is that I love you."

"I love you too, but marriage is a big step, Bill. There's a lot to consider."

"Like what?"

"Your job. Are you going to stay on at Denham as their private security investigator?"

"I plan to, yes."

"So I'd have to worry about you constantly, worry that you were chasing after criminals."

"That's better than having to worry about me chasing after women, isn't it? And don't

469

forget the discount Denham gives me. You'd be swimming in jewelry."

"Just what I've always wanted. Where would we live?"

"At my place for now. There isn't enough room at yours for the boys."

"Speaking of whom, how would they react to our getting married?"

"They love you, Nancy. They loved you the first minute they saw you. Like father, like sons."

"They're great kids and we did have an instant rapport. I wonder how they'd feel if you and I had kids of our own though."

"I can't speak for them, but I'm all for it."

"You don't have a problem with starting a whole new family?"

"Nope."

"You're sure you want more children?"

"I'm sure."

I didn't say anything. I had run out of questions, conditions, obstacles. As a matter of fact, I couldn't think of a single reason why I shouldn't marry Bill Harris. Yes, we had known each other for barely a year, but what a year it had been. We had fallen in love believing we were two other people. We had stayed in love after finding out we weren't who we'd claimed to be. And we had held fast to our love even in the face of robbers, murderers, and Space Mud.

"This is it then?" I asked after a few seconds. "This is the proposal?"

"This is it," said Bill. "The moment of truth."

"Something's missing," I said. "I didn't picture it this way, with the two of us standing in the lobby of your building like two people deciding what movie to see."

"How about if only one of us is standing?"

"Bill."

He got down on the floor and perched himself on bended knee, assuming The Position, all six-foot-four inches of him. People were staring at him. "Is this better?"

"Much."

He smiled. "Will you marry me, Nancy Stern? Will you go from being my wrong number to being my wife?"

"I will." As Bill got up to embrace me, I said a silent thank-you to the other Nancy Stern, without whom my transition from wrong number to wife would not have been possible.

We told Peter and Michael our news the next morning. They said, "Cool." I told my parents shortly after that. They said, "When?" I told Janice later that morning, after she'd come home from a night at

Stan's. She said, "Courage."

"Courage?" I said. I'd thought it was an odd response, even for Janice.

"You'll need it," she said. "Bill's as good as they get, but he's still a man. Men require courage on our part, Nance."

"Things aren't going well with Stan, is that it?" I asked.

"They're going fine with Stan," she said, "but the neuroses are starting to reveal themselves."

I smiled to myself. "In what way?"

"He never empties the dishwasher. He loads it, is a whiz at organizing what goes where and how to fit it all in, squirts the liquid Cascade in the little compartment, closes the door, and pushes Start. But empty it when it's finished? Not a chance, even if he's hungry and there are no clean dishes in the kitchen cabinets. He'll go out and buy paper plates before he'll empty the dishwasher."

"You've discussed this with him?"

"Sure, but he's in denial about it. He thinks it's *my* problem."

"I don't mean to take his side against you, Janice, but maybe it isn't a problem at all. Maybe it's just an eccentricity. You can live with an eccentricity much easier than you can live with a problem, you know?"

"Well, that's a switch: You giving me advice about men. Who'd have predicted it. You were the innocent little fawn, remember?"

"I remember. Boy, that feels like a long time ago, doesn't it?"

"It does." There was a bittersweet note in her voice, as if she thought she might be losing me, losing her best friend. "So have you and Bill set a date for the wedding?"

"Not yet, but there's one detail that is set. You're going to be my maid of honor. At least, I hope you will, Janice."

"I'd be crushed if you picked someone else. Of course, I'd rather be your *matron* of honor, but Stan's dragging his feet."

"Dragging his feet? You met him a month ago."

"Which means he's had thirty days to consider my proposal."

"You asked him to marry you on your first date? Just like you did with Gary, the nutritionist-sociopath?"

"You betcha."

"What are you going to do if he says yes?"

"Marry the guy."

"Oh, Janice. Do you love Stan?"

"Sure, why not?"

"I'm serious. Do you love him or are you settling? I'd hate to see you marry a man simply because he's willing to marry you. You're better than that. You deserve better. Don't you realize that?"

She laughed. "When you were the innocent little fawn, you weren't so blunt."

"But you don't mind, do you?"

"I don't mind."

CHAPTER THIRTY-ONE

Bill and I decided to get married over Labor Day weekend. The question was: Where? Everyone had an opinion. When we went to Maryland, so I could meet Bill's parents, the consensus was that we should have the wedding there. When we went to Pennsylvania, so we could spend time with my parents, the consensus was that we should have the wedding there. When we went to the New Jersey shore, so we could stay with Janice and Stan for a few days, the consensus was that we should have the wedding there.

The matter was settled when we went to Block Island, Rhode Island, so we could get away by ourselves. After four idyllic days there, we knew without a doubt where we would be married.

A charming island only seven miles long and three-and-a-half miles wide, "the Block," as it's often called, is a throwback to another era. Less precious than Nantucket, less celebrity-studded than Martha's Vineyard, it has no golf courses, no fancy restaurants, no gated estates. What it does have are spectacular beaches, verdant, rolling hills, anchorages dotted with sailboats, and weathered, shingled houses that have withstood their share of nor'easters. It's a salty place where the lobsters really are "just caught," a nature-lover's paradise, the coast of Maine without the long car ride. Neither Bill nor I had ever been there before, but from the instant we stepped off the ferry from Point Judith, we felt as if we'd found *our* romantic haven.

During our four days on Block Island, we scouted locations for the wedding, eventually narrowing the candidates down to two. There was the grand old Spring House, where we were staying, a Victorian hotel with wide verandas and sweeping lawns, both with views of the Atlantic; and the Sea Breeze Inn, a cluster of rustic cottages nestled in a meadow of wildflowers that peeked out over the ocean.

"You know what?" I said. "We can choose both. Let's have the wedding at the Spring House and spend our wedding night and honeymoon at the Sea Breeze."

"Great minds think alike," said Bill. "I was going to suggest the same thing."

There were details to work out, obviously, but by the end of the long weekend, we'd worked them out. We would have the ceremony on the lawn of the Spring House, cocktails on the seaside veranda, and dinner in the enclosed sunroom. After the party, our guests would stay at the hotel, while Bill and I would move over to the Sea Breeze — specifically, to Cottage #10, the most private of the inn's accommodations and the one boasting the best view. Tucked away at the rear of the property, it was a cozy spot with a bedroom, a living room, and a porch facing the water and meadow. Basic. Beautiful. Perfect.

Everything was arranged — the food, the ferry reservations, even the justice of the peace. I was marrying the man I loved on an island I loved with the people I loved around me. Was I happy? *Floating* was more like it.

When we got back to New York, I thought of nothing but the wedding, aided and abetted in my obsession by Janice, who had plenty of free time, having broken up with Stan.

"He didn't want to get married?" I asked as we stood in the Wedding Books section of Barnes & Noble one Sunday afternoon. Now that she was back in circulation, she was delighted to accompany me to her favorite haunt.

"He *did* want to get married. *I* didn't," she

said, surprising me. "I didn't love him, Nance. I knew it the second he proposed."

"The second he accepted your proposal, you mean."

"Exactly. I would have been settling if I married him. You were right about holding out for the one and only, so that's what I'm going to do."

"I'm really glad, Janice. I'm sure the breakup is painful, but you'll look back on it and realize it was for the best."

"Yup. In the meantime, there's a cute guy over there in Cookbooks. Stan couldn't cook to save his life."

Before I could stop her, she was off on another adventure. Or misadventure, depending.

Lucky me, I thought. I'm off the market. I have Bill. Forever.

I was whistling my way toward the end of the summer, the picture of contentment, shopping for my wedding dress, writing thank-you notes to people who sent us wedding gifts, packing up my clothes and books and odds and ends in preparation for the official move to Bill's apartment.

I was cleaning out the kitchen, emptying all the drawers and sorting their contents into either Save or Chuck cartons, when I finally tackled what I always called the junk drawer. You know, the one you stuff with coupons and batteries and ads for things you mean to buy but don't. As I rummaged through the drawer, throwing away practically every item in it, I came upon a letter . . . a letter I had, apparently, never gotten around to opening . . . a letter that was badly stained as a result of its close proximity to a leaky packet of soy sauce, the kind that comes with takeout Chinese dinners along with the duck sauce and the hot mustard.

Yuck, I thought as I examined the sticky envelope which, by the way, was crawling with ants.

I giggled. The paper was discolored, but I could easily make out the return address (Denham and Villier) and the postmark (New York City, December eleventh of the previous year).

So it was from Bill!

I laughed again as I realized that the probable reason I hadn't opened it was that I had just met and fallen in love with him. I'd been so consumed with our budding romance then, so consumed with the fear that he'd find out I wasn't the other Nancy Stern, that it was a miracle I hadn't tossed everything I owned into the junk drawer.

But this letter can't be from Bill, I reminded myself with a start. He didn't know who I really was on December eleventh. He didn't learn the truth about me until Christmas Eve, after Nancy was murdered. He didn't even know my name.

I tore open the hopelessly browned envelope and lifted out the letter, which was handwritten on Denham and Villier's once-creamy stationery.

"Dear Nancy," it read. "As you've heard, we have an old friend in common: Joan Geisinger."

I put down the letter.

It was for *her*, not me! Bill had mailed the other Nancy Stern a letter, it had been deposited in my mailbox, and I'd forgotten to give it to her! But why had he written to her when he had already met me? Why had he written to her when he had thought she *was* me, or vice versa? It didn't make sense.

I picked up the letter and continued reading.

"As Joan told you in her note, I moved to New York recently to become the manager of the Denham and Villier store on Fifth Avenue. She suggested that I contact you when I got to town, so you and I could have dinner some night. I tried calling you — she did too — but you're not listed in the phone book. Hence the letters from both of us."

Tried calling her? Oh, he tried calling her

all right, but he got me instead. And judging by the fact that he was about to marry me, he *liked* what he got! At least, that was my impression before I stumbled on this bombshell.

I read on.

"Anyhow," Bill wrote, "since I arrived in New York, my life has taken a turn, and I —"

He what? *He what?*

I'd never know, because the soy sauce obliterated the rest of the letter.

I flung it onto the floor and stared at it, as if it were alive, as if *she* were alive.

Had Bill actually asked Nancy out even after supposedly falling for me? More to the point, had he always known I was an imposter and not said anything? What was the story anyway?

I needed this, right? The week before my wedding?

When Bill walked into my apartment that night, I pounced. Before he could get out a "Hello" I handed him the letter.

"What's this?" he said.

"What does it look like?" I said.

"A letter somebody spilled something on. A letter from Denham and Villier, as a matter of fact," he said after noticing the letterhead.

"Good. Good. And who do we know at Denham and Villier?" I said. I was using my preschool teacher voice. I couldn't help it.

He took another look. It all seemed to be coming back to him. "*I* wrote this, didn't I?"

"That's right. You wrote it. And now I'd like it if you'd explain why you wrote it." I stood there, hands on hips, waiting.

"You mean I never told you?"

"Bill."

"I'm serious. I thought I did."

"You thought wrong."

He shrugged, put his hands up in surrender mode. "Could I sit down? It's been a long day."

"For me too." We both sat down.

"I'm sorry, honey. I honestly thought I told you. But then we haven't exactly had a routine courtship. Little details were bound to fall through the cracks, given all the other stuff going on."

"Right. Now how about those little details?"

He smiled. "Here's number one: I knew you weren't who you said you were, almost from day one. In other words, I let you pretend to be the other Nancy Stern. I played along."

"Let me pretend? Played along?"

"Yes."

"But I don't understand. It wasn't until after our third date, after Nancy's murder, that you figured out what I'd been up to."

" 'Fraid not. I knew you were assuming her identity after our *first* date. I used to be a cop, remember? I checked you out."

"Checked me out?"

"Ran a check on you. Habit, I guess."

I couldn't believe this.

"I found out that you were a preschool teacher at Small Blessings who was posing as the Nancy Stern who wrote magazine articles about celebrities, the woman Joan Geisinger had intended to set me up with. But I didn't say anything because I thought what you were doing was adorable. I thought *you* were adorable. And I was flattered that you would go to so much trouble to impress me."

"You were flattered?"

"Wouldn't you be?"

"Well, yes, maybe. But if you knew all along what I was doing and you had no problem with it, why did you storm out of my apartment that night I broke up with you? Why did you blast me for deceiving you?"

"Because you did deceive me. You told me you didn't want to see me anymore, and that wasn't true. You didn't trust me enough to admit who you really were. I was hurt and disappointed."

"Hurt and disappointed enough not to call me again? If I hadn't shown up at Denham with the brooch, Bill, we wouldn't have gotten back together."

He shook his head. "I would have called you. I was just taking a while to lick my wounds. Cops are tough characters, Nancy, that's all."

"So you knew," I said, still dumbfounded.

"I knew," he confirmed.

I tried to absorb this new information, tried to make it compute. "Okay, what about this? If you knew I wasn't the woman Joan wanted you to go out with and you thought I was so adorable, why did you write the other Nancy Stern the letter, asking *her* out?"

"I didn't ask her out. If you hadn't gotten whatever on the letter —"

"Soy sauce."

"Soy sauce, you would have read that I was backing out of asking her out. See, right before I moved here, Joan had dropped her a note telling her I'd be calling when I got to New York. But then I met you and fell madly in love and had no interest in calling her or any other woman. Still, I wanted to do the polite thing and write her a letter, since Joan had gone to the trouble of making the introduction. So I explained that someone special had come into my life after I settled in town and that I wasn't free after all."

"That was very gentlemanly of you. I've never heard of a man getting in touch with a woman to tell her he wasn't going to be getting in touch with her. Wait until I tell Janice."

"Do you feel better now? It was all very innocent on my part."

"Except that you let me think you bought my act." I had to laugh. So much for my Jimmy Carter story.

"I not only bought your act, I loved your act," said Bill, pulling me closer to him on the sofa. "I was crazy about you. Am crazy about you."

I sucked up his compliments like a sponge, particularly since he was fondling me as he was complimenting me.

"Any other little details you want to clue me in on?" I said, entwining my legs with his.

"None at the moment." He began to kiss me, starting at my mouth and moving down my neck.

"I suppose there is one little detail I should clue you in on, in the interest of full disclosure."

"Hmm?"

"You may have written to the other Nancy Stern telling her you wouldn't be getting together, but you did meet her."

"No, I didn't, honey. I already —"

"You did. In the elevator in my building. The night you picked me up for our second date. We were going to that hamburger place, remember?"

He stopped the kissing. The fondling too. He was trying to remember. "Vaguely."

"Do you remember the woman who was in the elevator with us? The blonde who said she was an interviewer?"

"Actually, now that you mention it, I do remember her. The one you said wrote a newsletter for psoriasis sufferers."

I nodded. "That was Nancy Stern. The other Nancy Stern."

"No kidding. She was better-looking in person than she was in all those newspaper photos. A lot better-looking. What a body."

I narrowed my eyes at him. "They were implants."

He laughed. "Come here." He kissed me again. "Will you marry me, Nancy Stern?"

"Too late to back out now," I said, holding his face in my hands, the face I planned to wake up next to for the rest of my life.

"Will you change your name to mine?"

"You don't like the name Nancy?"

"I meant, will you be Nancy *Harris* now?"

"Yes. And not a moment too soon."

Everybody says September is the best month to visit Block Island, because the August fog gives way to crisp, clear skies and the crowds thin out. But while the skies were crisp and clear when we arrived for the Labor Day weekend, the crowds were very much in evidence. It was the last big holiday weekend on the Block, the weather was glorious, and everybody wanted in. I couldn't blame them.

My parents were the first among our guests to check in at the Spring House, followed by Bill's parents, his two brothers and their wives and children, and Bill's sons. It was Joan Geisinger who had driven down to Virginia to pick up the boys. Bill and I had both wanted her to come to the wedding — we wouldn't have met if it hadn't been for her, after all — and she had offered to bring Peter and Michael with her. When Janice showed up an hour later, the party was complete.

That night, we had a festive dinner out on the deck at Dead Eye Dick's, a Block Island eatery overlooking the Great Salt Pond. We ate lobsters and dunked the meat in melted butter and dribbled the whole mess on our bibs. Bill's parents told stories about him when he was a child, and my parents told stories about me when I was a child, and there were toasts, lots of toasts.

We spent the next morning showing everybody the Block, then shared a picnic lunch together on the island's most dramatic beach — a long stretch of sand that lies 150 feet below the Mohegan Bluffs. You can see the coasts of Connecticut and Long Island from the rugged cliffs on a clear day, which *our* wedding day was.

But it wasn't merely clear, in the sense of being fair-weathered; it was clear in that it was free of the problems, the snafus, the petty slights that often plague wedding days. Everyone got along. Everyone was happy for us. Bill and I were happy for us.

The ceremony, too, went without a hitch. The justice of the peace who married us was a man who had been born and raised on Block Island and had the New England accent to prove it. As we all stood together on the Spring House's impossibly green lawn that sloped down to the equally impossibly blue sea, he spoke simply and unsentimentally about marriage in a way that moved me more than if he had trotted out the fussy old phrases. What I found most interesting was his discussion of the symmetry of marriage.

"*Webster's* defines 'symmetry' as the beauty of the form arising from balanced proportions," he said. "A good marriage has symmetry. A good marriage is where one isn't doing the giving of love and the other the taking. A good marriage is where the proportions are balanced."

He looked up at me, as if he sensed his words held special meaning for me, as if he knew that this union, unlike my last, would be one where the proportions *would* be balanced.

And then he asked me the Big Question: Did I, Nancy Stern, take Bill Harris to be my lawfully wedded husband, etc. I said I did. When it was Bill's turn to answer, he said he did. When it was time for the groom to kiss the bride, we reached for each other at precisely the same instant, neither of us hesitating even for a second, neither of us the initiator, neither of us the receiver. The kiss was the very essence of symmetry, which wasn't a bad way to begin a marriage.

EPILOGUE

The first invitation arrived in the middle of November, around the time that Janice and I were rehearsing the children for the Thanksgiving play.

"Bill! Come look!" I said excitedly, waving him over to the newly reupholstered sofa in the living room, where I was sorting through the mail that evening. Now that his apartment was officially our apartment, I was starting to do a bit of redecorating.

"What?" he said, sliding his arm around my waist and peeking over my shoulder.

"You're not going to believe this," I said. "The mayor is hosting a cocktail party at Gracie Mansion and *I've* been invited! It's some sort of celebration of the arts."

"Let's see." Bill grabbed the embossed, elegantly scripted invitation out of my hand and read it for himself. "Very impressive," he said, nodding. "How do you think you got on their guest list?"

"Beats me," I said, "although it's possible that Madison Copley's mother got me on it.

She's big in the arts, is on a special task force or something, and she's been very appreciative of the extra attention I've given Madison during their family crisis." Madison Copley was one of the seventeen children in my class. Her father had recently left her mother for the woman who had faux-finished the walls of their fifteen-room apartment. "I'll call her and ask."

As it was too late that night to call anybody, I waited until the next night. Mrs. Copley was delighted to hear from me but embarrassed that she'd had nothing to do with my receiving the invitation.

"I wish I *had* gotten you on the guest list, Mrs. Harris," she said apologetically. "You *and* Miss Mason. You're both wonderful teachers, and I'm grateful for all you've done for Madison, but the mayor's party is rather exclusive. I'm surprised that *I* got an invitation."

The following morning, I asked Janice if she, too, had been invited to the soirée. She hadn't.

"Strange," I said.

"No kidding," Janice concurred.

I would love to have gone to the party, but I wouldn't have known anybody, wouldn't have fit in, so I RSVPed that I couldn't make it — and promptly forgot about it.

Besides, there were other, more immediate issues on my plate. While Janice and I had a good group of kids at Small Blessings, we did have one problem child — not a problem child on the scale of Fischer Levin (no murderer for a parent, in other words), but a problem child nonetheless. Her name was Moonbeam Elkins, and she was the daughter of a best-selling author of science fiction novels. She was a sweet girl but a loner, who regularly chatted with an imaginary friend during snack instead of interacting with the other children. When I discussed her behavior with her father, the best-selling author, he insisted that Moonbeam's imaginary friend was an entity from a distant solar system and that I would be placing the universe in grave jeopardy if I broke their connection. O-kay.

Penelope was no help with the situation, what a shock. Mr. Elkins was a wealthy man and, therefore, a potentially big contributor to the school — to the library — and she didn't want me to alienate (excuse the pun) him.

What I'm getting at is that, despite my marital bliss, life went on almost as before.

Then, a week after the first invitation arrived in the mail, a second showed up. This one was requesting my presence at the Kennedy Center in Washington at a gala event honoring a veritable who's who of artists and actors and musicians.

"Maybe someone you knew in Washington put us on the guest list," I suggested to Bill, as the two of us stood there scratching our heads.

"*Us* on the guest list?" he said. "The envelope's addressed to Ms. Nancy Harris, not Mr. and Mrs. William Harris."

"True. Obviously, there's been a mix-up."

"Obviously. Your name must have gotten on a mailing list intended for people who give a lot of money to the arts."

"I guess. But I'll tell you something, Bill. I would certainly skip a day of school to fly down for this shindig."

"It does sound pretty glamorous."

"Yeah. A lot more glamorous than playing with Space Mud. Janice and I made a batch of it today, by the way. I thought of you."

"That's sweet. Someone stole a diamond brooch from the store today. I thought of you too."

The week before Christmas, I received a delivery of flowers — a dozen long-stemmed red roses for Nancy Harris. When Bill got home, I flew into his arms to thank him for the early present.

"You're such a romantic," I said, nuzzling

him. "You and your roses. I remember the last time you gave them to me. They were sort of a peace offering, remember?"

"I remember, but these aren't from me, honey. Sorry."

"Not from you?" I pulled away, then went over to re-examine the flowers, lifted out the card. "But it says: 'To Nancy, my dearest girl. I love you madly.' "

"Is it signed?"

"No, just a lot of XXXs and OOOs."

"I didn't write the card, Nancy."

"Are you sure?"

He laughed. "Have I ever called you 'my dearest girl'?"

"No, now that you mention it."

I was mildly disappointed that the flowers weren't mine, that Bill hadn't bought them for me, but I got over it. I didn't need roses from him in order to feel loved. He demonstrated his love every day, by how he looked at me, how he touched me, how he spoke to me. Our relationship continued to be a revelation to me.

"Want me to take those down to the doorman?" he asked, referring to the vase of flowers.

"Not necessary. I'll take them."

I trudged down to the lobby carrying the vase.

"Here," I said, handing the roses to the doorman. "These weren't for me."

"Ah," he said. "They're probably for the other Nancy Harris."

"The other Nancy Harris?"

"The one in 4B. She moved in a month ago."

"A month ago?" I was so stunned by this turn of events that I was reduced to repeating everything the doorman said. I mean, seriously. What were the odds that I would be living under the same roof with *another* woman with my name — even after *changing* my name?

"A month ago, maybe two," he said.

"A month ago, maybe two," I said, still processing.

"What must have happened," the doorman went on, "is that the florist delivered these to the wrong Nancy Harris."

The wrong Nancy Harris. Oh, no you don't, I thought. Not again. Not this time. *Other* Nancy Harris maybe, but not *wrong*.

Suddenly, the whole thing — the coincidence, the irony, the symmetry — struck me as hilariously funny and I broke out laughing, couldn't stop laughing. "What is the other Nancy Harris?" I said, trying to catch my breath. "A celebrity journalist?"

"She's a ballerina," said the doorman,

taken aback by my reaction. "A famous ballerina. She dances with the New York City Ballet."

"While I'm making Space Mud with Moonbeam Elkins." I launched into a new round of laughter. The joke was that I *liked* making Space Mud with Moonbeam. I also liked teaching with Janice and I liked making love to Bill and I liked getting up in the morning and living *my* life, not somebody else's.

"Are you all right?" asked the doorman, who was much more attentive than the ones at my old building but just as unaware of the complexities inherent in having two tenants with the same name.

"What did you say?" I asked, my guffaws drowning him out.

"I said, 'Are you all right?' "

"Oh, yes," I said, patting his arm. "Yes, I am."